Tess of the Road

Also by Rachel Hartman

Seraphina

Shadow Scale

TESS OF THE ROAD

RACHEL HARTMAN

RANDOM HOUSE 🏠 NEW YORK

Text copyright © 2018 by Rachel Hartman
Jacket art copyright © 2018 by Simon Prades

All rights reserved. Published in the United States by Random House Children's Books, a division of Penguin Random House LLC, New York.

Random House and the colophon are registered trademarks of Penguin Random House LLC.

Visit us on the Web! GetUnderlined.com

Educators and librarians, for a variety of teaching tools, visit us at RHTeachersLibrarians.com

Library of Congress Cataloging-in-Publication Data
Names: Hartman, Rachel, author.
Title: Tess of the road / Rachel Hartman.
Description: First edition. | New York : Random House, 2018. | Summary: "Tess Dombegh journeys through the kingdom of Goredd in search of the World Serpents and finds herself along the way"—Provided by publisher.
Identifiers: LCCN 2016041764 | ISBN 978-1-101-93128-8 (hardcover) | ISBN 978-1-101-93129-5 (lib. bdg.) | ISBN 978-0-525-57857-4 (intl.) | ISBN 978-1-101-93130-1 (ebook)
Subjects: | CYAC: Courts and courtiers—Fiction. | Fantasy.
Classification: LCC PZ7.H26736 Te 2018 | DDC [Fic]—dc23

Printed in the United States of America
10 9 8 7 6 5 4 3 2 1
First Edition

For Scott, who's been on this road with me a very long time

Prologue

When Tessie Dombegh was six and still irrepressible, she married her twin sister, Jeanne, in the courtyard of their childhood home.

Married her to Cousin Kenneth, that is. Tessie, draped in one of her father's law robes cinched with an incongruous red ribbon, played the priest. Faffy the snaphound was the flower girl (Tessie had cleverly given him a bouquet of snapdragons).

It was past midsummer, and the plum tree was dropping fruit onto the bricked walkways, little plummy bombs that fermented in the sun and got the bees drunk. They buzzed in slow orbits, the worst sort of wedding guest, and terrified the groom.

Tessie led the wedding party to the bee-free apex of the garden, where the green-man fountain, forever choking on leaves, glugged and fussed and spit water at intervals. Father Tessie—she was a clergyman, after all—clambered onto the low fountain wall and turned toward the happy couple, wrestling her expression into solemnity as she leafed through the weighty tome she carried, just like the priest at Aunt Jenny's wedding the week before.

Unlike the priest at St. Munn's, Father Tessie's book was not the *Compendium of Rites* but *The Adventures of the Porphyrian Pirate Dozerius and His Valorous Crew*, Vol. 1. She flipped pages until the story "Dozerius and the Gargantuan Hedgehog of Balbolia" lay open before her, and then she said, "Let us pray."

Faffy shook his bouquet like it was a squirrel. Petals flew everywhere.

Jeanne bowed her golden head, crowned with white carnations and pink mother-may-I. She clutched a bunch of yellow daylilies to the bodice of her nicest gown, the pale blue velvet with silver buttons that she'd worn to Aunt Jenny's wedding. (Tessie, dark-haired, had worn the same dress in green, and then torn the skirt climbing the wisteria trellis at Count Julian's, exactly as she'd been told a thousand times not to do.)

Kenneth, who hadn't been warned beforehand that he was getting married today, had been hastily clad in one of Papa's more festive doublets, a wine-colored silk; he was nine, and bigger than the twins, but still it hung to his knees. Docile as a cow, he'd let Tessie festoon his strawberry curls with sprigs of baby's breath, which made him look rather like he'd crawled in from under a shrub.

"Bow your head, Kenneth," Tessie stage-whispered to her cousin, who was gaping into space. "And you're supposed to hold her hand."

"I don't wanna hold her hand," said Kenneth, wrinkling his freckled pug nose.

He was usually so biddable that this resistance took Tessie by surprise. "You have to," she scolded. "The ceremony doesn't work without it."

Kenneth rolled his eyes and grabbed Jeanne's hand in one of his grubby paws. Jeanne flushed pink, which Tessie chose to interpret as happiness and not embarrassment. These two were less enthusiastic about getting married than she'd anticipated. This boded ill for her grand experiment unless she could turn things around.

She flipped a page and plowed ahead with the service, administering their vows. They mumbled their answers, but Tessie had a fierce capacity for wishful thinking and decided Heaven could hear them even if she could not. At last she uttered the final blessing, words of celestial power she'd memorized during Aunt Jenny's service: "By the authority entrusted to me by Heaven and Allsaints, let these two be joined in marriage. Let two hearts be as one heart, two lives as one life. What Heaven joins together, no earthly power may rend asunder. Blessed be every enterprise undertaken together and"—here was the important point, Tessie's entire purpose—"fruitful be thine issue. Under the eye of Heaven, so let it be."

Tessie beamed down upon her sister and cousin. They stared back, eyes enormous, as if they'd gleaned what she was about. *Issue* was code for babies, and Tessie, forever curious, was relying upon Kenneth and Jeanne for proof.

Mama had given birth two months before, and Tessie had been immoderately obsessed with how this had come to pass. The only hint Mama would give her had been the cryptic statement "You can't have a baby unless you're married."

Tessie had pondered these weighty words upon a block of ice in the cold store, sore from the spanking she'd also received. She couldn't make it add up. If babies came from inside your body (and Mama's belly, now diminished, was evidence of this), how did your body know that you were married? If Tess pretended she was married hard enough, could she fool herself into having a baby?

She had pretended very hard; indeed, no one could pretend like Tess. When she rose in the morning, she'd said, "Ah, how blessed am I to face another lovely day of being married!" She'd served imaginary dinner and scoldings to her imaginary husband, and said, "Good night, you old prune," to him every night as she drifted off to sleep. It all came to naught, though. Her belly didn't swell, and she eventually grew weary of her imagined spouse—he was such a trial to her, Saints give her patience.

Unlike her mother, Tess could abandon the old prune whenever she wished and return to her first love, piracy. That's exactly what she did.

However, Aunt Jenny's wedding had rekindled her interest in the mystical origins of babies. There were clues embedded in the service itself, hints of what had been missing from her original experiment. First was the priest's blessing, "fruitful be thine issue." Maybe the Saints needed to be given fair warning that someone was ready for babies now. Second was what had come after the wedding, the so-called wedding night.

She understood this only hazily. Aunt Jenny and newly minted Uncle Malagrigio (a Ninysh wine merchant) had gone off to some specially decorated bedchamber while the Belgioso cousins, aunts, and uncles laughed and winked, calling out bad advice and giving them lusty slaps on their backsides as they went upstairs.

Mama hadn't participated in the merriment but had turned pale and pinched-looking and gone off to nurse baby Nedward in a quiet corner downstairs. Tessie and Jeanne had exchanged a quick look that meant, *Mama's sad, whose turn is it?* It had been Tessie's turn, to her regret. Her great-grandfather Count Julian had just ordered another round of desserts to be brought out; she was going to miss the marchpane.

Tessie dutifully sat by Mama, ready to absorb whatever pain her mother radiated. Mama patted her head absently, as if Tess were her faithful dog, and muttered in Ninysh to Great-Aunt Elise on her other side: "Of course I'm happy. I'm happy I don't have to worry about my little sister anymore, or how we'd cope if she bore a bastard."

"You're so sour we could pickle beets in you," Aunt Elise muttered back. "What do you want, Samsamese-style scrutiny, flying the bloody sheets in the breeze like a flag of victory?"

Tessie's ears pricked up at "bloody sheets." That sounded piratical.

"What I want," said Mama, her voice sharp and hurt, "is accountability. I want the wicked punished for their sins. Is that too much to ask?"

And then *she* had appeared, like a spirit summoned to Mama's anger: Seraphina, Tessie's half sister. She slouched into the room, sullenly picking at her dessert plate. She always looked bored at Belgioso gatherings. They weren't her family, after all; Seraphina had a different mother, a terrible dragon mother. Tessie and Jeanne had found out at midwinter and weren't allowed to tell anyone, which was a misery.

That first marriage was Papa's unpunished sin, Tessie knew. Seraphina was like a thorn in Mama's toe, reminding her all the time what kind of man he was. It was awful enough that he'd married a saarantras, a dragon in human form, and then covered his tracks; now that his wife and daughters knew, they were bound to keep his sordid secret, or there could be dire consequences for all of them.

That was the wellspring of Mama's bitterness; it had driven her toward a pair of crankier, more vindictive Saints, Abaster and Vitt, who offered balm for her suffering, and suffering for the wicked who'd wronged her.

Tessie made soothing, sympathetic noises even as her mind began to wander in other directions. Two more insights had struck, and she had to ponder them. First, contrary to what Mama had told her, Aunt Jenny might have had a baby before marriage. A bastard, she'd called it; Tessie had heard the word but never understood it. Second, Seraphina was not entirely dragon. Papa had been involved in the making of her, which meant that it was very naive indeed to go around pretending you were married in order to fall pregnant. The male of the species (such as Papa, or one of Aunt Jenny's previous boyfriends, the ne'er-do-wells Mama had refused to have in her house) must be involved somehow.

Tessie knew who would know: Seraphina. She was eleven and always knew everything.

Tessie asked the very next day, but she picked a bad time. She wasn't so foolish as to interrupt music practice, when Seraphina might have literally bitten her head off, but she asked while Seraphina was reading. Of course, Seraphina was always reading, so it wasn't like there were a lot of other options. Tessie eased open Seraphina's door to check that she was there, and then crept up on her in the window seat.

"You could knock, gargoyle-face," said Seraphina, not looking up. "It's rude not to."

Tessie worried the laces of her bodice, almost too nervous to ask. But she'd come this far. She said in a barely audible voice, "Where do babies come from?"

Seraphina, long-suffering, sighed heavily. "Anne-Marie just had one." Seraphina never called Mama *Mama*. "It came from inside her, or did you fail to notice?"

Tessie chafed; she wasn't stupid. That wasn't the sort of argument to make to Seraphina, however, who could demonstrate in under a minute that yes, you *were* stupid, check and mate. "Like that quigutl we found in the basement last month, laying eggs," Tessie offered, trying to sound intelligent.

Seraphina shuddered. "Distressingly like. No silver blood, though, and no eggshells."

"Yes, but . . . but how did the baby get inside her in the first place?" asked Tessie, fretting.

"Papa put it there," said Seraphina, turning a page. "Like planting a seed in a garden."

This was it. This was the answer, though incomplete. Tessie pressed a little further. "But how? How do you plant a seed inside another person?"

"Saints' bones, you are six. You don't need to know all that," cried Seraphina, her patience abruptly exhausted. Tessie had stepped on the dragon's tail without knowing how. "This is why you're such a spank magnet, you know, because you never shut up. You're the cat curiosity is going to kill."

"I only wanted—" Tessie began.

"I wanted to read, but am I allowed ten minutes' peace? Indeed, I am not," said Seraphina, leaping to her feet, ready to push Tessie out of the room if she had to. There was no need for that kind of thing; Tessie scurried toward the door under her own power. "Knock next time," Seraphina called. "Or I'll tell Anne-Marie what kind of questions you've been asking."

"She'll just spank me," said Tessie bitterly from the doorway.

"Because you're a spank magnet!" shouted her sister, and Tessie dared linger no longer.

⚔

So this was Tess's grand, misguided notion on Jeanne's first wedding day: she'd bless the happy couple and then lead them upstairs to the big bed Mama and Papa used to share (Mama slept in another room these days, with baby Ned). Once there, they'd play it by ear. She believed there must be kissing involved, because Mama had always been scandalized if Aunt Jenny was seen kissing in public.

Tess led the docile pair upstairs, where she had festooned the bed with roses—well, four roses. Not quite a full festoon, but that was as many as she thought she could take from Mama's white climber without their being missed. Faffy followed them up, that naughty hound; he leaped onto the bed ahead of everyone, getting grimy footprints on the sheets, and wormed his skinny body between the pillows. Jeanne, who was terrified of Faffy at close range, shrieked while Tessie chased her dog out of the room, crying, "Bad boy! Stop scaring Jeanne!"

With the ruckus resolved and restorative hugs given to her sister, Tessie finally directed Kenneth and Jeanne into the bed. The newlyweds began looking uncomfortable, especially Kenneth, who was nine and may have known more about all this than he was letting on.

He said, "Tess, we don't have to play this part. I'd rather go on to the pretending-we're-married part. Jeanne could make me dinner." Jeanne nodded eagerly at this suggestion.

"We're playing wedding," said Tessie authoritatively, "not marriage, and the wedding night is the most important part, after the priest."

"Then you should take a turn being bride," said Jeanne, who instinctively let Tessie play all the most important parts.

"No," said Tessie, exasperation mounting. "I'm the priest, telling you what to do. Now kiss!"

But the two of them seemed suddenly to become a pair of magnets with like poles turned toward each other: they'd get no closer, repulsed by some invisible field. Kenneth protested that it was wrong to kiss Jeanne because he was not her cousin but her uncle. (This was true: he was Anne-Marie's youngest brother, whom Tessie had declared an honorary cousin.) "Really, you shouldn't marry your uncle," he said sensibly.

Jeanne, for her part, whined about Kenneth's breath. He had a distressing habit of eating onions like apples.

"Oh, for Heaven's sake!" Tess cried at last. "You're both a pair of babies." And then she dived onto the bed herself, crawled after Kenneth like a crocodile, and planted a big kiss right on his stupid mouth. Jeanne had been right about his breath, which was astonishing, but Tessie grabbed his ears like Dozerius clinging to the mast of his shattered ship and hung on for dear life.

Inevitably, that was when Mama burst in.

⚔

The spanking, even for a girl dubbed "spank magnet," was one for the ages. Tessie, over years of corporal punishment, had learned to absent herself during these events to make them hurt less; she'd be sailing the wine-blue seas with Dozerius, and the chafing on her buttocks was due to the splintery wooden benches of his ship, or (if it was particularly bad) to the piping-hot Throne of Embers that she'd sat upon to save him from injury.

This one, though, recalled her most unpleasantly back to the here and now, not because it was so severe but because Mama cried the entire time. Indeed, her fury flagged sooner than usual; her arm dropped to her side and her chest heaved with sobs. Tess threw her arms around her mother to comfort her, as if it were Mama who had just received a beating.

"Don't cry," said Tessie, patting Mama's cheek as tender tears welled up in her own eyes. "Whatever has made you so sad, I won't do it again. I promise."

"You are never to climb into a boy's bed or kiss him until

you're married, Tessie," said Mama when her breathing had stilled enough to let her speak.

"I didn't mean anything by it," said Tessie weepily, which was a lie.

Mama put her hands on Tessie's shoulders and looked her in the eye. "You must understand, boys and men are afflicted with bodily lusts. They will try to coax and cajole you into bed, but you must resist. 'If you won't renounce temptation, O woman, there is no saving you. The Infernum burns hottest for the unrepentant harlot,' says St. Vitt, Heaven hold him."

Tess, who'd failed to understand most of that admonishment, nodded gravely. She would learn those words; she would understand what Mama wanted and live up to it, if only Mama would stop being sad. "I won't go near any boys," she said. "Only Kenneth is my uncle, so . . ."

Mama rolled her eyes. "I'll talk to Kenneth. Of course you may still play together—you're family!—but there is to be no kissing. No . . . explorations."

No explorations seemed a bit harsh. What was Dozerius if not an explorer? Still, Tessie agreed to it—she'd have agreed to almost anything to see Mama smile—although a mote of bitterness niggled at her, the knowledge that Kenneth would not be spanked for his part in this.

Then again, he hadn't wanted to play along. She'd done all the kissing.

Mama had not laid it out explicitly, but she didn't have to, not when years of spankings had done the work for her: there was something particularly bad about Tess. She was singularly and spectacularly flawed, subject to sins a normal girl should never have been prone to. It was going to take far more work for her to get into Heaven than someone like Jeanne, whose goodness seemed to flow effortlessly from some deep inner well of virtue.

Tess was determined to make it, though. Jeanne wouldn't want to go without her.

The twins were in the habit of creeping into each other's beds for what they called their "midnight conference." The night after the faux wedding and epic spanking, Tessie wept in her sister's arms.

"W-why is she never happy, Nee?" Tess sobbed. "W-why do I always make it worse?"

"We'll find the way to help her," said Jeanne, stroking Tessie's dark hair. "I think she's unfair to you sometimes. She's mad at Papa, but it's easier to take it out on you."

This only made Tessie cry the harder. Jeanne held her sister's face in her hands and said, "You've got me, Sisi. We've got each other. It's us against the world."

"Us against the world," Tess repeated in a sopping sob voice. But there was strength in those words and in Jeanne's hands. She felt it. Little by little she calmed, until she found the road toward sleep, whereupon she dreamed of pirates and woke refreshed and ready to get in trouble all over again.

One

The twins had taken their morning stitchery to the Tapestry Salon, one of the less fashionable sitting rooms in the palace. Jeanne liked the quiet, and Tess the tapestries, which depicted a seagoing adventure involving serpents and icebergs and flying fish. A younger Tess might have gone in search of the weavers to ask them what legend they (or their forebears) had been trying to depict; she might have scoured the library for references or asked Pathka the quigutl, who knew an awful lot about serpents of every sort.

Tess the lady-in-waiting, however, sadder and sixteen, had no time for such involved and esoteric interests. Who would have dressed old Lady Farquist if Tess was selfishly haring off after her personal curiosity? More important: who would put Jeanne forward in the world and find her a husband?

Jeanne, embroidering at the other end of the couch, was

too sweet and mild to do it herself. If she were left to her own devices, no one would have noticed her at all.

"Lady Eglantine's soiree is tonight," Tess was saying as she basted a new sash onto Jeanne's blue satin gown. She'd add mother-of-pearl beads, too—she'd gleaned some off Lady Mayberry in exchange for a particularly succulent bit of gossip—and no one would recognize the dress when she was done. The Dombegh twins couldn't afford many new clothes, so Tess, the stronger seamstress, had learned to be resourceful.

"Couldn't we stay in for once?" said Jeanne, leaning her blond head against the back of the velveteen couch and gazing out the window at the snowy courtyard. "I'm tired of all this."

Jeanne was tired? Imagine the tiredness of the person who dressed her, altered her clothes, and carried her messages. The one who vetted eligible bachelors and navigated the treacherous web of palace politics with no thought for herself, doing everything for Jeanne's happiness and that their family might be saved. *That* person must be bloody exhausted.

Tess basted fiercely, stabbing the needle in and out, and kept her mouth clamped shut.

The twins had no option but to attend every soiree until Jeanne's future was settled. Tess frowned over her work, trying to find the words that would best persuade her sister. "I've heard a certain someone is going to be there," she said, tilting her head and batting her eyelashes.

Jeanne knew whom Tess meant, and blushed, but still she opened her mouth to protest.

And that was when the miracle happened: the door of the salon flew open and there stood a strapping young man of twenty-two, Lord Richard Pfanzlig, the exact same "certain someone" Tess had alluded to.

Tess hadn't planned this meeting; the spooky timeliness of his appearance raised the hairs on her arms. He looked windblown, flakes of snow glistening in his thick dark hair; his commanding nose shone red from the cold, and his cloak swirled dramatically around him.

Tess's heart quickened, though he wasn't here for her. She didn't want him for herself or envy Jeanne (more than usual), but he cut a romantic figure, and Tess was not immune to romance, in spite of everything.

He whipped off his cloak, tossed it toward a chair, and missed, but no matter. All eyes were upon his finely fitted maroon-and-gold doublet, his trunk hose, and his shiny, shiny boots. Or maybe his eyes, which smoldered at Jeanne from across the room.

Jeanne couldn't bear it. She squeaked and grew intent upon the shepherdess in her embroidery hoop. Tess sighed inwardly, praying her shy sister wouldn't spoil this opportunity.

"I heard Lord Chauncerat intended to ask for your hand," cried Lord Richard, clasping a fist to his chest. "Am I too late?"

So that was why he'd come. Tess resumed her stitching with some satisfaction. Lord Chauncerat, of course, had made no proposal; he was a Daanite, uninterested in women, but he kept it secret. Tess had found out, or more accurately, something in his gaze had reminded her of Cousin Kenneth and she'd guessed. For her silence, Lord Chauncerat had permitted her to take his name in vain and start the tiniest rumor that he might have a modicum of interest in Jeanne.

That was all it took at court. You put a copper coin in the gossip engine, every tongue polished it up, and it came out unrecognizably golden. By the time the rumor reached Lord Richard's ears, it would've been inflated to ridiculous proportions. He'd burst in as if expecting to interrupt the wedding itself.

Jeanne wasn't finding her voice. Tess bailed her out: "Indeed, Lord Richard, you have arrived just in time."

His face lit up as if Jeanne herself had spoken, and not Jeanne's oracle at the other end of the couch. Tess didn't mind. She'd have plunged her hand into her sister's back and moved her mouth like a ventriloquist's dummy's if that would have helped.

Lord Richard crossed the room in three strides and dropped to one knee before Jeanne. The embroidery stand was in his way; Tess edged over and hooked it with her foot. Jeanne's eyes widened as the frame drifted away, leaving her no choice but to meet Lord Richard's eyes.

She looked at her hands. Tess cursed silently.

It wasn't that Jeanne didn't like this suitor; the problem was entirely that she did, rather a lot, and that she'd been raised on the strictures of St. Vitt to keep her desires severely under wraps. It was devilishly hard to encompass both.

Tess felt for her, but this was important.

Lord Richard took Jeanne's hands—clever Richard!—and Jeanne looked up at last, flushing pink all over. She was beautiful even pink, Tess noted with some satisfaction. Richard seemed to think so, too, because he pressed her knuckles to his lips.

Tess tried not to watch, even though she was supposed to

be the chaperone, guaranteeing that nothing got out of hand. Privately she sort of wished things would get out of hand, just a little. It would have eased her heart to think that even pure, virginal Jeanne was a mere mortal.

As if Lord Richard could read Tess's mind, he released Jeanne's hands and was back on his feet again, two yards of decency between them. Tess sighed.

"Jeanne," he said gruffly, his heart evidently in his throat, "I want to marry you. Would you have a fellow like me?"

A rich, handsome fellow who seemed utterly smitten with her? Unless she was terribly stupid. Tess snipped a stray thread with her scissors; she hadn't raised Jeanne to be stupid. She hadn't made every mistake she could possibly make, hadn't given everything up, so that Jeanne could sit there, saying nothing, as if she were stupid.

"Say yes, Nee," Tess mumbled around the needle between her teeth.

Jeanne rose, her green day dress draping demurely around her, and curtsied to Lord Richard. There should have been no suspense, but Tess found herself sweating all the same, her eyes glued to the duo, tall and dark facing short and pale. Lord Richard fidgeted with a button on his doublet, which Tess found humanizing and endearing. If Jeanne should turn him down, it was going to take a lot of looking to find another suitor half this well suited.

In a voice so sure and strong that Tess couldn't quite believe it was her sister speaking, Jeanne said, "Lord Richard, I would happily accept your offer, but do you understand my family's situation? My father was unjustly stripped of his law license, and we've struggled ever since. I should feel ashamed to put too great a burden on your house, and so I cannot agree to marry you without being certain you know how many obligations come with me."

Tess's jaw dropped; this was not part of the script. That is, it was the truth—the family desperately needed Jeanne to marry for money—but it was nothing anyone would, or could or should, utter aloud. This was a game everyone played but no one acknowledged. Tess felt vaguely sick. She'd worried that Jeanne would look too mercenary, and here was Jeanne herself, laying it all out on the table.

Lord Richard, however, was smiling, and not a strained *what have I gotten myself into?* smile, but a smile full of warmth and gentleness that almost took Tess's breath away. "My dear, there is no burden your family could place upon my house that we could not easily bear, or that I would not willingly take on for your sake."

Saints above, he was perfect. Jeanne deserved no less. How had they gotten so lucky? If Tess felt a self-pitying pang for her own ill fortune, for Will and Dozerius and everything else she'd lost, she suppressed the feeling almost before she noticed it. This was not the time; the moment was all Jeanne's, as was right.

Jeanne, her courage spent, returned to her bashful, blushing self again. She stammered something adorably grateful; Richard, all passion, took her hands once more. He shot a glance at Tess, asking permission. Tess nodded curtly and turned her eyes resolutely to her hemming.

She didn't keep them there. She peeked through her lashes

and thought her heart would burst as Lord Richard chastely kissed Jeanne's cheek. Tess recalled such joys, even if she would never again experience them; indeed, she wanted more than that for Jeanne—he should kiss her lips at least!—but Lord Richard came from a devout household, as strict as theirs, and passion could not override his upbringing. Not today, anyway.

He didn't linger, either, because it would not do to have tales told. One of Jeanne's great appeals, in the absence of money, was that she had not the faintest whiff of scandal about her. She was innocence incarnate. Lord Richard wouldn't compromise himself by compromising her.

When he left, Jeanne turned toward her twin. Tess's smile froze when she realized her sister's eyes had filled with tears.

"Dear heart, those are tears of joy, I hope?" said Tess softly, holding out her hand.

Jeanne flopped onto the couch and laid her head on Tess's shoulder, where she began to weep in earnest.

Tess set her sewing aside and put her arms around her sister, saying, "No, no, why are you sad? If you dislike Lord Richard, we will find you someone else. Never mind the money, never mind how long it takes. Papa and Mama will find a way to send Paul to school. Seraphina will swoop in and fix everything—" She wouldn't, in fact, because she couldn't, and Jeanne knew this as well as Tess did, but Tess felt it incumbent upon herself to keep her mouth moving, to keep her sister's spirits up. "Something will come through for us. It always does."

Jeanne drew her handkerchief out of her bodice and held it to her streaming nose. "That's not it, Sisi. I'm happy to marry Richard. I believe I may be a bit in love with him."

Tess drew herself up a little, taken aback. "Whatever is the matter, then?"

Jeanne's cheeks were speckled like a rosy quail egg, her eyes rimmed in pink. "I can't help remembering that you're older than me, whatever we may pretend to the world. I don't deserve this honor and happiness, not when they should have been yours."

Tess's heart contracted, wringing out the unselfish joy she'd felt earlier. Wasn't this typical, though? Not only did Tess not get what should have been hers by birth, but now she had to comfort dear, tenderhearted Jeanne, who was upset by the unfairness of it. Tess did not often feel true resentment toward her sister, but in this moment she did. Soothing Jeanne's guilt, on top of everything else, seemed a bit much to ask.

"There, there," she said, patting her sister's back mechanically. "We both know I've gotten what I deserved. If I had really valued any of these things, surely I'd have had the good sense not to throw them away."

Jeanne sniffled and nodded. Tess turned her face away, unwilling to let her sister glimpse any anger in her eyes. It wasn't Jeanne's fault; every ounce of blame could be ascribed to Tess herself. Could be and should be. She ascribed it with all her might.

Only an ungrateful bitch of a sister could feel angry at dear, gentle Jeanne.

Tess walked through the rest of her day, waiting on Lady Farquist, laughing at gentlemen's jokes during dinner, steering Jeanne's footsteps toward the obligatory soiree. Jeanne and Richard exchanged lingering glances across the room but said no more than a coy word to each other. Tess didn't care what they did; she was marking time until she could finally be alone.

Around midnight, Tess closed the door to her little room, which was technically a walk-in closet; her "elder" sister got the suite's main boudoir. She fished around behind Jeanne's hanging gowns and three pairs of shoes and drew out a little bottle of plum brandy, which she'd won off Lady Morena. She rationed the stuff religiously, because one never knew when it would be possible to obtain another, but tonight she filled her little glass three times. The fumes streaked painfully up her nose (plum brandy was not as delicious as it sounded), making her cough every time she exhaled, but she didn't mind. She flopped onto her cot, pleasantly dizzy, and joy was finally able to rise up in her again, a single bubble of hope.

After two years at court, diligently securing her sister's future, Tessie would be free.

She trotted down the hill into Lavondaville the next day to tell Mama about the engagement. Jeanne couldn't go herself; she'd been promoted to maid of honor, which meant that while Tess had merely to dress Lady Farquist (and Jeanne), Jeanne had to accompany Lady Farquist around the court and be an amicable companion to the old woman. Jeanne's promotion was perfectly acceptable to Tess, as it showcased Jeanne to the court while Tess worked behind the scenes. It also enabled Tess to steal some time for herself without being missed.

Not that she often wandered into town. Once burned, thrice shy. She knew better than to go coursing after her own selfish interests. Telling Mama the good news, however, wasn't . . .

Yes, it was. Tess would be the one to make Mama smile, not Jeanne. She never seemed able to escape her own selfishness completely, whatever she did.

She was so bursting with news that she went to the wrong house first, to her childhood home near the shrine of St. Siucre, and knocked upon the door. She realized her mistake, and before the servant could answer, Tess beat a hasty retreat, leaving incriminating footprints in the snow.

Papa's first marriage, to a dragon in human form, had been illegal five times over; there could be no mistaking Goreddi law on this point. That he was a lawyer and had been deceived only made it the more embarrassing. Queen Glisselda, thanks to her friendship with Seraphina, had pardoned him and saved his life, but even she couldn't prevent the lawyers' guild from revoking his license and stripping him of his practice. He consulted on the Queen's new dragon treaty, but in this time of peace, that was hardly full-time work. He taught classes at the seminary on an irregular and adjunct basis, and sometimes—holding his nose—he advised his Belgioso in-laws in their business ventures.

Alas, the family had been quietly creeping into debt ever since Seraphina's scales came in, as Papa tried to placate a hurt, angry wife with clothes and servants and fine porcelain. The wife was not placated, and the house was mortgaged to the eaves. Everything still might have come out all right if the money he'd expected upon the death of his mother had come through.

He had gotten nothing but a letter from his elder brother, Jean-Philippe, Baronet Dombegh, saying, *The house in town was your inheritance, you idiot. Did you think she'd relent and write you back into her will? By the end, the old buzzard couldn't even remember your name.*

Tess kissed a knuckle toward Heaven for her grandmother. Uncle Jean-Philippe wasn't worth a flea on one of the "old buzzard's" tail feathers.

The house in town had been sold a year ago, after Tess and Jeanne had already gone to court. Half the proceeds had trickled into the gaping sinkhole of debt, and three-quarters of the rest was reserved for Jeanne's dowry, as the investment most likely to yield a strong return.

The new flat was only a few streets over; Tess took the back way, up alleys and through St. Brandoll's Church. The flat was on the other side of the close, above a mapmaker's, accessible via an outdoor flight of slick, rickety stairs festooned with icicles. Tess ran her finger along the wooden railing, sending a rain of ice shattering onto the flagstones below.

This door required no knocking. It didn't even lock properly. She let herself into the parlor-kitchen-dining room, where her mother was simultaneously kneading bread and tutoring Tess's younger brothers in arithmetic. There was a common misapprehension that a Goreddi housewife wouldn't know her sums, but any city-born woman knew how to keep an accounts book, and Anne-Marie was not just city-born but Belgioso, a surname synonymous with business. A merchant would be the first to tell you: the wife who could add and subtract—as well as multiply—was a credit to her house indeed.

Tess pulled up a chair across from Neddie. "I have news for you, Mama," she said, not caring that she was interrupting the lesson. Jeanne's engagement was so momentous it couldn't wait. Tess spilled the whole story, embroidering upon Richard's sense of duty and omitting the kisses, innocuous though they'd been. "They're going to announce it officially at the Queen's Treaty Eve ball," she concluded. Richard had sent a note saying so that morning. "You must come, of course. We'll have to stand up next to the duke and duchess and—"

"She might have told me herself," said Mama, slamming the bread dough onto the table and raising a cloud of flour dust.

"Jeanne's stuck working today," said Tess disbelievingly. There was no pleasing this woman, even when one had unalloyed good news. "You're hearing the news before anyone at court. I thought you'd rather know sooner than later."

"You thought to steal her thunder," muttered Mama, laying into the dough with her fists.

A spark of anger warmed Tess's chest; she'd chastised herself for this, but it still rankled when Mama pointed it out. "I'm here with Jeanne's blessing. You know she dislikes a fuss."

"'Envy is the termite of good faith,'" said the older of Tessie's brothers, the Abominable Paul, quoting St. Vitt. He smoothed his dark hair with one hand and smirked at her.

"I'm not envious," said Tess, glowering. "What's thirteen times seventeen?"

"Piss off," said Paul, who was almost thirteen and could muster considerable venom.

"Language, Paulie," said Mama, punching the dough. "It's two hundred twenty-one, and you're supposed to have that memorized by now."

Tess stared at her mother incredulously. "Language? Mild chastisement? When you sold the house, did you also sell your temper?"

"Tess," said her mother, with a quaver in her voice that made it clear she had not.

"When I was a wee lad, *Paulie,* I'd've been spanked for not knowing my maths," said Tess. She'd gotten smacks with the spoon equivalent to the product she'd missed; 221 had been the most she'd ever received. Every other number would disappear from her head when she was old and senile, but 221 was emblazoned there forever.

She didn't dare tell the whole story, though. Mama's blond hair was drawn up under a cap and snood, and Tess could see the little vein already pulsing at her temple, a gauge for how high the steam was rising. As much as Tess told herself a lady-in-waiting was too big and dignified to be thrown over her mother's knee, some part of her didn't quite believe it.

Of course, Mama didn't have to lift a finger to Tess, not when she had two fine deputies at that tiny table, ready to take up the mantle for her. "Maybe some of us are clever enough that we don't need arithmetic beaten into us," said Nedward the Terrible, who was ten, pushing sandy hair out of his eyes with the end of his pen.

"No amount of punishment could teach our Tess," said Paul. "That's why she ran off to St. Bert's, for some *learning*." This last word was accompanied by an unambiguous gesture.

That was cruel. Tess felt it keenly, even if she let her face show nothing. Worse, though, her mother said, "Boys! There's no call to be that mean to your sister!"—as if Mama were the good one, looking out for Tess, trying to spare her feelings. Keeping her hands clean. Tess glared at her mother, blaming and raging. The boys had learned to be nasty from someone.

And yet blame never stuck to Mama. As much as Tess wanted to hate her, she understood too well what Mama had suffered at the hands of her husband and by the humiliations of his elder daughter. Mama got that look about her now as she plopped the kneaded dough into the baking pan, the long-suffering, mournful look. "Drop this off at Loretta's on your way out," said Mama, handing the pan to Tess. Dismissing her.

The flat, unlike the house where they had once lived, had no oven. One might simmer a stew in the ashes of the fire, or roast something small—a hare or capon—on a spit when the fire was roaring, but there was no way to bake bread unless you took it to the neighbors'.

Tess hefted the pan, adjusting the towel over the top, but didn't leave yet. She needed an answer and would bear the hostile stares of her brothers until she had it. "Mama, I think I've fulfilled my duties tolerably well." Argh, no, that was a terrible start, hedging and qualifying. She tried again: "I've done all the family has asked of me, with no thought for myself. Jeanne will be well settled; there will be money to send these two miscreants to law school and seminary. Enough to buy you back some things you've had to do without—the carriage, your gowns, a decent kitchen, and a place to entertain your family." To say nothing of Papa's once-resplendent library, but she didn't dare mention it; Papa was forever ignominious and disfavored in Mama's eyes.

"In light of all that," Tess went on, not daring to meet her mother's eyes, "I was hoping—"

"What, that you might get married, too?" crowed Neddie the Terrible.

Tess flashed him a dirty look, but Paul was already taking up the cry: "No, she wants to run off in search of World Serpents. Don't you remember any of her old manias?"

"I thought she was crazy for boys, not monsters," jeered Neddie.

"She was mad for both," said Paul. "Nobody's sure which got her in trouble."

"Saints' knuckles, will you stop?" cried Tess, slamming the bread pan down on the table between them, making them jump.

She looked to her mother; Mama's eyes had gone icy and distant. "What an ugly temper you have. You're supposing that your time is up, your task is complete, and you are free to go?"

"Something like that," said Tess warily. These kinds of questions were usually a setup for a lecture on why she was wrong.

"And where do you propose to go, exactly?" said Mama, turning toward the fire and lifting the lid on the stew. It bubbled ominously. "You've spoiled your chances at marriage."

"Not everyone marries," said Tess. "I could work as a seamstress."

"Or a harlot," muttered Paul. Both boys burst out giggling.

Mama said nothing, which stung as badly as whatever she might have said.

There was no way not to hurt. Tess gritted her teeth against it.

Mama scraped at the bottom of the pot, where the stew was sticking. "The boys are right: seamstress today, slattern tomorrow. It happens to undefended women all the time." She straightened and stretched her lower back, her eyes on Tess's. "You fell once, and we picked you up. We can't keep doing that. A convent would keep you respectable and safe."

Tess opened her mouth to object, but her mother cut her off. "You've made your bed most abundantly, Tess. Don't imagine you're finished lying in it. Quoth St. Vitt: 'Thou shalt pay for thy sins ten times ten what they cost thee, but if thou hast fallen all the way to the ground, woman, there shalt thou lie.'"

"So I'm to lie and pay," said Tess, seething, "with no recourse."

"You knew this before you set off bullheadedly down the road to damnation," said Mama, cold as well water. "I brought you up in full knowledge of the scriptures. Whatever you've done, you've done with your eyes open and your chin set defiantly against me."

Tess's chin quivered now, her defiance spent. There was no talking to Mama once she started quoting scripture. All authority was ceded to St. Vitt, the most implacable and unsympathetic Saint in Heaven.

One would have thought, after St. Jannoula's War and the apparition of St. Pandowdy (Heaven shine upon his scaly hide), that the Saints might have relaxed their grip upon the hearts of Goreddis, just a little. The Saints of old had been revealed as ityasaari, half dragon, and that should have created more room for doubts, not less. Tess's half sister, Seraphina, was a Saint by that definition, and Tess felt that should have been enough to make anyone question the whole setup. Tess could have made a list of Seraphina's un-Saintly qualities—her morning breath and noisy chewing, how she'd twist your arm if you came into her room without asking, burps and farts and every common, earthy thing—but somehow the actions of one sister were not enough to cast aspersions upon an entire pantheon of Saints.

Tess's mother, after the war, had dug into her piety all the more deeply, like a tick burrowing into a dog's ear.

There were no arguments. Not only was Mama's faith intractable, but Tess knew in her heart that she was right. However bitterly Tess might protest, she had done this to herself and she deserved what she got. In a way, she was lucky: St. Vitt had advocated the stoning of women like her, but in this day and age her mother could never have gotten away with that.

Or rather, she could, but only if the stones were words.

In the end, Mama and the boys couldn't make it to the Treaty Eve ball for the betrothal. Two days before the happy event, they came down with influenza—perhaps contracted from the neighbor's toddler, who'd coughed on their fresh-baked bread, or perhaps brought home from Mass. Only Papa was well enough to come; he never set foot in church (which suggested the bread was blameless) and had too little meaningful contact with his wife to catch it from her.

Four couples announced their engagements at the ball. Lord Thorsten, apparently inspired by all the romance in the air, proposed to Lady Eglantine in front of everyone, which was merely embarrassing for Lord Thorsten. Tess could have told him he had no chance with Lady Eglantine; Tess knew everyone's business.

That was one thing she'd miss about court. Did nuns gossip? With her luck, that would be considered a sin. Tess grimaced, feeling like she'd already glimpsed the first way she'd get in trouble at the convent. It was nice to know these things in advance.

The families of the four betrothed couples stood upon the dais at the head of the hall while the whole party applauded. Tess felt sad for Jeanne's paltry showing, only two people, and Papa barely counted. He'd grown so thin since he'd lost his law practice that he could hardly be seen from the other end of the hall. Jeanne took his arm, however, and nodded at Tess, who understood to do the same, and maybe that was sufficient. Maybe they'd be remembered as the Dombegh twins, bearing a twig between them.

The in-laws-to-be were invited for a private reception in the Blue Salon, where Queen Glisselda would congratulate them personally. Jeanne went ahead with Lord Richard's family, who'd traveled from Ducana province for the betrothal announcement: his parents, Duke and Duchess Pfanzlig, and his middle brother, a congenial, pumpkin-headed fellow called Lord Heinrigh. Tess took her father's arm so he couldn't disappear and led him doggedly after.

"We couldn't skip this?" Papa muttered as they entered the

salon. "The announcement's made. Surely we've done our due dilige—"

"Jeanne needs you here," Tessie snapped. She had no patience for her father; everything about him irritated her, from his balding pate to his dated houppelande to his meek posture, like an apology for being alive. "You do little enough for us. You can suck it up and socialize."

She scanned the room for where they needed to be. Richard and Jeanne were talking to the Queen at the farthest point of the room. The duke and duchess and Lord Heinrigh stood near the center with a small group. They were the ones Papa should be meeting; Tess hauled him forward. Duke Lionel was speaking grandiloquently, and Tess slowed her steps, knowing it would not do to interrupt a duke. As the Queen's second cousin once removed, he outranked everyone but Her Highness and the prince consort.

"I disapprove the Queen's decision, and I don't mind saying so," he said, tossing his mane of white hair.

Tess froze, fearful of what the duke might say next. One criticism of the Queen reflected upon her own family: the royal cousins' peculiar relationship with Seraphina. Nobody, not even Seraphina's sisters, knew much for certain, beyond the fact that Seraphina lived in the royal family's wing of the palace. That was quite enough fodder for speculation, however—and enough to stain Jeanne's reputation if one were of strict and censorious mind. They'd been lucky, Tess felt, that no one had thought to paint them with that particular brush.

"Saints' balls, I've said so to her face," Duke Lionel pontificated, unaware of Tess's anxious presence behind him. "'It is wrong to let quigs roam free and terrorize innocent people,' I told her. 'Lock them in at night, like your grandmother used to, or this is going to come back and bite you in the arse.' And it will, too—perhaps literally!"

Gasps went up all around him, shock that he would dare to speak so bluntly of the Queen's derriere. "Whatever did she say to that?" cried an elderly baronet.

Duke Lionel shrugged his powerful shoulders. "She knows in her heart that I'm right. It's that idealist, the prince consort, who puts such notions in her head. Him, or St. Seraphina."

Tess bristled at hearing *Saint* appended to her sister's name, and yet it was a relief in this case. That would be why they weren't holding Seraphina's questionable relationships against Jeanne. They were believers. A Saint could, by definition, do no wrong.

Unlike Tess. Tess had to rely on keeping her sins well hidden.

She edged closer with her father. "I beg your pardon, Duke Lionel, Duchess Elga, Lord Heinrigh," she said, giving full courtesy to each. There was supposed to be a third son, Lord Jacomo, the youngest, but he seemed not to be present.

"Tess Dombegh, if I'm not mistaken," said Duke Lionel, like a man who felt he'd never truly been mistaken in his life. "Jeanne's fraternal twin, the younger. Is this your father?"

"Yes," said Tess, but Duke Lionel was already holding out his enormous hand, crushing Papa's flaccid fingers in his grip. Papa squeaked in alarm. Tess winced.

"Well met, sir," cried the duke. His heartiness seemed only to make Papa wilt further. "Your Jeanne is quite a girl. Richard is utterly smitten with her, and even my wife can find nothing to complain about. We could put a pea under Jeanne's mattress, and it would beat her black and blue by morning, no doubt."

He accompanied this pronouncement with an appalling wink. Duchess Elga, her salt-and-pepper hair pulled back under a Samsamese snood, seemed offended by this, and was perhaps on the verge of saying so when Heinrigh burst in: "We never thought he'd find anyone good enough for Mother! You should have seen the girls she rejected. I tell you, I've learned my lesson. Better to let her do the choosing, and save yourself a deal of grief!"

The duchess's expression moved from offended to livid, but Heinrigh seemed not to notice. He gave a wide, vacant smile, like a sweet-natured spaniel that has no idea how the drapes ended up on the floor with muddy prints all over them. He was appalling, and yet Tess found herself half wanting to scratch behind his ears.

"It is rare to find a young lady as pure in spirit as your Jeanne," said the duchess at last in a pained voice. "You've brought her up piously, Counselor Dombegh."

"We tried," said Papa, bowing his head. Tess struggled not to roll her eyes. Papa and *pious* didn't belong in the same sentence, and *pure in spirit*, she knew, was a euphemism for virginity. Pure in body was more to the point, but the duchess would never be so crass as to utter the word *body*. She probably never even thought the word.

Tess accepted a glass of sparkling wine from a page boy and took a quick sip. It settled her stomach, which had become lightly queasy at this discussion of Jeanne, as if she were some heifer at market. Nicely fattened. Never known the bull.

"Go fetch them," the duke said to his wife and middle son, waving his hand dismissively. "Bring Richard and Jeanne here to us." When they had dutifully departed, and most of the circle of nobles had scattered, the duke put his arm around Papa's bony shoulders. "Now, remind me, you are the father of St. Seraphina, are you not? Your first wife was the dragon?"

"Y-yes," said Papa, flashing Tess a panicked glance. Tess, who was enjoying the spreading warmth under her ribs, fancied he couldn't remember which wife had been a dragon.

"So what was that like?" said the old duke, poking Papa's stomach in galling and comradely fashion.

"Seraphina was a challenging child, in some ways—" Papa began.

"Not *that*," cried the duke. "Your dragon wife. How were things with her? Is it true what they say, that the saar are slow to warm up, but once they get going they burn hot as the sun?"

Papa looked like he wanted to sink through the floor. Tess would've happily dug him a hole, but she knew her duty. She'd have known it even drunk. She cried in a little-girly voice, "Oh, Papa, what is he implying? My innocent ears don't comprehend his meaning!"

Duke Lionel laughed. "Forgive me, maidy! I forgot there were those present whom the corruption of the flesh has not yet touched. I understand you have decided to remain pure and dedicate yourself to Heaven."

Tess widened her dewy eyes, the naivest naïf. "I have no greater ambition than to serve the Saints."

The duke nodded approvingly. "My youngest, Jacomo, is at seminary, studying for the priesthood. You'll meet him at the wedding. He is a most pious young man, and I'm sure you'll have a lot in common."

Tess felt her heart harden—she could have nothing in common with a devout student-priest—but she let her smile warm upon her face. The wine helped, oh so much. She could do everything required of her without rage or resentment; her feelings were as inconsequential as a fruit fly, drowning in the dregs of her glass.

Duchess Elga returned, Lord Richard and Jeanne in tow.

"Ah, sweet Jeanne!" cried Duke Lionel. "I was complimenting your father on your moral upbringing. It's rare and refreshing to find a lady of your station with such a pristine reputation."

This was also code for *virgin*. Tess marveled at how many ways there were to say it, and how it was the greatest currency her sister possessed.

It seemed almost a shame to get married and spend it.

"We want to set the wedding date for the feast of St. Munn," Richard was saying.

"No, indeed, that's less than four months away. Far too soon," said his mother, her thin lips bending into a frown. "People will think you're in a *hurry*."

The word *hurry* was pregnant with portent. It was astonishing how much meaning could be crammed into a single word. How did such words not crumble under their own weight? Tess swirled the last of her wine and wondered.

"We *are* in a hurry," said Richard, pushing his dark hair off his forehead. "First: I love this lady"—Jeanne blushed enchantingly—"and second, her brother Paul turns thirteen soon and hopes to get into St. Fingal's Law College, I understand."

Richard nodded at Papa, who nodded back. Paul was to follow in Papa's footsteps—avoiding, of course, the places where Papa had stumbled.

The duchess took on a pinched expression. "We live in permissive times, Richard, and I suppose I cannot dissuade you. When I was a girl in Samsam, we took counsel from the priest for six months, made pilgrimage to St. Abaster's, and submitted to the rite of *Breidigswaching* upon our wedding night."

"Mother," Richard said warningly.

"What in the world is *Breidigswaching*?" Tess asked, curious in spite of herself.

"Don't make her explain," groaned Richard.

"Don't be a squeamish baby," said the duchess, smacking him with the end of her long sleeve. "In Samsam, each family sends a representative to observe the consummation of the marriage, to ensure there is no falsification. You can't imagine how many girls—already sullied—smuggle a little knife in their bodices, that they might stab themselves in the leg and bleed onto the sheets. Sometimes their new husbands even help them." Here she glared at Lord Richard, who looked scandalized that any man worth his manliness would try such a thing.

"But what about me?" Lord Heinrigh asked fretfully. He was shorter than Lord Richard and had been obscured behind him.

"What about you? Volunteering to watch?" Lord Richard elbowed his brother in the ribs.

"No! But Mother wants me to marry a Samsamese earlina," Heinrigh said, pouting. "Are you telling me her family will send someone in to watch us . . . y'know . . ." He turned alarmingly pink.

"Of course they will," snapped the duchess. "Your father and I endured it. You will hold your head high and endure it."

"I nominate Jackie for our side," said Lord Richard laughingly, since Jacomo the student-priest wasn't there to defend himself. "He'll be keen, especially if he joins a celibate order."

"Your brother can bear holy witness while praying for your immortal souls," said Duchess Elga, her expression taking on the hardness of wood. This put an end to all ribald joking, to Tess's immense relief. She'd have had to find a way to stop it otherwise. Jeanne had tears in her eyes; they were upsetting her.

Only at the end of the evening, when the twins were walking through the dim palace corridors toward their suite, did Tess finally blurt out to Jeanne: "Your future mother-in-law makes Mama look positively sweet. And the duke! I guess if you have enough money and rank, you can say whatever the devil you want."

"Sisi," said Jeanne quietly, "I've talked to Richard and he thinks this is a good idea. What would you say to coming to Castle Cragmarog with us?"

"I'm not going to miss your wedding, silly," said Tess, whose wits had been slowed by wine. "They can't slap me into a convent that fast."

"I meant coming to live with us instead of joining a sisterhood," said Jeanne. "You could keep me company, and when the children come, you could be their governess. I would treasure your companionship in . . . in that new house."

With Richard's family, Tess completed the sentence in her head. Duke Lionel was pompous and offensive, Duchess Elga strict and bitter. Heinrigh seemed innocuous enough, if a little stupid, but this youngest brother, the seminarian, was surely an apple not fallen far from the tree. Tess chose a trait from each parent and settled upon *pompous and bitter.*

If Jeanne had suggested this only a day before, Tess would have leaped at the chance on the principle that anything was better than a convent. Having met the people she would have to share a house with, however, she found herself surprisingly uncertain.

Except no, here was Jeanne leaning heavily upon her arm and sighing, her fair, dear head drooping under the weight of her fears. How could Tess tell her no? What kind of barbaric heart could harden against Jeanne? She kissed the crown of her sister's head and said, "Mama won't like it, but of course I'll come, dear heart. Wherever you are is my home, always. Us against the world."

Two

Weeks passed. The twins turned seventeen upon the cold, dark feast of St. Willibald, halfway between the solstice and the equinox. They invited their family to the palace so that Lord Richard might attend the celebration without embarrassment. Seraphina came (bringing her weird, solemn dragon uncle, against everyone's wishes) and then announced, in the most tone-deaf manner, that she was—surprise!—going to have a baby. Everyone, down to Seraphina herself, had assumed a half-dragon was like a mule, half this, half that, all infertile, but apparently not. They were all sworn to secrecy on the matter; Seraphina would be leaving for Ranleigh Cottage, one of the royal country estates, and staying there for the duration.

This untimely pregnancy announcement made the torte go sour in Tess's mouth. Jeanne noticed her expression and whispered in her ear, "She might have told us tomorrow, when it wasn't our birthday." Tess smiled weakly at this, though Jeanne had misdiagnosed the malady. Seraphina always stole their thunder; there was no point minding that. Tess didn't even resent having to keep yet another secret for her.

It was Papa's undisguised pride that gutted Tess, and Mama's smile. The smile was entirely fake, but at least she was bothering to pretend.

Later, alone in her closet, Tess polished off the plum brandy. She awoke with a terrible headache and a festering sullenness. Still, she hauled up her own smile, like a leaky bucket from the depths of a stagnant well, and dressed Jeanne with every ounce of cheer she could muster.

⚔

A week before the wedding, when the earliest cherry trees and nodding jonquils were just coming into bloom, Lord Richard drove Jeanne and Tess from Lavondaville to Cragmarog Castle, in Ducana province.

Once it had been a castle in earnest, but like Castle Orison in Lavondaville, age and peace had transformed it into something more palatial than military. Only a semicircle remained of the battlements, which now enclosed formal gardens and fountains. The keep had relaxed into a great stone house with three wings, like a trident. Cupolas, corbie gables, and whimsical chimneys kept the roofline busy; rows of identical glazed windows reflected the sunset sky. The facade was of native Goreddi limestone, glowing warmly in the evening light, elaborated with strapwork and scrollwork around the great doors.

It was all very newfangled and said quite clearly: *Here dwelleth money.* Jeanne looked overawed; Tess buttressed her across the cobblestone carriage drive and up the steps.

"What a cozy home you shall make it," Tess whispered in her sister's ear, but Jeanne was too petrified even to smile.

The twins lived there a week before the rest of their family arrived, getting lost in the big house, strolling arm in arm past crocuses and daffodils in the garden, sitting in the saffron-silk parlor with Duchess Elga every evening while she read aloud from St. Abaster. They studiously avoided the terrible trophy room, which belonged to Heinrigh and was decorated floor to ceiling with the spooked, hapless heads of deer, boar, aurochs, lynx, and wolf. An entire black bear stood on its hind legs in the corner, claws and fangs bared but glass eyes distinctly sad. Jeanne was a shuddering wreck after seeing it and swore never to return to that room again, even if she lived here a thousand years.

Tess had gone back on her own, however, to confirm that she'd seen what she thought she'd seen: the head of a quigutl, openmouthed beside the hearth, used to hold the fireplace tongs. Tess hefted a poker, with half a mind to go find Heinrigh, then set it down in disgust. It would be no help to Jeanne if she killed Richard's younger brother before the wedding even took place.

She knelt and patted the creature's spiny forehead. "I know how you feel," she said.

Cragmarog would be her home, too, if the duke and duchess felt she fit in. She was given a room far away from her sister's, near the old nurseries. The young lordlings' old toys—hobbyhorses and little siege engines and more dolls than she would have expected—were nearly as creepy as the trophy room in the moonlight.

The hollow halls echoed melancholy, like her heart.

The rest of Tess and Jeanne's family, except Seraphina, arrived the day before the service. They would have been welcome sooner—indeed, the duke and duchess would scarcely have noticed four more people wandering lost in their house—but this way the Dombeghs were able to bring along the duke's youngest son, Lord Jacomo, who had to finish the term at seminary and could return home no sooner.

That was the official story, anyway. Unofficially, it was Lord Jacomo who brought the Dombeghs, because only Lord Jacomo had a coach sturdy enough to withstand the rutted country roads. If you dug deeper still, it became clear that only Lord Jacomo had his own coach, period.

When the coach rolled up, the denizens of Cragmarog went out to greet the new arrivals, Tess trailing after her sister like a proper lady-in-waiting. She didn't mind being last; she was going to have the best view of her mother and Duchess Elga, a meeting she'd been looking forward to with a certain sadistic glee. What would they make of each other? They were so alike, and so different, that it could go either way: they might be best friends or implacable enemies.

Tess hoped for the latter, not because she harbored ill will toward her mother—or not *only* because of that—but because friends might see a common target in her and work together.

The mothers approached each other cautiously, like two wolfhounds, the duchess fresh from the house and Anne-Marie dusty from the road (advantage: Elga). The duchess's gown, a textured emerald-green velvet, shone resplendently in the morning sun—but wait! Wasn't Anne-Marie's mien movingly humble? Younger and blonder than the duchess (advantage: Anne-Marie), she kept her glory of hair under a wimple and her face bare of any cosmetic but piety.

For what greater adornment need'st thou, woman, than the radiance of Heaven's approbation? So saith St. Vitt, who surely should know.

The initial superficial assessment round went to Anne-Marie, Tess decided. Duchess Elga narrowed her eyes cattily. Best friends they would not be.

"So you're the twin," drawled a scornful voice. A young man, who could only have been Jacomo the seminarian, had sneaked up on Tess and stood at her elbow. He had the duchess's piercing dark eyes and heavy scowling brows, and the same thick black hair as Richard (and Duke Lionel, presumably, before his mane went white). He was taller and fatter than his elder brothers; the seminary must employ excellent cooks.

"You have the advantage of me," said Tess archly, pretending not to know who he was. This was a subtle way of underscoring his rudeness; he ought to have led with his name.

His mouth arced into the bitterest smile Tess had ever seen. "Yes," he said. "I do have the advantage. Don't forget that."

His long stride carried him past her into the house, and Tess stood wondering what he had meant, a pool of anxiety condensing in her belly.

Dinner was the second proving ground for the dueling mothers-in-law. Duchess Elga sat at the head of the table, dominating the meal like a castle on a hill above a village. No, like a dragon perched on the ruin of the castle on a hill. She frequently turned her iron gaze toward Jeanne and Lord Richard. This was the first meal where she'd permitted the betrothed pair to sit beside each other, but there was to be no hand-holding or—Saints forfend!—kissing. The duchess didn't realize Tess's mama was of much the same mind about these things. Tess wouldn't tell her. Making the two women get along was outside the scope of her responsibilities.

Duchess Elga ostentatiously refused wine (causing Tess's mother to pause mid-sip), and then Mama recited St. Abaster's Triticum Benedictio over the rolls. Tess imagined them holding a devotional after dinner—secretly a competition, of course. St. Abaster's champion versus St. Vitt's. Who read with the most tear-filled, heartfelt piety? Who chose the most severe verses? They'd look devoutly toward Heaven and daggers toward each other.

This was the first meal where wine had been served, a concession for Tess's family. Tess was grateful; interfamilial tensions were more manageable with a little lubrication. By the end of her first cup, Duke Lionel's bloviations seemed almost witty. Pumpkin-headed Lord Heinrigh was no longer a terminal bore, droning on about hunting, but a congenial *bonhomme* regaling them with tales of high adventure and dead animals. Lord Jacomo scowled, but the wine made this seem rather comical. Clearly, his face had frozen in that position when he was young. It would have been tragic if it hadn't seemed so well deserved.

He seemed to be scowling at *her*. That was absurd, of course. Lord Jacomo could have no reason for such instantaneous dislike, especially when Tess was such a charming specimen of impeccable respectability. She flared her nostrils and made a frog face back at him, and he looked away in apparent confusion.

Pleased with any small victory, Tess traded her empty goblet for Neddie the Terrible's full one. Neddie didn't notice; he and the Abominable Paul were wholly occupied with kicking each other under the table.

Mama noticed, however, and tried to send Tess a message across the table using only her eyeballs. This might have seemed like an obscure means of communication, but Tess could read it perfectly well: *Don't you dare! Spoil things for your sister, and I shall never forgive you. All this could have been yours, but you threw your future away and broke my heart and—*

Tess quit reading; she knew how that epic ended. Mama assumed she was a liability, even after two years of concerted effort. The Saints might offer redemption for the fallen (even angry old Vitt, if you fulfilled his strict conditions), but there were no second chances with Mama, and no forgiveness. It didn't really matter what Tess did.

On that bitter note, Tess threw back her second glass of wine.

Tess retired early, pleading a headache, but in truth she could bear her mother's glare no longer. No amount of wine could mitigate that. As she climbed the stairs toward her lonely wing of Cragmarog Castle, the strained voices faded like a weight falling from her shoulders.

Tess crossed her dark bedroom and opened the curtains; she'd stowed a little green bottle upon the windowsill. She had discovered bottles squirreled away all over the house—brandy in a bookcase, sherry under the stairs. Tess had deduced that these belonged to Duchess Elga. Anyone who drank only water in public was the first suspect for enjoying a tipple in private.

Tess had some sympathy for that; it was one of her hobbies, too. In her off moments, when Jeanne had not required her solicitous care, she'd sought out the duchess's liqueur collection like a pig after truffles. Most bottles seemed to see regular use, so while she might sneak a sip here and there, she couldn't abscond with a whole bottle. This green bottle, however, had been tucked beneath the fuzzy bottom of the black bear in Lord Heinrigh's trophy room (FRITZ'S BEAR, the placard read, which Tess thought rather cute). It was caked in dust and had surely been forgotten. Tess had liberated it before her parents arrived, along with a crocus-shaped glass, but hadn't had a chance to try the stuff yet.

She poured a dram while the moon rose over the manicured gardens outside her window. A cloying scent tickled her nostrils. Tess frowned and sniffed at the glass to be sure.

Feh. Crème de menthe. No wonder the bottle had been abandoned. Beggars, alas, could not be choosers. That could have been her life's motto right there.

She toasted the moon and downed her whole glass in a gulp. The liqueur was, as anticipated, nasty, but she had one more, enough to soften the brittle edges inside her and put all feeling to sleep. She tucked bottle and glass behind the curtain and flopped back onto the bed.

This was Tess's favorite way to fall asleep, her head heavy and her limbs weightless, her bitterness sweetened, her regrets wrapped in muzzy wool until they were no longer recognizable even to her. The goose-down mattress was exactly like her mind, all . . . fluff . . .

The sound of her door closing startled Tess awake. "Why?" she cried in alarm, as if the reason for this invasion bothered her more than the identity of the trespasser.

"It's me," said Jeanne, lingering by the door. "Can I . . . that is, I hoped—"

"Yes, come in, I wasn't asleep!" cried Tess, who had been so soundly asleep that she couldn't figure out how to sit up. She found herself in a wrestling match with the sheets. The sheets won. She settled for patting the bed beside her. "One last midnight conference before you're married, eh? Just like old times."

Old times, Tess realized, had been but four years ago, and it had been Tess herself who'd put a halt to the practice of creeping into each other's beds. It would have been impossible to sneak out of the house otherwise. Still—it felt like a lifetime since then.

Jeanne timidly crossed the room, her linen chemise catching the moonlight like a ghost, and crawled into bed beside her sister. The sheets picked no quarrel with her. Tess offered her half the pillow, and they lay with their heads together in the near darkness, Tess's dark plait beside Jeanne's honey-colored one.

Jeanne's hand, when it reached for Tess's, was as cold as ice. "I wanted to talk to you, Sisi," she said. Over seventeen years, they'd accumulated dozens of silly names for each other, but *Sisi* meant Jeanne was serious.

"What is it, Nee?" They'd be using their private twin language next. Tess wasn't sure she remembered how to speak it.

Jeanne sighed like a butterfly might have. "I need to know that you're all right."

Tess was so astonished by this line of inquiry that for a moment she couldn't speak. What had she expected? An admonishment to behave herself tomorrow, maybe. "D-do you mean all right, right now," she asked, feeling foolish, "or in some kind of cosmic sense?"

Jeanne said, "You had a headache after dinner."

"I didn't really," said Tess. "I was tired of Duke Lionel droning on, is all."

Jeanne didn't laugh. Maybe she was smiling; it was too dark to tell. "I feared you were upset," she said after a pause. "You've been so solid this week, and I appreciate how hard you've worked. Richard's family likes you. I feel certain they'll be happy to let you stay. The wedding is going to be difficult, though—on everyone, but especially you—and I wanted to make sure you were all right."

Tess's mind had snagged on the idea that Jeanne's in-laws-to-be *liked* her. She was growing increasingly sure that she didn't like them. She'd borne the rules and formality at court for two years, but there had been a goal: to keep Jeanne looking pretty and persuade someone rich to marry her. Tess could tolerate anything if the end was in sight.

Living here among these sourpusses was the end. She'd have to be on her best behavior for the rest of her life. Whether she wanted to wasn't the issue; she wasn't sure she could.

"Sisi," said Jeanne, and Tess startled as if she had fallen back asleep.

Impossible. She knew exactly what she'd been thinking. "I wasn't asleep," said Tess.

Jeanne inhaled slowly through her nose, and Tess realized that her sister was sniffing her minty breath. And judging it, there could be no doubt.

"My sweet, I need to hear that you're all right," said Jeanne.

That wording rankled. Jeanne needed to hear the magic words to assuage her conscience, did she? *Oh yes, dear sister, go right ahead and get married. I'd love to be your children's governess. I never wanted anything for myself, truly.*

Bitter and ungrateful. Tess knew she didn't deserve all the help she got.

"I don't envy you, if that's what you're worried about," said Tess, not lying exactly. It wasn't envy so much as self-pity. Did that make her "all right" or not?

Jeanne exhaled. "I wouldn't envy me, either. Have you met my mother-in-law?"

Tess couldn't help smiling at this. "I'll be here to shield you," she said, squeezing her sister's hand. "And once you start popping out the heirs, she'll have nothing to criticize."

Jeanne tensed. "Sisi, does . . . does it hurt terribly?"

"What, having a baby?" asked Tess, lolling her head in her sister's direction. Jeanne had never asked her about that; silence had squatted between them like a toad.

"Oh. No," said Jeanne, clearly embarrassed. "I'm certain that must hurt. Remember how Mama screamed when Neddie was born?"

Tess had an inkling what Jeanne was really asking. Somewhat cruelly, she wanted to hear her say it aloud.

"I mean . . . ," Jeanne began again, meaningfully. She paused as if hoping that would be enough; Tess wouldn't give her the satisfaction. "You know what I mean," said Jeanne.

"No, indeed," said Tess.

Jeanne elbowed her; Tess played dumb. "I mean the wedding night," said Jeanne at last, in a voice like a terrified gnat. "Does it hurt as much as Mama always said?"

Tess had half a mind to say, *I never had a wedding night*, but Jeanne squirmed pitiably, making Tess relent at last. "If you mean the 'consummation,' as darling old St. Vitt calls it—" Tess broke off abruptly; she'd been about to answer facetiously, but another answer had leaped into her throat and was perilously close to coming out: *It hurts. Every single day.*

But that wasn't the answer to Jeanne's question. Jeanne was asking about the act itself, not . . . not her heart. Not her conscience, or what it felt like to see her future shattered in front of her like a mirror. Jeanne had the official sanction and blessing of both families, Heaven, the Saints; her situation was completely different.

"*That* doesn't hurt," said Tess at last. "I promise. You'll hardly feel it."

"But there's supposed to be blood," cried Jeanne, her voice nakedly afraid now.

Tess wrapped her arms around her sister, who trembled like

a baby bird. "There isn't always, even if you're a virgin. That part is a lie. And Richard will be gentle with you, if you ask him. He loves you, Nee. I know he does. That's what tipped the balance in his favor; otherwise I'd have urged you to accept Lord Thorsten."

This wrung a soggy giggle out of Jeanne; Lord Thorsten was sixty and bandy-legged like a beetle.

They lay a bit longer in silence, Tess drifting in and out of memories and dreams. The memories were of Will, mostly—the big hands, the small humiliations—but also the birth of Dozerius. The dreams . . . well, surely she dreamed that Jeanne muttered their old watchword, "Us against the world," and kissed her cheek.

Tess awoke hours later to the cacophony of country birds jeering at the dawn. Jeanne was long gone, her side of the bed grown cold.

Tess had been dressing her sister all week, but on the wedding day Duchess Elga insisted upon letting Jeanne use her own dressing room and her own lady's maid. Tess did not object; it would have been futile, and she had enough to do getting herself ready. The duchess had provided both Jeanne and Tess with gowns, which seemed generous on the surface of things, but Tess knew it wouldn't do to let the bride's sister look shabby. The other noble guests would talk.

Tess's revised theory, as she maneuvered herself into her farthingale—an imported Ninysh petticoat with willow hoops sewn in—was that the duchess was trying to torture her. The architectural underthings gave dressmakers an excuse to add an extra foot of fabric to the hem and an extra twenty pounds of beads, buttons, and embroidery to everything else. All that weight converged right at the middle; she felt crushed whenever anything bumped her perimeter, and she was bumping everything. She couldn't get used to how wide she was.

Tess wound her brown braids around her head and frowned at herself in the glass, knowing she ought to do her face but feeling exhausted by the notion. When she made up Jeanne's face, it was a hopeful, anticipatory act, but to do her own seemed to underscore the futility of everything. She powdered her cheeks (which were unexpectedly damp) and reddened her lips and called it good enough.

She sat on the edge of her bed, a difficult trick in a farthingale, and had another crème de menthe, staring out the window at the tidy topiary hedges. She had a second glass. She might have had more than that; it was a small glass and she was very far away. Her hands and mouth had come to some kind of understanding with each other and left her out of it.

She smudged off half her lip rouge onto the edge of the glass. She didn't care.

The service was to start at noon, Samsamese-style. Tess met Paul and Ned at their room and herded them down the curving central stair into the magnificent foyer, where a hundred or more newly arrived guests were milling around. She paused on the landing overlooking the room and let her brothers go down without her. It was a colorful crowd, mostly other landed gentry, but the magistrates of nearby Trowebridge had also been invited, along with some of the more prominent merchants.

That kind of social blending was still rare, but it would have been utterly unheard of just six years ago, before St. Jannoula's War. A lot had changed since then.

A trumpeter rushed in from outdoors and blared a lively fanfare, the new one, composed by Seraphina in honor of the Queen. The mob of wedding guests parted seamlessly down the middle and oriented themselves to face the door. Queen Glisselda, in a farthingale gown of evening-blue silk sprinkled with constellations of pearls, entered upon the arm of Prince Consort Lucian Kiggs. Tess's half sister, Seraphina, in an outdated maroon houppelande, walked several paces behind them, trying to be unobtrusive.

One good thing about Seraphina's houppelande was that it made her belly ambiguous. Was she or wasn't she? It might just be the hang of the robe.

Tess longed to tell someone, anyone, that Seraphina, so-called Saint, was no better than she should be. Would it have been a treasonous embarrassment of the Queen, though, to imply that her husband was unfaithful? For the baby must surely be Prince Lucian's. Of course, for all Tess knew, he'd had Queen Glisselda's blessing. Seraphina was so tight-lipped about the royal cousins that Tess could only speculate.

But then, they could do whatever they wanted. People might mutter, but no one would try to stop them. It must be nice.

Beside Seraphina walked a plump woman wearing a fabulously plumed hat and a red-and-green gown, its skirt cut so daringly short that her boots showed. This was Countess

Margarethe of Mardou, the famous explorer; Tess had heard her speak once at St. Bert's. The countess had her Porphyrian mother's dark complexion but was clearly Ninysh in her flamboyant dress and carriage. Goreddis, down to the Queen herself, were finally adopting the farthingale, and here the Ninysh had already moved on to calf-length skirts, raised square collars, and shiny, authoritative boots. There was no keeping up with them.

Seraphina's ploy to remain unobtrusive by entering behind the Queen and beside the most fashionable woman in the room wasn't working out for her. She was mobbed by wedding guests, ostensibly wanting to say hello but really wanting to shake her hand so they could later tell their friends and relations, "I know she claims not to be a Saint, but I swear I felt the grace of Heaven in her palm."

Seraphina, reserved by nature, tolerated it as best she could, but Prince Lucian was, even now, working his way back through the crowd to extricate her.

Tess clucked her tongue, refusing to feel sorry for Seraphina. She didn't have it so tough; she'd always been the special one. The smart one. Jeanne was prettiest and sweetest. That hadn't left much scope for Tess beyond "the one most likely to get spanked."

A momentary glimpse of a face in the crowd—blue eyes, cocky grin—caught Tess's attention, and her heart nearly stopped. Had William of Affle been invited to this wedding?

The face was gone. She forced herself to resume breathing, and with breath came reason. It was impossible; the Duke and Duchess of Ducana wouldn't associate with a poor student like him. Where would they have run into each other? And Will was surely off on some expedition or other, anyway. *The opportunity of a lifetime must have come up*—that's what she'd told herself for the last two years. It was the only excuse she could almost accept.

Will had left her, for who knew where or what, and she'd banished him from her heart and mind. He was not welcome back. If he were to show up out of the blue, Tess wasn't sure how she'd react. It would be like seeing a ghost.

She suspected she'd cry, actually. That only made her angry.

A light touch on her shoulder made her jump. It was merely Mama, who had a talent for sneaking up on people. "I was up at your room," she said, her ice-blue eyes accusatory, as if Tess had put her to a lot of trouble.

"I don't see why," said Tess, turning back toward the sea of guests. "I brought Ned and Paul down, like you asked me to. If you'd been here, you would have seen—"

"I found something very concerning behind your window curtain," said her mother.

"Ah," said Tess dully. Jeanne must have reported on Tess's breath from last night. *Us against the world, my fat behind.* "Again, why did you bother? You might have asked me."

"And gotten a lie in return?"

Tess shrugged. "I guess you'll never know."

Her mother took her arm, which Tess's farthingale made awkward. Indeed, as soon as her mother bumped her perimeter, Tess felt a great pinch at her waist. She wondered whether she'd put the thing on properly. Her mother wore a more sensible unhooped gown of blue velvet. Papa had pawned the last of his library to buy it, assuring them that it was a worthy investment. Jeanne was nearly married; this dip in the family fortunes would soon be over.

Tess accompanied her mother down the stairs, taking scrupulous care not to wobble; her hawk-eyed mother would be scrutinizing her for unsteadiness, trying to gauge the degree to which Tess was drunk, making contingency plans, no doubt. Tess carried herself steadily, refusing to give the old woman any satisfaction.

Old. Feh. Mama was thirty-five. She'd been seventeen—same as Jeanne—when she'd married Papa. Years of disappointment, however, had put fine lines around her mouth and a dark sorrow in her gaze. Her hair was not yet gray, but you'd never have guessed. She kept it under a wimple like a widow or penitent.

Tess refused to pity her mother, either. This made her a hard-hearted, ungrateful daughter, she knew. She'd been told often enough.

A five-note trumpet flare gave everyone to know that it was time to come to chapel. Tess and her mother lingered behind the crowd; the families of the betrothed were to enter last. Tess gazed dully at her counterparts-in-law, Lord Heinrigh and Lord Jacomo, the mild-mannered, ginger-haired middle brother and the tall, fat, storm-cloud youngest.

At least Lord Jacomo had stopped glaring at her; he was pacing and reciting under his breath, practicing for the service.

The thinning crowd revealed a smiling Seraphina, who approached Papa and took his arm. "How are you feeling these days?" Papa asked his eldest.

"Like a pile of bricks," she said in the low, quiet voice that always sounded like she was concealing a laugh somewhere. "You should see my feet. They're puffed up like morning rolls."

Papa chuckled, and Tess's stomach twisted sourly. Nobody had considerately asked after her health when she'd been pregnant. Nobody would have been charmed if she'd complained of puffy feet. Seraphina was every bit as unmarried, but nobody seemed to mind. She was the exception to everything; rules bent deferentially to make room for her.

Mama, full of her own kind of envy, tightened her grip on Tess's arm.

The families entered at last, walking in procession toward the gilt boxes at the front of the chapel. Lord Richard, decked out handsomely in a wine-colored doublet and slashed trunk hose, waited under the rotunda with Father Michael, the abbot of nearby St. Munn's. While the families took their seats, Lord Jacomo stepped up beside the abbot and led the opening prayer. At last Jeanne came in, resplendent in gold and green. Mama, Papa, and Seraphina stood up to be her witnesses, though only Papa was to speak: *Yes, this maiden has come to be married of her own free will, and not because we dragged her kicking and screaming.*

Those weren't the exact words, but Tess felt the sentiment behind them. Jeanne was a lamb brought to the knife, a bird to the cage. By her sacrifice would her family be redeemed.

Tess's mind wandered during the ceremony, especially when Lord Jacomo read from the scriptures; she wasn't sure what kind of student he was, but he'd mastered the "droning monotonously" part. Top marks for that. Maybe he was a natural talent. When he finally finished, the chapel disgorged everyone into the great hall, where servants had set up long tables for feasting and a merry band already played in the gallery.

Later, Tess barely remembered the feast, except that there was wine and that wine came as a relief, extinguishing the fires inside her. As soon as the guests finished eating, an army of servants dismantled the tables and cleared the room for dancing. Tess was a decent dancer, in fact, and her body merrily went through the motions, though her mind was disengaged. The room whirled around; the candles shone. It was pleasant, but she did not like being present.

In her vagary, she nearly ran into Countess Margarethe. "Steady on," said the countess, hat plumes bobbing, holding her goblet out of range so it wouldn't drip on her dress. "You're Tess Dombegh, are you not?"

"Yes, milady," said Tess, carefully giving full courtesy, pleased to have attracted the unexpected attention of such a highborn and fashionable personage. Countess Margarethe was equal in rank to Count Pesavolta, the ruler of Ninys, so she was practically a princess in Goreddi terms. Considering that Pesavolta had exiled or executed most Ninysh nobles over the rank of baronet, Margarethe was a rare bird indeed.

The plumed hat had obscured the view from above, but now at close range Tess saw that the countess kept her tightly curled hair very short and that it was the color of a copper coin, a shade lighter than her skin. Her gaze was unsettlingly frank and intelligent, and she stood with one foot slightly extended as if to show off her boots, which were highly polished and devastatingly pointy.

"I'm told you've studied a bit of natural philosophy," said the countess incongruously.

"I'm sorry—what?" said Tess, who had not anticipated this line of conversation at all.

"And that you were particularly keen on megafauna," the countess persisted.

Saying *megafauna*, though Countess Margarethe could not have known, was tantamount to slapping Tess's face. Her cheeks grew red as if she'd truly been hit. "What are you getting at?" Tess said shakily.

"I'm mounting an expedition through the Archipelagos and as near the Antarctic as we can manage," said the countess. "Departing as soon as the spring thaw reaches Mardou and we can sail."

When Tess did not respond to this information, Margarethe smiled up at her confidentially. "I'm inviting you to come with us, Tess."

Tess felt a kind of vertigo, as if the floor had been pulled out from under her.

"My uncle's ship is large," the countess continued, clearly unaware that the person in front of her was hurtling down a mental hole. "You won't be in the way. There would be plenty of work you could assist with, to say nothing of new skills to learn—cartography, navigation, languages, zoology. Seraphina says you're a clever girl, and that—"

"Seraphina made you invite me," said Tess, apprehending the truth, or leaping to a conclusion, at least.

"She's not in a position to *make* me do anything," said

Countess Margarethe, bristling. "But we discussed you, yes. She despairs that you've been painted into a corner, left with only two choices in life, governess or nun. That's nonsense, of course. There are always more options, but sometimes we need a hand up. I'm offering you a place on my ship because I can."

Seraphina had undoubtedly told the countess why Tess had only two options, laying Tess's shame out bare, and now the woman pitied her. Sickness and rage rose in Tess's chest. "I don't need your charity," she muttered.

Countess Margarethe scowled deeply. "What charity? I intend to make you work."

But Tess was hardly listening. She was glaring across the crowded room at Seraphina, seated in a tall chair beside Queen Glisselda, laughing and chatting. The prince consort returned from a refreshment quest with a goblet for the Queen and a tumbler of barley water for Seraphina. The Queen gestured adamantly and Prince Lucian nodded. Seraphina seemed to demur, but that didn't stop the prince from surreptitiously rubbing her back.

Countess Margarethe swirled the wine in her glass. "Would you like some time to think about it?"

It was going to be hard to say the words as if she meant them, but Tess brought all her stubbornness to bear. She had a duty. She loved her sister. "I can't go. I want to stay here for Jeanne's sake. She needs me."

Countess Margarethe's scornful expression cut her. "That's a grand ambition."

"That's virtue. And responsibility. Some of us have a strong sense of both, and don't go gallivanting after every selfish whim," said Tess, her face livid, her heart breaking.

The countess didn't say another word. She turned on the heel of her fine boot and stalked off.

Tess had other horrible things to say; she was nearly bursting with them, like a kettle left on the boil with a cork in its spout, ready to scald whoever came too near. At the same time, she was appalled at herself. She should scurry after the countess and apologize—but how could she face it? Anyway, it was Seraphina's fault for trying to fix the unfixable. She should know better than to meddle.

Tess wandered off in search of more wine and found it easily, found lots of it, found that it doused the fire to embers, dulled the kettle's shrilling whistle to a low, self-pitying whine.

There was no escaping the party until late. At least it wasn't the usual Goreddi nightfest; Tess was not going to last all night. This was all done Samsamese-style, in deference to Duchess Elga—the noonday service, followed by feasting and dancing and the happy couple "going upstairs" after sundown (Tess laughed at the euphemism). The party would continue until about midnight, with the showing of the bridal sheets, a barbarous custom to Tess's mind, but not as barbarous as the Samsamese rite they were omitting, the *Breidigswaching*.

Jeanne had been so horrified when Duchess Elga had described it—and her fear last night . . . Tess had been cruel where she should have been sympathetic. She knew that fear. She should apologize. Her shame was running very deep tonight indeed.

Through a fog of alcohol, Tess spotted the hulking form of Richard's youngest brother at the edge of the dance floor, and he distracted her from her purpose. She chuckled, remembering how Richard had volunteered "Jackie" in absentia for Heinrigh's *Breidigswaching* and made a lewd joke about it. It was funny because priests were celibate—or some were. Depended on the order. Tess had half a drunken notion to go up and tell Jacomo the story; he was so priggish that the story would surely horrify him, and that would give her some gross approximation of joy.

Priggish, or piggish? He was lucky to be so tall, so his fat could spread out evenly and pretend to be nothing but soft edges all around.

As she was making her way toward Jacomo, he was joined by Heinrigh, and the two stood conversing with their heads together. Tess was struck by an even more hilarious idea: if Jacomo's nickname was "Jackie," what must they call Heinrigh? "Heinie"? It had to be; it was a law of nomenclature. This gave her the giggles, which forced her to slow her steps until she could regain her composure.

She was near enough the brothers to overhear them talking. "Look, I don't want to dance with her, either, but people will talk if we don't," Heinrigh was saying.

"Let them," drawled Jacomo. "I care not a fig. Anyway, surely I have some kind of priestly exemption."

"Not yet, you don't," said Heinrigh laughingly. "Anyway, priests dance all the time, even in Samsam, so Mother couldn't fault you—and she could fault a newborn kitten."

"I didn't mean exemption from dancing," said Jacomo,

sneering down at his older but shorter brother. "I meant a moral exemption. She's not a nice girl."

"She drinks a lot, I noticed," said Heinrigh, shaking his pumpkin head.

"Oh, it's far worse than that," said Jacomo obliquely, looking around. Tess sensed he was looking for her and stepped behind a pillar where she could still hear them. Her cheeks blazed. What could he know? They'd been so scrupulously careful.

"If you know something about the sister or the family, you should have mentioned it to Mother," Heinrigh was scolding. "Before the wedding, obviously. It's rather too late now."

"That's why I didn't mention it till now," said Jacomo. "Richard introduced me to Jeanne months ago. I'm convinced he loves her. I could have spoiled the betrothal before it began, but I couldn't bear to."

"What a soft touch you are!" scoffed Heinrigh. "I had no idea."

"Only to a point," said the young priest. "You'll excuse me if I don't dance with the objectionable sister."

"You've certainly got my curiosity going," said Heinrigh. "What can she possibly have done to earn the permanent censure of a not-so-holy priest-to-be?"

"I'd rather not say," said Jacomo dryly. "It makes no difference now, anyway."

It mattered to Tess, however. Lord Jacomo surely knew everything—Will, the baby, everything. She leaned her head against the column, willing her trembling to subside. She found another glass of wine, and while it dulled the edge of panic, it also dulled her memory, which proved unfortunate.

The evening became a patchwork of things she could remember and things she could not. She danced determinedly, merrily, stumblingly, as if to show those brothers she didn't care, other people found her worth dancing with, she was fine. Her mind, though, tumbled the same thoughts over and over: she'd almost ruined Jeanne's prospects just by existing. How could she stay as governess to Jeanne's children if one of the brothers-in-law knew all about her? Jacomo wouldn't live at Cragmarog—he'd have a church somewhere—but he'd be home for holidays and family occasions, and she couldn't bear the idea of his knowing smirk across the dinner table.

A smirk was nothing. He could make her life miserable any number of ways.

These brothers! She hated them all. Richard, for being perfect enough to marry Jeanne; Heinrigh, for seeming friendly while being ready to think the worst of her; and Jacomo, for knowing and judging. The young men were very close in age, less than a year between each of their birthdays, what Goreddis called "Ninysh twins." It was funny because the Ninysh were amorous. Tess, being half Ninysh and an actual twin, found the term a bit offensive—and anyway, in the case of these brothers, they were surely Ninysh triplets.

Jacomo looked oldest, being tallest, which had turned out to be lucky. Tess, the taller twin, had to pass herself off as the younger so that Jeanne should reasonably be married first. Tess had worried that no one would fall for this, but the Pfanzligs had already set the precedent. Jeanne had gone to court first, everyone who mattered knew her longest, and it was that easy.

So you're the elder twin. You've deceived us.

Tess scoffed. "Not about anything that matters. It's not like Lord Richard's marriage contract specifies 'the elder Dombegh twin,' and we're planning to pull the old switcheroo in the bedroom tonight." She swayed a bit on her feet, grinning absurdly. "Although wouldn't that be a laugh. Jeanne goes behind the screen to change, and changes into me."

Tess's dance partner stopped cold, and the next sarabanding couple in line nearly ran into them. "If your family would lie about something this trivial, what else haven't we been told? Is your sister truly a virgin?"

"Wha—? Of course she is," said Tess, horrified by the question. Nobody could doubt Jeanne's virtue. Nobody. Who was this doubting lout?

She'd been dancing with Lord Heinrigh, but he'd become regrettably blurry, so she hadn't realized. She'd been thinking thoughts but had ended up speaking them aloud. How had that happened? What had she told him?

"I'm not a romantic like Jacomo," said Heinrigh, his congenial face congealing into a scowl. He squeezed her arm painfully. "I don't care if Richard loves her. This isn't about Richard. This is about our family, and the deceit you've been spinning around us."

"Oh no," said Tess, the world swirling around her like it was rushing down a drain. "Please. Don't punish Jeanne for my sins. Don't ruin my family. This marriage is going to save Papa, and send the little boys to school, and make Mama smile again, and . . ."

But she was speaking to the empty air. Heinrigh had flounced off, in search of the duke and duchess.

⚔

All the yelling happened in the third parlor, the peach-colored one nobody liked, far from the guests. Duchess Elga stormed back and forth before the cold hearth, terrible in her rage; the duke was solemn and stern. Lord Richard sat on the couch with his arm around a weeping Jeanne. Mama and Papa found opposite corners of the room to stand in.

Jacomo and Seraphina took the last chairs, leaving Tess nowhere to settle. She staggered around and vomited in a vase.

Lord Heinrigh, buzzing like a hornet, demanded of Jacomo: "What else do you know?"

"This isn't enough for you?" said Jacomo wearily, running a hand over his double chin.

"You implied there was worse! You have a duty to your family."

"You weaseled it out of her, you hero. I've nothing to add."

Tess was too drunk to appreciate what he wasn't saying. She lay down on the floor; the room did not stop spinning.

"Why would they lie about something this trivial, if not to cover up something worse?" Duchess Elga's shouts seemed to travel through water to reach Tess's ears. The ensuing discussion arrived from afar; words lapped over her in waves.

The only argument she heard distinctly was Seraphina's: "My father's first instinct is to be thorough and change the records. That's how he kept me safe. He didn't need to, here, and shouldn't have, but putting Jeanne forward was the right decision. Tess isn't temperamentally suited for marriage. I mean, look at her."

Tess was crawling toward the window. She leaned out and vomited into a bed of tulips.

There was more yelling; Tess shut it out, concentrating on the cool night air upon her face. It was the only thing keeping her from catching fire.

Richard apparently pleaded eloquently for his bride, and since the ceremony had already gone forward, the marriage stood—provisionally. The wedding night still had to be fulfilled, and if at the end Jeanne's purity was in doubt, the whole thing might still be declared null and void.

To ensure there was no cheating, the duchess invoked her terrible Samsamese right of *Breidigswaching*. She would have stood over the bed like a vulture, watching everything herself, but Jacomo (one of the cooler heads in this crisis, though he glowered like a bulldog) interceded and volunteered, and everyone agreed that maybe the duchess's righteous rage would only make things more unpleasant than they already were.

From the distaff side of the marriage, Seraphina offered, but Jeanne tearfully requested Tess, and their parents decided this was a just consequence. Tess, to her everlasting regret, was given a cup of tea and time to sober up a little. This entire mess was her fault, and they weren't going to let her forget.

The bride and groom climbed the decorated staircase at midnight, in the Samsamese fashion; Tess and Jacomo were secreted up another, darker stair.

She was directed behind a carven screen, unadorned

rosewood full of small perforations shaped like four-leaf clovers. The grand canopied bed was visible through them if she squinted. Tess resolved to look that way as little as possible, turning her gaze instead to the distressingly narrow bench where she was to sit. She was still drunk enough that the world wobbled, and the gilt bench seemed to buckle under the weight of her stare, as though it might tip at the slightest provocation and send her sprawling.

She edged toward it, one hand ready to wrestle her farthingale into submission, the other hand—the one with the teacup—extended for balance. The bench cringed as she sat gingerly, like a sparrow on a fence.

Fat Jacomo plunked himself violently beside her. The bench was springy and bounced; Tess barely kept all her tea in the cup, and nearly went over backward.

Tess regained her balance and glared at Jacomo. He'd had every opportunity to reveal her shameful history to his parents. Maybe he'd kept quiet for Richard's sake, or maybe he meant to make her suffer. He could hold his knowledge over her like an axe, keeping her ever in fear of the day it would fall.

She made an ugly face at him. Jacomo ignored her, drawing his beetling brows and squinting at the scene beyond the screen. His fleshy mouth puckered in distaste.

Tess couldn't help it; she looked. Richard, doublet off, his pleated shirt hanging loose around his trunk hose, led Jeanne by the hand across the room. She'd been undressed by maids (this was no longer Tess's job, nor would it be again in this lifetime; that door had closed) and wore only a white linen shift.

She followed her new husband reluctantly, glancing back at the screen with a look Tess knew only too well.

Does it hurt terribly?

"Just lie back and think of anything else," Tess muttered into her teacup.

"Don't talk," said Jacomo, turning his baleful gaze on Tess. "I don't want to hear a peep from you. It's your fault we're here."

"No, indeed. It's your vile brother's," said Tess, unable to stop herself from poking the bear with a stick. "Or your harridan mother's."

"Mother was pleased with this marriage and satisfied with the bride's virtue," said the student-priest, folding his fat arms over his fat chest and leaning back until his shoulders rested against the wall. "You had to blab to Heinrigh. You couldn't stay quiet a few hours longer for your own sister's sake."

"You don't know what I've done or would do for my sister's sake," hissed Tess. Her fingers clenched around her cup, as if she might dash its contents in Jacomo's face.

"I know more than you suppose." He had the gall to smile.

Tess snorted unattractively. "Whatever you imagine, it can have no reflection on Jeanne."

"My mother would disagree," he said, leering nastily. "Does the name 'Lord Morney's Little Bit' mean anything to you?"

In fact it did not. Something inside her unclenched slightly. Maybe Jacomo didn't know anything after all. "'Little Bit' sounds equine. Are you referring to his horse?"

Jacomo made a horsy sound through his lips. "I have it on

good authority that you played the harlot to Lord Morney and half the lads at St. Bert's."

"Lies," she said. She downed the last of her cup, relieved. He knew half-truths at most. Rumor had rendered the tale plausibly deniable; resemblance to real persons, living or dead, was coincidental. Tess set her cup on the floor; she caught a brief glimpse of the scene beyond the screen and averted her gaze. "Where do you get your inaccurate gossip?" she said.

"I drink at the Mallet and Mullet," he said, and this time Tess flinched. He couldn't have seen her there; it had been almost three years.

Jacomo smirked, malice written on his florid face. "Sometimes I drink with Harald Fjargard and Roger Ivy. They tell amusing stories about one Therese Belgioso. Don't deny that's you; I'm not an idiot, and you're no mistress of disguise."

Tess's mouth went bone dry, and suddenly she was at the Mallet and Mullet again—*in Will's room above the kitchens, the floor strewn with books and clothes. There is giggling coming from behind the privacy screen. Will leaps out of bed to find Harald and Roger—his best mates—hiding behind it. He spreads his arms and lets them take in his nakedness. "Happy now? May it be the last thing you ever see!"*

He swats the pair with his shirt and they flee, laughing.

Tessie weeps disconsolately, mortified that they've seen her, seen all. Will comes back to bed, gathers her on his lap, says, "It gladdens my heart to see you weeping. Do you know why, little bird? You're the same shy, innocent girl I first met, so modest and pure." He kisses her bare shoulder. "You are still a virgin in your heart, my little bird, my wife!"

Tess forced her mind back to the present, reeling and nauseated; she longed to crawl into a hole and die. She could only keep her eyes fixed on the floor, her skirts, or Jacomo's black-clad knee.

She was not going to play Roger Ivy to her sister's wedding night.

The student-priest studied her expression as if examining a vase for cracks. "That hit a nerve, I see," he said. "Is your conscience bothering you, 'Maid' Dombegh?"

His sarcasm and self-satisfaction felt like another layer of filth on her skin. "Is this how you spend your time at seminary?" Tess said through her teeth. "Getting the dirt on everyone?"

"It passes the time," he said stiffly, raising his chin so it was merely doubled, not tripled.

"You're going to be a terrible priest," she said, clenching her hands in her lap.

He leaned in, grinning, his teeth small and precise in his round face. "Maybe. But at least I'm not a dirty whor—"

Her fist was in motion before she even registered his words, as if her body had made the decision without her, certain she'd approve. And she did approve, in principle, though in practice the collision with Jacomo's nose hurt her knuckles.

He leaped up, blood gushing down his chin and running into the channels of his white ruff.

The treacherous bench gave way at last and pitched Tess onto her back. She battled her farthingale down and wrested herself back to sitting just in time to see Jeanne, her face pale and her eyes enormous, clutching a bedsheet to her bosom, peek around the edge of the screen.

Three

That night, Tess dreamed.

Drunk as she was, she would not ordinarily have remembered her dreams, but this was unusually vivid. She discovered (in dreamland) that her left foot was wrapped in filthy bandages; she could not remember why. When she unwrapped them, it turned out the bandages had been keeping her foot bound to her leg, and that without them the foot was completely unattached. It lay there on the pile of bandages, inert.

How long had her foot been separated from the rest of her? How had it happened, and how could she have forgotten?

She'd cut her own foot off with a cleaver. She remembered doing it, now that she thought it over, but what a thing to forget! It must have been the most terrifying moment of her life, the moment she realized it had to be done and that she would go through with it. It must have hurt (she couldn't remember, but logically it must have). How had she found the courage and the will to bring the knife down?

She spent the rest of the dream trying to recapture that feeling—the definiteness, the surety and determination. The commitment. When you decide to cut off your own foot, there can be no hesitation; it's one swift, decisive blow or a lifetime of mangled regrets. She had done it, though. She had been that strong, if only once.

Sunlight made her eyelids flutter, and she rolled over irritably, not wanting to wake up. She was just on the verge of recapturing the feeling, how she had brought the cleaver down unflinchingly, how she had been tragic and mighty, and in that moment how her bones had chipped and shattered, but it was all done in an instant.

Severed.

Her eyes popped open, and for a moment she didn't know where she was. Tangled in bedclothes, she lay sideways across a strange bed, her head half lolling off one edge. Above her the ceiling swam with cherubs, and for a nightmarish moment she thought she was back at her grandmother's house, in the room where Dozerius had been born.

She flailed about, panicking, until she was half sitting up. The room swirled around her, and her stomach churned within her.

This was not that room. There were no cobwebs, no midwives, no empty cradle in the corner. She didn't know this room at all. She flopped back, relieved, but her stomach was still apoplectic. She rolled slowly, then more urgently, scanning the floor for the inevitable chamber pot, found it, vomited.

Ye Saints, she'd been drunk. She had not quite achieved sobriety yet.

She rolled onto her back, wiping her mouth on a corner of the sheet, able to contemplate the cherubs with a bit more composure. They frolicked on puffy clouds, chasing each other. She scanned their faces again and again, until she realized she was looking for Dozerius. She wasn't going to find him. She felt ashamed to have hoped.

In fact, she couldn't remember what he'd looked like, exactly. Red. Squished. Like a wizened old man fashioned out of ham. These cherubs, insofar as they were babies at all, were much older, milk-plump and smiling, with curling hair. She despised them for it.

Tess rubbed her eyes hard with the heels of her hands until spots danced in her vision, and then she pried herself out of bed. She had the shadow of a headache, and it was going to get worse.

She used the chamber pot, feeling slightly sorry for whoever had to clean it later. For all she knew, it was her. She was in her linen chemise; her farthingale gown had been dumped unceremoniously on the floor beside the wardrobe. It was too complicated to put back on, and it was all full of regrets (she was slowly recollecting the pieces of these: Countess Margarethe, Heinrigh, and something else she couldn't find yet). She opened the wardrobe and found nothing but a man's short houppelande in brown. Good enough. It would cover what she wanted covered. She pulled it over her chemise as an improvised dressing gown, staggered across to the door of the room, and pulled it open.

She didn't recognize the corridor. This was not Cragmarog Castle. This was nowhere she had ever been before.

As if on cue, a trickle of harpsichord notes reached her ears. It was like a trail of bread crumbs through the house, and she knew whom it must lead to. She followed the spidery music up the dim, carpeted hallway, down a curving stair, and into a high-ceilinged chamber with tall windows full of morning sun.

No, more like noonday sun.

Seraphina, in pale, loose morning robes, sat at the instrument with the bench well back to accommodate her belly. Her brown hair, darker than Tess's, curled over her shoulder in a plait; her face, rounded with pregnancy weight, shone like the moon. She flicked her dark eyes toward Tess but did not break tempo. Closer to the empty fireplace was a round table with one dirty place setting and one clean, the remains of breakfast. Tess went straight over, poured herself a cup of tea, and gulped it down.

"Help yourself," said Seraphina, too late. "If you want something hot, I'll ring Anna."

Tess's tea was lukewarm and bitter. It might have set the tone for Tess's reply: "Where are we, and why did you drag me here?"

"This is the Queen's summer home, Ranleigh Cottage," said Seraphina, pausing her playing to pick up a charcoal pencil and jot some notes on the page in front of her.

Summer home must be the royal family's code for "place to hide pregnancies." Tess had heard the name Ranleigh Cottage, anyway; Seraphina had been living here for two months and would stay on until she gave birth.

Tess glanced at the thick Zibou carpet, the satin drapes and ornate furnishings. Maybe it was a cottage by a queen's standards, but not by anyone else's.

"As for why," Seraphina continued, letting the last word stretch as if she intended to let the question be her answer, "I'm going to guess you have some idea."

The memories came flooding back to Tess in a rush: she'd broken Jacomo's nose and ruined Jeanne's wedding night. The blood rose in Tess's face, and for a moment she couldn't speak. Seraphina met her eye from across the room and seemed to glean the questions Tess couldn't ask, for she folded her hands upon her stomach and said, "Jeanne is fine. She's married. Your being a violent drunk didn't nullify that."

Tess exhaled and lowered herself shakily into a chair. Her headache was beginning to assert itself. "Am I to be charged with assault?"

Seraphina's mouth crimped with amusement. "One would think you were a lawyer's daughter." She paused, as if waiting for Tess to laugh, but Tess didn't find that funny. "It seems there are to be no charges. Lord Richard came vociferously to your defense, claiming Lord Jacomo provoked you. I can only assume he's been wanting to pop his brother in the nose himself."

It was a relief, but not enough of a relief. Tess glanced over the food on offer. Cold toast. Hothouse strawberries. It was all quease-inducing. She stuck with tea, although the second cup brought her to the dregs of the pot. She added milk and gulped it down. "Are Mama and Papa here?" said Tess, setting down her cup and glancing around apprehensively.

"No, it's just us," said her sister, running her fingers across the keyboard again. "I offered to take you on. Everyone else is too angry to speak to you right now."

"I see," said Tess, slouching aggressively and crossing her arms. Of course they'd fob her off on someone else, the way they had when she was pregnant. She was too awful to even look at. "'O miracle-mongering St. Seraphina, won't you rid us of this troublesome Tess!'"

Seraphina raised her head and stared with big-eyed incredulity. The twins had always called this her "baffled owl face," not to be confused with her "cogitating owl face" or her "get-out-of-my-room-before-I-bite-you-with-my-terrible-beak owl face." She was owlish to her core.

"You haven't been yourself for some time, Sisi," said Seraphina. Only Jeanne was allowed to use that name; Tess bristled. "You've been unhappy. Everyone is at their wits' end trying to help you."

"Oh, indeed, 'everyone' has been trying to help, have they? They're worried I'm unhappy? They have a funny way of showing it."

"They've tried to talk to you. If you can't tell, that may be emblematic of the problem," said Seraphina, infuriatingly calm as ever. She was half dragon, and it was easy to tell which half. "As soon as anyone brings up the past, you get defensive and shut them out."

"What a load of self-serving nonsense!" cried Tess, leaping to her feet and pacing before the empty hearth. "I have set aside any hope or wish or ambition for myself, bent all my purpose toward securing Jeanne her damned husband—so Neddie and Paul might be educated—and in return I am to be packed off to a convent. But no, you say, they've been worried about my feelings and want to help. Cack on ice. They could help by giving me some other choice in life!"

"You had the option to stay on as governess, until you got drunk and punchy. I tried to give you another choice," said Seraphina, cool as marble, "and you spit on it and sent it back."

She meant Countess Margarethe. Tess's headache seemed suddenly to extend to all her limbs. "I don't want your pity," said Tess contemptuously.

"Well, that's fortunate, because you don't have it," said Seraphina. There was a tartness to her phrasing, but she smiled as she spoke, as if she found Tess's tantrum vaguely amusing. "I don't pity you at all."

"Because I brought this all on myself?" Tess sneered.

"Because you're not as bad off as you imagine," said Seraphina, marking up her music sheets some more. "You're seventeen. Your whole life is still before you."

Tess wanted to shout at her sister again, wanted to rage and tempest and scream, but her throat had tightened. Her whole life still before her? That was such a lie.

At seventeen Seraphina had been crossing the Southlands on bold adventures, stopping a war, summoning giants, modestly demurring when called a Saint, and charming the royal cousins. She couldn't see how blessed she was. She had no idea what it was like to throw away your future in the blink of an eye, to be relegated either to serving her sister or to serving with a sisterhood.

Seraphina had it easy; she got to live by different rules from everyone else, because she was different. Anytime Tess had protested the unfairness of things—*How come Seraphina gets tutors? Why is she allowed to walk to St. Ida's by herself and I'm not?*—Mama had answered, low and fiercely, "Because she's not like us."

Envy was such a bitter draft. Tess hated it, but it wasn't the only part of herself she hated; it could get in line behind everything else. She turned to the table, surreptitiously wiping her eyes, and pretended to take an interest in toast.

Seraphina pushed back her bench and rose like some antique camel, steadying herself against the instrument with one hand. She waddled toward the table. "You may stay here until you're ready to face the parental wrath," she said gently, pulling out the chair opposite Tess. "You won't be in anyone's way until the baby comes."

"The baby might come tomorrow," said Tess, picking the crust off her toast.

Seraphina's gaze went owlish again, as if she were trying to remember what had happened with Tess's baby, or trying to gauge the best way to talk about it. Tess smiled mirthlessly. Even Seraphina, for all her brave words, surely had to tiptoe around the subject.

"I never heard what your birthing was like," said Seraphina, not tiptoeing in the least. "I hope you'll tell me—"

Tess bristled. "I don't remember it," she blurted. Seraphina was right that Tess didn't want to talk. That didn't make her *right*.

Seraphina said, "You don't have to talk to me. We can avoid each other entirely. Whatever will give you peace and space and time to think. I'll put off Papa and Anne-Marie; the Little Sisters of St. Loola will wait until you're ready."

Tess squirmed. The inevitable was no less inevitable for its postponement. She was getting what she deserved, but she still felt like lashing out: "You know you always hurt Mama's feelings by calling her Anne-Marie. You're so quick to underscore that you're not one of us."

Tess glanced up from her mangled toast. Seraphina wouldn't look hurt—she was too much the dragon for that—but she grew preternaturally still.

"You think you're so superior," said Tess, hell-bent on being cruel. "Look at you, here in the Queen's summer palace, ready to bear a bastard's bastard. You're no different from me, but nobody would dare to call you whore."

Seraphina opened her mouth and closed it again. Her brows drew down as if she were considering the merits of Tess's argument, weighing that final word against her conscience.

"Maybe Blessed Jannoula was right," said Tess. "Maybe you're a Saint. I guess we'd better let you do whatever you want, just in case."

That was below the belt, and Tess knew it. Seraphina's relationship with St. Jannoula had been painful and complicated, and she hated being called a Saint.

Still she said nothing.

"You know who else was a Saint?" cried Tess, pounding a fist on the table. "St. Vitt. And you know what he said about women like you? 'In this order shall they enter Heaven: first the virgin, whose purity equals that of the final abode; then the chaste widow, who returns to her pure state after her duty is accomplished; and lastly the faithful wife, who of necessity must stain herself with the repeoplement of the world—'"

"*Repeoplement* is quite an astonishing word," said Seraphina, quirking a tiny smile.

"'And who may not enter Heaven?'" Tess continued bull-headedly. "'The faithless wife, the unchaste harlot, the craven, shameless whore. For them are the furnaces prepared, for them the long days contemplating woe.'"

"Indeed," said Seraphina, who seemed to relax in the face of Tess spouting scripture. "You do realize that that positively contradicts St. Loola's credo: 'Thou mayest reach Heaven only by the mercy of the fallen.' If you're to join the Little Sisters, you may require some adjustment to your theology."

"You always do this!" cried Tess, flailing in frustration. "You divert every argument into some irrelevant side stream. I don't care if St. Vitt's diction is archaic, and I don't care if the Little Sisters of St. Loola contradict him—"

"Yes, yes, you only wanted to call me whore," said Seraphina, waspishly now. "You've done it. Twice. Well done. Are you finished? I have a present for you, but I'm feeling less and less like giving it to you."

Seraphina strode over to the harpsichord again, pulled a small wooden chest out from under it, and plunked it down at Tess's feet. "As your fellow 'fallen' woman, I know what it's like to be the one who doesn't get married," said Seraphina, hands on her hips. She tapped the trunk with her toe. "I thought Jeanne shouldn't be the only one getting gifts today."

Tess glanced warily at her sister's face, but there was no trace of guile there. There never was, even when Seraphina was lying egregiously.

Tess sighed dramatically, disliking to lean over with her

head so achy, but her pregnant sister wasn't going to bend over the chest again. Tess unfastened the brass clasps and flung open the lid. Inside was a pair of dark leather boots, knee-high and supple, finely tooled, soft as a quigutl hatchling. They smelled delicious.

"I've been admiring Countess Marga's boots since the day I met her," said Seraphina. "She finally told me who her boot-maker is. Since you and I have about the same-sized feet, I had the boots measured off myself."

Tess had picked up one of them and cradled it like a child, but this additional narrative from Seraphina soured her on the gift. There was nothing so fine it couldn't be spoiled by family. Tess let the boot flop out of her hand into the trunk. "Thanks," she said cuttingly.

Seraphina did not appear cut at all, but one never knew what was going on in the middle of her. She smiled as if choosing to believe Tess liked the gift, and then returned to her instrument.

Tess made a point of leaving the boots behind when she quit the room, but hours later she found they had migrated to her cherub-infested bedroom. "Don't follow me," she said, shoving the box under the bed. The boots said nothing in return.

It is the nature of boots, however, to speak subtly. Tess lay awake that night, thinking about them. They seemed to be a suggestion, tooled in leather.

It's time to walk away from all this, they said.

"Shut up," said Tess, and for a while they did.

You dreamed about feet. That means a journey is imminent, said the boots.

"No, I dreamed about cutting off my foot," said Tess into the darkness. "I'm maimed. Ruined. I can't go anywhere."

But that wasn't quite true. That missed the flavor of the dream entirely. Her dream-foot hadn't hurt; she'd tied it back onto her leg and walked on it as usual. Hacking it off had been an act of tragic courage, taking all her determination and will.

All her Will. She chuckled, which was absurd because it wasn't funny.

It's time to cut ties, said the boots-of-her-heart. *That dream was a suggestion, too. It's going to be hard, but you're brave enough.*

"But do I have the Will?" Tess said, making the joke twice. It was no funnier the second time. William of Affle had brought her nothing but grief; she didn't want him back. She should not have been laughing—and it's possible she wasn't. There's a line between laughing and crying, and Tess was right on its razor-thin edge, teetering back and forth, expecting any moment to land squarely in one or the other. Tears ran down her face, her diaphragm began to ache, and she couldn't catch her breath. She buried her face in the pillow and only succeeded in soaking it with tears and giving herself hiccups.

You'll only avoid the convent by walking away, said the boots sagely.

"Boots can't tell me what—*hic*—to do," said Tess.

The next morning, however, she tried them on just to see. The left fit perfectly. The right would have fit, but there was an obstruction in the toe. She upturned the boot, and a pewter ring dropped out, pinging across the floor. She scurried after it and saw that it was a thnik, one of the cheap ones now ubiquitous in the Lavondaville markets.

Seraphina had the mate, presumably, but Tess declined to test the thing. The implication seemed clear. Seraphina expected Tess to take her boots and go, and if she ran into trouble, she could call home with this thnik.

That was almost enough to make her stay. Such was the contrarian nature of Tess—especially against Seraphina—that she would have tossed out ten babies and drunk their bathwater rather than take a hint. She would have cut off someone else's nose and swapped it with her own, the better to spite everybody's face. She would have walked twenty miles backward through a snowstorm for a bowl of bitterness if there were a proverb about that—and maybe even more so if there wasn't. The proverbs were going to have to keep up with Tess; she outstripped them at every turn.

Tess put the boots back in their box and shoved it under her bed. She threw the ring hard at the cherub-crusted ceiling. It ricocheted and landed who knew where.

Still, Tess found herself in the kitchens with nothing to do later that day, and—because she was bored, merely—she stole some little cheeses while the cook's back was turned. She nosed around in spare rooms and came up with a satchel and some sturdy kirtles, the sort that would make her look like a respectable laboring countrywoman. She nicked a broad straw hat from the garden shed; it would be missed by the gardeners, but presumably they could tell the Queen it had been eaten by marmots and she'd requisition a new one.

"The royal gardening-hat budget," Tess imagined Queen Glisselda telling Seraphina, "has gone right through the roof. It's the marmots, you know. They're insatiable."

The next day Tess pinched some oatcake, some stockings, and a bottle of wine. Upon the fourth day she took a wool blanket and filched a second bottle of wine. The first bottle was, perhaps not mysteriously, already empty.

A map of the Southlands—Goredd, Ninys, and Samsam, plus some of the southern islands—took up almost an entire wall of the cottage's library. Tess found herself studying it, especially Ninys, her mother's ancestral homeland. She spoke serviceable, if rusty, Ninysh. She didn't have family there anymore; her great-grandfather Count Julian Belgioso had been exiled along with all his progeny for a variety of crimes, real and imagined. They'd come from Segosh, which was easy enough to find, being the capital. Whoever had drawn this map had represented the city with fanciful buildings and spires; Tess touched it as gently as one might pet a skittish finch, as if it might flutter off.

You could start over in a city, expunge your past, be anybody. Her Belgioso family had done it, coming north. Contrary to Mama's claim, women sometimes did leave home to live unchaperoned. Tess had heard tales, and they didn't always end in disaster.

She'd spent the last two years altering Jeanne's clothes; she didn't enjoy it much, but she could work as a seamstress.

An actual seamstress, not a harlot. The Abominable Paul could go die in a fire.

If Seraphina noticed Tess sneaking and plotting, she gave no sign. The eldest Dombegh sister, stately at twenty-two, kept to her routines: composition in the morning, a garden walk in the afternoon, a visit with the midwife after supper. Tess saw her at meals and managed, with effort, not to quarrel with her again.

Upon the fifth morning, Seraphina perused a letter at the breakfast table. "You will be interested to hear this, Tess," she said, gesturing with her teacup. "Papa and Anne-Marie—"

"Not interested," said Tess through a mouthful of kipper.

"—intend to come here tomorrow," Seraphina continued, as if Tess had not spoken. "Not to fetch you home—I've told them you may stay as long as you wish—but to bring two abbesses to meet you: Mother Philomela of St. Loola's order, and Mother Nancy of St. Agnyesta's." Seraphina raised her guileless brown eyes to Tess's face and smiled. "Well, that's encouraging, isn't it? They make cheese at St. Agnyesta's. You'd like that better than plague, I should think."

Tess wasn't listening about the cheese; she'd gotten stuck on the word *tomorrow*. She was out of time. The letter didn't say they were coming to fetch her, but the letter was a liar, if she knew her mother. Seraphina couldn't protect Tess from their parents; living in the Queen's house didn't give her a queen's power. Anyway, it wouldn't matter what Seraphina did. One look at Mama's tearful, disappointed face and something would crumple inside Tess. She would swallow her despair and comply, because Mama's despair was heavier, and Tess's conscience couldn't bear adding to it.

What was this power called Mama? Why couldn't Tess stand against it? She had bucked against Seraphina for the last several days, and the very act of pushing back made Tess feel alive. But there was no pushing against Mama.

Tess picked needle-fine bones out of her breakfast fish and realized she could leave tonight, under cover of darkness. She could be over the fields and halfway to Trowebridge before her parents arrived. Why wait for darkness? She could tell Seraphina she was ill.

"I'm going to miss lunch," said Tess, pushing back from the table. "And supper."

"Are you, indeed?" said Seraphina, buttering a scone. "I thought you looked unwell, but I didn't like to mention it."

Tess scowled ferociously, hating the way Seraphina saw through her, but Seraphina couldn't be bothered to look up and face the withering glare. "You know what you are?" said Tess, who couldn't leave without kicking her sister once more. "Insufferable and smug. You think you're so sensible and that you know what other people are going to do, but you're wrong. You don't know anything. I am going to astonish you someday, and you will fall right over dead from the shock of it."

Seraphina looked up, deliberately finished chewing her scone, and said, "I'll die happy, then. That's good news. Of course, now I shall be expecting it."

Tess stuck out her tongue, rudely blew a farewell serenade, turned on her heel, and went.

Four

Tess quit the house, her family, and her entire life before lunch.

It would be exactly like Papa to arrive early, so Tess eschewed the front drive. She cut across broad lawns, through a yew hedge and a garden of old, twisted rosebushes (not even leafed out yet), across a field of sheep bleating anxiously to their lambs, and over a stile in a stone wall. The field beyond the wall was full of scrub and bramble, and Tess had hopes that this marked the edge of the Queen's summer estate. You never could be sure with the Queen, though; anything not explicitly owned by someone else was hers by default.

The stile was an A-shaped wooden ladder over the wall, and Tess paused at the top, the whole of Ducana province spread at her booted feet. Farmsteads and village churches dotted the rolling hills, while hedgerows and stone walls divided them into a chessboard of fields, the yellow-green of new shoots alternating with black, sodden earth. The sky glowed warmly blue, as if it were determined to make the day not merely fine but over-the-top, ridiculously beautiful.

Even Tess's self-pitying heart found itself a little bit moved.

The cathedral spires of Trowebridge, the biggest town in Ducana province, rose to the southwest. That had struck Tess as the logical place to go first; she might buy supplies there, and then take the main road south. As soon as she descended this hilltop, the town would disappear from view. The direct route passed by Cragmarog Castle (which she could make out, coiled like a snake in the midst of trees), and that was no good. Her parents—or, more humiliatingly, Jeanne's in-laws—might be encountered upon that road at any time.

Tess, having studied the map, knew the other landmark to look for in this landscape. Directly south was a hilltop ruin, Pentrach's Dun, which she could reach via footpaths, ancient right-of-ways leading straight through farmers' fields. From that hilltop, she should be able to see another road, running westerly to Trowebridge.

She had to go the long way, two sides of the triangle, because the hypotenuse was forbidden her. This struck her as perfectly symbolic of her entire life.

The sun shone; she put on her gardening hat against it. Her satchel straps dug into her shoulders, and the hedgerows snatched at her skirts as she passed. A great cloud of blackbirds ascended, screaming, and scared her. The wind slapped her cheeks, damp soil clogged her boot soles, and the hem of her kirtle grew steadily dirtier.

In spite of all this—in spite of herself, really—her heart began to lift as she walked, or maybe a weight began to fall away. She'd done it. She'd gotten free of her family (*for now*, a voice at the back of her mind nagged). Dirt and discomfort and uncertainty were nothing to her.

She was almost smiling to herself as she passed a gang of peasants, red-handed men in smocks and clogs. They were in the next pasture over, shouting and whipping the cows with willow switches, driving them away from their hapless calves. Two men would then grab a lone calf by its knobby legs, bucking and kicking, upside down in their arms, and haul it into another enclosure. The cows mooed, low and despairing, their udders heavy with milk for their babies, and the babies cried for their mothers—an inhuman cry, but unmistakable to Tess.

Tess didn't understand what mysterious agricultural purpose required tearing bovine families apart. She watched with one hand to her heart and the other to her lips, and she was struck by both the cruelty of the men and the realization that she was a woman, walking alone.

She started walking faster, hoping none of them would look her way.

As if they could read her thoughts, one of the men began to sing:

> *A little pretty bonny lass*
> *Went forth upon the dewy grass*
> *I followed her down to the dell*
> *She snubbed me with a fare-ye-well*

Whereupon the rest of the farmhands took up the chorus:

Upon the heath, the holt, the hill,
My girl, I'll do whate'er I will.

Tess's face puckered at these lyrics and fell at the next verse (which was too bawdy for general consumption). She hunched her shoulders and kept walking. She thought she heard someone whistle after her, but maybe it was merely the call of the hedge shrike.

No, that was a whistle. Tess didn't look back.

The world was full of men. She'd been so desperate to get gone that she hadn't given that consideration the weight it deserved. All unbidden, Mama's voice spoke in her head: *Men are scoundrels, and they only ever want one thing. They will try every trick in the book to seduce you, and if you won't go willingly, they'll find a way to take you anyway.*

She shuddered. Mama hadn't said such things often—preferring to focus on Tess's own inadequacies—but of course they were the corollary to everything St. Vitt had always said. *Why* should women avert their eyes and dress modestly and suppress their desires, if not for the sake of men? How was the wolf to blame, if the sheep were roaming free?

Thou shalt not tempt wasn't a commandment of any Saint she knew, but it could've been.

Maybe she could find a way to live alone and support herself—she still believed that—but walking across the entire Southlands, with no protector, to get there? Suddenly it didn't seem like such a clever idea. She wasn't going to last out here.

She paused in the shade of a hedgerow, out of sight of prying eyes, to peel a cheese and munch an oatcake. It was a filling enough lunch, but fast walking and the warm spring sunshine had made Tess powerfully thirsty. Salty cheese and dry bannock didn't help.

All she'd brought was wine. She held the bottle up to the light; the sun shone enticingly through green glass and liquid dark as night. It wouldn't quench her thirst particularly well. The sensible thing to do would be to go looking for water. Every little farmstead surely had a well ... and a red-handed cowherd, or a lecherous shepherd, or any other sort of man with a bawdy song in his head and a gleam in his eye as he realized she was at his mercy.

Some of them were surely fine—most of them probably were—but you couldn't tell by looking, and that was the problem. She drank about half her wine, staggered to her feet, and carried on, trying to stay out of sight now, keeping to the shadows of hedgerows.

As she sneaked, her mother's voice came to her: *You can't tell if a man might be good or evil, but do you know what they can tell by looking at you? That you're not where you should be, and therefore not what you should be. You aren't at home, so you must be public property. No one's taking care of you, therefore anyone might claim you.*

A gang of men with rakes suddenly crossed the road in front of her, moving from one meadow to another. Tess pressed herself into a hedgerow to avoid them. One of the younger ones winked at her; nobody was fooled.

They know, said her mother. *You're an old shoe that might fit any foot. A sucked marrow bone. A gob of chewed honeycomb, its sweetness long gone. No wonder Will left you; he knew what you really were.*

"Stop it," Tess muttered, wiping her eyes. She pulled the bottle back out of her pack and glared at it accusingly. She'd had an agreement with wine: it would be a good friend to her and mute these kinds of voices, but it wasn't doing the trick today. It had ceded the floor to them and stripped her naked of defenses.

She drank the rest, still hoping it would do what it was supposed to.

Her mother's voice followed her the rest of the way to Trowebridge. Tess felt it like hot breath at the nape of her neck, smelled it in wafts of woodsmoke and manure. It wrapped around her ankles like a vine, making her stumble, and snagged the hem of her skirt as she climbed over stiles. The voice told her to hide whenever masculine farmhands came into view, called her a contemptible insect for hiding, and then flew above her like a flag to make sure everyone knew.

Tess missed the ancient beauty of Pentrach's Dun, missed a salmon sunset and the aching curve of the river, so wholly occupied was she with wrestling the unseen.

She reached Trowebridge at dusk and stood on the eponymous stone bridge staring at the shadowy buildings, her heart in her boots. Even if she had enough money for lodgings, which she very much doubted, she didn't have the wherewithal to knock on strange doors and ask.

Running away was the worst idea she'd ever had. She regretted everything.

An idea bubbled up from her sludgy mind—didn't storybook

trolls live under bridges? It would provide shelter enough for one night, anyway. She picked her way through the weeds and crawled under the bridge. It was humid, but more spacious than she would have guessed. Tess exhaled, finally feeling safe. *Like a cockroach in a crevasse,* her mother said, unable to resist one last kick while Tess was down. The wine bottle was long empty (she checked one last time, to be absolutely sure), so Tess chucked it toward the river, where it shattered on unseen rocks.

The earth under the bridge was cool against her cheek, at least.

To Tess's immeasurable disappointment, she woke up.

She could tell without even opening her eyes that she'd made herself ill. Her throat pricked and stabbed as if she'd swallowed a prickly gorse branch. Every inch of her hurt. Her feet were blistered from the stiff new boots, her muscles sore from seventeen miles of hills. The hard ground had compounded her aches; her joints felt swollen and wrong.

Sleeping longer might have helped, but rumbling wagons and tramping feet rudely imposed consciousness upon her. She lay on her side, curled in her blanket with the gardening hat for a scratchy pillow, listening and resenting and wondering if she could avoid getting up. She curled tighter. Surely she never had to move again if she didn't want to.

And she might not have, either, had the man not grabbed her from behind.

Panic lifted her to her feet before she could even think, and she stared at the ragged, twig-thin man who'd crept up in the night to sleep next to her. He was old, with barely a tooth in his head, and he yawned grotesquely, his mouth a dark hole in his white furze-bush beard. His right hand, clutching a corner of her blanket to his chest, was missing two fingers. He was disgusting.

Tess's head pounded from the sudden movement, and her fear condensed into rage.

"Give me that," she growled, grabbing at her blanket. It was trapped under his body.

He croaked, incongruously, "Annie?"

Tess shoved him off, rolled him over, but the fellow had an iron grip on the corner of the blanket. She tried prying his knobby fist open, which only made him shriek and flail about. His forearm smacked Tess's aching head so hard her ear started ringing, and the next thing she knew she was kicking him once, twice, thrice in the ribs. His thorax made a hollow sound.

Tess backed away, panting, horrified at herself. She'd never . . . she'd been so angry . . . she could have broken his rib cage as easily as crushing a wicker basket.

"Oh, Annie," said the vagrant mournfully. He'd curled into a bony ball, his cheek pressed into the dirt. "I know I deserve that."

Tess snatched up her blanket and whipped it furiously, shaking the dust out.

"What is this place?" he said. He sounded like a child. The dust made him cough.

Fold blanket. Into satchel with both hands. She had to get out of here.

The old man ran his three-fingered hand through his wild white hair. "Did the dragon chase you here? I saw it and came running. I thought I could save you this time."

The more he talked, the worse her conscience stabbed. She'd kicked a delusional geezer who didn't know where or when he was. She was a terrible person. Tess swung her pack onto her back and scuttled out from under the bridge. The old man called after her—"Annie!"—but she pretended not to hear.

Tess hauled herself out of the shadows, desperate to leave bridge and beggar behind, up the rocky embankment onto the road. It was so bright up here, she couldn't open her eyes all the way. She staggered onto the bridge, into horse and pedestrian traffic. Food carts lined the roadway, and the smell of cooking twisted her stomach painfully; she couldn't tell if she was hungry or nauseated.

Tess hurried like one pursued, pushing past the broad buttocks of horses and the shopping baskets of young wives, toward the market square. Around her, children laughed; the sun shone on the market tents; bright flags flapped in the spring breeze; swallows swooped and sang overhead. Every beautiful thing felt like a fist clamped around Tess's heart, squeezing.

She stuck her face in the market fountain, not caring how uncouth she looked, and gulped water frantically, like she was trying to drown.

She'd kicked an old man. He'd been no danger to her, and she'd viciously attacked him, and she'd done it (if she was being honest) in part because he was so feeble. Of all the men she might have liked to kick, she'd kicked the one who couldn't fight back.

Tess raised her face from the fountain, gasping, and wiped it on her arm. Women with water jars stared at her; she hurried away, ashamed. She didn't make it ten steps before she had to pause and lean against a market stall, shaking and sweating and unable to catch her breath.

She was despicable. How could she go on?

At that very moment, Tess chanced to raise her eyes and look across the crowded square. There, shining like Heaven's own messenger, sat that most eminently kickable of men, her father, upon a borrowed horse. Relief coursed through her, and an unaccustomed tenderness.

He'd come to find her and save her from herself. He'd been worried; he loved her.

Her lungs unclenched and she took an enormous, restorative breath. This had to be a sign from the Saints. She'd made her point—and made a mess of everything, as usual—and now it was time to concede defeat. She was too tired to keep fighting.

Tess made a beeline toward her father, ready to place herself in his gentle and capable hands, but herds of milling shoppers stood in her way. "Papa!" she shouted, waving, but he neither heard nor saw. He turned his horse up a side street. She was losing him; even a liberal application of elbows couldn't clear a path through the crowd quickly enough. She noted where his hat plume disappeared, and the spot became her pole star, guiding her.

He was long gone by the time Tess broke free of the square. Praying he'd kept to this road and hadn't turned up any side streets, she ran past mercers, tailors, leatherworkers, her boots thunking on the hard-packed dirt of the road, her head thumping painfully. About a mile along, it curved south, dead-ending at a wide wooden building with a statue at the apex of the roof. Papa was nowhere in sight, but the horse he'd been riding was tied up out front alongside a tiny donkey.

Tess's feet slowed at the sight of the Saint on the roof, recognizing her big green apple even before reading the plaque: ST. LOOLA'S HOSPICE FOR THE INDIGENT AND INCAPACITATED.

Papa wasn't looking for Tess; he did not yet realize she'd run away. He'd come for Mother Philomela of St. Loola's. Of course the nuns had to be fetched from town. They wouldn't have been wandering the fields near Cragmarog, grazing and mooing.

Tess wasn't sure what to do. He wouldn't be relieved to see her, as she'd . . . Her lungs tightened again. She should have known better than to hope. He might not even take her back home, not when this was where he ultimately wanted to leave her.

The door opened, and Tess darted behind the horse. She pulled her blanket out of her satchel and wrapped it over her head like a widow's shawl.

A widow's shawl with a light plaid weave. This would fool no one.

Papa approached the steed to untie it, but he was on the other side, engrossed in conversation with an elderly nun, Mother Philomela of St. Loola's, as per yesterday's letter. "We're at our wits' end," Tess heard Papa saying, his voice strained. "My wife insists this daughter was simply born bad—"

"No one is born bad," snapped the nun. Tess peeked at her over the horse's back; she was at least sixty and built like a grain stack, an impression enhanced by her yellow habit. She was looking at Papa shrewdly. "Anyway, you don't agree with your wife. What's your theory?"

Papa hesitated; contradicting Anne-Marie always made him anxious. "I suppose ... I assumed our Tess misbehaves for the pure, anarchic joy of disobedience."

He thought she was bad on purpose? He might as well have reached across the horse and slapped Tess. She'd never heard what he really thought of her before.

"So you have no idea, either," said Mother Philomela flatly. "Tell me more about her. I suppose she's out drinking till all hours, entertaining young men, dressing like a slattern?"

"Erm," said Papa, removing his hat and scratching his balding head.

He didn't know, Tess realized, her ears growing hot. He had no idea how she dressed or what she did all day, or why. Mama was bitter and mean, but at least she paid attention.

"She punched a priest," Papa finally said weakly.

"Feh. Who hasn't?" Mother Philomela had untied her donkey and was stroking its nose. "Well, never mind. The parents never know. I'll get to the bottom of it. Our order is salubrious for wild and selfish young ladies. Nothing like a hospice full of graypox victims to give you some perspective. Life is short, by Heaven's mercy, and we are distressingly fragile."

The nun leaped onto her donkey like a woman half her age and began to sing in an unexpectedly clear soprano:

The flesh is but
A sack of goo,
A feast for worms
To delve into.

Remember, mortal,
As you strive,
That you, ambitious goo,
Must also die.

Papa mounted his horse, his lips pinched as if the song disturbed him. Tess had been standing frozen, listening to them talk, and had forgotten to pull the shawl across her face. Papa looked right at her as he turned his steed.

He looked her in the eye.

Maybe he thought she looked familiar; his frown deepened, and his gaze lingered. Maybe he thought, *That woman could be Tessie's twin, almost,* or the question arose in his mind halfway to Ranleigh Cottage, *Wait, did I see . . . ? No, it couldn't have been.*

He didn't recognize his own daughter out of context. He rode on, unseeing, unknowing. Tess gaped after him, her voice caught in her throat, insubstantial as a ghost.

Five

Tess flopped down in an empty doorway at the edge of the market square and leaned her aching head against the frame. Papa had left her shaken.

She'd always known she was particularly flawed—it was the fabric of her life—but she hadn't been bad on purpose. Even if she'd been a bit wild as a child, that was a long time ago. Did Papa think she enjoyed shaming herself and her family? What kind of joy, anarchic or otherwise, was to be had from ruining yourself?

And yet Tess couldn't quite believe herself born bad, either. Her entire existence had gotten off on the wrong foot, somehow, but it wasn't uniformly awful. She'd taken good care of Faffy; she'd saved the life of a quigutl laying eggs in the cellar. She'd gone to Mass—well, no, Mama had dragged her. But would someone born bad have given two years of her life un-selfishly helping Jeanne find a husband?

Unselfishly? You whined the whole time, whispered her mother's voice at the back of her mind. *And you almost spoiled it for her in the end.*

Then there's Will and the baby. And just this morning you kicked a helpless old man.

Tess closed her eyes against the painful sunshine, deeply weary. Cosmically weary. She'd run away from home, and now she wanted to run away from running away, but it was no use. Tess (born bad) was always with her, wherever she went.

Wine might have helped, temporarily, but she had hardly any coin in her little purse. She could've afforded beer, but ... She cringed, remembering yesterday's state of mind, Mama's voice in endless pursuit. Being drunk wouldn't guarantee peace of mind, and besides, she'd be undrunk and penniless before she knew it, and then what would she do? Tess (b. b.) would be waiting for her, worse than ever.

There was only one permanent way to run away from your-self. Tess considered it carefully. The knife she'd brought was short and dull, and she didn't know where to stab herself effec-tively. It would be embarrassing to only mostly bleed to death before scabbing up. The bridge she'd slept under wasn't high, although there were convenient rocks to dash herself against. Dashing seemed an uncertain art, though. With her luck, she'd merely break her ankle and have to lie there in agony until someone discovered her.

Mother Philomela's song had made death sound as easy as it was inevitable, but Tess had (she felt) a special talent for doing things wrong. The *bad* in *born bad* was more than mere sinfulness; she'd bungle her own death, given half a chance. She did everything wrong.

She stared at the mockingly blue sky. Dying took commitment. It was easier to go on living incompetently. What if she put off deciding until tomorrow? She needed time to get her nerve up and work out a foolproof, painless way to do it. Until then, she'd walk on—badly.

Tess staggered to her feet, brushed dirt off her backside, and drifted back into the market. She bought a pork pie, devouring it joylessly, and a water skin, which seemed sensible. Then, having used up almost all her capacity for planning, she bought some more little cheeses, the foodstuff requiring the least amount of thought or ambition.

There. Incompetence fulfilled. She'd last one more day.

You'll never make it to Segosh, said her mother's voice. She swatted the gadfly thought away. She couldn't think about Segosh right now; one foot in front of the other was all she could manage.

A booth full of shiny quigutl devices stood nearby, and Tess's feet, operating separately from her will, took her in for a closer look. Most of their wares were communication charms, shiny thniks and thnimis heaped in pewter boxes or strung from the ceiling in matched pairs, tinkling like Saint's-day chimes. Tess didn't care for those; her childhood friend, Pathka, had given her a taste for the oddities. A statue that spoke your words back to you, billed as an aid to memory. A four-legged dancing fish, sold as a children's toy or back massager. A whistling, jack-knifing mechanical shrimp that had no purpose whatsoever.

Pathka had scuttled out of Tess's life before most quigutl craft had become legally available to the public, but she'd given Tess a small collection of curiosities during the years they'd been friends. Seraphina had collected such trinkets, too, but her docile statuettes were boring compared with Tess's restless pets. (Tess drew the obvious parallels between herself and her sister, of course; it was so seldom that she came out ahead of Seraphina in any way that she'd clung to this one victory with a fierce, if misplaced, pride.) Pathka had given her an ever-inching brass caterpillar, a scorpion-cow named Stingy, and a *fthootl* (Pathka's word) that fluttered like a drunken butterfly and would poke you in the eye given half an opportunity.

"It's supposed to poke you in the eye," Pathka had explained. "It's part of a game we play, called Poke Me in the Eye. The object is—"

"To poke someone in the eye?" Tess had cut in, like the young smarty-biscuit she'd been.

"No, no," said Pathka. "You're supposed to catch it with your eye cone before it can poke your eye." She had demonstrated; the quigutl had bulgy eye cones like chameleons, and the aperture could widen and narrow, apparently at will. When the *fthootl* made a stab at her, she clamped down on it. "It's good for building up ocular dexterity," Pathka explained.

"What happens if it gets all the way through?" asked Tess, morbidly fascinated.

"Blindness," said Pathka pleasantly, as if she were talking about cake.

The memory made Tess smile in spite of herself. Most Goreddis found the lizardy quigutl frightening, but if you could get past the surface—learn their language, to start—they were deeply odd. Far stranger than anyone imagined. Tess felt privileged to know this.

Three quigutl ran the market stall in Trowebridge: a youngster who clambered up the booth's support columns and fetched additional stock from under the thatched eaves, a middle-aged female who bargained with human customers using a bulky translation engine, and the podgy old patriarch in charge of the money box. He stood upon his hind legs at the back of the booth, dressed in an approximation of Goreddi garb. Breeches were awkward, due to his tail, so he wore a skirt; his shirt frothed with lace and had large openings in back for his second set of arms—his ancestors may have had wings, like the great dragons, but modern quigutl had twiggy dorsal arms with long, dexterous fingers. An absurd little hat perched on his forehead, between his eye cones, his head spines arrayed like a fan behind it. He had more than forty spines—a sign of great age—but the reddish streaks on his throat pouch showed he could still sire children.

The sight of these creatures, even the absurdly dressed older male, sent a wave of nostalgia over Tess. She sidled closer, not to buy anything but to listen to them talk. She'd taught herself Quootla so she could communicate with Pathka. She had the wrong mouthparts to speak it, of course, but Pathka had understood Goreddi. Most quigutl in Goredd did; they didn't have much choice.

Beside Tess, a well-to-do man in a pink doublet and a sugarloaf hat rattled a box of thniks and said, "Forty-seven is too much. The last transmission box I bought didn't have the range you claimed. I didn't want to buy from you again, since you seem bent on swindling honest folk, but the wife insists on supporting local industry. I'm going to be in Lavondaville next week, and I'm inclined to see what the quigs there are selling."

Tess cringed. Quigutl didn't like being called quigs, which was also the Mootya term for *dirt*, but Goreddis would insist upon being contemptuous or lazily ignorant.

The female swiveled an eye cone toward the patriarch, who licked his nose. She hefted her translation engine, like an oversized accordion, rapidly manipulated keys on one end, and squeezed the bellows. A voice wheezed: "Forty-seven, and we include a free jenny."

From the rafters, a pole descended and a mechanical creature shimmied down, a monkey with the head of a dog, its jaws working frantically. Tess had seen jennies before; they were for fetching jars off high shelves and dusting in unreachable corners. Often they bit people.

The customer wrinkled his delicate highborn nose. Tess wondered if he'd attended her sister's wedding; he seemed to be someone important. In any case, she couldn't resist muttering behind him, "Ask for a door worm instead. They're much more useful."

The man recoiled as if Tess smelled bad, which may indeed have been the case, and furrowed his brow. "What's a door worm?"

Tess's eyes went big and innocent, a strategy she'd often employed to charm old ladies at court. "If you lose your key, you stick the worm into the lock and it opens the door for you."

A door worm would also destroy the lock and sometimes

the door, the wall, and the floor; it would burrow until it broke, and some of the blighters were distressingly durable. The man was considering the possibilities, though. Everyone, it seemed, had a door they'd like opened, generally one they weren't entitled to look behind. The worm was an unsubtle means of entry, but he would come to appreciate that too late.

Of course, it was not nice to inflict mischief on an unsuspecting stranger, even if he rather deserved it. Tess had to admit she was getting a touch of anarchic joy from this. She wrestled her conscience and was about to recant her suggestion, but the man raised his chin like the prow of a ship and said, "Throw in a door worm, and I'll pay forty-five."

The female rolled her eye cones toward the patriarch, whose throat pouch swelled minutely in response. "Your hard-driven bargains will assuredly ruin us," wheezed the engine, while the female hissed at the youngster in the rafters, "Toss down a worm, Athla."

The man left with his bounty, looking smug. Only a practiced eye could discern that the quigutl looked equally pleased, their head spines at a cocky angle. "Forty-five is a lot! We could buy you a ruff, Kashth," chirped the young one.

"It would look better on Futha," said the female, glancing at the old male, who was drumming his fingers dreamily on the money box. "*Ko* has a longer neck."

Ko was the pronoun quigutl used for each other, although Tess could never bring herself to use it. The word was hard to say correctly with human mouthparts, but more uncomfortably, it was ungendered. *It,* to Tess's mind, implied a thing, or at best an animal. It seemed disrespectful.

Tess was just turning away from the stall when the translation engine blared at her: "Young maidy, what will you buy? Thniks, thnimis, toys, tools, specialty items?"

"No, thanks," Tess said, walking backward, hands raised. "I haven't any money."

The two adults pursed their beaky mouths demurely, but the little one scuttled down the pole headfirst, crying, "How does she live without money? You said it was impossible!" The exclamation was delivered with an accusatory glare at Kashth.

"It's not easy," Tess interjected, hoping to head off a squabble. Quigutl generally had no compunctions about fighting like cats, but these two were mismatched and the booth was full of things they could break. "I haven't been without for long, and I hope to remedy it soon, but ..."

She trailed off because all three quigutl were staring at her, openmouthed.

"She understands Quootla!" cried the little one, prone to excited exclamations.

"How do you know our speech, human?" asked the female warily, without the engine.

"A quigutl friend taught me. Her name was Pathka," said Tess.

"Pathka!" crowed the youngster, Athla. "Pathka lives with us in the Big House. You should come see *ko*. Kashth, can she come home and meet everyone?"

Tess's heart leaped. She hadn't seen Pathka in years, since before St. Jannoula's War; the little quigutl had disappeared without a trace. When war had forced the citizens of Lavondaville into the tunnels, Tess had ventured beneath Quighole, where the quigutl had their nests (dragging a frightened Jeanne along with her). None of the quigutl had known where Pathka had gone. If she was here in Trowebridge, Tess had to see her.

Kashth, the female, was saying, "Yes, go see our house. We bought a house, you understand. In a street. The biggest house owned by quigutl in Goredd. We were clever to move here, where houses are cheap. Every quigutl in Trowebridge lives in our house, or under it. Even Pathka, who has antiquated fancies and sometimes slinks off to the sewers. Futha had to break *ko* dorsal arm to make *ko* obey."

Futha, at the back of the booth, grunted acknowledgment.

"But now *ko* stays home and makes wonderful things," little Athla piped up cheerfully, as if Kashth had not just said something appalling.

"I see," said Tess, worried now. Quigutl could be cruel—Pathka's mother had bitten her in the face—but this kind of violently enforced discipline was not something she'd heard of before. Tess decided to withhold judgment until she saw how Pathka was taking it; it was Pathka's judgment that mattered, Tess had learned long ago, not squeamish human standards.

The patriarch, who'd been speaking to Kashth with hand signals, made a gesture of assent. The youngster in the eaves gave a whoop, leaped down, and took Tess's hand in one of its pad-fingered ventral ones. "Futha says we may!"

"I'll follow you," said Tess, gently disentangling herself. It wouldn't do to walk through town holding hands with a quigutl, even in these liberal and enlightened times. Also, the hand was sticky. She surreptitiously wiped her own on her skirts.

The youngster bounded ahead, looking back often as if to

make sure Tess didn't slip away. Tess wouldn't; she couldn't bring herself to be rude to quigutl. Dragons were one thing—the saar didn't care—but quigutl had emotions, even if the naturalists denied it. Dragon and human scholars alike hadn't put in the hours of observation Tess had.

The Big House was, indeed, "in a street" in the sense of being along a main road. It stood five stories tall, half-timbered with diamond-pane windows and cheerful yellow shutters. The window boxes were planted, though it was early for blooms, and swallows nested in the eaves.

The houses on either side were for sale, Tess noted with sorrow but little surprise.

The youngster ushered her inside, and Tess paused in the front hall, breathing rapidly through her nose to put her sense of smell to sleep. The ground floor was deserted, although the hatchling insisted on opening every door and showing Tess their collection of fine human furniture: exquisite hardwood chairs, claw-footed couches, painted screens, inlaid tables, fancy boot jacks and coat trees, credenzas the size of small islands, paintings of Samsamese earls, suits of antique dracomachia armor in lifelike poses ... more furniture and objets d'art than Tess could take in at once, let alone identify, jumbled together in the most unusable fashion.

"Four parlors," said the little one, cocking its spines. "Does anyone else have four?"

"Indeed not," said Tess. Cragmarog and the Queen's residences didn't count. "You can't sit in them, though. That's the reason for parlors, as I understand it. To sit in."

"*We* can't sit on chairs like that," scoffed the youngster. "It's in casc we have guests."

They went upstairs, where there were workshops for making devices. The dormitory floors were farther up, the hatchling said, but Tess didn't need to see those. The quigutl would have made themselves nests so they could sleep in heaps; the house would barely look like a house up there. Tess followed the youngster down a short hall into a sunny room filled with, intriguingly, quigutl-style furniture: couches or benches, allowing them to lie on their bellies with their hands free to work. Several of the lizard-like creatures were working here. Some had affixed magnifying lenses into the openings of their eye cones, to do delicate, close-up work on thniks. Some worked on larger objects—jennies, groglets, pilchards, woles—or welded joints with the jet of fire at the end of their hollow tongues. Hot metallic smoke curled toward the ceiling.

Across the room, a smallish quigutl swiveled one eye at Tess, then the other, then raised the front of its body upright and cried, "Tethie!"

Tess's mouth fell open. This quigutl was a male, with ruddy streaks on his throat; he couldn't be the same Pathka, who'd been laying eggs when Tess first met her. And yet he knew her name (the notorious quigutl lisp was only apparent to Tess when they tried to pronounce Goreddi words; her name was a challenge). She knew the voice, and even though it sounded like a heron choking on a frog—a double-strong croak, as it were—it brought a lump to her throat.

What other quigutl would know her name or be happy to

see her? At least . . . maybe he was happy. He'd made no move to leave his couch.

"Pathka, is it really you?" Tess managed.

"I might ask the same thing. You've grown so tall," said Pathka, head spines waggling playfully. "But come closer so I can sniff you. I can't leave my bench."

Tess picked her way among the working quigutl, who ignored her, and saw that Pathka wasn't exaggerating: a manacle around one ankle bound him to the workbench with a chain. Tess knelt beside him, holding out her arm to be sniffed and studying his scaly face as he did so. This was Pathka, all right; there was the broken head spine, and the scar behind her ear where her mother had bitten her.

His mother. Its mother?

"Youuuu," said Pathka in a long exhale, "have been having adventures without me."

"None worth the name," said Tess, smiling apologetically.

"Nonsense. You're a mother, I whiff. Congratulations!"

Tess withdrew her arm, embarrassed. So much had happened since she last saw Pathka; there seemed suddenly a great chasm of time and experience between them. "What are you doing here?" she said, gracelessly changing direction. "How is it that you're male now?"

Pathka clapped his mouth, quigutl laughter, and said, "I became male three years ago. It was overdue. The others teased me, 'Do you want to lay another clutch of eggs, after it nearly killed you?' But I worried *thuthmeptha* would hurt."

Tess didn't know the word *thuthmeptha*; few non-quigutl

did. Even the greater dragons of the Tanamoot, who stayed one sex their whole lives, didn't quite comprehend it. Quigutl couldn't change into humans like the saar could, but the drive to change was still in them. They changed back and forth from female to male several times across their life spans, and evidently *thuthmeptha* was what they called that process. It was like the metamorphosis of a caterpillar in its chrysalis, though the caterpillar, that rank amateur, only manages it once.

Tess filed the word away for later. "But how did you come to Trowebridge? You left without saying goodbye, and no one knew where you'd gone." Her words came out accusingly, as if Tess's life might have turned out differently had Pathka not gone missing. Pathka would surely have kept her out of trouble.

Tess misremembered: Pathka was always more likely to get her into trouble than out of it.

"They knew," said Pathka. "A whole nest of us came east together. We were tired of the city and heard life was simpler in Trowebridge."

Around the room, the other quigutl, who'd been unsubtly listening in, slapped tails in agreement.

"Simpler how?" asked Tess, glancing uncertainly at the others. Pathka was the only one chained to a worktable; things surely hadn't turned out the way he'd hoped.

"I can't speak for others," said Pathka, "but I wanted to escape the tyranny of money."

The other quigutl shifted uncomfortably, now anxious to pretend they *weren't* listening.

Pathka continued, too loudly to ignore: "There was a time

when we used our hands, minds, and fiery tongues for the joy of it. When following our nature was its own reward. Now we ceaselessly quest after coin. I find this a hollow existence."

Around the room, quigutl body language rose and swelled like a wave. Tess had been quite adept at interpreting it, but it was a long while since she'd been faced with so much of it at once. Here was a skeptical shoulder roll, there a spinal arch of irritation (or anxiety? She was out of practice). Nervous tails moved side to side in quick flicks, angry ones in a steady, deliberate wave.

Tess gleaned from this symphony of motion that the whole room was suddenly tense and defensive. Pathka had insulted everyone.

"You oversimplify our history and clog it with nostalgia," croaked an old female across the room. "You omit the generations of quigutl who were compelled to their craft by dragons; the way humans and dragons would like to harvest our labor without compensation; the way they've scorned us for living like beasts, without the refinements of civilization."

The gathered quigutl puffed their throat pouches and chattered agreement: "True. We have money now, a tangible good. They have to respect us and take us seriously."

Pathka swiveled an eye cone at Tess and wobbled it sarcastically. "And so the quigutl of this age mistake bemusement for respect, resentment for tolerance, and money for joy."

"Whereas you mistake dreams for reality," countered the old female. "You'd take us back toward powerlessness and subservience, to lose ourselves in myth. What joy is there in that?"

"Brethren, it is time for dinner," said a much younger female, appearing in the doorway.

"Yes, go," Pathka called after the rest, who slithered off their benches and bolted for the door. "Eat on schedule. Sleep on schedule. Poop on schedule."

"Stop harassing them, Mother," said the young quigutl who'd called them to dinner.

"Teth," said Pathka, gesturing at the youngster, "do you remember Kikiu?"

The juvenile reared up and folded her ventral arms across her chest, a very human pose. Tess didn't recognize her or her name. Pathka said, "*Ko* is my offspring, the one who survived. The one you persuaded me to spare."

Tess blinked incredulously; she'd half forgotten that argument, partly because she'd never seen the hatchling again. "You really didn't eat her! I assumed you were humoring me."

"I might have eaten *ko*, my promise notwithstanding," said Pathka slyly, "but I'd had seven already, and my belly was full."

Kikiu snorted as disdainfully as any human adolescent. "So it's this human's fault."

"Her fault you're alive? Yes, poor you. I'm sure it's been awful," said Pathka.

Smoke curled out of Kikiu's nostrils, and she kept one wary eye on Tess while she said, "I'll bring up your dinner, Mother. There's goat stew and fresh bread from the baker's."

"I want fungus," said Pathka crankily. "And dung."

"We don't eat that anymore," said Kikiu, turning up her snout.

"Which is why you're always so dyspeptic," said Pathka.

Kikiu departed with a haughty swish of her tail, leaving Tess and Pathka alone. "She still calls you Mother, even though you're male?" Tess asked, trying to work out the nuances.

"I laid her egg," snapped Pathka, "so I am her mother. That can't change."

He pushed himself off his belly and reeled in the chain affixed to his leg. "Quick, Teth, close the door and brace it with something. I'm so pleased you're here; I need help with this."

Tess did as he asked, dragging one of the work couches in front of the door. "What are you—?" she began, but there was no point finishing, as Pathka focused his tongue-flame upon one of the links of his chain, pulling to stretch the link open.

It didn't budge. "Stupid steel," he snarled. "Stupid high melting point."

"What can I do?" Tess asked. Pathka couldn't answer, as his mouth was occupied again, but he pointed with one of his dorsal hands. Tess retrieved the indicated hammer.

He held the chain taut across the pommel of his workbench, flaming until the steel glowed orange, and then indicated where Tess should strike. Her weak blow sent up a shower of sparks. Pathka redoubled his flame; the metal glowed white, and the bench began to smolder. Tess gritted her teeth and struck again, flattening the link but not breaking through.

Gravelly voices became audible through the door, and then came pounding. Pathka trembled with the effort of sustaining such a powerful flame. Tess rummaged frantically for a better tool and found a pair of cruel-looking loppers. With difficulty, she snipped the white-hot link in two.

The steel clattered to the wooden floor, which began to smoke. Pathka gasped for breath, pulling himself loose; he still had a manacle around his ankle, but he was free of the bench.

Behind Tess, the door splintered and cracked under a heavy blow.

"This way," cried Pathka, flinging up the window sash. He could easily climb down the wall, and lost no time in doing so. Tess stuck her head out; the alley below was full of trash, and it was a long drop. She scanned the wall to either side, looking for a surer way down, and saw footholds to the left. It had been a long time since she'd climbed out a window; it had only led to trouble.

The door burst off its hinges. The work couch kept it propped up, but a gap at the top allowed quigutl to swarm toward her across the ceiling. Tess reached into her satchel, grabbed the last of her coins, and cast them into the room, hoping that their natural affinity for metals, or else their newly "civilized" greed, would keep them busy for a minute or two.

Then she said a hasty prayer and swung herself out after Pathka.

Six

Tess scrambled down alleys after Pathka, who seemed to have a clear idea where he was going. He led her out of Trowebridge and down the southern river road, running on four legs; his long body rippled like an otter's. He kept looking behind him, clearly expecting to be followed.

Tess's legs still ached from her long hike yesterday, the blisters on her toes screamed agony, and she wasn't sure exactly how much danger they were in, but she grinned in spite of herself as she ran. She'd found the dearest friend of her childhood and they were doing exactly what they'd always done—fleeing from mischief. In that moment she felt like she'd stepped back in time, or like she was fleeing all the intervening years as well.

The river road ran relentlessly clear and straight. If they meant to lose pursuers, surely it would be smarter to cut through sheep pastures and hedgerows.

"What good would that do?" said Pathka when she mentioned it. "They'd sniff us out. Our best hope is to put distance between ourselves and town. Most won't follow us far. Even the most stubborn will decide we aren't worth the effort beyond a certain distance, say, eight-point-two miles."

"That's bizarrely precise," puffed Tess.

Pathka wriggled his head spines. A quigutl giggle. "Maybe I can quantify laziness."

Their run devolved to a walk when Tess got a stitch in her side. Trowebridge receded and disappeared behind them, but still they kept on. Near sundown, they reached a confluence of blocky water mills, two on the near side of the river and one on the far side, joined by a bridge. A single imposing house stood among several outbuildings. After a short argument about where to spend the night—the flour storage barn was out, as Pathka was prone to exhaling sparks in his sleep—they settled on the second barn, where the animals stayed.

Tess had argued against it, first because it would stink, and second because they had to tiptoe across a gravel yard to get to it, and Pathka couldn't tiptoe, exactly. Pathka, however, took a quigutl shortcut over the top of the house, where his sticky, padded toes made no sound. Tess was left to crunch across the yard by herself, directly in front of the tall dining room windows. She paused to watch the miller and his grown sons carving into a venison roast. A serving lad brought wine around; beeswax candles illuminated their merriment. These millers were better off than her own family had been these last several years.

By now her family must know she was gone. She wondered how they were taking it. Mama would be furious, of course, and

Tess felt some regret that she couldn't be there to see it. Papa would be cringing before Mama's wrath, Seraphina placid and unmoved, Jeanne . . .

Tess blanched. She'd spent the last two years thinking of Jeanne first, and then she'd run off without giving her twin a single thought. She should have left a note, at least. Tess's throat tightened. The sun might cease to rise, but Tess would never cease to do the selfish, thoughtless, wrongheaded, hurtful thing.

She swallowed that guilt down, along with the rest of it, and reminded herself that she had put off dying of shame. She could reassess in the morning, but for now, she had to walk on. Or tiptoe on, as it were. The gravel complained loudly.

The livestock barn was well built and tidy, full of goat smell but no goats; they'd be out to pasture now that it was warm enough. Alas, there was no hay in the barn, either, but Tess and Pathka climbed into the loft anyway, out of view should anyone enter the barn in the night.

Tess broke out her meager provisions; Pathka was ecstatic about the cheese, which made her smile. His enthusiasm was constant, even if so much else had changed.

⚔

Tess had met Pathka when she was . . . how old? It was going to take some calculation.

Seraphina had broken out in scales the winter before; every family event was measured from that mile marker. Tessie and Jeanne weren't supposed to know, so of course they did. Their elder sister may have been secretive and aloof, but the twins were perceptive. Also, they were nosy, and Seraphina had been too ill to chase them off when they'd sneaked into her room.

In her feverish delirium, she hadn't noticed them. Jeanne had gently smoothed Seraphina's hair off her sweaty forehead. Tess had gone straight for the incipient scales sprouting through Seraphina's arm. They were silver, surrounded by red, angry, weeping flesh.

Jeanne gasped and covered her eyes; Tessie, bolder, touched one. Seraphina cried out, making Tessie jump and Jeanne shriek. Even more frightening was the suddenly looming figure, a man who'd been sitting so still they hadn't noticed him. He unfolded himself from his chair, grabbed each girl by an ear, and steered them into the corridor.

Mama was arriving with a tray for Seraphina, which she dropped in alarm. "Don't touch them, you fiend!" she cried, pulling the twins out of the man's grasp. "If I had known what you were, you should never have set foot in my house."

"I'm the only one who can help her," said Orma, scratching his beard as he turned back into the room. "Find a way to tolerate my presence, madam."

Mama, quivering with rageful words unspoken, bent down to pick up the broken crockery. Jeanne fetched a towel and Tessie a pail of water. They helped her sop broth off the floor, watching helplessly as angry tears washed Mama's cheeks.

"Don't cry, Mama," Jeanne had ventured at last, putting her arms around Mama's waist, which was beginning to bulge with the baby that would be Neddie. "Seraphina's going to be all right. Dragons make good doctors, Papa says, and—"

"He's not her *doctor*," said Mama bitterly. She glanced

behind her, wiping her cheeks with the back of her hand. The door to Seraphina's room was closed. Her soft face hardened; she led the twins down the hall into the nursery and closed the door. Baby Paul was asleep in the cradle, but no matter. This was the kind of news that could only be whispered. "Saar Orma is Seraphina's uncle, girls. Claude—" Mama's voice broke; the twins, in panic, threw their arms around her as she started to weep again.

"You must never tell our Belgioso family," said Mama when she had recovered enough to speak. "Promise me, girls, that you won't breathe a word of this to anyone."

"Of course not, Mama," said Jeanne, and Tessie shook her head vehemently.

"Your father's first wife was a dragon," Mama whispered, clutching them tightly. "A vicious, unscrupulous saarantras who tricked him into thinking she was human." Mama's mouth worked spasmodically; her reddened eyes grew fierce. "Or so he claims. I have no choice but to believe him. He's a clever man, though, your father, and I don't understand how he couldn't . . . there must be differences between dragons and real people."

Tessie met Jeanne's eyes, and they had one of those moments—commoner when they were young—where they shared a thought. *He still loves that dragon woman*, they thought together. *Mama knows, and it hurts her.*

Mama was kneeling now, her arms around their shoulders. "Girls, remember: this mortal, material world will let you down. Husbands, love, life—everything and everyone will disappoint you eventually. Only one thing never fails. Do you know what that is?"

The twins answered dutifully, "Heaven."

Mama nodded, steel in her pale eyes. "Faith is the only rock in life's tempestuous sea. Heaven is perfect and eternal, and it awaits us if we keep our troth to it."

Jeanne piped up, "Papa doesn't believe, does he?"

She knew the answer perfectly well, but the twins played this game to calm their mother. The question put Papa in his place and made him manageable.

"His faults are for the Saints to tally," said Mama, her tone now pitying and superior. "Our job is only to forgive, not to judge."

This was Tessie's cue to judge him with everything she had. "Papa is a terrible sinner, Mama, and I hate him!"

"Oh, no, you mustn't hate, dearest," said Mama, in command of herself again. "He may be an unbeliever, and he may have let bodily lust blind him to his first wife's nature—"

That was a new angle on Papa. If Tessie could have swiveled her ears like Faffy the hound, they'd have been on high alert now, pricked up and straining to hear more.

"—but your duty is to love him, warts and all, as is mine," Mama concluded, to Tess's disappointment, kissing each girl on the forehead and rising awkwardly to her feet. In the cradle, baby Paul began to wail. Mama picked him up, and the little girls took the opportunity to quietly escape, hand in hand, back to their own room.

Seraphina had fallen ill upon Treaty Morn in the dead of winter, and Pathka had crawled into the basement early the following summer—before Aunt Jenny's wedding and Tess's failed baby-making experiment—so Tess had been not quite six and a half years old.

Mama was laid up for a month before Neddie's birth. Her old Belgioso aunties took turns skulking around the house, making enormous pots of soup, going on violent cleaning sprees, and putting the twins to work. Seraphina, back on her feet, always contrived to wriggle out of chores; her dragon uncle's music lessons took precedence over anything else. Besides, the Belgioso side of the family, without knowing why, found Seraphina strange and spooky. Nobody dared press her into service against her will. Tessie and Jeanne, on the other hand, were fair game and big enough to send for water or bedsheets or onions, whatever the avenging aunties needed.

Cabbages were Tessie's excuse for being in the basement that day. They were in a crate up front, by the stairs, and she needn't have spent more than three minutes fetching one, but Aunt Mimi was there today, the most unpleasant of Mama's aunties. She was also, fortuitously, the easiest to avoid. She had bad knees; all you had to do was contrive to get yourself sent up or down, and you were out of range of her cane and her braying voice.

Jeanne had landed the plum assignment of taking Mama her tea. Aunt Mimi liked Jeanne best, because she was sweet and compliant and blond like a proper Belgioso. Tessie didn't begrudge this any more than one might begrudge a rose, but it meant she had to work twice as hard to get away from the old woman. As Auntie made soup, Tess kept asking about ingredients that she knew were in the basement. Unfortunately, a whole box of onions had been hauled up the night before, and Aunt Mimi had only conceded a need for cabbage after making Tess slice ten onions paper-fine.

Tess felt she had earned this basement respite, and she intended to take full advantage.

She dawdled in dark corners where there were no cabbages (as she knew perfectly well). She was Dozerius the Pirate, hero of her favorite Porphyrian adventure stories. His gender was no obstacle, although she carefully refrained from imagining herself afflicted with bodily lusts, just as Mama had always carefully refrained from reading any of the lustier passages aloud (or so the twins had discovered, now that they could read to themselves).

Tess-as-Dozerius had been sent in search of the Jeweled Cabbage of Condamaciatius (Tessie's approximation of a Porphyrian name) but couldn't get near it because it was guarded by the Buxom Serpent of Flittifluttius. (*Buxom*, she had deduced, meant "pretty," because that was how ladies were described in the paragraphs Mama didn't read.) The serpent was so pretty no one could bear to harm him, even though he ate every awed adventurer who came near.

"Don't look, don't look, he'll dazzle your eyes," Tessie sang to herself as she skipped among the crates, casks, and hogsheads of the cellar, bearing a little lamp and brandishing a broomstick-spear. "Come out, fell beast! Dozerius commands you!"

She swatted the side of a half-empty ale cask with her broomstick, which made a pleasant thunk. She smacked it again for good measure, then climbed a chest, treading upon the hem of her skirt and tearing it. From up here, she could cast lamplight over the clutter. She moved her arm in a great circle, making the shadows bow obeisance to valiant, stouthearted Dozerius.

Tessie climbed one tier higher and accidentally knocked off a jar of pickles, which shattered, attracting the attention of Aunt

Mimi, who was unfortunately not deaf. The old lady shrieked down the stairs, *"Piquietta!"* That was Ninysh for "little devil girl," the Belgiosos' usual epithet for Tessie. "Get back here!"

"I'm looking for the cabbages, Auntie," Tessie hollered back.

"They're at the bottom of the stairs, you monster," shouted Mimi. "I can see them from here. If it weren't for my knees, I could get one myself."

"I don't see them," cried Tessie.

"Liar! You're playing down there, closer to your friend the devil. If you love the basement so much, fine."

The light waned; Mimi was closing the door.

"Let's see how long your lamp lasts, and how you like it after that." She barred the door with a heavy thump.

Tessie's heart leaped. She could not have asked for better. Aunt Mimi would assume she was contained and forget about her. Tess could do what she liked.

"You don't imagine, you old behemoth, that there's only one way into the basement?" Tessie muttered, squeezing through a forest of spare chairs toward the back of the room where a passageway connected to the old tunnels under the city. Before Queen Lavonda's peace with dragonkind, the citizens of Lavondaville used to hide in those tunnels to escape dragon fire.

The passages were in ill repair, but they hadn't been filled in. Tess had done enough exploring—even at six and a half—that she'd come this way before. A short spur led to a bigger tunnel under the street, and then a narrow vent opened behind St. Siucre's shrine down the block. She'd escape that way, come into the house at the back, sneak upstairs, and play with

Jeanne—assuming Jeanne had been sensible enough to drag out her own chore and hadn't obediently returned to the kitchen by now.

You never knew about Jeanne; she was often reflexively well behaved. Tessie loved her for it, but it could be inconvenient at times.

"Damned inconvenient," she said aloud, relishing the freedom to curse.

She was heading for the tunnel when a spooky sound stopped her short. It came from the darkness ahead, a kind of *eeh-eeh-eeh*, and then a *k-k-k-khhhee*, and then a *thoo-eee-thoo eee thaaaah*, most perplexing and uncanny.

Tessie pressed herself against the back wall of the cellar and inched toward the doorway, wishing she dared extinguish her light. The creature would see her approaching.

What would Dozerius do?

Tessie counted to three and then leaped into the doorway, brandishing the broomstick and crying, "Yah-*ha*!"

Curled on the floor in front of her, shivering uncontrollably, a small quigutl had made a makeshift nest of rags, leaves, paper, and (Tessie noted with interest) a shredded cabbage. The creature had already laid a clutch of eggs—seven whole, one broken—but there was one more egg bulging half in, half out of its body. Tessie stared unabashedly; a neighbor kept hens, so she'd seen eggs laid before, but never such large ones.

The quigutl hissed at her. Tessie came no closer, so it arched its back and carried on with its business. It strained and groaned and growled, but the egg didn't budge.

Tessie got tired of standing, so she squatted to watch. Did it usually take so much time to lay an egg?

"That must hurt," she said, not expecting the beast to understand her. It whipped its head around to face her, however, and . . . was she imagining things? It nodded.

It buckled under the strain of another contraction and shrieked eerily. The egg was making no progress. Something was wrong.

"Do you need help?" asked Tessie. Her lamp was dimming; she'd be no help in the dark.

The quigutl chittered, clearly panicked, and Tessie's heart quickened. She had to do something—the egg was going to tear the poor creature in two.

"I don't understand you," she said, trying to keep her voice soothing, "but my sister can. I'm going to get her, and we'll help you. I'll be right back."

She edged around the nest and then sprinted toward the larger tunnel, up the winding stair to St. Siucre's shrine and then toward home. Tessie didn't bother with the back door—no time—but burst through the front. She bolted upstairs and into Seraphina's room without knocking.

Seraphina barely glanced up from her book. "What is it, Rudeness?"

"Quigutl . . . dying in the basement . . . talk to it . . ." Tessie was out of breath. "Please."

Seraphina frowned. "Better tell Papa. It'll stink up the whole house if it dies. He'll hire somebody to remove it."

"You don't understand!" wailed Tessie. "It doesn't have to die. We can save it."

Seraphina rolled her eyes, marked her place in the book with a ribbon, and followed Tessie downstairs. Tess paused in the parlor for more lamp oil, then led Seraphina outside, toward the shrine of St. Siucre. If Seraphina thought this was a peculiar way to get into the basement, she gave no sign; indeed, she'd opened her book again and was reading as she walked.

The quigutl lay where Tessie had left it, panting and doubled up in pain. Silver streaked the half-laid egg now, the quigutl's blood. It didn't look gory to Tess, but Seraphina recoiled.

"Ask what we can do to help," said Tess, yanking her sister's arm to pull her closer.

"You just asked," said Seraphina, wrinkling her nose. "It understands Goreddi."

"Fine," cried Tess impatiently. "What does it need?"

Seraphina's brow crumpled in concentration as she listened to the creature's jabbering. "Oil," she translated. "Cooking oil, not lamp oil. And hot water."

"Argh, those are in the kitchen," cried Tess, stamping. "Aunt Mimi barred the door."

Seraphina sighed loudly and handed Tess her book to hold. "I'll handle her, but all the quigutl midwifery falls to you. I didn't sign on to stick my arm up anyone's cloaca."

"Thank you," said Tessie. "Only hurry!"

Seraphina took the lamp, leaving Tess and the quigutl in the dark. The creature moaned and thrashed its tail. "Poor thing," said Tessie. "Don't fret, little beastie. She'll be back straightaway."

Tess reached out, thinking to comfort the poor creature by petting it, but the quigutl didn't want to be touched. It scuttled out of reach and growled at her.

"Oh! Sorry," said Tessie. She didn't take it personally; the creature was hurting.

She rummaged in the pocket of her apron, where she sometimes squirreled away snacks for later, and came up with a lump of damp, crumbling cheese.

"Are you hungry? You're working hard."

She held her hand as close as she dared and soon felt a snuffle of hot breath as it cautiously approached her again. A rough tongue, like autumn leaves, swept the cheese into an unseen mouth. Tess laughed in amazement.

Seraphina, who'd taken her merry time sauntering across the basement, was now banging on the door and shouting, "It's Seraphina! You've locked me in. . . . No, Tessie isn't here. You must have been mistaken. I always read in the cellar. Just open up, would you?"

It seemed an eternity, waiting helplessly while the quigutl groaned and grunted its agony, but Seraphina returned with a second lamp and some expensive Porphyrian olive oil, and then with a pot of steaming water and some thick woolen bandages, lunessas, like Mama used for her monthlies when she wasn't pregnant.

The quigutl jabbered urgently and Seraphina nodded.

"Take it by turns rubbing the egg with oil and applying a warm compress to the skin around the opening. Watch the blood—it's poisonous," said Seraphina. "Also, hand me back my book. Thank you."

Seraphina settled in to squint at her book. The toil fell to Tess, but she didn't begrudge a minute of it. She calmly wiped blood off the egg, wrung out the bandages, dabbed and stanched. There was a piercing smell, like hot, metallic sewage, that made her stomach turn, but she got around this by imagining herself a battlefield surgeon, or a heroic farmer saving sheep ... scaly, stinky, snappy sheep.

The quigutl would occasionally chirrup, and Seraphina would translate without looking up: "More to the right with that compress," or "Now press on its belly just below the sternum."

"What's a sternum?" cried Tess, afraid of getting it wrong.

Seraphina indicated her own, and Tess dived in, perhaps too enthusiastically. The quigutl screamed, but that was the final push. The egg popped out, glistening with oil and quigutl blood.

The shell was stony gray and lightly pitted. Tess wiped it clean with her apron, realizing too late that this would leave some difficult-to-explain stains. The quigutl lay on its side, exhausted, its ribs rising and falling rapidly.

"Any more eggs in there?" Tessie asked.

The quigutl shook its weary head.

Tessie felt weary, too, but also exhilarated. She was almost sorry it was over.

"I'm Tessie," said Tess, resisting the urge to hold out a hand for the quigutl to shake. That surely wasn't how quigs greeted each other. "What's your name?"

The creature swiveled an eye cone at her, as if it couldn't believe she was still talking.

Tess stood up reluctantly, untying her filthy apron and

wadding it into a ball. She had taken up one lamp, and Seraphina the other, when the quigutl raised its heavy head once more and spoke.

Tessie glanced at Seraphina, her face lit eerily from below. "What did it say?"

"That's its name," said her sister. "I can't translate it. It's just a name."

"Say it again?" Tessie asked the quigutl softly, hating to impose upon its exhaustion.

The quigutl enunciated: "Pathka. *Fthuma tikith pa Anathuthia kiushth.*"

"It's called Paska," said Seraphina, converting its hard-mouth sounds into softer human phonemes. She paused, chewing the inside of her cheek, as if the rest were harder to translate, then said, "And it commends you to the great snake . . . Anassussia?"

"Anathuthia," the little quigutl corrected her.

Seraphina shrugged it off. "I have no idea what kind of bizarre reptilian benediction that's supposed to be, but there you go."

"Thank you," said Tess, who knew it was a gift, anyway. She smiled at Pathka, and the quigutl twitched its head spines in such a way that she knew, without understanding how, that it was smiling back.

Seven

"Thank you for helping me escape," said older, male Pathka in the loft of the goat barn, once they'd eaten their meager supper. "That's the second time you've named my life."

"I what your what?" asked Tess, pausing with her dusty blanket half out of her satchel.

"*Name* is a nuanced verb in Quootla, sorry," said Pathka. "I mean, that's the second time you saved my life."

"Were they going to kill you?" Tess asked, appalled.

"Eventually," said Pathka. "Perhaps not literally. I don't know how long I could have kept pushing against them, or when I might've decided my convictions weren't worth the fight."

Tess shook out the blanket, spread it, and lay down, folding one side over herself and leaving a lip for Pathka to lie on. He curled up next to her like a hot, spiky dog.

"So I saved your life that time in the cellar?" Tess mused, staring into the dark. She knew she'd saved Pathka's life, in fact, but wanted to hear that she'd done one good thing as a child. *Surely, if you were capable of one good thing, you couldn't have been born bad.*

Pathka was in her face, his scaly snout bumped up against her nose. "Don't doubt it. That last egg was too big for me to pass; I could tell it would be, even as its shell was forming. I nested alone because I thought I might die, and I didn't want to give Karpeth the satisfaction."

"Karpeth?" asked Tess, wanting to pull away from Pathka's fetid breath.

"My sibling," said Pathka, backing off. "Karpeth was a . . . what do you call someone who thinks deeply and can't stop talking about it?"

"A priest?" said Tess, mystified. "A philosopher? Dragons and naturalists also—"

"Philothopher," said Pathka, seeming satisfied with the Goreddi word. "We don't have a separate word for that; *quigutl* used to be enough. We were all philothophers once, but things have changed. We are adrift, and the thinnest breeze may blow us where it will."

Tess recognized that last sentence as a line from Dozerius, and smiled to herself. She and Pathka had both loved stories when they were young; she'd traded Dozerius tales for the old quigutl myths about great serpents beneath the earth.

"Karpeth's ideas have proved to be sticky; they cling to my brethren like a second set of scales. When the war ended and the Ardmagar Comonot made it legal for us to sell our devices in the Southlands, Karpeth decided this was our chance. We could accumulate money and become more like the saar," said Pathka, pushing himself away from Tess's side restlessly.

He began pacing the loft. "We would be ruthless, logical, dominating, miserly. Hoarding. No mercy for the weak. Thus did the saar achieve greatness while we crawled in the shadows, eating garbage.

"But look at me: small for my age, never the strongest. My mind and heart were mighty, though; I argued well against my sibling, and there were those who agreed with me.

"Karpeth ambushed me and got me with eggs, knowing it might kill me to lay them."

"Saints' bones!" cried Tess, appalled that her friend had endured a violent ravaging—by a sibling, no less—and was speaking about it matter-of-factly, as if it were nothing unusual.

"I wouldn't have minded dying," said Pathka, misinterpreting Tess's horror, "but *ko* would have invited everyone to watch and *fthep* me in judgment."

Pathka demonstrated *fthep* with a stinging tail-whip to Tess's leg.

"Did Karpeth come to Trowebridge?" Tess asked.

"Karpeth is dead," said Pathka, in a tone that forbade follow-up questions. "*Ko* ideas endure, however, and when I push against them, I get worse than a mere *fthep*."

"Why would they chain you up and force you to stay?" asked Tess. "Wouldn't it have been more agreeable to everyone if you'd left?"

"That," said Pathka, "is a story for another time. I'd much rather hear what you've been up to these last six years than relive all my worst memories of Trowebridge in one evening."

Pathka shook himself like a dog and then burrowed his snout in her armpit. "I was right: you had a baby. Don't deny it; I have the keenest olfaction in nature."

"You can't really smell baby under my arm," said Tess, forcing levity into her tone, pushing back against the familiar leaden feeling creeping into her gut.

"It's your mammary tissue," Pathka explained. "It changes when—"

"Fine. Stop," said Tess. Suddenly there were tears burgeoning in her eyes. She wrapped her arms around her head as if to physically hold them in.

She dared not cry. Three years of pushed-down grief had accumulated pressure, like water behind a dam, and she couldn't release just a trickle. It would gush uncontrollably, split her up the middle, and kill her, like trying to pass a too-big egg.

Pathka sniffed her head anxiously. "What's wrong?"

"Sorry," said Tess. "Sorry. I—hold on. I'll be fine in a minute."

"No, I'm sorry," said Pathka hastily. "I don't smell young child on you. I hadn't considered the implications of that. You don't have to tell the story if it hurts you."

She needed to say something, though, or the story would squat between them like a malevolent toad, poisoning the very air. Maybe it would be a relief to tell someone like Pathka. Surely he wouldn't judge her. She didn't want to feel anything while she told it, however, which was a challenge.

She racked her brains, composing an official, unsentimental version. The only way through was to judge herself. She said, "I was stupid."

"I don't believe that," said Pathka, patting her foot.

Tess took a deep breath of goat-tinged air. "Foolish, then. After the war, I started sneaking out to St. Bert's and attending natural philosophy lectures. Your old World Serpent stories drove me to it, in part." Another deep breath. "I wanted to know more about them and other wonders the world might hold." And she'd been bored, and mad at her mother. There was no point going into all that.

"See?" cried Pathka. "You wanted to learn the laws of nature. Not stupid!"

Tess smiled wistfully at his innocent faith in her, but didn't refute him. If she paused, she'd lose her momentum. "I met a boy, William of Affle, and—"

What could she say about Will that wouldn't hurt? *He was handsome, and he took care of me?*

No.

He promised he'd marry me?

Double no.

We were going to travel together in search of the World Serpents someday?

Ha.

Pathka offered an interpretation: "You loved him, like princesses loved Dozerius."

Tess considered. She was still so angry that he'd left, so humiliated and mortified, that she couldn't quite remember feeling love. She probably had. It didn't matter.

"I loved him, and I did everything my mother ever told me not to do."

"How else were you to determine it couldn't be done?" said Pathka reasonably.

"Y-yes," said Tess. That wasn't exactly what had happened with Will, but it gave the story a clean logic and put the blame squarely where it belonged. "I was the cat curiosity would kill, Seraphina used to say. Anyway, not listening to your mother leads to pregnancy, I learned."

Flippancy wasn't helping; tears threatened again. She puffed her breath like Chessey the midwife had advised during childbirth.

"The body wants what it wants," said Pathka sagely.

That irritated her. Her good judgment had not been overcome by bodily lusts; Pathka was misunderstanding. Arguing meant delving deeper into the story, however, and . . . She couldn't. It was time to fold up this memory and wedge it into the darkest corner of her mind, out of sight.

"I threw my future away," she said curtly, summing up. That was the whole story, the real story. "Jeanne got to be 'eldest' and marry a duke. I had to wait on her at court."

Tess launched into an account of Jeanne's courtship and wedding, which she could tell with humor, at least. Pathka listened raptly, squawking sympathy at Tess's humiliations, flailing his tail in excitement when she punched Jacomo in the nose.

"There," cried Pathka, as if he'd been waiting for it. "You're still yourself after all."

"What, a priest-puncher?" she said.

"No, no." Pathka head-butted her ribs. "I feared that your misfortunes had cured you of your taste for adventure, that you'd decided to live a small, circumscribed life, like the penitent Julithima Rotha."

Julissima Rossa had been one of the pirate Dozerius's

lovers. Guilt had driven her to give up adventuring, and then, when Dozerius wouldn't leave her in peace, she'd taken her own life, *the gleaming knife pressed to her ebony breast.*

Tess had found that description terribly romantic as a child, but she hadn't thought about the story in years. She wouldn't die that beautifully; she always did everything the wrong way.

"Surely you ran away to go adventuring, like we always spoke of," Pathka was insisting.

Tess emitted a bitter laugh. "Pathka, dear, I can no more go adventuring than I can fly. It was one thing to dream of it when I was little and didn't know better. Now that I have more sense of what's possible"—*and how bad the results can be*—"there's no way. Even in the Dozerius stories, women never hare off on adventures by themselves. It's too dangerous."

Pathka cocked his head to one side. "Julithima Rotha fought alongside—"

"Julissima Rossa killed herself!" cried Tess. "Julissima Rossa proves the rule: women plus adventure equals disaster."

Pathka was silent, as if pondering her vehemence. "Why did you leave home, then?"

"Because these boots seemed to demand it," Tess joked weakly. "I barely had a plan, beyond escaping my family and avoiding the convent."

"You were on your way to somewhere," Pathka pressed. "You can't walk away without also walking toward."

Tess snorted. "Assuming I could get anywhere without being ravaged, robbed, and left for dead in the weeds, I suppose . . . I had some notion to head south, to Ninys."

Pathka bounced excitedly, barely able to contain himself.

"I'm going south! The world brought you to me for a reason. I wasn't meant to go alone; no quigutl should have to be forever alone."

"You're going where?" asked Tess, baffled.

"Back to the beginning, back to the wellspring of my people, to Anathuthia!" cried Pathka. "Anathuthia, Anathuthia, Anathuthia!"

Tess sat up. Beams of moonlight cut through chinks in the planked wall, and Pathka danced in and out of them, flashing and slashing like some ancient spirit, a creature out of myth.

"You don't mean . . . ," said Tess through a laugh.

Pathka stopped dancing and grabbed her face. His padded ventral hands felt hot against her cheeks. "The World Serpent. The one beneath our continent, the one who will restore us to ourselves. I dreamed she was under a field of waving wheat, the Ninysh high plains."

"Do quigutl dream?" asked Tess. The great dragons didn't.

"Only when we're alone. We don't dream all together in a nest—and yet I did," said Pathka. "That's why this is important: because it's impossible."

No, it was merely eccentric. A woman walking the roads alone was impossible. If she traveled with Pathka, though, she wouldn't be alone.

"Think it over," said Pathka as Tess lay down again. He turned in a tight circle and lay beside her with his tail in her face. "You suggested finding the World Serpents a long time ago. This dream means Anathuthia is ready to be found."

Tess had indeed been keen to search, before Will had run off with her future and all her courage and enthusiasm. Tess laid a hand on Pathka's ridged spine, her bones leaden with weariness. "Sleep, friend. Let's decide in the morning."

It wasn't the only decision she was putting off till then.

Pathka rested his chin on her ankle and soon began to snore.

There is no snore quite like a quigutl's. The greater dragons snore, of course, but they rumble so deeply that the sound is more tactile than auditory. Quigutl snore in chords, like sad, deflating accordions with several jammed keys, a tune to keep teeth on edge and make skin crawl.

Seraphina could have identified the exact notes; Tess, alas, had to suffer in ignorance.

Not at first, however. She was so exhausted that she slept through the wheezing—to say nothing of Pathka's gnarled feet in her face, his spiky head upon her leg, and his body temperature like a portable furnace.

Once she'd slept enough to take the edge off her exhaustion, the snoring woke her, and sleep fled. She mulled over Pathka's words. *You're still yourself after all,* he'd said, as if he'd worried that she'd become something else in the years since they'd last seen each other.

Of course she had. One didn't fall as hard as she'd fallen and come out the same. When she was little—when Pathka had known her—she'd still had hope that maybe, if she tried, she could be good enough to see the Golden House and dwell forever with Allsaints and Jeanne. That maybe her mother—or anyone, really—would be proud of her someday, moved to say,

She wasn't the sweet one, or the smart one, but she contrived to be worthy in her own way.

Punching a priest had not been worthy, or good, or even entirely reasonable, so what had Pathka gleaned? That she was as childish and impulsive as she'd always been? That she still stupidly aspired to be like Dozerius, answering the world with her fists?

Dozerius hadn't always punched his way out of trouble, though. He could be wily when he had to be, or suave, or sneaky. Dozerius's chief virtue was resourcefulness. *There's never just one trick to try, comrades,* he used to say.

Tess rolled over, abandoning the blanket to Pathka. She didn't want to be Tess anymore; Tess was nothing but trouble. Why couldn't she be Dozerius instead? It didn't seem so childish an aspiration, here in the wee hours. It certainly beat dying.

If there were impossible, unpassable roads ahead of him, would Dozerius quail and quake and cry? Indeed, he would not. He'd find another trick to try.

Tess extracted herself from the bits of Pathka that were still draped over her—a dorsal arm, his tail—and crept down the loft ladder. She opened the barn door slowly, cringing at the vocal hinges, and slipped outside. A slender moon lingered near the horizon, giving a little light, but she had no idea how to gauge the time by it. She hurried across the gravel yard, toward where she remembered seeing a laundry line.

The time had come, Tess thought, for her own *thuthmeptha*.

The clothes were stiff from hanging and damp with dew. She found braes and breeches and a padded jacket, but no shirts. Never mind, this would do. She hustled back to the barn and changed into her pilfered outfit. "Yarr," she muttered piratically as she pulled the breeches on. They were snug across her behind, but they fastened with adjustable buckles, which helped.

She solved the shirt problem with her little knife, making a nick in her chemise at mid-thigh level and tearing the fabric along the bias. Years of sewing hadn't been for nothing. She tucked the shirt into the breeches and tried the jacket. It was padded and fitted, somebody's feast-day best, and it smashed her breasts encouragingly flat. They'd been nothing remarkable to begin with; post-baby they'd deflated further. She wouldn't miss them.

Sin is etched into woman's very form, St. Vitt liked to say.

To the devil with her form, then. She would be a new person, with a different shape.

She climbed the loft ladder, carrying her knife and the spare linen, wondering what to do about her hair. Men often wore their hair long, especially in Ninys, but Tess didn't have a strong enough chin to pull it off. Her dark waves gave her too soft and feminine an aspect.

She sat in the loft with her legs dangling down, held out her little knife, and . . . hesitated. This felt serious, a boundary crossed, no going back. She'd never considered herself that attached to her plait, but apparently it carried symbolic weight. She'd be someone else without it.

Good.

She took a breath—determination! decisiveness!—and tried to saw the damned thing off. A few strands severed, reluctantly, but it was like trying to chop down a forest with a hatchet. Tess stubbornly persevered.

In the farmyard, a cock crowed. Time was passing, and she'd made little progress.

"Let me." Pathka's voice at her shoulder startled her.

"What will you do?" asked Tess, lowering her hands. "Bite it off?"

Pathka deftly undid her braid, and Tess soon smelled the sharp reek of burning hair. He was using his flaming quigutl tongue.

"Do hold still," he said between bursts.

Hair drifted down, soft, smoldering snow. Pathka, gentle and precise, took a handful at a time, puffed through the strands, and pinched off the singed part close to her head. Tess never felt a flame lick her scalp.

When he'd finished, Tess raised trembling hands to her head. It felt like a fuzzy peach. This would take some getting used to. "I should have stolen a cap," she said.

"You don't need a cap," said Pathka stoutly. "You look lovely."

That beggared belief. Tess fell back into the pile of hair, laughing. "I appreciate the thought," she said at last, wiping her eyes.

The door of the barn shrieked as it opened; Tess sat up in alarm. A weedy young man, his mouse-brown hair more awake and upright than any other part of him, groggily shuffled into the barn.

He lifted a lantern, squinted through the dust she'd kicked up, and said, "Who's larfing?"

Pathka had scurried up the roof joists and hidden in the rafters, leaving Tess alone in the lamplight, uselessly frozen. She teetered on the edge of panic, but only for a moment. The lad was too young and scrawny to be intimidating. He looked like Neddie, but stretched; his hair had clearly been up all night having adventures without him.

He'd think she was his peer, not some scared, vulnerable girl. She needed to act the part.

Tess straightened her shoulders and said haughtily, "Is there a law against laughing in barns? One may not laugh in church, but in a barn one should be free to laugh as one sees fit."

She spoke in her most highfalutin accent, trying to pitch her voice low. A persona was developing in her mind, someone who would wear these breeches and this jacket with these boots. The boots sharpened her focus. A ridiculous situation was surely no hindrance with boots like these. She could kick her way out of anything.

The lad, who had maybe fifteen years, looked flummoxed. "What're you up there for?"

"I was about to leave, in fact," said Tess. "I'd hoped to be off before sunrise. I'm running away from home and I'd rather not be seen."

The lad's bovine eyes widened, as if he'd considered running away himself and had a certain respect for it.

"Won't your mother miss you?" he said, a bit quieter. His own mother had evidently been the sticking point for him.

"My mother is Elga, Duchess Pfanzlig," said Tess, her face dramatically mournful. "I daresay she shan't miss me, the old harridan."

Her audience seemed suitably awed by Tess's parentage, or by her boldness in calling the duchess names. Doubt crept into his eyes, however, and Tess worried that she'd overstepped. She was dressed in peasant clothes, after all, not like the son of a duke.

It wasn't her style that perplexed the lad, however, but a specific garment: "Why're you wearing my jacket?"

St. Daan in a pan! Of course she was, and of course he'd recognize it even with bits of straw and hair clinging to it. It was striped, for one thing. She was half inclined to toss it down to him, but feared being known for a girl, even in the semidarkness. Her chemise-shirt was too lightweight to conceal the obvious; the jacket was integral to her disguise.

"I saw it outside," she said, keeping her voice stern. "And I liked the look of it, so I took it. I can do that, you know. I'm the son of a duke. A dukeling, if you will."

The lad bobbed his head, not daring to contradict her, and for one giddy instant Tess thought, *That was easy. What else could I get away with?*

A mean girl might've demanded money or tribute. A practical girl might've sworn him to silence. Tess, however, was a tenderhearted . . . boy. She pitied the misplaced awe in his eyes.

"Listen," she said, easing off the pomposity, "I need this jacket. I lost mine in a terrible overclothes accident, and there's no going back. However, my father the duke would not wish any miller to go jacketless. Bring me parchment, pen, and ink, and I will write to my father, enjoining him to repay you."

The boy looked horrified, and she wondered what she'd said wrong this time. He soon, and stammeringly, made it clear: "I—I'm not a miller, m'lord. I'm only the grist lout."

A servant. She'd seen him at dinner, now that she thought

about it, waiting upon the miller's grown sons. He could not bring her writing materials without stealing from his masters.

"That's no good," said Tess, furrowing her brow. "Do you have a psalter of your own?"

"My ma does," said the boy. She'd be the cook, most likely.

"Run and fetch it, then. The Saints surely left me a blank half page to write upon."

The boy turned to go.

"And bring some bread," Tess called. "Or venison scraps. Or anything edible, really. I'm not as finicky as one might anticipate in a nobleman."

Tess had nothing to write with, even if the lad returned with a blank page.

"You, Pathka," she called into the eaves. "You can burn my hair off, but can you make me some charcoal?"

"I have some in my throat pouch," the shadows replied. "Good for an upset stomach."

"Do quigutl get queasy?" asked Tess, amused by the notion. "You eat garbage. Surely you have cast-iron bellies."

"Indeed," said Pathka dryly, scuttling down the wall. "But in these modern times, as we affect the trappings of 'civilization,' we challenge our digestion with human foods. Cheese, for example. We wouldn't normally eat mammalian secretions."

"Why didn't you tell me I've been poisoning you all these years?" Tess cried, half distraught, half angry with him.

"Because I really like cheese," said Pathka.

Tess had packed, retrieved the charcoal from Pathka, and descended from the loft by the time the boy returned. He gave Tess a day-old loaf and a dry sausage, and then handed over his mother's book. Tess tried the back cover first, but that page was filled with a hand-drawn family tree. This peasant lad—Florian, by the book's reckoning—was descended from Samsamese earls on his mother's side, six generations back. Tess wondered if the knowledge galled him.

She flipped pages and found space upon the verso of the final hymn to St. Eustace, patron of the dead, who had more pages of poetry than most.

When Tess and Jeanne had trained to be ladies-in-waiting, their most surprising lesson had been handwriting; knowing different hands enabled one to pass notes at court. Tess, immediately grasping the potential for mischief and intrigue, had eagerly exceeded her twin, learning seventeen hands to Jeanne's eight. She knew exactly how the sons of a duke would form their letters, so she wrote in her best courtly masculine hand:

To my revered parents, the Duke and Duchess Pfanzlig of Ducana:

Please give the bearer of this book two new doublets and three new pairs of breeches (or the monetary equivalent therein) as a reward for kindness shown me on the road. I have vouched for your generosity and rely upon it. Your affectionate and honorable son,

Tess hesitated over which name to sign, but supposed it could only be Jacomo, who would soon travel back to seminary in Lavondaville. Jacomo (she decided) was the sort of humor-less killjoy who would keep his signature square and uptight.

Too bad she couldn't have counterfeited Heinrigh, who probably used a dozen flourishes. Tess enjoyed flourishes.

"Whatever you do," she admonished the lad, handing back the book, "don't tell my parents I was hiding in your goat shed. If they demand an explanation, say I was thrown from my horse, but I'm better now and on my way to seminary and they needn't concern themselves."

The boy Florian stared skeptically at the note. "Can you read that?" asked Tess.

"No. For aught I know, it tells them to have me strung up."

He was canny, if illiterate.

Tess read it to him, accounting for each word with her fin-ger. Doublets were nicer than jackets, and he was to receive more than she had taken.

He still seemed unconvinced. "I'll have Father Barnard read it over before I take it, beggin' Your Grace's pardon."

"You are a prudent and cautious individual, Florian," said Tess warmly, filled with sisterly fondness. "You're right not to trust Lord Jacomo on the strength of his lordliness alone."

Florian returned to his chores; Tess and Pathka slipped out into the foggy morning.

"That was cleverly done," said Pathka after about a mile down the river road. The sun had burned off the mist; gravel crunched beneath their feet. "I'd have bitten him, if need be, but this is better. He was only a hatchling."

Tess filled her lungs with clean morning air. She hadn't

slept much, but she was delighted with her new clothes, and her new self.

"Have you given Anathuthia any more thought?" said Pathka, bounding ahead of her and turning in a circle. "What have you decided? What what what?"

He was all motion, arching his back, bobbing his head, waggling his head spines hopefully (or maybe plaintively), twitching his tail. These added up to one big emotion; there would be a quigutl name for it, something oddly specific and semipoetic, like *when you can't find your nest because your siblings moved it for a prank*, or *when your eggshell first breaks and you see the world is distressingly big.*

Tess felt it with him, but the Goreddi word eluded her.

No, it didn't. He was anxious. Transcendently so, like he might explode from it.

He was afraid she'd say no.

Was this journey that important to him? It looked like it. Tess hadn't grasped the gravity, and still didn't fully understand his reasons, but it didn't matter. Of course she would help.

She would pretend to herself later that this was a well-considered decision, that she'd systematically tallied up the benefits of traveling with a companion, plus the satisfaction of her once boundless curiosity, and an extra dollop of hope that she might find a World Serpent before Will (wherever he was, Heaven punch his smug face), but that was all retroactive rationalization.

Pathka, her oldest friend, who'd known her when she was still herself, needed her. Her heart answered.

"All right," said Tess. "Let's go find her."

She'd half expected Pathka to start running in circles of unbridled quigutl joy. Instead, he stopped stock-still, a churning, glopping sound coming from his insides, and then he vomited right at her feet.

Tess skipped back a step, alarmed. Pathka hurled again, and then a third time.

"What's wrong?" Tess cried. "Is it the cheese?"

"No, no," gasped the quigutl, "it's just"—*splort*—"an excess of emotion." *Glargh.* "You do a similar thing when you feel too much. It comes out of your eyes."

Tess boggled at him. "You mean—crying? You're *crying*?"

"Obviously, I'm not crying," snapped Pathka, who was now into dry heaves and growing short-tempered. "That's the closest analogy. The body can't hold it in anymore."

His fit wound down; he scooped up a mouthful of sand and gravel, gargled with it, and spit it out again. Tess stood over him protectively, but nobody came down the road. They walked on when Pathka was able.

"You probably want an explanation," he said after they'd climbed another rise.

"You don't have to tell me if it's too painful," said Tess, recalling what he'd so kindly said the night before.

Pathka's underside rippled with another spasm, as if the sick was returning, but he settled down. "It's about Karpeth, and how *ko* died, but whenever I remember the story, I'm there again, and I can't—"

"I know," said Tess quietly. "It's all right."

"I will say, for now, that you are saving my life for a third time."

"If this were a children's story," said Tess, "the third time would mean I get a wish."

"Of course you do," said Pathka, scampering up the road ahead of her.

Even though she knew, or thought she knew, that the little quigutl was humoring her, Tess clasped a hand to her heart (she felt it beating even through Florian's jacket) and wished with all her might. Not for the classical piratical standbys—vengeance, fame, or fortune—but that she might shed the past like a skin and walk on with nothing, empty and new.

The breeze tickled her newly shorn scalp, as if in answer. It seemed a good sign. She would walk on one more day.

Eight

*T*he world was a failure, at first.

 It had wanted to be useful, kindly, and beautiful, a habitat for the plants and animals it envisioned in its mind's eye, but it couldn't bring its ideas to fruition. It collapsed into a petulant ball of fire and water. No air, no land.

 The sun and moon looked down on it pityingly. "You boasted that you could make life," they sneered. "But what could thrive upon a tempestuous wreck like you?"

 One thing did survive among the flames and storms, though: memory. The world had a memory of what it had once intended and entirely failed to be. The memory hardened and cooled into seven strands, and each strand became a serpent. Then the world was frightened, and didn't want the memory anymore, but there was no stopping the serpents, no controlling them. They ate fire and water and cooled it into earth and air, like worms renewing the soil.

The world screamed in agony and fought them, but the serpents knew what they were doing.

"Hold very still," they advised the world. "Let us do our work, coursing through you like blood and breath. Only when we have carved you into pieces can you be whole again."

The frightened world tried to believe them. It stopped struggling, although its fiery heart still trembled, and let the serpents do their work.

That was the first World Serpent story Pathka had told Tess, the beginning of her long fascination. Tess had never heard such a tale, obvious and elusive at once, raw and wild and elemental. It went nowhere, and yet it was everywhere. She demanded to hear it again and again.

The second time Pathka told it, however, the serpents weren't memories. They were knowledge. Tess blamed her poor Quootla, assuming she'd misunderstood, until Pathka told the story yet another way. It changed with every telling: the serpents were conscience or calamity, a plague that healed or a darkness that brought light.

Only toward the end of her time with Pathka, before the war broke out, was Tess brave enough to ask about the changes. "What were the serpents, really?"

"The word we usually use to describe them is *thmepitlkikiu*," said Pathka, "which means 'something that kills any words you try to put upon it.' It's too great, too terrible, too much. You can shout words into the void forever and never fill it up."

"So you've called the serpents something different each time—"

"To give you some idea how complicated they are," said Pathka, throat pouch puffing affirmation. "They ate the entire world, after all. They contain everything."

Tess fidgeted, working up her nerve to ask the most important question: "But are the serpents real, or just a story?"

Pathka's eyes swiveled quizzically. "There's nothing 'just' about stories. Stories are the most real."

"But . . . literally real? Could we go find them, out in the world?"

"We could indeed," said the little quigutl.

"Then that's what I want to do," Tess had declared. "Surely they won't seem so vast and incomprehensible once we look them in the eye."

"Or they might seem even more incomprehensible," Pathka had said.

"It will be our greatest adventure," said Tess. "We'll go after them when I'm grown."

"Of course we will," said Pathka, but there had been something shifty in her aspect.

Tess hadn't understood in the moment that Pathka was about to leave for good.

Finding the serpents had been more than a childish fancy to Tess (although it had also been that). The serpents were like a mirror that revealed your insides instead of your outsides,

Pathka had sometimes claimed. Once you glimpsed the truth about yourself, your understanding was complete and you could finally be at peace.

There were things Tess wanted to understand, answers she needed, even if she could not easily formulate the questions.

Not that the Saints of her own faith didn't provide answers. St. Vitt, in particular, had messages tailored to her shortcomings: *Yes, child, your very nature is flawed. Yes, young woman, your body is the cradle of sin and depravity. You must work tirelessly, every minute of every day, to have any hope of seeing Heaven's Golden House.*

She didn't like those answers, even as she feared they were true.

But Pathka vanished. St. Jannoula's War came and went. Faffy died—rest he on Heaven's sun-drenched cushions. Tess grew, inexorably, reaching her full height and new womanhood by thirteen.

Growing up brought nothing but tedium and disappointment. That is to say, lady-in-waiting lessons.

Once St. Jannoula's War was over and peace had broken out again, the lawyers' guild convened an ethics panel to discuss Papa's first marriage. Mama saw the future as clearly as any seer: hard times were coming. She'd have done anything to secure her children, but the children had parts to play, too. Tess, as the elder twin, would have to marry well, and the best place to find a rich husband was at court.

The Dombegh twins had enough pedigree to merit a lowly position: Papa's older brother, Jean-Philippe, was a minor baronet, Mama's grandfather an exiled Ninysh count. Even so, Seraphina (their connection at court) had to pull every string at her disposal to get them in.

This took time; Seraphina's political capital grew but slowly, and she insisted on finding places for both twins. "I know there's only dowry for one, but they'll be happier together. A sulky lady-in-waiting won't catch anyone's eye," she'd said sensibly.

Mama had glared at Tess as if preemptively blaming her posture for her future hypothetical failure to find a husband. Tess, though it galled her, sat up straighter.

After much late-night debating—or shouting, as it was called in lawyer-free households—Mama convinced Papa that investing in a course of good manners would be to the entire family's benefit. Mistress Edwina, a dowager baroness down on her luck, came to live in their attic and whip the girls into geniuses of etiquette.

Tessie had envied Seraphina's tutors as a child, but now that she had one of her own, she hated it. Manners were a noisome and fiddly art. There was a lot of sitting still, something to which Tess was constitutionally disinclined, and a great deal of mannerly calculus involving her own rank vis-à-vis the ranks of others. There were sixteen variants on courtesy, all of them used at court.

Tess had heard of half courtesy, even quarter courtesy, but five-sixteenths courtesy was going to be the death of her.

"When you begin, you will be maids of the robes, or maids of the bedchamber if you're lucky," said Mistress Edwina, who was ancient and wrinkled as a raisin. "Through diligent and impeccable discretion, you may move up to maid of honor, meaning your lady relies upon you particularly. You will be her confidante, trusted with her correspondence and intrigues."

Tess's mind had already wandered; she could just manage to keep herself anchored to her seat by practicing ecclesiastical hand or satin stitch, but listening to Mistress Edwina's minutiae at the same time was beyond her limits.

Jeanne, on the other hand, asked brightly: "Is a maid of honor a maid of the court?"

"An apt question!" cried Mistress Edwina, pleased that Jeanne was so keen. "A maid of the court merits her own maid of the robes, whereas a mere maid of honor does not."

Tess made Jeanne explain it later, at their midnight conference. Jeanne fretted, "You need to listen and take this seriously, Sisi. The whole family is relying upon you."

"Oh, fie," Tessie had cried, tweaking her sister's nose. "If the family relies upon me, then surely I may, in turn, rely upon you. It is us against the world, after all. It always has been."

Jeanne's smile grew pained in the semidarkness. Tess tickled her worries away.

Tess was all empty bravado, though. Every day, as Mistress Edwina droned on, Tess felt more incapable and inadequate, as if clinging wet rags were being piled upon her. Each was nothing in itself, but together the pile weighed a ton and dragged her down.

Adulthood was going to smother her.

It was Cousin Kenneth, unexpectedly, who gave Tess an inkling that she might escape the soggy rag heap of duty. Kenneth at sixteen was as benignly towheaded and apple-cheeked as ever, but fully six feet tall and strong from unloading cargo crates. He would come over after working the Belgioso warehouses to mooch dinner off Mama, his older sister, and slouch around the parlor. Sometimes he'd lure Tessie and Jeanne into a game of backgammon or grouse chess. The twins made an ineffective team. Jeanne whimpered if Tessie got too aggressive, Tessie pulled her punches to reassure her sister, and Kenneth, that rapscallion, seized every opening.

One evening, when Mama had taken the other children to late Mass, Tess stayed home, ill with her monthly flux, which seemed determined to kill her. She'd been plagued with it for nearly a year now, whereas Jeanne's had not yet materialized.

"Each in its own time, as Heaven wills," Mama had said.

Tess wished, uncharitably, that Heaven had picked Jeanne first. While she enjoyed being so much taller than her sister that she looked years older (rather than mere minutes), it wasn't worth the cramps and misery.

She was curled on the couch with a hot compress against the small of her back when there came a knock at the door. "Papa! The door!" she cried, but her father was in his library, culling beloved books with an eye toward selling some. She pried herself out of the upholstery, groaning, and opened the door to Kenneth.

"You're come awfully late," she snapped, concealing the hot compress in the folds of her skirt so he wouldn't see it, guess why she'd stayed home, and feel uncomfortable or disgusted.

"I suppose there's no supper left?" Kenneth brushed past Tess, heading for the kitchen. "Only I haven't eaten since noon, Tes'puco, and I'm famished."

Tessa-puco was Ninysh for "stupid-head"; Kenneth had bestowed the nickname on Tess when she was nine, after one of her pranks had landed him in the river. It was a term of endearment now, one only Kenneth was allowed to use.

"Were you out with the dark barges?" asked Tess, wrapping her arms around her aching belly while Kenneth dug through the pantry. If the Belgiosos were smuggling, the barges had to be unloaded at night. It was early to have finished that kind of work, though.

"Noph," Kenneth said around the end of a sausage, piling rolls and cheese on a plate. "In fact, I cut out early. Uncle Leo will flay me tomorrow, but it was worth it. Is there any mustard?"

Tess located the mustard, curious as to what Kenneth would find worth a flaying. "What did you sneak off to do, you naughty thing?" She rubbed her lower back. It didn't help.

Kenneth, oblivious to her discomfort, waggled his eyebrows at her. "Astronomy lecture."

That hardly sounded worth skiving off work for. "Never. You were meeting some boy at the Soggy Lamprey."

"Saints' bones, I wouldn't lie to you, Tes'puco," said Kenneth, kissing a knuckle toward Heaven. "It was the public lecture at St. Bert's. A pair of astronomers—one saar, one human—talked about using lenses to examine the sky."

"A spyglass, you mean? Like a pirate?" It always came back to pirates for Tess, even when she was thirteen and taller than her mother and should have outgrown such nonsense.

"It's true, I swear. The dragons say there are other worlds out there, and you can see 'em, even without the glass. They're the traveling stars, the ones the pagans took for gods and the Saints called Heaven's lanterns. They're other worlds, Tess, circling the sun."

Tess shook her head unconsciously, not because she didn't believe him but because her imagination was caught already. Other worlds! Pathka would've loved the thought of sailing the skies, exploring and marauding upon other seas like some Dozerius of the air.

"You still don't believe me," said Kenneth, leaning against the kitchen table and licking his fingers clean. "There's two lectures per week, open to the public. They aren't always about the skies. Next one's on electrostatics, I think. You should come with me."

Tess burst out laughing. "That's not even a word! And how am I to come?" Her belly twinged. "Mama would never allow it."

"Pshaw. She's not such an ogre. I can handle her," said Kenneth, waving dismissively.

He returned the next day, pointedly winking at Tess's doubts, and helped clear the table and wash the dishes, which raised Anne-Marie's suspicions. After dinner, when the family gathered in the parlor—even Papa, who typically would have retreated to his library but couldn't bear to face the new gaps—Kenneth flopped onto an armchair and said languidly, "So. Which of my little cousins wants to come to a free lecture tomorrow evening at St. Bert's?"

Nobody jumped to their feet or raised their hand or cried, "Me!" Tess kept quiet, petrified to give any sign or get her hopes up.

Anne-Marie, darning socks, frowned. "Is that what you're

skulking about for?" she asked her baby brother. "You don't want to go alone?"

"Quite the contrary, I already went alone," said Kenneth, jutting his chin. "For my boldness, I was rewarded with some edification. I peered at the moon through a spyglass."

At this, young Paul and Ned pricked up their ears.

"It's all pitted on the surface, like it had the graypox," said Kenneth smugly. "But you wouldn't know from ogling it with your naked eye."

"Kenneth! Language!" cried Anne-Marie, clapping her hands over Neddie's naked ears.

"It's what the astronomers say, sis," drawled Kenneth. "Nothing to be squeamish about. Anyway, tomorrow's nothing so scandalous as moon-gazing. They'll explain electrostatics, the power that runs quigutl devices. They'll have machines you can play with."

He aimed his last words at the boys, whose eyes grew eager. This, Tess understood, was Kenneth's strategy for getting her to the lecture: preying on Anne-Marie's indulgence of the boys—an indulgence well remembered from his own boyhood.

It was working. Paul and Neddie were at Mama's knee, clamoring to play with the wonderful devices.

Anne-Marie frowned, unsure, but Kenneth saw the seams in her resolve and began picking at them: "If you don't want to go, sis, I don't mind taking them. I'll keep a close eye out, or if that won't put your heart at ease, maybe Tess would be so kind as to help me. That's one boy apiece. No way we can lose them. What say you, Tes'puco, old love?"

Tess, a natural thespian, knew exactly how to answer. "I have to escort the boys all the time! Surely it's Jeanne's turn."

"I don't mind doing it," said Jeanne.

"No," said Mama crisply. "Tess will accompany her brothers. Caring for younger siblings is a duty, Tess, which you shirk at every—"

Tess suppressed a look of triumph. She had this speech memorized, but she groaned as if she couldn't believe her ears.

Outside Anne-Marie's line of sight, Kenneth winked. He'd been right; he could handle his sister.

"But this is just one lecture," Tessie fretted the following night as they traversed the dark streets behind the bounding boys. "How do we convince her next time?"

"Already wanting to attend a second when you've yet to see the first?" said Kenneth laughingly. "At some point, little coz, we won't have to convince her. She'll be accustomed to the notion that going to St. Bert's is something you do. Or, failing that, we find a way to sneak you out. Ever climbed out your window?"

She'd tried. "Jeanne's a light sleeper," Tess grumbled, but a radical notion occurred to her. Did she and Jeanne have to share a room? What if she moved into Seraphina's old room? Had her existence become so stifling that she could consider abandoning her sister and their midnight conferences?

She had to do something. She felt like a rat in a trap.

They arrived at Old St. Bert's, in the heart of Quighole. Time was, this neighborhood had been locked up at sundown, its wrought-iron gates chained shut. After the war, however, Queen Glisselda had decreed an initiative of normalization.

Quighole would no longer be cordoned off, public lectures would occur at the old church in the close, and the human denizens of Lavondaville would learn both natural philosophy and how not to be afraid of the saarantrai and quigutl around them.

That was the theory. The lectures had not achieved broad popularity yet.

This one was sparsely attended, so Tess and Kenneth took the boys up front. A saarantras, silver bell pinned conscientiously to his shoulder, stood upon a dais behind a long table covered in strange apparatuses. Behind him loomed a large slate upon a stand, whereupon his assistant, a young man of nineteen or twenty, could jot notes and make diagrams with chalk.

Tess had met saarantrai before—Seraphina's crabby uncle, for one—so she wasn't unduly fascinated by Professor the dragon Ondir. His monotonous voice and the esoteric nature of his subject didn't capture her attention, either; the hard pew made wiggling almost inevitable. Indeed, Tess's first lecture might have been her last, had not her attention been wholly captured by what stood behind him.

The altarpiece had been removed, since the building was no longer a church, and replaced by a vast mural, a gift from St. Fredricka before she'd departed for her home in the Archipelagos. The painting depicted the myriad creatures of land, sky, and sea, cavorting in their legions. In the center, human and dragon clasped hand and talon in friendship. Everything was in motion around those two poles of stillness. The birds looked ready to flutter into the heights of the nave, the ocean to spill out across the seats. The auroch capered with the frog, and the bee danced with the wolf. It was a harmonious, deathless world, a dream.

Tess found it deeply moving. Indeed, it colored everything Saar Ondir had to say about electrostatics. "The world is made up of infinitesimal particles, smaller than we can see or envision," he began, his voice nasal and atonal, but Tess felt she could see these particles, like gnats and bright butterflies, soaring through the mural's skies.

"Lodestones are drawn together by an invisible force called magnetism," the professor droned, and Tess thought she saw it manifested in the schools of mackerel and flocks of starlings, lines of motion, attraction and repulsion, the great whirl of life.

The mural was teeming. She wanted to walk straight into that world and never look back.

Paul and Neddie wiggled during the lecture but enjoyed the machines later. Paul turned a crank, building up enough charge in a wand to give his brother a snapping shock; Ned made a tube glow by moving a magnet over a coil of wire, then dropped the heavy lodestone on his brother's toe.

This was their usual nonsense. Tess barely gave it a second thought, automatically scolding or comforting by turns. Her eyes were still on the mural. There was something she couldn't quite make out in one corner, a vague suggestion of coiling behind the seals and belugas and icebergs. Sometimes it looked like the water, like her eyes playing tricks on her, but sometimes she was sure she saw it.

Each glimpse gave her shivers. She felt a flame reigniting in her heart, something the wet rags of stultification had all but extinguished.

"Excuse me," she said quietly to Professor the dragon Ondir's assistant, tall, with knowing blue eyes, who had swooped in to rescue a spinning engine from Neddie. "What's that in the corner of the painting? That's not supposed to be one of the World Serpents, is it?"

"World Serpents?" said the young man in a light, merry voice. "I've not heard of those."

Of course he wouldn't know the name; it was the translation from Quootla, which nobody bothered learning. "A quigutl told me stories," she began, but the fellow interrupted her.

"Quigutl can't speak Goreddi," he said, as if explaining to a child.

"I taught myself Quootla," said Tess crisply, nettled by his tone.

"Did you indeed?" he said, managing to sound both astonished and contrite. "You must be older than you look."

"I'm sixteen," said Tess, who wasn't.

"So that's a no," he said impudently. Tess wrestled a smile, secretly pleased that she could pass for sixteen. That was nearly grown-up. It didn't occur to her that a thirteen-year-old who knew Quootla would have been even more impressive.

"There are seven World Serpents," Tess explained. "And they . . . they hold the world together. They have wondrous powers."

She cringed at how silly it sounded, like magical creatures out of a Dozerius tale. He wasn't going to take her seriously.

"Come look at the corner of the mural," she said.

Tess led him around the table and showed him where the picture seemed ambiguous. There were stories about St. Fredricka's paintings, that they moved or wept or changed, and indeed the image seemed to come and go most disconcertingly.

The young man tossed his fair hair out of his eyes. "There is a faint something. Damned if I can tell what it is." He rubbed his cleft chin. "They tell tales in the Archipelagos of a monster under the ice. St. Fredricka came from those parts, you know. Maybe she included a hint of the old legends for her own amusement. Artists do silly things like that all the time."

"But if the southern peoples have stories, and the quigutl have similar stories, don't you think there could be something to it?" Tess implored.

"Dragon scholars have never mentioned anything of the kind," he said. "If creatures like this existed, bigger and more powerful than the saar, don't you think—"

"That the dragons would admit they weren't the greatest monsters in the world?"

His startled expression lit a flame of satisfaction in Tess's heart. She'd got him thinking.

"The quigutl say dragons deny the World Serpents because they can't bear to be second at anything," she added.

Ondir's assistant smiled, quite alarmingly. "Well, aren't you an unorthodox little thinker. What's your name, then?"

Tess felt instinctively that she ought not give her real name. Word would get back to Mama that she'd spoken to a young man. She wasn't sure how that was a crime, exactly, only that Mama would make it so. However, she wasn't entirely quick on her toes making up a name, and said, "Therese Belgioso."

"That's a lovely name." His smile widened and warmed. "Welcome to the lectures, Therese. Do I glean correctly that you're interested in animals?"

Pathka and Faffy—how she missed them both!—sprang to

mind and produced a knot in Tess's throat, so she could only nod vigorously.

"Well then, let me extend a personal invitation to my talk on mountain megafauna next week," said the young man, his eyes twinkling. "I hope you'll be back for that."

Tess was struggling to regain her voice and think of a clever response—something a real sixteen-year-old unorthodox thinker might say—when Saar Ondir called, "William, finish socializing. I require your assistance with the pulser before these children break it."

That was Tess's cue to fetch her brothers. She grabbed Neddie, and Kenneth steered Paul; they left St. Bert's an hour after the boys' bedtime and headed back across town.

"I want to attend the lecture on animals next week," Tess told Kenneth.

"I saw you examining the mural."

Tess felt herself blush in the darkness, even though his tone was not suggestive.

"There are loads of lectures on animals, or explorers talking about the fantastical creatures of distant isles. And there's not just the public lectures. There are classes—night classes, for honest working people—on any subject you wish. I've been thinking of taking one on astronomy. I can't work at the warehouse forever," Kenneth added quietly, so the little boys' big ears wouldn't overhear. "I hate it. There's talk of sending me out for collections, because I'm strong. Imagine me breaking the fingers of poor villains who can't pay."

Tess couldn't; Kenneth could be self-absorbed, but he had a gentle heart. Such violence would surely shatter it.

"I need to get away from the family," he was saying. Belgiosos always called themselves *the family*, as if there were no other. "Anne-Marie had the right idea, marrying outside the business, even if your father turned out to be a rummy choice."

Tess scowled at his description of her father. He and Mama did not love each other anymore, if they ever had, but it hurt to hear it said so plainly.

"If you take a class, maybe I'll take one, too," said Tess.

"Braver together, eh?" said Kenneth, elbowing her and grinning, and for a moment she was painfully reminded of Jeanne, of *us against the world*. Jeanne had never been a partner for her exploits, though. Pathka had been, but Pathka was gone.

Tess could endure anything—all the manners and morality lessons in the world—as long as she had a secret joy, something she loved that was hers alone. Sneaking out to St. Bert's was just the thing to make her life delicious once again, and if it should happen occasionally to bring her into contact with learned young men who would answer her questions and treat her like she was all grown up, so much the better.

She held the word *megafauna* in her heart like the key that would unlock her prison.

Nine

Tess and Pathka followed the river until it turned east, and then took the road south over a low ridge. The land beyond flattened and stretched. The sky was enormous here. Tess, who'd grown up in a city, had always thought of the sky as a kind of ceiling, painted blue above her, but out here it was clearly a dome. It went all the way to the ground.

Pathka had set out in a frolicsome mood, but by late afternoon he was growing cagey. He left the road in favor of creeping under bushes and through ditches, and kept glancing back.

"We're being followed," he said at last, emerging from a muddy culvert.

Tess leaped to a panicked conclusion: "Papa!"

Pathka's head spines flared. "No. My brethren. I knew a few would be tenacious."

Tess squinted against the glare. The road behind them

stretched straight and empty for a mile or more. "I don't see anyone."

"I smell them," said Pathka. "If the wind shifts, they'll smell me. They're following my tracks, so I'm leading them on a chase." He sprang over a stone wall into a pasture, scattering sheep.

The plain ended in low, lumpy hills, thrown up by a river barging heedlessly along. Tess recognized the phenomenon from geology lectures, which amused her.

The road crossed the river at a frothy ford, putting Tess's boots to the test.

Pathka didn't let her return to the road but led her upstream, through the shallows. "If they can't immediately smell us, they might give up," he said. He was up to his neck, swimming with an elegant serpentine ripple. "Even the stubbornest must be tired of following me by now."

The bank was thick with horsetails and mud that almost sucked the boots off Tess's feet. They climbed out into a coppice, a domesticated forest, which made for easy walking, and by the time they glimpsed the road again, it was nearly dark.

The coppice was made of firewood; Tess gathered some for a campfire, and Pathka's tongue set the small pile alight. They had nothing to cook, but a fire can dispel a great deal of gloom, and Tess, feet blistered and muscles aching, needed to stave off a darkness encroaching on her heart.

It was her mother's voice again. It had been quieter today, or Tess had been distracted, but as soon as the sun had set, it had lit into her: *What are you doing out here? You don't know the first thing about survival. You'll be eaten by a bear.*

Ah, death. She smiled mirthlessly, and reckoned she could put it off again, until morning at least. She felt squirmy, though, and wished they had some wine. There was only water, and the last of Florian's bread and sausage, and some cheese (which she felt guilty giving to Pathka now). They ate in silence, and then Tess spread her blanket and lay down, still restless. She was too tired to walk another step, and yet she felt like running, punching, kicking things.

It was that gadfly voice, still buzzing. She swatted at the air, which helped not at all.

"Would you tell me a World Serpent story?" Tess asked Pathka.

Pathka poked the fire with a stick. "Which one? The creation of dragons and quigutl? How the dragons turned their tails upon the truth?"

The dragons had indeed, Tess recalled wryly. Professor the dragon Ondir had vehemently denied the World Serpents' existence, and the scholar Spira, Will's archrival, had written papers demonstrating their physical impossibility. It had been enough to make even Tess doubt.

"Tell me a story that proves they're real, that we're not chasing a phantom," Tess said, settling with her pack under her head.

Pathka, usually a blur of motion, grew still and solemn. "For once, let us squat upon time/no-time," he intoned, and Tess nearly burst out laughing.

She'd tried to teach him to begin stories with "Once upon a time." As a child, alas, she'd been unable to explain exactly what the idiom meant, so Pathka had invented an idiosyncratic Quootla translation. He couldn't conceive of being "upon" unless there was some verb to go with it, hence "squat." Since "time" in this case really indicated timelessness, Pathka had put the word in contradictory case.

Quootla had a suffix, *-utl*, that could be glued to the end of anything—nouns, verbs, adjectives, pronouns, small rodents— and meant the word itself plus its opposite, simultaneously. It didn't always translate into Goreddi. *Time/no-time* almost made sense; *blue/orange* or *fall/rise* or *dog/whatever-the-opposite-of-dog-is* were perfectly intelligible in Quootla but boggling to nearly everyone else.

Even Seraphina, who had mostly refused to help Tess understand quigutl speech, was baffled by contradictory case. "It's an illogical quigutl innovation," she'd said. "Proper dragons wouldn't tolerate such nonsense. Their brains would implode."

Tess's mind had been malleable in those days, however, and she'd made peace with the usage, even if her understanding would never be perfect.

"Squatting upon the smug face of time-*utl*," she said now, grinning up at the merry stars.

Pathka's eyes closed; his skin glowed orangish in the firelight. "The World Serpents are sometimes called the Most Alone, but they weren't always solitary. The greater dragons and quigutl lived with them for an age of the earth. Long after the dragons abandoned them, chasing after rationality, the quigutl stayed. We cared for our great mothers until our wings shriveled into spindly arms, and our fierce flame became precise and gentle. We would lie upon them, skin to skin, and our dreams would twist and entwine together like smoke.

"I know they're real, Tethie, because we all ache with their absence when we're alone. Sometimes we even dream of them, if there are no other quigutl around."

"I thought you said your dreaming was impossible," said Tess.

"It was, because I dreamed in the nest, not on my own. Sleeping in heaps silences the dreams, mutes our loss, and lets us forget that we aren't meant to be apart—"

A dark shape suddenly shot out of the underbrush like a ballista bolt, hitting Pathka squarely in the side and knocking him into the fire.

Pathka landed hard, scattering burning branches, but popped back up like an uncoiling spring. His adversary hissed and scratched, spines splayed in fury, and tried to bite Pathka's neck. They rolled, kicking up dust; thrashing tails struck the fire and sent up sparks.

Tess leaped uselessly to her feet and flailed around for some way to stop this. She couldn't throw water on them; she only had what was in the water skin. She flung her blanket at the assailant quigutl like a net, succeeding only in catching the corner on fire.

Pathka, who'd started out giving as good as he got, abruptly stopped fighting. He rolled onto his back, legs spread and throat stretched out, leaving himself almost mockingly vulnerable.

"Fight me, Mother!" his attacker squawked in frustration. It was Kikiu.

"I did fight," said Pathka evenly. "We've had our *fatluketh*, and now we're done."

Kikiu hesitated, panting, then bit Pathka viciously on the thigh. Pathka skreeled in pain.

"*Now* we're done," said Kikiu, spitting a scrap of Pathka's skin into the fire pit.

Silver blood beaded upon Pathka's leg. Tess fought down horror, dumped her pack out on the ground, and began ripping the leftover linen from her chemise into strips.

"The others turned back at the river, but I saw through your little ploy," said Kikiu.

"Aren't you clever," said Pathka.

"Merely determined to hold you to your obligations," snapped Kikiu, flaring her head spines.

Pathka ignored this last bit of aggression, but Tess glared daggers and wished she had head spines. She'd have shown Kikiu como flare. Pathka needed care, though, so Tess turned her attention to where it would do good.

Pathka let Tess wrap his leg without snapping or biting, all the fight drained out of him.

Kikiu cleaned blood off her claws with her flaming tongue and nudged the scattered fire sticks back into the pit. "You left before I could fight you," she said at last. "You did it on purpose, knowing I couldn't get my *fatluketh* unless I followed you."

Fatluketh was the rite of adulthood, Tess recalled: hatchlings fought their mothers and then they were free of each other. Pathka's damaged head spine came from such a fight.

"Would you believe I wasn't thinking of you?" said Pathka, wincing as Tess tied off the bandage. "It is possible, perhaps, that you are not the center of the universe."

"You never intended to fight me," cried Kikiu. "You've abandoned the nest. What kind of quigutl are you?"

"That was no nest," said Pathka. "I'd advise you to abandon

it as well, and its false ideals, though I know you won't. You're afraid of your true nature."

"True nature!" Kikiu scoffed.

"You may mock," said Pathka, "but I'm doing what I've been called to do, going in search of the Most Alone."

Kikiu flinched upon hearing the epithet, as if her mother habitually used the name as a weapon, but she recovered her sneer soon enough, and turned her attention to Tess.

"How did Pathka persuade you to go looking for imaginary monsters?" said Kikiu waspishly, black-hole eyes watching Tess shake out the blanket. "Do you know why we chained *ko* to that workbench? Because we found *ko* at the bottom of the deepest well in Trowebridge, passed out from a self-inflicted wound, poisoning the townspeople's water with blood."

Tess stared at Pathka in alarm; Pathka wouldn't meet her eye.

"*Ko* might have died," said Kikiu, "and the rest of us been driven out of town, and for what? A bizarre superstition based on ancient stories."

"I chose a poor location. It was as far underground as I could get," said Pathka, looking shifty. He tried to reassure Tess: "I was called; I heard it in my dream. There's a very old story that says when the World Serpents call us back to them, we must answer—"

"And when we find them, the world will end," said Kikiu. "You gloss over that part."

"It won't necessarily end," said Pathka, his voice pleading now. "The stories say the singular-*utl* will end. That word is teeming with possible interpretations."

"What is more singular and plural than the world itself?" said Kikiu.

"The World Serpents," said Pathka quietly. "Or the one who searches for them."

"Are you listening, human?" said Kikiu, wheeling toward Tess. "My mother seeks to kill us all, or die, or maybe both. You've unleashed *ko* upon the world—more fool you—but even if the world is safe, can you bear to walk a friend toward death? I couldn't do it."

Tess couldn't begin to respond. Kikiu had pulled the floor out from under everything Tess thought she knew about Pathka's journey, and left her standing on empty air.

"All I know is that I've been called," said Pathka, his voice almost inaudible, like grit in the wind. "How do I live with myself if I don't answer?"

"You live/die," said Kikiu bitterly, using contradictory case. "Like the rest of us."

"You do feel it," said Pathka, rolling onto his side. His limp, exhausted body seemed melted into the dirt. "The malaise. The dis-ease. The creeping certainty that we've gone wrong."

"I feel worse things than that," said Kikiu, glowering. "You don't know the half. But I bear them. I submit to the rules, and don't go crying after myths and phantoms." She leaped to her feet and shook herself off. "My *fatluketh* is done, and I am done with you. You have no further maternal claim upon me."

"Good," said Pathka. "Go."

Kikiu spit into the dust, turned tail, and fled.

Tess clasped her hands around her knees, unsure what to say to Pathka. She'd been wrestling her own urge to die, making herself walk on, but what a cruel farce if she was simultaneously walking Pathka toward death.

Pathka broke the silence. "It's not as dire as Kikiu made it sound. The end of the singular-*utl* is likely a metaphorical dissolution, or a merging together. Maybe it's the entanglement of dreams I mentioned."

"Likely. *Maybe,*" said Tess, poking Pathka with his own hedging words.

"It's been a millennium since we left them Most Alone," said Pathka, grinding his body into the dirt, making a depression to sleep in. "I can't pretend to know what will happen. But I've been called: I've got to go. You know what that's like. You answered the call of your boots."

"That was a joke!" said Tess, unexpectedly offended.

She spread her blanket on the ground, trying to smooth her irritation at the same time, but it didn't help. Maybe food would help. She rummaged in her pack for more, and was alarmed to find nothing. She dumped her belongings out on the ground; only a single cheese remained, and no money to speak of.

She lay down to sleep, but the gadfly with her mother's voice was biting her again: *You're going to starve. You're a terrible friend.* The story hadn't silenced it; worry over Pathka and food was making it worse. Tess felt herself curling tighter and tighter, like a spring made of bitterness, until she had no choice but to snap.

"Should I have let that egg kill you? Is that what you really wanted?" said Tess, feeling cruel as she said it. "Why else would you name your daughter Kikiu, 'death'? Don't imagine that morbid detail was lost on me. What a name to carry around.

No wonder she resents you, when you force her to remember the time she accidentally almost killed you."

Pathka opened his eyes; he'd been asleep. "Kikiu doesn't resent me," he said at last, ignoring the rest of Tess's barbs. "It's more like . . . *ko* has grown too big and feels trapped in *ko* own skin. It pinches. Kikiu needs to shed that polluted nest, but of course *ko* won't. *Ko* has assimilated to their unnatural ways, and anyway, it's easier to blame me. What's a mother for but to be blamed?"

With that, he rolled onto his side away from the fire, signaling sleep more aggressively, and Tess was left to fend off her unwieldy feelings alone. She lay a long time, staring through branches at the night sky, until her temper was soothed by the cold impartiality of the stars.

First thing in the morning, as she was burying the ashes of the fire, Tess kicked up two stray bits of metal. One turned out to be a tiny key; Kikiu had apparently spit it into the dirt on parting. It unfastened the heavy manacle around Pathka's ankle.

"That was kind of her," said Tess.

"Symbolic, actually," said Pathka, tossing the key and manacle into the ashes. "Now I'm completely free. Not that I'm complaining."

Tess had palmed the other bit of metal, a pewter ring, which must have come from her pack. That meddling Seraphina had evidently sneaked it in there when she wasn't looking.

"Pathka, be honest," said Tess, worrying the thnik behind

her back. "You said I was saving your life by journeying with you. Kikiu says I'm leading you toward death. Which is it?"

Pathka's throat pouch quivered as he breathed. "I said you were *naming* my life, which is similar but not identical to saving. We name something to make it real, to give it meaning. You can name my life and I might still die. Those aren't mutually exclusive."

"You're not making me feel better," said Tess miserably.

"Then how about this," said Pathka. "You'll be naming your life as well. Anathuthia will hold a mirror to your heart, answer the unanswerable, plane the rough places."

"Destroy the world?" Tess was still skeptical.

"The world is surprisingly hard to destroy," said Pathka gently. "Whereas saving it can be done a bit at a time. Anyway, don't be afraid. We're walking away from death, not toward it. Death is going back to Trowebridge."

Tess rolled her eyes at the Quootla pun, and the tension broke. Pathka asked if there was any breakfast, and Tess brought out the last cheese.

Under its pristine wax shell, alas, the cheese was riddled with worms. Pathka gobbled it down, maggots and all. "They're full of cheese, so they taste like cheese!" he announced. Tess couldn't bring herself to try any. They walked through budding coppice toward the southern road, ignoring the ominous rumblings of Tess's stomach, or any thoughts of what it would take, in the absence of coins, to fill it.

From her pocket, the ring niggled at her.

Ten

Pathka, who had an inner furnace to stoke, could not be satisfied with one grubby cheese. He rooted around in flooded ditches by the side of the road for rotting tubers and corms. Strands of algae dribbled from his chin like a horrible green beard.

Tess tried not to watch him eat, or smell his breath afterward.

Later in the year, the countryside would become a banquet of delicious things: berries, honey, wild onions, nuts. The fields Tess passed, alas, had but the first inklings, a verdant hint of bounty to come, or they were black and sodden, heaped with clotted dung (Pathka, disturbingly, ate his fill of dung). The scattered patches of forest held no edible treasures that Tess could discern; the blackberry canes barely had leaves yet, let alone berries.

She might have milked a sheep—not that she knew how. She considered it as she paralleled a pasture, watching the new lambs nurse and *not* watching Pathka sneak around the field eating dried-up ovine afterbirths.

He was making the ewes cagey. Could a stampede of sheep kill you? Even if the answer was no, Tess felt certain they'd make an exception for her. That would be an embarrassing way to go, and she'd already decided to walk on today. She didn't dare risk it.

Capering lambs, endemic to the Goreddi countryside in spring, leaped into the air for pure exuberance, as if stung by bees of joy. They were happiness incarnate upon the new grass. Tess's heart was lifted at first, but by her second hungry day, she took little pleasure in their antics.

By the third day, Tess was so ravenous that the pewter ring in her pack began whispering: *One word, and Seraphina would fetch you. You were never hungry at home. You never got blisters or raw places where your boot tops chafed you.*

"Quiet, ring," Tess muttered through her teeth. There was no going home. She'd be delivering herself up to the convent.

Plenty to eat at a convent, said the ring, sensibly.

Nearby lambs bleated raucously and kicked up their silly heels in agreement. "Quiet, lambs!" Tess cried, walking faster.

Beyond the next rise, a well-to-do yeoman farmstead stretched along a burbling creek, tidy and bucolic, like something out of a painting. Cherubs would not have been out of place in the blossoming peach trees, or a sunbeam bursting out of the clouds to set the thatched roofs ablaze with gold.

Tess froze in her tracks, not for awe but because she'd

caught a waft of baking bread and found herself paralyzed by want.

"Pathka," she half whispered, and Pathka appeared beside her, like a fairy godlizard. "It's all right to steal if you're very hungry, isn't it? Heaven would forgive me, surely?"

"Is that why you haven't been eating?" said Pathka. "I thought maybe you were fasting to let your gut fauna recuperate."

Gut fauna was not a quigutl phrase Tess knew. Even with copious explanation—"Your intestines are full of tiny bugs"— her ears rebelled from understanding. It couldn't be true. Pathka was teasing.

"I don't want to steal from serfs and villeins," she said. "They're poor."

"Poorer than you?" asked Pathka shrewdly. "Not likely. Anyway, I reject 'poor' as the artificial creation of humans and dragons. Hunger exists, though, and a hungry creature is entitled to eat."

Tess was so hungry, in fact, that the smell of bread was making her dizzy. She couldn't follow Pathka's argument, but she could follow him toward the farmstead.

"You grab some bread," he was saying, like a general laying out battle plans. "I'll sneak into the henhouse and the cold storage. I'll meet you on the other side of the stream, in that stand of beech trees."

He disappeared into the weeds behind the walled garden. Tess shook herself, trying to focus, and crept into the farmstead.

Stealing from a yeoman farmstead wasn't the same as stealing from serfs, though Tess didn't appreciate the distinction; country folk were all "peasants" to her. A yeoman farmer did not own land—that belonged to his lord—but he owned the house and stock and was free to give up farming if he liked. Serfs were more like trees: they couldn't move, owned nothing but their leaves (so to speak), and could be cut down at will. A yeoman might have serfs in his charge, belonging to the land he rented. The yeoman made use of their labor, oversaw the payment of debts and the resolution of disputes, and acted as a subcontracted agent for the local lord.

Tess was not, therefore, stealing from the abjectly poor this time. Knowing would not have eased her conscience, though. Her head was full of scriptural admonitions against thievery, recited helpfully in her mother's voice, as she crept across the farmyard.

The brick oven had been emptied; a girl cleared out the ashes with a hoe. Tess passed behind her, walking when the hoe scraped, pausing when it paused. She still smelled bread, and it didn't take the olfactory prowess of a quigutl to tell it was coming from the main house.

Her nose led to an open window and five perfect loaves cooling on a breadboard inside. Tess almost reached in, but at the last minute glanced up and saw the woman of the house stirring a cauldron over the fire. Tess ducked, heart pounding, and listened hard. The woman hummed as she worked; the sound came no closer. Tess stood up to one side, out of view, and peeked cautiously around the frame. The woman hadn't moved.

Silent as a shadow, Tess leaned over the sill and wrapped her fingers around the nearest loaf.

It was hot; she winced but didn't cry out. She fetched the loaf back quickly, so as not to burn herself. In her haste, her elbow bumped the rod holding the casement open, and the window fell on Tess's shoulder. She gasped. The woman turned, saw Tess, and bellowed like a bull. Tess valiantly kept her grip on the hot bread, pulling it out and letting the window fall shut.

Then she ran.

There was no time for care or consideration in this run. She noticed farmhands, dimly, and dodged behind the barn, the henhouse, the well, a wheelbarrow, whatever she could to avoid them. Maybe they saw her, maybe they didn't; they were running indoors to answer the woman's cry, and Tess's presence might not have sunk in until they reached the kitchen and heard the story. Then they probably thought, *Wait, I did see a boy in a striped jacket, now that you mention it, and he looked a proper villain, and maybe I should set the dogs loose and they'll sort him out.*

Tess's lungs burned and her vision was spotty by the time she reached the beech grove where Pathka had said to meet. She didn't dare stop so close to the house. She ran—or, more accurately, staggered stubbornly onward—until she reached a cattle guard, a bridge of narrow slats that a cow, being bulky, would shy away from crossing. She crawled into the ditch under the bridge and lay in the weeds, panting. Sunlight poured through the slats in slanting stripes.

When she had breath enough, she laughed, and when she could laugh no more, she tore into that bread like a vulture into a bloated carcass. The interior steamed, scalding the roof of her mouth, but she didn't care. She'd never tasted such sweet, rapturous bread in her life.

Her head nested in spindly weeds; beyond them the sky glowed preternaturally blue through the slats. As her chewing slowed, she noticed a bee crawling along a blade of grass above her head. She counted its stripes, amazed to see them juxtaposed with the stripes of sky. The bee's were a warning, the sky's a promise she could not yet fathom, and for a moment everything seemed connected, aching beauty and imminent danger, the fragility of the bee and the scalded roof of her mouth, the transcendent savor of bread and the fact that she was literally lying in a ditch.

The moment made such a deep impression that she never forgot it, but she couldn't explain it except with the single word: *there.* She was there. Present in herself. She wasn't always, so it was worth remarking upon.

Pathka caught up soon after, an iron pan in his dorsal hands, and in the pan fresh eggs, smoked meat, a wedge of soft cheese, and a jar of peach jam. There was no bread left for the jam, but Tess happily scooped it out with two fingers and ate it like that. The bee had buzzed off, or she might've extended a jammy finger to it, as if it were a friend.

She closed the jar and stowed the rest in her pack for later. "Are they still looking for me?" she whispered to Pathka.

"They're looking for a quigutl," he said, his voice like a gravel road. "I showed myself and left musk about to confuse the dogs. Try to be stealthier, if you don't mind."

"It was my first time!" Tess protested, crawling out from under the bridge.

"It was almost your last," said Pathka mildly. "I suppose you'll improve with practice."

Tess slept hard that night, her belly full and her whole being exhausted by running and danger. Pathka let her sleep a whole hour past sunrise before pouncing on her.

"I spotted several cave entrances when I was foraging," he cried, sitting on her chest. "Today we find the best one and begin our journey toward Anathuthia."

"Pluhhh," said Tess blearily. She'd been having a terrible dream—her mother had dismembered her, put her in a basket, and lowered her into a pit where a monster lurked, all the while berating her for choosing to be sacrificed this way. She'd been so deep, in both sleep and pit, that she was having trouble pulling herself out.

"I thought we'd begun," she muttered. "And that Anathuthia was south. In Ninys. Under a wheat field."

A terrible idea occurred to her; she tried to sit up but was prevented by Pathka's weight on her ribs. "You don't intend us to travel underground to Ninys," said Tess, flopping back.

"No, no. Do you remember what I was doing in Trowebridge that upset everyone?"

"Bleeding in the well?" Tess eyed him suspiciously.

"That's what I did, but it wasn't what I was *doing*," said

Pathka, climbing off her. "I was calling to Anathuthia. We can't go to her without calling her first; we'd never get close. I need to get deep underground to do the—the needful things."

Tess sat up, still suspicious. He was blazing with tics and wriggles, body language she couldn't quite parse. "Does it involve bleeding?"

"Kikiu made it sound worse than it is," said Pathka.

"Then make it sound better."

"It's called *kemthikemthlutl*," he said. Tess untangled the word with some difficulty: a dream within a dream that is also the opposite of a dream within a dream. "I need to go deep and sleep," Pathka went on, "and also bleed, but only a little. It will let Anathuthia know I'm coming, and she, in turn, will indicate more precisely where we should go. I hope."

The thought of blood made Tess shudder, but she decided this was some kind of ritual, a symbolic sacrifice not meant to kill him, and that reconciled her a bit.

"Fine," she said with more bravado than she felt. "You can try it, but if I perceive that you're in danger of dying—"

There was no way to finish that sentence. She had no idea what she'd do.

She ate hastily, packed up, and followed him toward a stream leading into the trees. They soon reached a humid glen where a cave mouth gaped under a crumbling overhang.

Tess had never been in a cave, though Goredd was riddled with them. Soft limestone underpinned this part of the Southlands, and it was carved by trickling, persistent streams that joined into underground rivers, the unseen arteries of the world.

Some were reputedly enormous, bigger than any river on land, rushing through darkness toward who knew where.

Caves made for fascinating lectures at St. Bert's, but the actual cave mouth exhaled a breath of decay. The prospect of entering that empty darkness made Tess shudder. "What if there's a cave-in?" she asked Pathka, who was winding dry fern fronds upon the end of a stick. "Limestone caves are prone to those. Water weakens the rock, and—"

"We won't know what hit us, because we'll be dead," said Pathka, his nimble dorsal fingers tying the fronds securely. He set them aflame with his tongue. "Or we will know, and we'll die in protracted agony. There's no point worrying about it beforehand."

He handed Tess the torch and plunged into the darkness without a backward glance.

Tess, intensely discomfited, got up her nerve and followed.

The cramped, muddy cave pierced deep into the hillside and soon left daylight behind. A giggling rivulet traipsed across the floor; Tess avoided it at first, then decided that's what boots were for. Pathka adhered himself to the ceiling and crawled upside down. Tess worried about singeing his tail with her torch, but if the flames licked him, he seemed not to notice. He wound among jutting thumbs of rock, none dramatic enough to be called a stalactite. Tess hit her head twice, because her attention was occupied downward. Minnows swam in the rivulet, and a fat white salamander. She laid her hand on a rock, and something disturbingly leggy scuttled over it.

Tess recoiled, inhaling sharply; the torch revealed an

enormous ghostly cricket, almost transparent. She laughed then at her own apprehensions. The darkness was full, fuller than she would ever have guessed, and she found this curiously comforting.

They reached the egress and burst out into sunshine again. Tess felt strangely exhilarated and sorry to be out so soon. Pathka seemed twitchy and cranky. "You didn't try your dream-in-a-bloody-not-dream thing," Tess said.

"It wasn't right," Pathka said, rubbing himself in the grass. "I can't reach her here."

Tess didn't mind. She extinguished her torch and said, "Let's find another."

There were many such crevasses to choose from. They tried two more that afternoon, to Tess's immense delight, but Pathka soon became frustrated. "These limestone crannies are too shallow," he grumbled. "I suspect we need something deeper."

The word gave Tess a chill, eagerness and dread combined. Deeper would be more dangerous, without question; she both wanted and feared it. Pathka, however, seemed done for the day. For now, Tess had to settle for deeper south. She followed Pathka through tall grass, across a stony field of sprouts, and back to the road, into the heart of the heart of the country.

Eleven

Every morning, as she'd promised herself in Trowebridge, Tess made the decision to live. It was getting easier, even if thieving was difficult and dangerous and she never got any better at it. She had Pathka, and she found joy in walking the road.

This eccentric quest was a pilgrimage, she decided. Pathka hadn't said so explicitly, but Anathuthia was more than megafauna to him. She was practically a goddess, which was astonishing if you knew anything about quigutl. They weren't as purely rationalistic as the greater dragons, but one didn't expect religion of any kind in reptiles. Tess had been taught from childhood that belief was uniquely human.

Quigutl religion would have made an astonishing lecture at the Collegium. Tess sometimes imagined herself on the dais in front of St. Fredricka's mural, dumbfounding everyone. Spira would be in one corner, mouth open in disbelief. Ondir (implausibly) would have fainted dead away, and Will . . .

She always stopped imagining when Will showed up, and turned her attention back to the real world, where Pathka was zigzagging merrily ahead of her.

Over the years apart, she'd all but forgotten what Pathka was like, so lively and nosy, always in motion. He reminded her, achingly, of Faffy—not that Pathka was a pet (an offensive notion to a quigutl), or that he physically resembled the long-legged, narrow-waisted snaphound. Together they'd been a trio of pure mischief, frolicking in the courtyard, exploring tunnels under the city. They'd formed a continuum, with Faffy at the animal end, Tess at the human, and Pathka definitively demonstrating that there was no great distance between the poles.

"If you have a personality, you're a person," Seraphina had once told Anne-Marie in defense of dragonkind. Tess had taken this deeply to heart. Faffy and Pathka were both persons to her, the main difference being that Pathka could talk.

Pathka had understood Goreddi and had known the Southlander alphabet well enough to improvise spelling. Tess had quickly gained insight into Quootla without Seraphina's help.

Which was just as well, because Seraphina, prickly as a thistle, didn't like quigutl. "I can't stand listening to them," she'd said, tuning her oud and barely glancing at Tess. "Their language is nothing but Mootya with a bad lisp, and it drives me to distraction."

"It's not Mootya at all," Tess had answered crossly. "They have their own language, and it's called Quootla, and you don't understand anything."

That was one time Tess had been indisputably right, and that heady feeling had goaded her to learn contradictory case, future-past tense, the secret words quigutl never uttered in front of dragons—anything Seraphina wouldn't know. Seraphina hadn't taken it graciously; she always had to know one thing more than you. She had the facts.

Mama had the moral answers. And Tess was always wrong.

The farther she walked, the more irrelevant that seemed.

Walking was a good in itself, right and just and necessary. The road gave her no small measure of joy. Every day brought new vistas—the white conical roofs of oast-houses, a fox with her kits, an undiscovered color in the evening sky. Anything might be around the next bend; she could walk forever and never reach the end.

The road was possibility, the kind she'd thought her life would never hold again, and Tess herself was motion. Motion had no past, only future. Any direction you walked was forward, and that was as must be.

Walk on became her credo; she repeated it to herself every morning upon deciding to get up and exist for one more day.

Her days began before dawn, when the birds started arguing. Tess would eat whatever scrap of food she had left and listen to animated avian conversation all around her.

Birdsong was a language, unquestionably. She could discern calls and answers, aggression and capitulation and seduction. Warnings. Rapture. She wondered how long it would take to learn such a language without the advantages she'd had with Pathka.

If you'd paid as much attention to family and duty as you paid to dumb animals, said her mother's voice in her mind, *you might not have been such a disappointing daughter.*

That kind of thought was her cue to get going.

"Walking on now," Tess told Mama-in-her-head, kicking dirt over last night's ashes. "I think I'll live one more day."

She'd slept in an orchard, and disintegrating apple blossoms had shed petals over everything like snow. Heavy dew made them cling to her blanket and pack.

Pathka was nowhere to be seen, but he often woke earlier than she did and went foraging. She'd start walking. Pathka always found her.

The sun began to rise in earnest; Tess loved the way it illuminated treetops first, turning the foliage white-gold. The sky behind was warmly blue, and in the west a gibbous moon lingered in the branches like a pale fish caught in a net.

Like a delicious secret. Tess blew it a cheeky kiss.

The sun was well up and the moon long set by the time Tess reached a peasant hamlet. This was not a village as a city girl like Tess understood it. There was no church, no tavern, no fountain or market square, but a collection of house-barns, wherein people lived under the same roof as their animals, clustered around a green for common grazing. The fields were cultivated in long strips, so no single household got all the best land. There'd be an ancient vaulted chamber under the green, a place to hide in the event of dragon attack, used for hay storage now. It was an antiquated arrangement, the old high-feudal style.

At one corner of the green stood the communal bake oven, like an upturned clay bowl, its aging whitewash streaked with soot. It belched smoke like a little dragon.

Tess paused in the road, her stomach souring. If walking was the best part of her day, stealing was the worst, and she was sorry to stumble into it so soon. She didn't dare pass this place by. Who knew how far away the next opportunity would be?

Pathka still hadn't caught up, which concerned her. If he was off bleeding in some cavern by himself, she was going to be thoroughly cross. They had a deal.

An unspoken deal, she now realized. She'd have to change that.

Tess glumly began picking her way toward the oven. Most of the peasants, dressed in smocks and clogs, were working the long strip fields, spreading manure (the breeze confirmed) and hoeing cabbage sprouts. Someone should be watching the lambs on the green and minding that oven. Tess couldn't see anyone yet.

The hamlet was a maze of low stone walls. Tess duck-walked alongside them, but inconveniently there were no gates, only jutting stone stiles, difficult to clamber over discreetly. She poked her nose over a wall, like a mole taking stock of the upside world, and then flattened herself against the top and rolled over into the next yard. She crossed three walls this way without spotting the shepherd.

As Tess topped the fourth wall, however, she glimpsed a

pair of girls about her own age across the green. They'd been sitting in the shade of the wall, deep in conversation, and were now getting to their feet, crooks in hand.

They saw her at the same moment she saw them.

Tess dived over and quickly crabbed on all fours. She scuttled around a corner and out of sight before the girls reached the near edge of the green.

"We seen you spying, Mumpinello," cried one of the girls. "You can't hide from us in our own home. We will flush you out."

"And then beat you with a stick," called her shorter companion enthusiastically.

The girls, who clearly knew their business, hopped onto the wall and began walking around on top, crooks in hand, peering into every enclosure.

Tess crawled frantically; the only way to elude them was to keep moving. She reached one dead end and then another, until her only options were a muddy culvert (which would surely ruin her jacket) and a pigsty where a sow nursed her piglets. Sows—even a city girl knew—were famously fierce. Even if it didn't bite her, it would scream, and Tess would be found.

She'd lost this game of hide-and-seek. There was nothing left but make it no worse.

She stood up, hands raised in a gesture of submission.

The peasant girls ran toward her over top of the walls, sure-footed as goats. They were laughing, which Tess took as an encouraging sign.

"Oh, fie, it's not Mumpinello at all," said the taller and stouter of the girls, gathering her homespun skirts and leaping down to stand by Tess. "State your sneaky business, stranger," she said, tossing her fair braids behind her shoulders, "and submit to our righteous judgment."

"This is the court of the shepherdesses," said the smaller, darker one cheekily. She stayed atop the wall, her crook leveled at Tess's head. "Behave, villain. I'd hate to have to scream for my da."

"I can assure you—" Tess began, but the short one swatted her on the head.

"None of your oily talk," said the lass beside Tess, putting her hands on her broad hips. "We ask the questions. Why were you spying on us? If it were for lecherous purposes, I warn you, we will string you up."

"By your walnuts," cried the shepherdess on the wall, the tiny dog barking loudest.

"I can assure you"—some instinct helped Tess dodge another swing of the crook—"I have no vile designs upon your persons."

Here the shepherdesses looked unexpectedly crestfallen. Tess blinked at the pair of them, uncomprehending. "I—I only wanted some bread," she said. "I'm hungry."

"So you thought to rob us!" cried the small, elevated one, shaking her crook menacingly.

"Our father will thank us for catching a robbing bastard," said the bigger girl at Tess's elbow, practically purring in Tess's ear. "You'll never persuade me and Blodwen to let you go."

"Actually," said Tess, whose father was a lawyer, "it would have been theft, not robbery. Robbery implies violence, and I am not prepared for violence in any way."

Blodwen, on the wall, threw up her hands; the girl beside Tess snorted disgustedly. There was some game they were trying to play with her, Tess suddenly realized. Her capture was the most exciting thing since Mumpinello, whoever that was, and now she was disappointing them.

"B-because I've given up my former violent ways," Tess added hastily, improvising. "After killing that man. I vowed never to be violent again, and went to become a priest."

The girls pricked up their ears and exchanged a meaningful look. "Old Father Martius," said Blodwen from the wall, nodding portentously. "He's probably a killer, too, Gwenda."

"So many priests have secret pasts," said Gwenda, her wheaten brows arched mournfully. "But what did you do, Father? Was it a crime of passion or of cold-blooded calculation?"

Tess, secretly amused to be called Father, molded her mouth into a frown with some difficulty. "Passion, of course," she said.

The shepherdesses clapped and grinned with morbid glee. Tess realized they would not be satisfied until they'd wrung every gory detail from the tale. She cleared her throat. "It's a long story, and I could tell it better if my throat weren't so dry."

The girls eagerly took the hint. Blodwen pranced along the wall to fetch Tess a drink, while Gwenda led Tess over a stile into the sheep enclosure where they might sit in the shade and resume tending lambs while Tess talked. Blodwen returned with a rough-hewn cup of barley water—you could never be sure if a priest would drink beer—but it was cooling and delicious and Tess couldn't complain.

Tess licked the last drops off her lips. She'd had time to

think of a good story. "I fell in love with Julissima Rossa, wife of the Duke of Barrabou, and she with me."

It was a Dozerius the Pirate tale; they surely didn't have imported Porphyrian storybooks out here. The girls listened raptly to how Tess had gone half mad and attacked the duke with a sword over breakfast, only to have Julissima Rossa repent her infidelity when she saw the old man bleeding into his porridge.

"You cruel, terrible man," cried Julissima Rossa, putting a jeweled dagger to her ebony breast. "You've killed my husband and ruined me, and I curse you for it."

The shepherdesses gasped at Julissima Rossa's suicide and clutched at their hearts in pity to hear that her family had barred Tess from the funeral.

"The duke's son still pursues me," said Tess in conclusion. "And he will continue unto the ends of the earth until he has vengeance, a bill paid in my very blood."

"Won't the church protect you, Father?" said Blodwen with tears in her brown eyes. "Does it mean nothing that you've repented?"

"It matters not a jot," said Tess, her voice breaking slightly, overcome by her own imaginings. "What's done cannot be undone. A moment's lapse in judgment, and you're lost forever. I should probably lie down in a ditch and wait for my fate to overtake me."

"Never!" cried Gwenda, with such vehemence that three nearby ewes, startled from their grazing, trotted away across the green. "Blodwen, fetch Father . . . um . . ."

"Father Jacomo," Tess offered helpfully, feeling a little

foolish to be invoking Jeanne's brother-in-law yet again. She needed a deeper well of emergency names.

"Fetch Father Jacomo some bread," said Gwenda, hauling herself to her feet. "I know which stores Auntie Dee won't miss."

The girls rushed off and returned with bread, eggs, and a jar of pickled beets bundled into a clean kerchief. Tess felt a pang of guilt: this was a big gift from people who couldn't spare much. She began to stammer an apology, but the girls wouldn't hear it. They walked Tess to the edge of the hamlet, eyeing the road in both directions as if expecting any moment to see the junior Duke of Barrabou thundering toward them on a charger.

"Ah," said Tess, pressing a hand mournfully to her heart, "if things were different, and I hadn't taken orders, I'd give you each a kiss for your generosity."

"You joined a celibate order?" cried Blodwen, apparently disappointed.

"Of course he did, stupid," said Gwenda, swatting her. "He's genuinely penitent, and his crime was amorous as well as violent."

"I belong to St. Vitt," said Tess, flashing a pained smile. "No half measures for me."

"As must be, Father," said Gwenda, bowing her head. "Heaven mind your road."

"When your enemies come looking, we won't tell them where you went," piped up Blodwen as Tess turned to go. "We never saw you here."

Tess walked backward, waving goodbye, and then set her face southward again.

The shepherdesses' merriment wore off, and Tess found herself curiously unhappy, itchy in her very soul. Fields of buttercups nodded under the noonday sky; Tess drifted past, unseeing, spooling out uncomfortable feelings like a weaver untangling her weft.

She'd been so wrapped up in her story that she'd inadvertently told the girls something true: it mattered not a jot that she'd repented. A moment's lapse in judgment, and her future had been lost forever.

The shepherdesses, though, had forgiven her transgressions— or rather, Father Jacomo's transgressions. He'd killed a man in a fit of passion, he was a murderer, but the sin was adorable on him because of course he hadn't *meant* to, poor darling. He was the victim of his own strong emotions, which made him terribly romantic.

And the worst was, Tess had felt it, too. She'd been as caught up as the shepherdesses—the story was an old favorite, in fact—but at the same time something had changed. Some part of that tale galled her. She felt like she was seeing with two different eyes: an eye full of stars that still saw the romance, and a new eye, one she'd acquired while walking, an eye full of . . .

It was full of fire, she decided. Her second eye saw the flesh of this story burned away, held the bones up to her own story, and saw the injustice.

She'd committed a crime of passion, too, but hers had created life, whereas Father Jacomo—Dozerius the Pirate, really—had taken life. In fact, accounting accurately, the pirate had two lives on his hands: he'd driven Julissima Rossa to kill herself.

So why could Dozerius be forgiven, when Tess could not?

This question put her in a spiraling, simmering rage. She threw the jar of beets against a tree, and it shattered, red pulp everywhere, like brains or like her heart. It was a terrible waste, but she didn't like beets anyway and she wanted to be wasteful. Or she wanted to lay waste to . . . something. Anything. Everything.

Pathka found her soon after and assured her that he hadn't been bleeding underground. She didn't listen beyond that. She brushed off his nosy questions and walked in a haze, barely seeing the road, and then finally it was nighttime and she slouched by the fire, still steaming.

Pathka went to sleep, but Tess couldn't. The foundational stories of her life had betrayed her; the inside of her head jangled with dissonance. Whose fault was this? Whom could she break her ire upon?

It was probably her own fault for being gullible. That just made her madder.

It occurred to her, all of a sudden, that she still had the pewter ring. Once she'd gotten enough to eat, it had stopped beckoning her home, so she'd half forgotten about it. She scrabbled through her pack, found it, rolled it between her fingers, desiring but not daring. It was the middle of the night, the rudest time to wake her sister. Seraphina wouldn't get mad, that was not her way, but she was bound to say something to make *Tess* mad, and then Tess would have someone to yell at.

That would make her feel better.

Tess flipped the switch. The thnik hummed in her hand. Once, twice. Half a dozen times.

Finally, a voice crackled through. "Sisi?"

That wasn't Seraphina. Tess's throat seized up.

"Tess, is it you?" said Jeanne, her voice small and plaintive. "Seraphina said you had the mate to this ring, but I call and call and you never answer. Please, where are you? We've been so worried. I cry every night, imagining what might happen to you out there. Mama says to consider you dead, but—"

Tess flung the ring away, as if it burned her. The sandy soil stopped it from bouncing. Tess ground her heel upon it, stomped and crunched, her breath heavy and ragged. Jeanne's voice crackled and went out.

A wash of cold regret hit her hard. Why was she so accursedly impulsive? She should have spoken to her sister. Jeanne was hurting, and it was her fault and she could have reassured her, but this flash of rage had . . . Why had she . . .

Mama says to consider you dead. That was why. She could help everyone out by making that a fact.

Suddenly Pathka leaped into the fray, crying, "Destroy it!" He torched the smashed thnik until it was a glistening puddle of molten metal. Dry leaves around it caught fire. Pathka did a hideous dance on his hind legs, capering among the flames like an ancient painting of a salamander spirit, vicious in his glee.

"Down with shoddy, soulless thniks!" he cried to the night. "Down with the foul profits that lure us away from our truth and our calling! Let us build only what our nature bids us build, and let us be true to our nature before all else!"

Tess sat down hard, appalled at herself and bewildered by Pathka's reaction. He blew cool air over the melted mass, solidifying it, and placed it in his throat pouch. He noticed her staring, and said reassuringly: "You were right to break that thnik. They mass-produce those to sell at the market, as if we might buy human esteem if only we had enough coin. I will make you a better device—two better devices. Once we discover deeper caverns, we'll want to search in our own directions and find each other again."

He held Tess's gaze. "That wasn't what you were angry about, though, was it?"

"Not exactly," said Tess, morose and regretful now. Dear, sad Jeanne! Reassurance had been in Tess's power to give, even a kind word or two, but she'd acted before her mind could . . .

It was like kicking the beggar under the bridge. Something terrible in her kept bursting out, beyond her control. It never went away, even if it quieted while she walked. Walking only suppressed her inherent awfulness. It wasn't a cure. Maybe there was no cure. She'd been born bad, and she was dragging her bad carcass through the wilderness to no avail.

She flopped onto her blanket, hurting all over, feeling like she'd slid all the way back to the beginning. It was going to be hard to make herself walk on tomorrow.

Pathka was at her side, padded fingers soft against her cheeks. "Is it that boy?" he said incongruously.

"What boy?" said Tess. She swatted his hands away, even though their touch was a comfort. She didn't deserve comforting.

"The one you loved, who abandoned you," said Pathka. "You've been furious all day, long before Jeanne called you. Is he the wellspring of your anger?"

Tess was sure she hadn't said Will had abandoned her. That

wasn't even the word she used when she thought about Will; she always said *disappeared*.

"You're making assumptions."

"Deductions," Pathka corrected her. "And of course I am. It's my duty, as your friend."

Tess squirmed; there was a rock under her blanket. "Do you remember the story of Julissima Rossa? How she killed herself, repenting her infidelity, whereas Dozerius—who'd killed her husband—went traipsing off after treasure as if nothing had happened?"

"What are you getting at?" asked Pathka.

"Why do we forgive Dozerius?" Tess's voice was like the embers of the fire.

"I don't understand the question," said Pathka. "Who forgives Dozerius?"

"Everyone," said Tess. "Nobody says, 'Saints in Heaven, this man is terrible,' and stops reading at that point. If we can forgive him for killing an old man, why can't we . . . why . . ." She couldn't finish, not if she wanted to keep her composure.

Pathka tilted his head sideways, confused. "*I* can't forgive Dozerius. I'd have to bite him, but he hasn't wronged me, so . . . the idea makes no sense."

Tess noticed for the first time that Pathka said *forgive* in heavily accented Goreddi, as if there were no comparable word in Quootla. "Is this not a concept among quigutl?"

"We bite each other," said Pathka. "It amounts to the same thing. It gets the poison out of your system so that it doesn't eat at you anymore."

"What if you can't bite the one who wronged you?" asked Tess, mystified. "What if . . . you don't know where they are?"

"Or they're dead, or human?" said Pathka. "Then you're biting-*utl*. That can lead to death—your own, if you're lucky, or someone else's. If you can't bite whom you need to bite, you end up biting whoever comes near."

Tess had done that, she suddenly realized. She'd been the bitingest biter at the wedding, because the person she really wanted to bite was . . . No. She wasn't going to think about him.

She'd been terrible. She felt worse than she had in weeks, like everything was caving in on her again. Right on cue, her mother's voice cut in, cut deeper than ever: *You ruin your sister's wedding night, and then you can't speak two words to her? How do you sleep at night?*

She wouldn't tonight, certainly.

"What do you do, Pathka," Tess half whispered, "if the person you most desperately need to bite is yourself?"

"Then you bite yourself," said Pathka. "With your mind."

"Beat myself up, you mean?" said Tess bitterly. "Recite my long litany of regrets? I do that all the time."

It made her wish she were dead. She wrapped her arms around her head.

"No, not that," said Pathka. His breath burned against her neck. "I mean grasp on to yourself. Clamp down. Hold on with everything you've got."

The fire snapped; crickets chirped.

"And then let go," said the fierce, hot wind in her ear.

Tess said nothing. Pathka crept back to the other side of

the fire. She waited until she heard him snoring, and then she let the tears flow.

Mama's criticism was too painful to hold on to and too primal to let go of. It was the rock Tess had been pushing uphill her whole life, and she had an inkling that this could not be resolved in a single night. Not even close.

But there were plenty of other things she might examine in closer detail if she dared. Specific ways she'd been terrible. Specific things she'd done.

Will.

He popped into her head occasionally, and she always beat him back into the shadows. That was an era of her life best forgotten. She'd been so stupid and naive and—

Her very reluctance suggested this was important. She should hold on to the memories she didn't want to remember.

And then, maybe, she could finally let them go.

She conjured Will to mind, on purpose, for the first time in a long time.

Twelve

That first taste of freedom, at the electrostatics lecture, had only made Tess hungrier. Lady-in-waiting lessons went from tedious to torturous. She couldn't concentrate on any of it. She dropped stitches, bungled lineages, and used the wrong fork for everything.

"There are cures for inattentiveness," said Mistress Edwina after three days of this. "A hard rap across the knuckles with a wooden spoon does wonders. I merely mention it."

In fact, she *didn't* merely mention it. The old woman demonstrated upon Tess's fingers shortly thereafter—when she'd been about to use the fish fork to eat songbird pie—and even Tess had to admit it was very motivating.

When the day of the megafauna lecture arrived, Tess squirmed like she was full of ants. She could finally go out and forget all this for a while. Evening couldn't come soon enough.

Mistress Edwina, of course, chose that morning to give an unannounced courtesy test—*Which degree do you give the third son of the Earl of Blystane? What about his nephew?* After about twenty-five curtsies with accompanying flourishes (several of which Tess knew she'd got wrong, because Jeanne had been flourishing in a different direction), Tess lost all patience.

For her next answer, she gave eleven-sixteenths courtesy, reasoning that the Scion of Ziziba probably wouldn't know which degree to expect anyway, since he came from far away.

Eleven-sixteenths, absurdly, was Tess's best flourish; it was used least, and was therefore an amusing and hilarious thing to know.

Mistress Edwina seemed to take it as sarcasm. She wasn't wrong.

The old woman grabbed Tess by the ear and pulled her upstairs to a tiny storage room. She didn't have to say a word; Tess had been here before. Tess went inside and sat on a tiny trunk, her knees awkwardly wedged between stacks of dusty baskets.

The dowager stood in the doorway, a slip of angry darkness against the light.

"Do you think this is a game?" said Mistress Edwina. Her voice was quiet and steely, like a knife being drawn.

"No," said Tess sullenly, rubbing her sore ear.

"And yet you persist in taking nothing seriously," said the old woman. "You're the one who has to marry, Heaven help us."

Tess slumped back against the wall. "I wish I wasn't."

"Penury suits you, does it? Well, your family doesn't agree. You're going to court, like it or not, and impeccable etiquette is the only tool you'll have at your disposal. Not your looks, not your temperament."

Unlike Jeanne, the dowager didn't say, but Tess knew the comparison was being made.

"My nature is a liability, you mean?" said Tess bitterly. "No one could love me as I am?"

Mistress Edwina gave a snort of frustration. "You read too many stories. Nobody has to fall in love with you," she said. "There will be no prince on a white charger, sweeping you off your feet. This is business, not romance. You have merely to find a suitably wealthy suitor, and then persuade him that you'll make a decent mother and won't embarrass him in public. That's all, Tess. That's destiny. Sit there and reconcile yourself to it."

Mistress Edwina closed the closet door, leaving Tess in darkness.

Tess didn't mind. The old woman had inadvertently given her something to ponder. Had stories really warped her expectations and made her dissatisfied with her lot?

Or were they her road map out?

At thirteen, Tess had already read a hundred variations on this theme: a princess is required by her family to marry someone terrible, she objects and gets herself locked away in a dark tower (or storage closet), and then Dozerius (or some analog) comes along and rescues her with the power of love.

True love was a time-honored way of escaping nearly everything—ogres, witches, bandits, tedious obligations. Her parents wouldn't like it, but surely even they had to acknowledge that love conquered all.

Hadn't Papa married that dragon-woman, after all? Hadn't Mama married Papa? Love won out every time, never mind their subsequent regrets.

Tess wasn't so naive as to imagine that if she stayed in this closet, her true love would magically intuit that she was here. Waiting for a literal prince was impractical, and anyway, she wasn't a literal princess. If it was up to her to go out and find her own rescuer, so be it.

In fact, now that she thought about it, she might just know someone suitable.

Tess stood up and rapped softly upon the door. Mistress Edwina loosed the bolt and threw the door open. Tess blinked in the light.

"Well?" the dowager demanded.

Tess kept her expression rigorously neutral. "I've seen the error of my ways, Mistress Edwina, and am ready to cooperate."

The old woman cocked a deeply skeptical eyebrow but let Tess come downstairs, back into the circle of her favor. It took every ounce of Tess's willpower not to smirk.

Evening finally arrived.

Tess climbed out the window of Seraphina's old room, met Kenneth at St. Siucre's shrine, and crossed town with him. He chattered on about his day at the docks, and Tess smiled and nodded in all the right places, barely listening.

She was too caught up in her hopes. This evening could change everything. Maybe.

Please? she said, to any Saint who might be listening.

The hall at St. Bert's was packed to the rafters, and not with mere townspeople, there for a free lecture. Young men, the students of St. Bert's Collegium, had filled the hall to hear the talk on megafauna. Tess noted their excited energy, students grinning and elbowing each other.

This William of Affle was quite a dynamic speaker, apparently, if he inspired such a buzz of anticipation.

That was one quality to recommend him. Tess was keeping a tally in her head.

There were no empty seats on the floor, so Tess followed Kenneth up to the gallery. The last two together were up against the balcony railing, but by the time they'd maneuvered through the crowd, one of the seats had acquired an occupant, a slender fellow with an aristocratic nose and long dark curls.

"St. Masha's stone," Kenneth swore. "Take the seat, Tes'puco. I'll stand."

"Are you together?" the long-haired young gentleman asked Kenneth as Tess squeezed past his knees. "Take my seat and sit by your lady friend." He rose to let Kenneth sit.

"I'll be fine," said Kenneth. "She's just my cousin."

"Please," said the fellow. He was near Kenneth's age, maybe a year older, and almost as tall. His face held a quick intelligence; his flowing hair made him downright pretty. "You've clearly been working all day, whilst I've been sitting on my arse listening to humans debate saar. My day was tiresome, but not tiring, if you follow me. You surely need the seat more than I do."

"I'm Kenneth." He was blushing to his ears.

"Rynald, Baronet Averbath," said the young man, smiling.

"Sit. Maybe I'll settle myself here in the aisle beside you. Were you at our astronomy lecture last week? You look familiar."

Kenneth was either in awe of him as an astronomer or shy of his beauty. Lord Rynald seemed charmed by his discomfiture, in either case. Tess sighed wistfully.

Kenneth was naturally, effortlessly lovable. She was not going to have it so easy.

She chewed her lip and watched the stage.

It had been a day of debates, as Lord Rynald had said, and this—the public lecture and final event—was no exception. Two podiums had been set up. Will, tall and blond, stood at one, beaming and waving at people in the audience; he had a lot of friends (a second mark for the tally, or maybe a third; tall and blond surely counted for something).

At the other podium stood a stocky person with a doughy face, dressed ambiguously in an old-fashioned floor-length robe.

"Scholar Spira, a dragon," Lord Rynald told Kenneth.

Professor the dragon Ondir raised his hands for silence. The rowdy students roared and stomped, a last hurrah, before settling down. "Today's final pair, scholar versus scholar, are my two doctoral candidates. The dragon Spira"—a smattering of applause and jeers—"will debate William of Affle"—raucous cheering now—"about megafauna of the mountainous regions, whether to exploit or preserve them, and how this may best be accomplished. Scholars, proceed."

"Thank you, Professor," William called after Saar Ondir's departing form. "Of course, we're required to omit the largest mountain animals of all—dragons—which is like omitting vultures from a discussion of birds, but I'll do my best to pretend you don't exist."

Scholar Spira, in a voice as flat as vellum, said, "Let me begin by—"

"Did you hear something?" cried William. His human cohort laughed uproariously.

It was a rather stupid joke, but Tess found herself grinning for the first time all day.

"Our dragon professors suggested these debates," Lord Rynald was telling Kenneth. He had to shout to be heard; Tess leaned across to listen. "They're meant to sharpen our critical faculties, but a keen wit stabs harder than a finely honed argument. The dragons have been slaughtered today, by human reckoning."

Scholar Spira began speaking, in a grating, nasal whinge, in favor of conservation—a counterintuitive position for a dragon, Tess felt. Didn't they like exterminating whole species? Maybe just humankind.

Tess couldn't recall Spira's arguments later. The scholar's voice was like a nail on slate, and William of Affle spent the entire time pulling disrespectful faces.

Rude, Tess thought, which should have been a mark against him, but there was that grin tugging the corners of her mouth again.

"Is anyone still awake?" said William when he finally took the stand. His voice was like a rich ocean breeze after the doldrums of Spira's monotone.

Tess would have found it utterly charming if he hadn't been arguing for exploitation. The great animals, per his thesis, were nothing more than a resource, and had been placed here by Heaven for humans to use as they saw fit.

"Of course I exclude dragons," he said with a saucy wink. "Since I must."

His friends in the audience laughed, but Tess found his argument unkind and, frankly, disappointing. He'd understood that she loved animals, and this had made her believe, perhaps mistakenly, that he loved them, too.

Lord Rynald was saying, "And there he goes, playing the provocateur. He's full of beans, and his human audience eats them right up."

Ah. Maybe that explained it. He was arguing for the win, rather than from conviction.

Tess had to admire his gall, even if it seemed a dangerous way to go.

William placed his hands on the podium as if bracing for the most provocative argument of all. "Let me conclude by suggesting, Spira, that you dragons may have an ulterior motive behind your ethic of 'conservation.'" He raised his chin and his voice: "I assert that there are animals—fabulous creatures, like beings straight out of myth—that you saar are actively hiding from us."

His friends laughed; William looked mildly irritated at this.

"You think I'm kidding," he said. "But our two races work together at this Collegium, ostensibly to share knowledge and build trust. This requires good faith on both sides. How is humankind ever to catch up if dragonkind won't tell us the whole truth?"

The word *truth* reverberated through the silent hall, and then a confused mutter went up. He didn't mean that, surely?

Spira, caught flat-footed, shuffled notecards on the lectern and said, "Um. What?"

"I refer, of course, to the World Serpents," said William.

Tess sat up straighter, eyes wide. He'd . . . he'd taken her seriously.

"I realize none of you know what I'm talking about," said Will, holding up his hands to still the crescendo of baffled murmuring. "Goreddi scholars have never delved deeply into this, but I've had inklings. Last week, an observation by one of our keenest minds confirmed my suspicions and gave me courage to speak."

He meant Tess. *Keenest mind* was an exaggeration, ridiculously elevated, but Tess felt it profoundly anyway. She pressed a hand to her heart.

He'd said he hadn't heard of World Serpents, though he'd known the Pelaguese legend. Maybe she'd misunderstood. Maybe he just hadn't put it all together.

"It's unfashionable to look to legends for truth," he was saying, "but haven't our own Saints proved literally real? The ancients knew a great deal about the natural world; there may be things to learn when old tales tell the same story.

"Look to this mural." He gestured broadly at the teeming mural behind him. "St. Fredricka included hints of a creature coiled under the ice, an animal the Pelaguese people once considered a god, who held the gift of prophecy and the key to eternal youth. Well, our pre-Saint pagans told of a similar monster under the earth, whose blood could heal wounds or cure disease. If either of these legends is even partially true, it would be the greatest discovery of our lifetimes. If they're altogether true, the possibilities are unfathomable."

William paused dramatically. "Friends, this world may be riddled with great serpents of untold power, and the dragons don't want us to know about them."

The hall erupted, and not with approval. The human instructors were shouting angrily, scandalized that Will would accuse their allies of such a thing. Laughter came in two flavors: mocking and highly amused. The saarantrai, as expected, stared in stony silence.

"He can't be serious." Kenneth had to shout to be heard. "How could such creatures exist?"

Lord Rynald shook his curly head in bewilderment.

"And isn't he asking for trouble, accusing the dragons of deceit?"

"If the saar were prone to anger, maybe," Lord Rynald shouted back. "They won't even bother to dispute him. Well, no, Spira might write a paper. Spira's kind of a pedant."

Tess, irked by their skepticism, cried, "World Serpents are real. He's telling the truth."

Lord Rynald blinked his dark, pretty eyes. "If you say so."

Tess turned away in irritation, folding her hands on the balcony railing. She rather wished William would look up, but four of his friends had rushed the stage, and they were singing a rude song about Spira (complete with choreography) that they must have prepared in advance.

O Spira, come near-a
And lift up your skirt.
Are you male or female
Or fat, shameless flirt?
It's bad enough, Spira,
Just being a saar;
You mince like a maidy—
Come prove what you are!

Spira, speaking quietly to Professor the dragon Ondir, ignored them. Tess might've pitied him (her? It was hard to tell) if mockery could've hurt a dragon's feelings. She ought to have been shocked by such a naughty song, at least, but once again she found herself wrestling a grin.

He was incorrigible. Mischievous and bold and everything she'd been told time and again she shouldn't be. Everything she'd ever admired about Dozerius.

What would he do if he knew she was trapped in a dark tower? She hardly dared hope.

William looked up exactly then, and met Tess's eyes across the crowd. His smile deepened, and he winked at her. She felt warm all the way to her toes.

The song had broken the back of the debates; there was no restoring dignity. Ondir said a few stern things about rules and order, but nobody minded him. The crowd, having gotten more scandal than it could have hoped for, began to disperse.

Kenneth seemed in no hurry to leave. He laughed and chatted with Lord Rynald at the back of the nave, finding reasons to hang about and keep talking. Tess stood by, fidgeting, glancing at William, who was still at the front of the hall.

She thought about walking up to the dais but couldn't quite bring herself to do it. Six-year-old Tessie would have, half a lifetime ago, before the ungovernable wildness had been spanked out of her. Before she understood what manners were for, and that you can't make a good impression by acting like a silly, bossy little girl.

She bit her lip, struggling. Keeping a lid on her impulsiveness wasn't trivial.

Then Will was crossing the room toward them. She did not boldly meet his eye but looked away demurely, as she'd been taught.

She risked a glance to see if she'd made a good impression.

He smiled at her, as warmly as the sun after storms. Tess had never been the recipient of such a smile. She'd behaved like she was supposed to, and had been rewarded.

She could do this. She had the tools. The possibilities were unfathomable.

"I'm so pleased you came, Therese," William said, drawing near. "You recognized the object of my little paean to encouragement, I trust."

"Indeed, thank you," said Tess, striving to keep her voice steady and dignified. "I'm astonished I could be of any help to someone like you."

That was laying it on a little thick. She cringed, worrying that she'd misstepped, but he seemed not to mind.

"You may yet be more help," he said. His fair hair flopped

endearingly. "The faculty library has been of some use, but I'm sure your quigutl friend told you more useful tales than anything I've uncovered there. I'd love to compare notes sometime."

Tess's heart fluttered. Actually fluttered. She'd always thought that a silly metaphor, but now she felt it. "I'd like that, too."

"What are you doing next?" he said. "We could go to the Mallet and Mullet."

Tess cast a lightly panicked glance at Kenneth, who was engrossed with Lord Rynald. William caught on and said cordially, "Of course, your young man must come along, too."

"He's just my cousin," said Tess hastily.

"All the better," said William, his voice regaining its warmth at once. There was nothing suggestive in it, and yet Tess found herself pleasantly flustered.

"Will!" cried Lord Rynald, finally noticing they'd been approached by the hero of the evening. He held out a slim hand, which William clasped in his larger one.

They were all taller than Tess. She felt like a mouse.

"Very amusing," Rynald said. "Ondir will make you pay for humiliating his pet toad."

Will shrugged. "Spira humiliates itself just by existing. The truth had to be told. Come to the Mullet, you and your friend. I'm gathering a posse."

Minutes later, William, Tess, Kenneth, Lord Rynald, and a gaggle of friends and hangers-on were in the street laughing raucously. Someone threw a shoe at them from a window, which only made them laugh harder. Tess was the only girl in the group, but she wasn't frightened. Kenneth wouldn't let anything happen—if he could pull himself out of Rynald's eyes—but anyway, what was going to happen? They were delightful, these lads; they spoke to her like an adult and not a recalcitrant child. She felt every year of the sixteen she was pretending to be.

She felt like queen of the world.

Will ordered everyone cakes and ale. Tess, who'd never drunk anything but small beer and well-watered wine, found the ale appallingly bitter. She struggled not to gag. It was strong and likely to make her tipsy in any case, so she paced herself and made sure she ate enough cake.

The students of St. Bert's quaffed freely, growing more hilarious by the hour. Stories were told of pranks played on professors and other students, of the foibles of Spira (who seemed a genuinely eccentric and uncouth person). When the stories veered toward amorous conquests and the suspected proclivities of one female dragon professor, Tess grew uncomfortable, crumbling her cake and avoiding everyone's eyes. William, bless him, noticed and swatted the tale-teller on the back of his head, saying, "There are gentle ears present, villain."

He was considerate; that went straight to her heart's tally. She flashed him a grateful smile, and he reflected it back tenfold, like a magic mirror.

It was late. Tess was going to be a wreck in the morning, she could already tell. Several lads pushed back from the table, complaining about early laboratory hours. Anything before noon was early, Tess gleaned; they didn't often see the hour when she woke up, unless they came at it from the other direction.

Tess waited for Kenneth, who was whispering with William

and Rynald. Finally her cousin approached and said, "Listen, ah, Tes'puco—"

"*Therese*," she hissed, flicking an anxious glance back at William.

"All grown up, are we?" said Kenneth, not sarcastically, but amused. He hadn't stopped grinning all evening. "Well, listen, I want to talk to Rynald a bit more—"

"About astronomy? Maybe he'll show you his telescope," said Tess before she could stop herself. She was tipsier than she'd thought.

Kenneth gaped incredulously. "Cheeky! But what I mean to say is, would you mind very much if I didn't walk you home?"

She felt a lightning bolt of panic—she couldn't cross town alone in the middle of the night!—but Kenneth continued hastily: "Will offered to walk you. Would that work?"

Tess felt a different jolt then, but she put a lid on it immediately. Kenneth would see no trace of eagerness in her face. "I suppose," she said, with carefully measured reluctance.

And so Kenneth went off with Rynald—stargazing, moongazing, gazing into each other's eyes—and Tess and William went the other direction. "May I offer you my arm?" William asked her.

She longed to take it, but would that be too forward, too soon? She couldn't risk it.

He didn't insist, but walked at her side, leaving a decent gap between them.

"Do you really think the World Serpents exist, or were you trying to make Spira look stupid?" Tess burst out before they'd gone two blocks. "Lord Rynald said you're full of beans."

So much for keeping her boisterousness under wraps. Stupid ale. He would surely be horrified by her unladylike forthrightness.

To her astonishment, William laughed. "I've found no proof that World Serpents exist—*yet*. But it's worth looking into. You saw how nettled the dragons were." Tess wondered how he could tell. "Even in this time of peace, they're still our rivals. We should seize any opportunity to get one up on them. Including," he said, drawing nearer, "gleaning what we can from nontraditional sources—folklore, quigutl testimonials, and the sprightly, unexpected intelligence of young women."

He meant her. Tess shivered pleasantly.

The stars glittered; it was like a night out of a story. Tess would have liked to spin in exuberant circles, to skip or whoop, but she couldn't let herself.

She also couldn't let him see her house, where the doorplate read *Dombegh*, or he'd know she'd lied about her name—and her age. It was easy enough to learn how many children her father had and how old they were. Tess led William up the street to the shrine of St. Siucre.

"That's a rather small shrine for a warren of Belgiosos," he said mock-seriously.

"There's a tunnel to my house," she said, pointing up the wrong side of the street in the wrong direction. "Sneaking through the cellar is quieter than climbing through a window."

Provided no one had barred the door to the kitchen. She said a little prayer.

"I've kept you out too late," said William solemnly. "I hope you won't be in trouble."

"Never," said Tess optimistically. "Thank you for walking me home, William."

"Will, to friends," he said. He reached boldly for her hand and pressed it between his. "Will I see you again? You still owe me some quigutl myths, but more than that, I'd love to show you St. Bert's. Whatever your curiosity demands, let me know and I can guide you. I live upstairs at the Mullet, easy to find."

"Then I will find you," said Tess with what she hoped was an arch smile.

He pressed her fingers to his lips, lightly, like a butterfly landing.

Tess felt her insides effervesce.

"Forgive me," he said, releasing her.

"Nothing to forgive," said Tess.

She flitted into the shrine and leaned against the door to catch her breath.

Sprightly intelligence. She still wasn't over it.

She raised her gaze to the wooden statue before her. St. Siucre was always depicted as a wizened old woman, with bent back and bright eyes. She was a quiet kind of Saint, the sort nobody much thought about, and she was Tess's patroness, to her infinite embarrassment. She'd much rather have had someone witty and gregarious, like St. Willibald, or mighty like St. Masha; even Jeanne's stolid St. Gobnait would have been preferable to this ancient, grandmotherly, forgotten Saint, whose great claim to fame was that she'd help you find things you'd lost.

For the first time, this struck Tess as apropos. She was the patroness of *memory*. Tess lit a candle and stuck it in the box of sand; there were only two others there. "Sweet St. Siucre," Tess began, using the traditional epithet. It was aspirational: all memories should be sweet ones. "Never let me forget this night," she prayed, getting down on one knee. "How he kissed my fingers, how he took me seriously, how I'm feeling right now."

She paused, heart beating hopefully. "I think . . . I might love him. I hope so. I want to."

She fidgeted, her knee sore against the flagstones. She wasn't sure how to end the prayer; she'd never been a great one for listening in church. "Bless us all forever and ever, let it be, thank you. Um. Good night?"

Then she lit a second taper in the shrine and used it to light her way home.

Thirteen

"Awake, awake!" Pathka was in her face again. It was no earlier than she usually woke; it only felt earlier, since she'd been up half the night, remembering.

"I've had an idea," said the quigutl as Tess rolled away from his breath. "I saw a big house yesterday while foraging. They'll have the metals I need to make the thniks I mentioned."

Tess packed up groggily, too sleepy to argue. The morning fog made it hard to follow Pathka; he had to keep circling back so she could see him.

He was like a perpetual-motion machine. Some of Will's friends had been trying to build one, but the spoilsport dragons kept giving away the punch line: it would never work. Nobody had thought to harness a quigutl.

She liked fog. In the city, she'd always found it cozy, filling the spaces between known objects and making the world feel closer and smaller. It was like a veil over a familiar face.

Now she had no notion what might lie behind the gray. Maybe wonders and dangers yet unimagined; maybe nothing at all. She imagined the world didn't exist, that the fog congealed as she walked into it and created everything on the fly—a logical blocky barn, the fanciful fingers of trees. The mists imagined objects into being as she passed.

What a wonder, to walk into the unseen unknown. Nothing was set in stone.

After all her rage and grief last night, that was a profound relief.

The fog thinned enough that she could tell Pathka was leading her off the main road, down an eastern spur. It was well maintained, covered in pea gravel, like the carriage drive to a manor house.

He'd said something about a big house, she recalled now that she was more awake. Her steps slowed. "We're going where, exactly?"

"Don't worry. Nobody's home," said Pathka. "There's an old caretaker, but—"

"I'm not breaking into a manor." The slope steepened; gravel skittered beneath her boots.

"It's more of a hunting lodge," said Pathka, as if that were better.

They reached the bank of a large, sluggish river, mists dancing on its dark face. The road ended there, and it looked like they could go no farther. A stout rope, tied to a post, stretched over the water and disappeared into the fog, presumably tied to something on the other side.

"Ferry crossing," said Pathka, explaining the rope. "You can haul yourself across with the rope if the ferryman's not here to row you—and he's not here, don't fret. Too bad the boat's on the far bank."

This seemed like a natural place to balk. Tess went stiff-legged like Faffy when it rained.

"Pathka, I'm a terrible thief. You've seen it firsthand. I've had dogs set on me a dozen times. I'll trip on a rake or almost fall into the well. Remember the time I scared up a field of crows and the farmer chased me with an axe?"

"I was beside you, befuddling the dogs and tripping the farmer," said Pathka, curling around her ankles. "And I want you here, Teth, in case anything goes wrong. We are nest to each other."

"I—I'm honored that you'd say that," she said. "But stealing to eat is one thing."

"I'll do all the stealing," said Pathka. "It will be just this once, I promise."

"But how do we get there?" She kicked the water with her boot. "I don't swim."

"Hold the ferry rope," said Pathka. "Anything that can't get wet, I'll carry on my back."

The offer didn't extend to Tess's person, alas. She handed Pathka her pack and, somewhat reluctantly, her boots. He might as well have her stockings, while she was at it, and Florian's jacket, and then, since she'd gone that far, she decided to strip down completely and have a bit of a bath. She hadn't had a bath since Ranleigh Cottage.

"I'm glad you reached that conclusion on your own," said Pathka, stuffing her clothing into her satchel. "I didn't want to have to tell you how terrible you smell."

"This, from a quigutl!" scoffed Tess.

"Exactly." Pathka sounded relieved. "You see how dire it is. Also: your monthlies are nearly here."

Tess froze, appalled that he'd mention such a thing.

"Don't doubt this nose," said Pathka, unfazed by her glare. "You'll want to plan for them, because it'll be hard to maintain your disguise if your breeches—"

"Stop talking. Now, please," snapped Tess, rubbing her goose bump–covered arms.

Pathka clasped her belongings to his back, boots on top, and swam into the mist. He was out of sight before Tess, already shivering, managed to stick her feet in. The water was cold, and the rocks on the bottom were slimy. She waded up to her thighs, excruciatingly slowly, clutching the towrope. The current wasn't strong this close to the bank, but she disliked not seeing the other side. It felt like walking into the underworld.

The sun, which had been dithering in the trees, rose higher and began melting the fog. Tess felt unpleasantly exposed; the water was only up to her hips.

Even though it meant letting go of the towrope, she crouched in the shallow water so she wouldn't have to see herself illuminated, white belly, flat breasts. Her body horrified and embarrassed her. It was the locus of her badness.

And here she was, in the middle of nowhere, stark naked in a river. She never learned.

She waded in deeper until she could stand with only her head and neck exposed. She had assumed she'd be able to reach the towrope again, but it hung just out of range. The current tugged and sucked at her ankles like a baby, and then she was in too deep, standing on tiptoe, face lifted to the sky. The weight of water constricted her lungs, and she felt a twinge of terror.

Pathka had deposited her things on the far bank and was chugging steadily back to help her along. He was going to arrive too late.

She teetered, her only options sink or swim. It could go either way. She had not yet decided to walk on today; Pathka had gotten her moving before she could make her daily promise. She was not going to find an easier way to die than this. She had merely to let go, let herself be pulled down and pinned underwater in darkness. She would be swept away and never found.

Swept away was a fortuitous choice of words: it made her mad. She'd been swept away once—hadn't she been up all night remembering it? She'd let herself be, hoped and desired to be; that's how it always went in romantic stories.

She'd never be that passive again. It was far, far better to choose.

She'd seen Faffy swim, years ago, when their mischievous trio had discovered an abandoned coracle, like a tortoise shell, bobbing on the Mews River. Pathka had swum out and nudged the tiny (pirate) boat toward shore. Faffy was having none of it.

Tess had carried the whining dog aboard, but the moment she let go, he sprang over the side and lit out for shore, frantically churning his skinny legs.

If a bony snaphound could swim, Tess could, too. In a fit of optimism, she lifted her toes and went under immediately. Water flooded her ears and nose, but she imitated Faffy's motions, hands circling like millwheels, legs kneeing back and forth like an infant's. She held her breath and believed, and when her head broke the surface, she yelped in triumph.

"Coming!" cried Pathka, snaking toward her.

Tess, flailing, might soon have tired and sunk, but Pathka reached her. She clasped his dorsal hand and let him tow her shoreward. The water felt like a rolling caress, like the fingers of a god, like she was not just clean but new. She rolled onto her back, chest toward the sky, let her limbs drift open, and for a moment forgot to be disgusted with herself. Let sun and clouds get a good look. She was the river, and the river had nothing to be ashamed of.

"It's shallow enough that you can stand now," said Pathka, but Tess didn't want to. She'd worked out how to float, limbs spread wide like a water-strider with her back arched toward the sun.

She spent the rest of the morning swimming. Pathka didn't complain. In fact, Pathka—the sensitive nose—washed her clothing and laid it on rocks to dry. When Tess finally crawled out of the river, exhausted and noodle-limbed and a bit sunburned, her linens were dry, but her breeches and jacket were not. She half dressed, enough that nonexistent passersby wouldn't be scandalized, and then she used the last of the spare linen in her pack to make herself three small pillow slips, lunessas, for her supposedly impending monthlies. She filled them with moss.

The sun had slipped past zenith by the time she finished. She apologized to Pathka for using up the day, but he was unperturbed. "At least the caretaker won't smell us coming."

"He'll smell you," said Tess, still chafing on this point.

"Even if he does," said Pathka evenly, "he won't know what he's smelling."

Tess followed Pathka up the weedy verge, less noisy than the gravel drive. The lodge wasn't far; in fact, Tess's river bath would have been visible from the lone turret had anyone been watching. She felt an unnecessary, belated pang of embarrassment.

The hunting lodge was absurdly fortified with battlements and a dry moat. Pathka led Tess down the ditch, through a patch of what turned out to be nettles (thank Allsaints for good boots, but the nettles stung her knees through her breeches). He ducked up a hole in the embankment; Tess followed on hands and knees. "I found this yesterday," said Pathka from the darkness ahead. "I thought it might lead down to a cave, but it leads up to the kitchens."

"You couldn't take what you needed then?" asked Tess, helping push open a trapdoor.

"Didn't occur to me until you smashed that ring," said Pathka, his tail disappearing through the opening. Tess followed him into a pantry. Pathka, his tongue alight, led the way to the kitchen door.

The kitchen had grimy diamond-pane windows and an obvious rat problem. "Go up front," Pathka instructed. "If the caretaker comes in, that's where he'll enter. You can run back and warn me."

Tess had no objections. She didn't want to know what Pathka was stealing, although she was practical enough to pinch a few pantry items for herself. She wandered up a corridor, past rooms of ghostly, sheet-covered furniture. She wished the servants had covered the deer heads in the great hall, too; this lodge's owners made Lord Heinrigh look like an amateur.

She finally found the grand entrance foyer, which was decorated with ancient carven stonework—ogham posts, green-man bosses, and a "Yawning Nancy," as the pagan figurine was euphemistically called. It wasn't her mouth yawning. She'd likely been a fertility goddess at one time, but her real name was lost to the ages. Tess kept her eyes religiously averted.

She'd been there a quarter of an hour, admiring the tapestries, when suddenly a deep bell tolled in the heights of the tower. Tess nearly jumped out of her skin, fearful of the caretaker, but it wouldn't be him ringing. He'd have a key. It must be a visitor.

A visitor would eventually go away or try the caretaker's cottage. Tess settled onto a bench and ignored the bell when it rang again. She ignored the knocking and hollering. Only when she heard a hard grinding sound, like chewing, did she grow concerned. Something was gnawing the door; daylight began to show through in a spiral around the lock. Tess leaped to her feet, but before she could bolt, the door was kicked inward with a tremendous crack.

"I told you that door worm would be to our beneficence," said the door-kicker in a gruff voice. He was a tall man of nearly thirty, wiry and hairy-armed, with a face like a peevish mule.

"But where are we to get another?" whined a second man, fat and sweaty, behind him. They were dressed in grimy peasant smocks and braes; their caps had once been grain sacks.

"Fortune favors the fortunate, Rowan," said the tall man, blinking as his eyes accustomed to the interior dimness. "Who's there?"

Tess's wits had frozen in place along with her body, and she couldn't think of any name but her own. She didn't dare tell them that. Her voice squeaked, distressingly girly, as she managed to stammer, "W-what do you want?"

"We wanted you to open the door, you worthless jackanapes," said Rowan, the fat one. "Look what you made us do. Your lord won't be pleased."

His long-faced partner drew a knife from a thigh sheath, pointed it at Tess's throat, and held her gaze as if waiting for her to flinch. "You don't belong here," he said with surprising certainty, wiggling the end of his knife against her skin. "A servant wouldn't be so derelicious of his duty unless he were drunk. You're a squatter—come out of the cold."

Rowan drew closer. He, too, had a knife strapped to his meaty thigh, although he didn't draw it yet. He was staring hard at Tess's chest, as if he could see through her clothes.

He can't tell, she thought desperately, like a prayer, trying to keep panic in check.

"That's a nice jacket," said Rowan at last, and Tess almost collapsed with relief. "Don't get blood on it, Reg. I want it."

He reached his thick fingers toward her buttons.

"Touch me and I'll scream," Tess said, cringing at how feminine that threat sounded. "The caretaker will gut you," she added, trying to beef up her rhetoric.

"Maybe, maybe not," said Reg, tapping her chin with the flat of his blade, unconcerned.

"My quigutl is behind you, ready to attack," said Tess. This was a lie. She hoped Pathka had had the good sense to flee, in fact.

Reg didn't blink at this, but Rowan looked around apprehensively.

"He's trained to do what I say, and his bite quickly runs to gangrene," said Tess. "Which is your favorite limb? I'll make sure he gets it."

Both ruffians reflexively clamped their knees together. Tess might have found this amusing in better circumstances.

Reg abruptly resheathed his knife; maybe he feared imminent quigutl attack, or maybe he decided she wasn't worth his time. "You're clearly our fellow malcontempt," he said, gazing over her head into the great hall. "I respect that, and you may keep whatever you've taken. There's plenty enough here. Rowan, bring in the old man."

Tess was too busy taking deep, shaky breaths to wonder whom he was talking about.

Rowan and Reg looked out at the bright afternoon sunshine. "Damnation, he's bogged off again," said Rowan, trotting outdoors. After some yelling and thumping, Rowan returned with a beardy old man in tow, pale and skinny, his right hand missing two fingers.

It was the beggar from Trowebridge.

The oldster met Tess's gaze and held it. Surely he didn't recognize her. He'd been half asleep and addled, and she'd looked like a girl. He put a skinny finger to his lips, though, as if they shared a secret.

Rowan steered him by the arm while Reg directed his attention around the front hall, pointing out distinctive artwork and asking, "How about this unicorn tapestry, Griss? No? Were you an aflictionado of green-men?"

"He *is* a green-man," muttered Rowan under his breath.

"You'd prefer Yawning Nancy?" said Reg, and they both laughed.

They were appalling. Tess shuddered to think that if they'd arrived an hour earlier, they would have spied her bathing. She thought about bolting while their backs were turned, but didn't like her odds. She wasn't a fast runner, and they'd surely give chase. That was basic hound logic, learned from Faffy: if you ran, you were prey.

They led Griss into the great hall and continued the odd interrogation. *Are these your armchairs? Your hearths? Your spooky buck heads?* The old man shook his head after every question and said, "I d-don't know. I think I own a fire … fire … fire door like that."

"Damn it all." Rowan kicked over the lacquered fire screen—

the word Griss had been looking for and hadn't found—and it clattered to the floor.

"Temper," said Reg, his frown plowing furrows beside his mouth. "I told you, his brain's a wormy cheese. What we need are lords and ladies who recognize *him*. He comes from quality, trust me; someone will know him."

Tess boggled. Had they broken in to determine whether this was the old man's home? Were they trying to return him to his family? She supposed a noble family might offer a reward for a missing lord, but she couldn't believe the old man had ever been lord of anything.

"Dear Lord Grissypants," said Reg, pinching the man's sallow cheek. His fingers left a red welt. "You've put us to a great deal of trouble. I think we deserve a little condensation."

They went upstairs to look for it, leaving Tess and the old man alone, to her great surprise. Were they so sure she wouldn't run away?

Griss made no move to flee; he shakily seated himself in one of the velvet armchairs and unsmilingly waved Tess over. She considered ignoring him, getting herself well quit of this house and these villains, but guilt won out and pushed her to the old man's side. He seemed recovered from the ferocious rib-kicking, thank Allsaints, but what might these two villains do to him if they never found his manor house?

And what could she do about it? She owed him an apology, at the very least.

He rose at her approach, grabbed Tess by the shoulders, and shook her. "What are you doing here, Johnny?" he hissed. "These are dangerous men. I've been trying to lead them away from you, and Annie and baby Lion, and now you . . . you . . . you . . ."

His eyes went vacant and fearful, as if he saw something that wasn't there, or had suddenly lost his bearings.

"I swore I'd kill you if I saw you again," he said mournfully, "but I'm not sure I have the . . . the . . ." He patted his concave chest meaningfully.

Tess pulled out of his grasp; his gnarled hand wasn't strong enough to hold her. "I'm not Johnny. My name's, uh, Jacomo."

Griss looked crestfallen, which compelled her, absurdly, to reassure him. "Easy mistake to make. Same first letter."

"Jacomo?" said the old man, scrutinizing her. Even his eyelashes were white, the eyes behind them dark as well water. "Sweet St. Siucre! Forgive me, child: you've grown so tall I didn't know you."

Griss approached again, raising shaky hands to her face. She let him touch her cheeks with hands as dry as paper. "You look like your mother."

"My mother . . . Annie?" asked Tess. It was the only name she had to guess with.

Griss's face fell. "Oh, Johnny. Haven't you heard? Annie's dead, and it's your fault."

In Trowebridge, Tess had found him frightening. The truth, now that she was talking to him, was of a different flavor, and nearer her heart: he was like Grandma Therese.

Before the baby came, Tess had spent two months at Dombegh Manor with her paternal grandmother, who'd been convinced that Tess was her dead sister, Agnes. Uncle

Jean-Philippe had called his mother's condition *antiquitus extremus;* Chessey the midwife had preferred *second childhood.* Tess had thought of her grandmother, somewhat poetically, as having come unbuttoned from time. She always thought it was some other year, other place, other people.

Griss was not some contemptible creature worthy only of her pity. There was a person in there, however confused he might be.

Tess guided Griss back to his chair. "I'm not Johnny, but tell me all about him."

Tess knelt, holding his withered hand. His beard was matted, and he was missing several teeth (his remaining teeth, emboldened by the extra room, had rebelled against the tyranny of standing in line). He licked his lips with a pale tongue and said, "I mistook you for my brother. Your face—I thought I—this keeps happening. Nothing stays where I put it. I'm sorry, Ja . . . Ja . . ."

"Jacomo," said Tess.

"You were the most honest of your household, with the greatest . . . the greatest." He patted his heart again; apparently he found that word too slippery to hold. "I'm glad they haven't beaten it out of you. We try, don't we?"

"We try what?" asked Tess, barely following. He seemed to mean some Jacomo he'd really known, not his brother Johnny again, but it was hard to be sure.

Griss stared into the cold hearth. "We try to do right, and we . . . we . . . they gang up on us, fear and pain and revenge and . . . and then we find we've done wrong."

Tess felt her own slippery heart constricting. His words touched close to the truth she'd meant to tell him. She had only enough courage to whisper: "I need to tell you I'm sorry."

"For what?" he asked, his face slack and baffled.

She took a shaky breath. "I kicked you in the ribs, back in Trowebridge, and then I ran off and left you because I couldn't face what I'd done."

Griss's shaggy brows drew down as he studied her face. She thought for a moment that he might recognize her, but then he said, "Was I in Trowebridge?"

"Trowebridge isn't the main thing," said Tess. "Do you recall someone kicking you?"

His expression went dreamy; he touched his side with his three-fingered hand. "It wasn't a . . . no, no, I saw the dragon. It took Annie, and I . . . I ran after it. Then I couldn't work out how to get home. Someone moved the mountains."

It should have been a relief to know that she hadn't left him permanently wounded or terrorized, but still Tess squirmed with frustration. It was like apologizing to a wall: how could he forgive her if he didn't remember she'd wronged him? How could she assuage her guilt without his forgiveness? It didn't evaporate when she apologized, instead continuing to rack her fiercely.

Loud cursing resounded from the front of the house, followed by a whistle and raucous barking.

Tess's blood froze in her veins.

The caretaker had come to check on the lodge and found the broken door.

Fourteen

"Quick!" Tess grabbed Griss's arm and pulled him up the dark corridor toward the kitchen. She heard Reg and Rowan coming down the stairs, but she didn't look back. In the foyer, the caretaker's dogs bayed. She hoped the hounds would keep those villains occupied.

Pathka was nowhere to be seen in the kitchen, although there was a golden plate on the floor with a bite out of it. Tess hoped that meant he'd fled, and she'd find him outside.

If she spirited Griss out of the bolt-hole in the pantry, maybe she could get him away from those two clowns. That would ease her stinging conscience.

It was hard to convince Griss to go down the hole, though, and harder still, once he was down, to persuade him to crawl forward. He blubbered in terror. "I don't know where I am," he sobbed. "And I don't know where Annie is. Annie doesn't live here anymore."

"Follow me," said Tess, squeezing past after failing to budge him any other way. From above came crashing, yelling, and the baying of dogs, a terrible altercation, caretaker versus vagrants. With luck, it would keep them all occupied until she and Griss were well away.

She emerged into the weedy moat-ditch. Griss crawled out after. She hauled him to his feet and found him light as a child. Pathka was still nowhere to be seen. Tess ran for the river, hoping the old man would keep up, but he skidded and fell on the steep gravel drive. Tess rushed back, wrapped his arm around her neck, and helped him to the strand, barely keeping her feet.

Pathka wasn't at the ferry, either. Tess, full of panicky energy, managed to shove the heavy craft halfway into the water, praying that the little quigutl would turn up.

Pathka could sniff her out; he could swim the river, no problem. Still, she dared not launch the ferry until she was sure nothing untoward had happened to him. "Pathka!" she cried, her voice echoing down the riverbank. There was no answering rustle in the underbrush. She was loath to return to the lodge but saw no other option. He might be trapped, or hurt.

"Stay here," she admonished Griss, seating him on the raft. "If you see a quigutl, yell."

He nodded, but his gaze was vacant. She might have been directing the wind.

Tess ran toward the lodge, not troubling to conceal herself. If the caretaker appeared, she'd be a concerned passerby who'd heard noises.

Reg and Rowan burst out the front, laughing hysterically. Each carried a bundle of pilfered goods wrapped in a blanket, and Reg's smock was spattered rusty red. The fact that it wasn't quigutl blood was cold comfort.

"Go!" Reg called to his companion, hopping on one foot while he sheathed his blade. "Go, go, go!"

The underbrush across the drive rustled: it was Pathka, signaling her to stay put, step back, let Reg and Rowan barrel past. She might have done it had not Griss cried out, "Run, Johnny! If they catch you poaching, you'll hang for sure this time!"

Tess didn't know the quigutl gestures for *I can't just abandon him* or *I feel responsible*. She hoped Pathka could read it in her face. She darted toward the ferry ahead of Reg and Rowan and started shoving the craft again, but it was heavier with Griss on it, and then Reg and Rowan caught up and launched the vessel.

They assumed she'd been trying to help, not flee with their captive, which was probably for the best. They kept laughing as they hauled the ferry hand over hand along the towrope. Tess tried to catch her breath; Pathka swam behind, glaring, like an ill-tempered crocodile.

Griss grabbed Tess's hand and clung to it. On the far bank, he wouldn't get off the boat. "C'mon, milord," said Rowan coaxingly. "Don't look so frightened. 'Tain't blood on Reg's smock, but some wine he spilled. We're your dearest friends. You remember us, don't yeh?"

"Wreck and Ruin," said Griss. He winked at Tess, and she realized that, at this moment anyway, he was lucid enough to mock his captors. Apparently his fog of senility could part sometimes, letting a keen sense of humor glimmer through.

He reminded her so strongly of Grandma Therese that her heart ached.

Rowan seemed not to get it. "Always foretelling doom," he muttered.

"Could we hasten away from this river?" griped his companion. Reg had swished his shirt in the water and was wringing it out; rusty drops stained the gravel. His body was pale as a toadstool, and marked with scars. "The hounds are dead," he said, "but I'm not a thousand percent sure I killed the caretaker. He'll know we crossed the river. We need to vanish."

The men shoved the ferry back into the water, to drift downstream and confuse pursuers. Pathka crept up beside Tess and hissed, "I got what I needed. Let's go."

Tess knelt as if to scratch Pathka's head spines and whispered, "I want to get the old one out of their clutches. I hurt him when I first set out from home; I need to make amends."

Pathka's eyes twitched skeptically. "We can follow them for a while, if your conscience demands it, as long as they're traveling south. Once I finish our thniks, though, I want to go underground. I don't want them with us—not even the old one."

"Understood," said Tess, standing up.

The two ruffians were halfway up the hill already, towing Griss between them. Griss balked, craning his head to look for her, and whined plaintively, "Johnny?"

Tess set her shoulders and followed doggedly, Pathka rattling up the hill behind her.

Rowan kept glancing warily back at Pathka; Tess's threat to his favorite limb had clearly made an impression. Reg steadfastly ignored Tess and Pathka's presence, although he held Griss's upper arm so tightly his knuckles whitened, and he scanned the woods on either side of the road as if he would have liked to bolt. Perhaps he would have tried to run if Griss could have gone any faster than a shuffle.

Evening fell, and the ruffians kept walking into the gloaming. Tess wondered if they meant to walk all night, until Rowan started whining. Reg answered him with a sharp hiss, and they had a quiet, intense argument just beyond her hearing.

She hoped it wasn't about whether to kill her. She needed to give them reasons not to.

There was a clearing not twenty feet off the road. At Tess's gesture, Pathka got to work building a campfire there. Tess sliced up the sausages she'd pilfered and began frying them. Reg and Rowan, still arguing, ignored all this, but Griss stared longingly. His eyes reflected the fire like a nocturnal animal's.

The smell of sausage finally grew irresistible enough to draw Reg and Rowan toward the circle of firelight. They still looked wary, so Tess smiled enormously and waved a hand around the pan to show she was willing to buy her way into their good graces. Her food would be gone by tomorrow if they took her up on it; she tried not to think about that.

"What're you playing at?" said Reg, eyes narrowed, staring at her across the fire. He held out an arm to stop Rowan and Griss coming any nearer without his say-so.

"Supper?" said Tess, trying to keep her voice low. It occurred to her that cooking for everyone was a rather feminine strata-gem. Was she holding the pan handle too delicately?

There were many ways to discredit her disguise. Her hand sweated against the cast iron.

"Look, friends," said Tess hastily, "we're traveling in the same direction. I figured we may as well pool our resour—"

"And which direction is that, precisely?" Reg had not re-laxed his posture or his glare. His voice was the tail of a cat about to pounce: only the most minuscule twitch of excitement showed what danger you were in.

Pathka stepped up to Tess's side and glared back, his tail twitching more obviously.

"'Toward fame and glory, comrades,'" Tess said carefully, quoting Dozerius the Pirate, "'but toward treasure will do, in a pinch.'"

There was a long silence. Tess wondered whether they could hear her heart pounding.

Then both ruffians burst out laughing, and Tess laughed, too, desperately, hoping this meant she'd put their minds at ease. They drew near the fire, at any rate. Rowan flopped onto his fat bottom and pulled Griss down to sit beside him.

Reg sauntered around the perimeter of the firelight with studied casualness, until he stood beside Tess. The back of her neck prickled; she tried not to cringe too obviously. Pathka, on Tess's other side, growled, but Reg ignored this, squatted down, and put his mouth near her ear.

"Who are you really?" he snarled. "No comrade of ours. Your speech is too well bred."

"Innit, though?" cried Rowan, helping himself to a slice of hot sausage. "'Which of your *limbs* is your *favorite*?'"

He mocked her in a high-pitched voice; Tess hoped he meant to be insulting, and that she didn't really sound like that. Her disguise wouldn't last if her voice was like a little girl's.

Pathka's angry spine flare made it hard to think. Tess put a hand on his head to calm him. She needed to tell a plausible story before her friend decided to take matters into his own jaws.

A hundred Dozerius tales at her disposal, none of them the right one. If she made herself sound important, they might seize her for ransom; if she seemed too dangerous, they might decide to kill her preemptively. Reg had pulled out his knife and was twirling it idly.

"I'm called Jacomo. I was raised in the church, but I lost my faith upon reaching, erm, manhood," she finally said. It was hard to sound confident with a knife on one side and a protective quigutl on the other. "The prior ordered me to go on pilgrimage and find it. Instead, I've discovered a talent for breaking and entering, and many fine things to steal."

Rowan burst into ugly laughter. Reg stopped playing with his blade and used it to stab a few sausage slices. Tess let herself relax a little.

"So how did you acquire a pet quigutl, Father Filch-My-Jewels?" asked Reg with his mouth full. "And what holy relics did you bring us from that hunting lodge? The chalice of St. Gilded Goblet? The bones of Saints Amethyst and Pearl?"

"Have some respect. He'll be the Archbishop of Pilfering-Booty someday," cried Rowan. He laughed uproariously at his own joke, clutching his sides as if he might burst like a ripe plum.

"Enough," Reg snapped. Rowan shoved his sleeve into his mouth, stifling himself.

"There's your *pet*," hissed Pathka. "So obedient. So docile."

A knife whizzed past Pathka's head and stuck, vibrating, in a tree behind him.

"If you mean to share our road, Brother Bat-Dung," said Reg, striding over to retrieve his weapon, "I don't want to hear this monster speak. Are we clear?"

"Extremely," said Tess, before Pathka could speak again. Pathka glared vitriol at her, and she didn't know how to reassure him. "We won't be with you long."

"That's what I hoped you'd say," said Reg, sheathing his knife at last. "We may walk the same way awhile, but you're not our comrade. We're not sharing the reward."

Tess would have asked, *What reward?* but Rowan was sneering: "Griss is our mad nobleman. We found him first, and you can go hang, by St. Masha."

"Is that your scheme? Locate his family and collect a bounty?" asked Tess.

The ruffians didn't answer, though. They were busy polishing off the last of her sausages.

⚔

Tess would have absconded with Griss that very night, but the men tied him to a tree. "What in Heaven's name—" Tess began, appalled at this indignity. Rowan, glimpsing thunderclouds over his partner's head, took her aside and confided, "Lord Griss wanders if we don't. You're not the only Johnny he sees, y'know. He chases Johnnies all over creation, and he's like to chase one over a clift."

Griss smiled sadly from across the fire. "It's all right, Jacomo," he called. "I asked them to. It's embarrassing to wake up Heaven knows where, next to someone you don't recognize."

It was the closest he'd come to remembering.

Even so, Tess might've untied him if she hadn't had to lean over a man with a knife to do it. Reg and Rowan plunked themselves down at the base of the same tree.

She didn't like her odds. She spread her blanket next to Pathka on the far side of the fire.

"Can I speak now?" Pathka growled. "We should leave. I don't care that it's dark and your heart is gnawed by remorse. The tall one will eventually kill one of us on impulse, while insisting it was logical."

"I can't," Tess said levelly. "Griss is in serious dang—"

"Burn him!" Pathka hissed. "You have no duty toward him. Your guilt will kill us."

Tess nestled under her blanket, thinking. She didn't feel this as duty; indeed, *duty* might have sent her running the other way. And it wasn't mere guilt. She felt . . . like her heart and conscience demanded it. Like this was where she was supposed to be. How could she turn her back when someone right in front of her needed help? Especially when that someone reminded her so keenly of Grandma Therese, who'd kept her going through the worst days of her life.

⚮

Tess had been fourteen, barely, when she'd had to confess all to her mother.

Bad girls in stories always fell pregnant on the first go; sometimes (depending on the story) they'd done little more than enter a man's room and close the door. It wasn't clear to Tess (until it was) what they'd been getting up to, only that judgment was swift and sure.

Saith St. Vitt: *Sin, and you sin before the eyes of Heaven. Heaven does not blink.*

Several months of Will passed without consequence; Tess carried on in merry denial. When her monthlies were finally delayed, she didn't mind. Who'd miss that mess? After three months' delay, however, she began to wonder and then to fear. If she was pregnant, wouldn't she be ill? Mama had been vomiting till the bitter end with Ned. Tess felt nothing but a gnawing anxiety. She grew quiet and then withdrawn. If Will noticed, he didn't ask what was wrong.

Finally she could maintain her denial no longer. She determined to ask Will; a naturalist might have some insight. Before she could tell him, though, he disappeared. Paid up at the Mallet and Mullet, no forwarding address. No one knew where he'd gone, not Roger and Harald, who'd wondered aloud whether she might require a new paramour, nor yet the saar Spira, who'd ogled her wall-eyed, as if he could smell her secret.

Even Will's adviser, Professor the dragon Ondir, had had no warning. "He didn't defend his thesis," the old saar said flatly. "Tell him he won't get his degree until he does."

In desperation, Tess asked Kenneth to eavesdrop at the Belgioso warehouses. She didn't believe Will had owed Count Julian money, but she was out of ideas. If Will was at the bottom of the river, at least she'd know. No one had killed Will, though, as far as Kenneth could discern.

Tess's gowns grew tight around the waist. She had to tell somebody, or go die in a gutter like the slattern she was. The latter, distressingly, seemed like the pleasanter option.

She'd tell Jeanne first. Jeanne would be sympathetic, even if she didn't know what to do.

She crept into her sister's room, but Jeanne was already asleep, illuminated by moonlight. Tess sat gingerly on the edge of the mattress, hoping Jeanne would open her eyes. She didn't, which pierced Tessie to the heart. Once Jeanne would have sensed her there; once there'd been a bond of steel between them, but Tess had selfishly broken it. Ashamed, she skulked back to the room where she now slept alone, which had once been Seraphina's.

As the patron Saints of comedy and tragedy would have it, the next day brought a carriage with the royal crest to their door. No fanfare—it was only Seraphina, deigning to descend from on high. Papa was at Count Julian's, humiliating himself for employment, but Seraphina wasn't here for him today. Mama led her into the parlor, offered tea as if she were a duchess, and hollered for the twins—unnecessarily, since they were listening at the door. Jeanne bounded in first; that is, she glided like a swan. Only the keen eyes of her twin knew this for unbridled enthusiasm. She perched on the edge of a chair, vibrant as a canary. Tess, by contrast, slouched in and tried to bury herself in the cushions of the couch.

"Tessie, sit up," Mama admonished. Tess wiggled as if she were trying.

"I come bearing news," said Seraphina, eyeing Tess. She looked suspicious, though she couldn't have been. No one yet knew the news Tess was bearing.

"I've secured two positions," Seraphina continued. "Jeanne may accompany Tessie to court, beginning next month. They'll attend on Lady Farquist, who's like a dear old auntie to all the young lords. You'll finally meet some eligible bachelors, Tess." Seraphina capped off this pronouncement with a suggestive wink; Anne-Marie swatted her arm.

Tessie burst into tears.

She couldn't go. There was no way. In another month, her belly would be swollen beyond easy concealment, and then? How long did it take to grow a baby? Mama had been pregnant forever with Neddie.

"Tess, stop being melodramatic," snapped Mama. "However moved you may be, these over-the-top displays are inappropriate. People will think—"

Tess flopped onto her side, keening, which cut the lecture short. Mama's mouth hung open, as if it began to occur to her that Tess's sobbing portended something serious. Jeanne rushed to Tess's side, faithful and unquestioning, pushing Tess's damp hair out of her face and handing her handkerchiefs. "My love, what's wrong?"

Seraphina raised her eyebrows, as if waiting for someone to explain this outburst.

"I can't...," Tess moaned. She was sweating and dizzy, and was Jeanne wearing perfume? It was ten times stronger than it needed to be; it turned her stomach. "Mama, I can't go."

"What do you mean, you can't go?" said Mama dangerously. "We've been training you to fulfill this duty for almost two years."

Tess heaved for air, fearing she'd faint, wishing she would. Jeanne propped her up, muttering soothingly. Tess's thoughts jumbled—how did her mortifying story begin? With the World Serpents, or Kenneth, or natural philosophy? With "Will promised he'd marry me" or "Will is gone, and no one knows where," or ... Saints in Heaven, Will was gone and he'd taken everything with him and left her to carry this on her own and she couldn't....

She was burning up, a sour-salty taste rising in her throat. "Mama, I'm sorry. I've ruined myself. I've ruined everything," was the last thing she managed to say before all of her breakfast and all of her dinner and all of the food she'd ever eaten—it felt like—plus all her guts and dreams and future came hurtling up out of her depths and splattered upon the wooden floor.

⚔

Jeanne, it was determined, would go to court on time; someone had to. She'd take Tess's place as Lady Farquist's maid of the robes, and Tess's place in the hierarchy of marriageability and family-saving. Jeanne, presumably, should have been the elder twin to begin with, if she hadn't politely allowed Tessie to exit the womb first. It was just like Jeanne to do that.

It was just like Tessie to elbow past her sister, thinking of no one but herself.

Papa, in an unprecedented convulsion of paternal conscience, wanted to find Will and either kill him or drag him back to marry Tess. Mama felt this would merely draw attention to their daughter's disgrace, jeopardizing Jeanne's prospects. Seraphina suggested Tess might go on pilgrimage, which was met with eye-rolling all around (nothing says surprise pregnancy like a pilgrimage), but then she hit upon the idea of Dombegh Manor, and that seemed to suit everyone.

Everyone but Tess, who didn't count. She'd forfeited everything.

Belgiosos swarmed over Lavondaville like termites in a hollow tree, but Tess had never met the Dombegh side of the family. Papa's elder brother—Jean-Philippe, Baronet Dombegh—and his ancient mother, Therese, were ensconced in the deep country and never came to town. Tess's story could be whatever her parents decided it should be; no one would check.

In an act of (wholly characteristic) filial piety, therefore, Tess had insisted upon attending her Grandma Therese's final days, or so the story went. Tess would come to court later—dear, tenderhearted girl!—to attend upon her sister. She was as selfless and giving and dutiful as one could hope for in a daughter, and Anne-Marie Dombegh (née Belgioso) felt blessed every day.

Tess, now famously pious and compliant, was bundled off to Dombegh Manor in the middle of the night.

⚔

Uncle Jean-Philippe, Baronet Dombegh, was a portly, mustachioed man, what Papa might have looked like if he'd spent forty years eating, drinking, and chasing women instead of fretting, lying, and cringing. The baronet met Tess outside the house and, even though she was clearly exhausted from her nightlong ride, he walked her to the village first. "Your grandmother is napping," he explained, "and she'll be a shrieking, disoriented harpy if we wake her too soon."

Tess barely heard him. She stumbled along, sights rolling off her like water off a goose's back. Uncle Jean-Philippe introduced her to the midwife, Chessey, a stout, middle-aged woman with a mess of chestnut hair going gray at the temples. Her eyes were bright and clever as a crow's, and she had a faint mustache, which made her look a little like a bear.

"You'll be in excellent hands, niece," said Uncle Jean-Philippe. "She's caught all my illegitimate issue, twenty-six and counting. 'Old Bastard-Catcher,' I call her."

"There've been twenty-three, m'lord," said Chessey, curtsying. "You must've got your imagination pregnant, too."

Tess was too numb to find the joke appalling; she didn't even feel hurt when her uncle called her "little slut" as they were leaving. Chessey's mouth turned down in a scowl.

Tess's grandmother Therese had awakened by the time they returned. A harried maidservant led the bony old woman into the parlor. "It's your *granddaughter*," the maid explained loudly—for the umpteenth time, to gauge by her exasperation. "Claude's little girl."

"Who?" cried the dowager baroness. She was in her dressing gown, her cobwebby hair loose around her shoulders; her eyes rolled like a panicking horse's. When she spotted Tess, she froze. "No, it can't be," she said, tears welling up. "Agnes, my love. You came back."

She threw her arms around Tess as if greeting a long-lost sister—no, not *as if*. She was doing exactly that. Her grief pierced Tess's veil of numbness, and then they were both weeping and clutching each other under the scornful eye of Uncle Jean-Philippe.

"I'm so pleased you like your namesake, Mother," he said nastily.

Grandma Therese scowled, as though he were some intruding ape, and led Tess to a musty couch. She pulled Tess onto the seat beside her and whispered loudly, "Ignore that lout I married, Agnes. He's a liar who only wanted to hide behind my good name. I should've followed your example and been happy, rather than let his title and money tempt me."

"I can hear you," cried Uncle Jean-Philippe across the parlor. "And you've mistaken me for Father again, you old buzzard. Do you even remember the names of your sons?"

"There was little Claude, who ran off to the city," said Grandma Therese, tapping a white finger against her chin. "Then my eldest, born a villain . . . what did I name him?"

She looked at Tess sidelong, her eyes two chips of opal, and

Tess suspected that her grandmother knew his name, knew she was playing a game. Jean-Philippe stepped close, arms akimbo, ready for a quarrel.

"I remember!" said Grandma Therese brightly. "The elder was called Jean-Philander, and he was a beastly sack of malfeasance, like his father."

Uncle Jean-Philippe raised a hand as if to strike her. Tess, with a cry, wrapped her arms around the old woman to shield her from the blow. Her uncle stayed his hand, using it to tug his mustache as if that had been his intention all along. "She's yours, little slut," he said, rocking on his heels. "That's what you're here for, officially. I wish you joy of her. She's pleasant now, believing you're Agnes, but Heaven help you when she decides you're her mother."

Though she hated to credit Papa with wisdom, Tess soon realized he'd kept his children away from Dombegh Manor for a reason. She was already growing afraid of her uncle. Luckily, Jean-Philander was easily avoided: Tess had only to stay by his mother's side.

Left to herself, Tess might've filled her days with weeping or plotting ways to end it all—the manor had nice high gables overhanging flagstone yards, or there was always that old standby, the well. Her grandmother needed her, though, and Tess found the old woman's company surprisingly pleasant. They were like merry children together, even if one was pregnant and the other a venerable seventy-eight years old.

Grandma liked having her hair brushed; she'd close her eyes and practically purr. They had tea parties and tried on all the jewelry and antique gowns. Grandma Therese liked to embroider, but everything came out muddled, patches of uneven satin fill, a thicket of wild herringbone, a scattering of seed stitch. Eventually she'd realize it looked terrible and weep with frustration. Tess would trade hoops and turn her blobs into fanciful animals and landscapes, delighting her grandmother, who seemed not to recall her part in creating them.

Tess envied her forgetfulness, a bit. It would have been such a relief to forget Will, Mama, all her shame and loathing, but Tess was doomed to remember everything she didn't actively push down. St. Siucre had answered Tess's prayer, her blessing a curse.

Grandma Therese's other favorite pastime was napping, which Tess felt herself well suited to. They'd doze off in the parlor in patches of spring sunshine, a lovely, comradely way to pass an afternoon. Tess did not at first realize that her grandmother was tired because she was up half the night, wandering the gardens in her nightdress, weeping and lamenting. The spooky sound woke Tess three or four times before she dared open her shutters and peek out.

What she saw frightened her more than any ghost. Her grandmother was going to get lost or hurt or eaten by wolves. (Tess's imagination still worked, even while she was pregnant.)

Grandma Therese's door had a bolt, but the maid refused to employ it. "It's an insult and an indignity to lock the dowager baroness in her room," the woman insisted, glancing over her shoulder. "Besides, I've tried it. She screams and bangs on the door all night. The baronet will have none of it. She can't hurt herself in the garden." The maid looked back again and lowered her voice further. "Her son is the greater danger—to all of us—if she annoys him too much."

"You couldn't stay in her room at night?" Tess pleaded.

The maidservant looked offended. "If she needs me, she'll ring. Plus she snores. I need rest, too, you know."

Tess began bunking down on the floor outside her grandmother's room, waking to chaperone the old woman's wanderings. Grandma Therese always took the same route, through the topiaries to the rose garden, where she circled for hours. Sometimes she walked until dawn, despite Tess's pleas to go back indoors.

The midwife, Chessey, checked up on Tess weekly, prodding and measuring her beneath the peevish gaze of the cherubs on the ceiling. At their sixth meeting, she declared everything right as rain, "except that you're clearly not getting enough sleep." She glared from under her single stern eyebrow.

"I'll nap more," said Tess. Her eyes refused to focus; she gave up trying to keep them open. "Only I'm afraid for my grandmother." She told Chessey the whole sorry story (with her eyes closed)—how threatening Uncle Jean-Philippe was, how he let his own mother wander the night unsupervised. "Surely St. Loola's has a hospice nearby?" Tess asked. The midwife wore no habit, but she would have been trained by the nuns, without a doubt.

"Tried that," said Chessey, mouth flattening. "Your uncle threw our Mother Superior out on her ear. St. Loola's isn't prestigious enough, he claimed. He has a point—a rotten, selfish point—but plenty of holy houses would take her. St. Clare's, St. Katy's. He could scrape up enough dowry that monks might take her, even, and she'd be out of his sight forever, but he won't spend the money. I think he wants her here, suffering where he can see her."

Soon after, Tess was on her way to her grandmother's room, carrying the quilt she slept in and two bolsters. Dombegh Manor was a chimerical structure, like a house made of other houses; the corridors didn't match up, and some were rarely used. The shortest path between Tess's room, the chamber of peevish cherubs, and her grandmother's took her through a dark, unused part of the house, where the doors were nailed shut (ever curious, she'd tried a few).

Her uncle stepped out into the corridor ahead of her, and she stopped short, afraid.

Uncle Jean-Philippe looked harried; he'd clearly come in from outside. His boots were muddy, his cloak sodden. Tess pressed herself to the wall, hoping he'd pass by without speaking, but he saw her. His breath was so heavy with alcohol that she could have ignited it. He grabbed her roughly and cried, "I know you're devoted to the old crow, little slut!" He spit while he ranted; his nails dug into her. "She looks so sweet and innocent to you, and I look like the devil, but who made me? Who made your namby-pamby father? When you grow up with a bitter, backbiting bitch of a mother, what hope is there for turning out well?"

He began to weep. "Every good thing I ever tried to do, she ground under her heel. Any tenderness in my soul was a plump partridge for her to sink her teeth into. She's a monster, and it isn't fair that her mind is going. She can forget her cruelty, rename herself a senile Saint, and I can't. I can't."

He released Tess and staggered into the darkness, periodically trying to force open an unopenable door.

Tess was quaking like a mouse. Outside, thunder rumbled.

Tess hurried to her grandmother's door, arranged herself on the straw pallet the maid had put out for her, and tried to sleep. Lightning illuminated the windows, and branches tried to claw their way in, but it wasn't the storm keeping her awake. Tess's thoughts were a jumble of terrible mothers and unforgiveable cruelties. Why shouldn't Grandma Therese remake herself? She'd been kind to Tess; that wasn't nothing. Was there redemption for anyone in the end, or would there always be some Jean-Philippe of your own creation, injured and obsessed, out for blood? Tess's mind mixed mother with child, Saint with sinner, cruelty with kindness. Between her turmoil and the storm's fury, she hardly noticed how her back ached and stomach cramped.

She awoke with a start; the windows glowed with predawn twilight. Had Grandma not come out? Tess struggled to stand, pausing to catch her breath as her abdomen seized. The pain should have been frightening, but she had practice ignoring her body.

She tapped timidly on the bedroom door. No reply. She opened it a crack and listened for snoring. All was silent. It was too dark to see, so Tess crept through to open the heavy drapes. Grandma Therese had accumulated seventy years' worth of souvenirs—vases, knickknacks, a bearskin rug, poufs, a globe, a suit of armor—and Tess bumped most of them crossing the room. Even a half-deaf old woman should have been awakened by the noise.

Tess whipped back the curtains, and wan half-light fell across an empty bed.

Grandma Therese must've sneaked out during the storm, without Tess hearing. "No, no, no," Tess repeated down the corridor, down the stairs, through the house, into the grounds, waddling as fast as she could, pausing whenever shooting pelvic pain stole her breath away. It felt like her monthlies times a thousand. She'd have to remember to mention it to Chessey next week.

The gravel paths were riddled with puddles; Tess's slippers were soon soaked, but she could only imagine how wet and cold her grandmother would be, out all night without shelter (unless she was in the gazebo; no, she was not). "Therese!" Tess shouted—the old woman rarely responded to "Grandma." At the rose garden, her heart sank; the plants were only waist-high, so she should have seen anyone on the paths.

Anyone upright. Tess plodded the perimeter doing grim due diligence, her heart quailing.

Someone had dug a pit in the middle of the path at the far end of the garden. Not deep, but too wide to walk around. An old woman might not notice it in the dark. An old woman might fall and break her hip, or her neck. Whoever had dug it might or might not have anticipated that it would fill with water in the storm—only an inch, but an inch was enough.

Tess teetered at the edge of the pit, staring at her grandmother's body, the pale hair like wet weeds, the soaked clinging chemise spattered with grit. Tess would have wept, but she was gripped by a terrible contraction at just that moment, so she screamed.

Fifteen

Sharing food with Reg and Rowan didn't gain their goodwill. Tess's supplies were gone by breakfast, and the two ruffians, their own packs still full, had not a morsel to spare for her. If they'd hoped to drive her off, though, they were sorely disappointed. Tess stayed on them like a tick, determined to free Griss.

Alas, she needed to eat. By the second morning, her stomach rumbled unbearably; she'd have to abandon them and go steal something for herself. She hit up a farmhouse for bread and cheese, but the farm wife spotted her and chased her with a rolling pin. Tess was forced a mile out of her way, and when she found the road again, the three men were nowhere to be seen.

They couldn't have gotten far; Griss, in particular, shuffled slowly. Half a mile along, Tess and Pathka reached a village. Normally they would have skirted it, on the principle that

Pathka was going to alarm people, but the village was nearly empty. It was a fine, warm day, and everyone was out on the surrounding hills doing farmwork.

In the middle of the village, Pathka abruptly veered toward a large, sturdy building, a public house, and Tess understood: the men had stopped for lunch. She found them in the taproom, Reg and Rowan drinking ale, Griss dozing with his chin on his chest.

Tess sat at their table, startling Griss awake. He smiled blearily. Reg and Rowan picked up their mugs and pointedly changed tables, which was ridiculous; the room was empty except for the four of them. Tess sighed, envying their ale a little bit, and then felt a tug on her sleeve.

"Johnny," Griss whispered, "you can't keep poaching. You're going to get . . ." He mimed wringing a chicken's neck.

"If you know some better way to feed myself, I'd like to hear it," said Tess sulkily.

Griss kept worrying her sleeve until she looked up. He pointed out the window. Beyond the thatched houses sloped a field of tall grass. Upon the hillside, a line of village men mowed with scythes; behind them, the women raked and tossed cut grass into piles running the length of the meadow. Tess could just make out snatches of song.

"You don't need to . . . to . . . There's honest work to be done, Johnny," whispered Griss. "The world is full of work, waiting for you. I've told you a hundred times."

"Have you?" said Tess absently, entranced by the rhythm and efficiency of their movements. It was like a dance—cut, turn, rake, repeat.

And that was how old Griss, whom Tess had set out to save, may have saved her in turn. As inept as she was at stealing, she'd never given farm chores a second thought. Hitherto unconsidered possibilities now opened up before her.

She discovered that she loved turning hay, loved the feel and weight of the seven-tined pitchfork, loved the way fresh grass smelled green, demi-dry smelled sweet, and crackling-dry smelled good enough to eat. She loved the rip and swish of the scythes, the songs (she never stayed long enough to learn the words, alas), the way the women giggled at her preference for the feminine task of turning the piles (Tess wasn't strong enough yet to keep up with the cutters). She loved the way her shoulders ached, and the way her skin felt when she finally scrubbed it free of dust in some secluded stream at the end of the day.

She'd walk into the dewy fields first thing and work all morning in exchange for a share of the midday meal. Aside from the unexpected pleasure of physical labor, she was glad to finally get along without stealing. Well, mostly. She did steal a leather jerkin that had been left on a stump, because the weather was getting unpleasantly warm for Florian's jacket, and she needed something that would hide her breasts without giving her heatstroke. She left a small bouquet of field poppies as a thank-you but knew that didn't make up for it.

After lunch Tess would hurry after Reg and Rowan. They never walked more than three or four miles and usually stopped for the night by midafternoon, so she caught them up easily. If she couldn't tell which tavern was getting them drunk, Pathka would sniff them out.

Not without grumbling, however. "They're going to kill you," he'd say. "Who will help me call Anathuthia then? Not the oldster. Not your ghost."

Reg and Rowan seemed determined to drink away the loot they'd stolen from the hunting lodge. Tess hoped they'd get so drunk that she could spirit Griss away, but it wasn't that simple. They preferred inns to camping, and they barred their door at night.

Tess sat with them at tavern tables in the evenings, so they knew she still had her eye on them. They avoided speaking; Tess would listen to the village fiddler and nurse her single ale, if she'd been lucky enough to muck out the stable or perform some other chore for the tapmaster.

One memorable evening, a priest gave the news: a child was born unto Queen Glisselda! A girl, not yet named. The tapmaster, in a fit of celebratory generosity, proclaimed a round on the house, and Tess—who couldn't hold it like she used to— found herself in conversation with Reg and Rowan at last. "What would you say if I told you the child wasn't Glisselda's at all?" said Tess ill-advisedly. "What if I told you it was Seraphina's, being passed off as the Queen's?"

Luckily, Reg was twice as drunk as she was. "I'd tell you to go drown yourself in St. Pandowdy's Pond, because you've uttered the most serene blasphemy ever heard."

"Blasphemy?" cried Tess. "It's 'disrespect to Her Majesty,' not blapshemy. I mean phlasbemy. Damnation!" She couldn't say it twice, which was embarrassing.

"Idiot," said Reg, taking a superior air. "St. Seraphina couldn't possibly get pregnant."

"She's half dragon," offered Rowan. "She'd be infertile, like a mule."

"Even worse!" cried Reg. "You dolts, she's a bloody Saint. You think she'd have filthy woman parts under her skirts? Never. She'll be pure as the driveled snow, virginal and unsculleried. You owe penance for your disgusting thoughts, Heaven slap you silly."

Tess had sense and sobriety enough to bite her tongue. She'd seen Seraphina in the bath and would have vouched for anything but breasts, which weren't her sister's strong suit. "Plant some cabbages in those fields!" Tess had once sassed Seraphina, and then, ye Saints, she'd been spanked so hard. It was the one time she knew for sure that Seraphina had told on her.

This foolishness got her no closer to rescuing Griss. Tess stalked out, slept it off, and dogged them again the next day.

Once, by some miracle, Reg and Rowan left without Griss. Tess, who'd been watching the tavern door, rushed in. Someone screamed upstairs; Tess took the stairs two at a time and found the proprietress shrieking at poor Griss, who was tied to the bed, lying in his own filth and weeping in terror. This was Tess's chance to free him, but he needed to be cleaned up, and she could not, in good conscience, leave the proprietress with the mess. Tess promised the woman a chip of gold (praying Pathka had some; he'd been using various precious metals to construct the thniks), and together they untied Griss, took up the sheets, carried his bedding down to the fire, and hauled up fresh straw from the shed. They sluiced poor Griss in the yard by the chickens, toweled him off, and dressed him in a pair of breeches the tapmaster had grown too stout for.

Tess found Pathka up an apple tree and asked for a crumb of gold. "They're going to kill you," he said, handing her a chunk the size of her thumbnail. Before Tess could ask him to bite off a smaller piece, noise made her look up. Across the green, the proprietress was shouting at Wreck and Ruin and beating them with a broom, but they drew their knives and took Griss away between them.

Tess ended up giving the proprietress the entire gold chunk. This was the last straw. Tess couldn't wait for the right circumstances to present themselves; the longer she took, the more abuse Griss endured. He wasn't going to last.

Tess was going to have to make her own opportunity.

Before she left the village, Tess asked the proprietress what lay to the south—landscapes, manor houses, hospices? "If you mean to save that old granddad, let me help," said the woman, placing the gold on the counter beside Tess's hand. Tess began to protest (although, to be fair, the nugget had shrunk significantly), but the woman wouldn't hear of it. "Call it charity," she said. "There, by Heaven's grace, go we all eventually."

Tess left the village with a plan, some money, and a hopeful spring in her step.

⚔

"I've heard tell of a palace nearby," Tess told Reg and Rowan once she caught them up. They were well into their cups at the Hefty Heifer in the village of Faverly. Tess had availed herself of a mug of ale, just one, funded by charitable donation. She was about Griss's business, after all, and she needed courage.

"The *palace*," she reiterated, since they were ignoring her, "belongs to the Duke of Barrabou. According to locals, he's fantastically rich, and—here's the best of it—he lost his father a few months ago. I don't mean dead, I mean lost."

Rowan eyed her sidelong. "Sounds like carelessness."

"Indeed," said Tess, keeping a straight face. "The old duke wandered the rose garden at night. No one minded, thinking at worst he'd get caught in the thorns. One day, though, the gardener left the gate open. The old man wandered into the forest and was never seen again."

She had Reg's attention now. He picked his nose with his thumb meditatively and said, "I suppose you want something for this information?"

"I ask no reward," said Tess hastily, as if to fend off their generosity. "I'll just sneak in the back while you've got everyone occupied in front, and walk off with a few golden forks."

The men laughed and hailed the tapmaster for more ale, whereupon Griss whispered in Tess's ear: "There is no Duke of Barrabou."

"You need to keep that very quiet," Tess whispered back. "Can you do that?"

Griss nodded solemnly; Tess might've worried, but she was sure he'd forget the Duke of Barrabou even quicker than his promise.

They headed across country, under Tess's direction, toward a distant southern ridge. It would take most of a day to reach it, the proprietress had told her. Tess had been on the road long enough to estimate distances with some accuracy; it sounded like a four- or five-hour walk to her, even at Griss's slow shuffle. The chief foot-draggers, though, were Reg and Rowan. The ridge was farther than they usually walked in a day. By noon their feet hurt and they were thirsty, and why hurry? The Duke of Barrabou's palace wasn't going anywhere.

Tess didn't dare let them stop at a tavern, though, lest they learn the duke didn't exist. "It's a haul today," she said, "but tomorrow's an easy downhill stroll to the manor if we camp on the ridge. I know you hate camping"—she raised her voice over their protests—"so I bought a bottle of pisky to ease your pains."

They seemed somewhat placated by the promise of pisky. "Too bad I've nothing but dried sausage to go with it," Tess muttered to Griss, taking his bony arm. "If I were really Johnny, I'd poach us a stag, how about that?"

Griss shook his leonine head. "Snare the . . . the little ones with ears. Those are loyal."

It took some asking before Tess understood: he meant hares, and that it was *legal*. "If I knew how to set snares, Griss, I'd have been eating like a king out here."

The old man glanced mischievously at Pathka. "Does your baby dragon have any . . ." He mimed tugging something long with both hands. "String. No, metal string."

In fact, Pathka could make wire from the scraps in his pouch; he extruded some when they stopped for lunch and a bit of a nap. Griss, too keyed up to sleep, showed Tess how to make a wire snare. His hands remembered how—a small loop, twist, thread through a bigger loop.

He explained how to set it. "Look for where they . . . they make a beat. A path. You shouldn't be there at night. That's how it got Annie." He grew melancholy. "I could have told her where it hunted. It had been in our dale awhile; I'd been tracking it."

He'd switched seamlessly from hares to the dragon that had eaten his sister. "Why did she go there?" Tess asked quietly. "Tell Jacomo what happened."

"Johnny was poaching. I'd turned a blind eye, but then I lost my fingers." He mimed a bear trap closing. "I told on him. I thought Papa would yell and—" He mimed throwing a punch. "But he told the duke. Johnny was going to hang. Annie went out to warn him away, and—" He made a snatching motion with his three-fingered hand. A dragon got her.

Tess had never heard him put the whole story together. It was as if making the snare had opened a door in his mind, if only for a moment.

They reached the ridge with daylight left. Tess helped Griss set the snare—upon a hare's beat, not a dragon's—and within a couple of hours they'd caught one. Griss twisted its neck sharply (Tess watched with mixed revulsion and curiosity; she needed to learn this, gruesome though it was). He skinned it with Rowan's knife so swiftly that Tess could hardly comprehend what he'd done. It looked like he'd turned the poor creature inside out.

However refined his speech and manner, *this* was what he'd done most of his life, Tess felt certain. Reg, too, was watching, eyes narrowed, likely having similar thoughts and new doubts about the Duke of Barrabou. Tess thanked Heaven that it would all be over tonight.

They feasted on roast hare, and Tess saw to it that Reg and Rowan finished the bottle of pisky (she took none herself; she needed her wits tonight). Getting them falling-down drunk was hard; they had a mighty capacity and years of practice. Tess, wishing she'd sprung for two bottles, tried to keep them sweet-tempered by telling Dozerius stories about fish the size of islands, rhinoceroses and camelopards, beautiful and compliant women. Rowan went from rapt to merry to benevolently snoozy, but Reg's scowl deepened. He seemed utterly unimpaired.

When the spirits and stories had run out and the fire was down to embers, they tied Griss to a tree as usual. Rowan settled beside him and began snoring. Reg, though, stalked over to Tess and pressed the tip of his knife to her throat. She went still as a hare.

"Dunno what you're playing at." His voice raised the hairs on her neck. "If I were plying my comrades with booze and tales, it'd mean something was up. I warn you, lad: I sleep with one eye open. If you so much as get up to piss in the night, I will gut you. Clear?"

Tess dared no more than nod in answer. He'd sleep more soundly than he claimed—half a bottle of pisky wasn't nothing, even to him—but she'd have to wait, listen, and be sure. Pathka had agreed to burn through the rope so she wouldn't have to lean across Reg and Rowan to untie Griss. It was the old man who worried her. He'd be disoriented when she freed him; he might cry out in fear. Stuffing a rag in his mouth would frighten him all the more.

She'd have to play it by ear.

Around midnight she awoke to rain spattering her face, fat drops, hard as pebbles. The leafy canopy had blocked lighter rain, but now it was getting through; thunder rumbled above the urgent hiss of the rain-shower. Rowan and Reg cried out inarticulately, swatting at the air, unsure where they were or how they'd got here.

Then the storm got serious.

The wind whipped branches around. Clumps of wet leaves slapped Tess's face and body, while above her tree limbs groaned and cracked ominously. Lightning struck a tree at the top of the ridge, and then another, which briefly caught fire. Close thunderclaps left her ears ringing.

Tess rushed to Griss's tree. Reg and Rowan had fled into the darkness after the second lightning strike, Heaven knew where.

Pathka had seized the opportunity to start burning the ropes.

"Come on," Tess cried above the howling wind, tugging Griss's hand. "Can you walk?"

Lightning illuminated his horrified face. He flailed about, striking the side of Tess's head. She clenched her teeth and grabbed him; it was like wrestling an otter, wet and slippery, surprisingly strong, and determined to wriggle free. She hefted him over her shoulders, the way a farmer carries a calf. He bucked at first, but went limp as she staggered to her feet.

Rain lashed her body, rolled down her face in torrents, down her jerkin, down her boots. She nearly tripped over a root that turned out to be Pathka, trying to herd her in the right direction. Thunder and lightning had confused everything; downhill looked the same on both sides of the ridge.

She followed Pathka's tongue-flame like a will-o'-the-wisp, through stands of trees, around boulders, as fast as she could go without falling. She thought she heard Reg and Rowan, far away, screaming. She hoped they'd run down the wrong side of the ridge, gotten separated, or maybe fallen off a cliff.

At the bottom of the hill spread a field of cabbages, as the innkeeper had described. Tess's feet churned mud as she ran, black clods flying. She kicked cabbages right off their stems but managed not to slide and fall. The thunder and lightning moved farther up the ridge; she heard Griss shouting, "Watch the sky, Annie!"

The promised village, Muddle-on-the-Fussy, came into view whenever it lightened, bulky thatched cottages, and there, by the river, a wide complex with a Saint at the apex of the roof. Tess reached the courtyard gate, set Griss on the stoop, and knocked with everything she had, hoping they could hear her over the storm.

"I'll wait here," said Pathka from a nearby yew bush. "They won't want me inside."

Before Tess could argue, the gate opened and out came a novice, her yellow habit eerie in the torchlight. "Mercy on a wet night," she said, holding the door for Tess and Griss, not even asking their business. No one knocked on a night like this unless it was an emergency.

A quarter of an hour later, they were in the hospice hall, a long room with eight beds, three occupied. Griss, bundled in quilts before the hearth, shivered and whimpered as a second novice spooned soup into his mouth. The young ones had night duty, apparently. The one who'd let them in questioned Tess about Griss's condition and origins; Tess felt chagrined at how little she knew. "He's no family of mine; he might be from Trowebridge. I don't know how old he is. His name may or may not actually be Griss," she said. And she told them, more than once, "There are two men after him. You mustn't let them take him. They tie him up at night, and I think they're going to kill him when he turns out not to be rich."

"You don't believe he's rich?" said a sharp, surprisingly familiar voice from across the infirmary. Tess turned to see a stout, older nun passing between the rows of beds. The room was nearly dark, but the woman's shape and bearing confirmed Tess's recognition: this was Mother Philomela, whom she'd seen with her father in Trowebridge.

There are moments that bring into question one's free will, and whether the world doesn't have some sentience behind it, trying to send a message. This was such a moment for Tess.

They'd never met face-to-face, and Tess looked very different now, but still she clambered to her feet, extended her hand, and said, "I'm Jacomo," as if she might preempt the possibility of recognition by giving the woman an assumed name.

The old Mother Superior ignored Tess, approached Griss, and felt his forehead. "Are you wealthy, venerable Father? Will you be leaving us an endowment?"

"I've nothing," he said hoarsely. "Nothing is worth having since I killed Annie."

He told a garbled version of his story. It was his fault Annie was dead; he'd sent her to her doom. He'd wanted to teach Johnny a lesson, see, but no matter how much you wanted to do right in this world, the world would find a way to crush you.

Mother Philomela neither confirmed nor refuted this hypothesis, but smoothed his hair out of his eyes, took his pulse, listened to his lungs—which she pronounced very bad—and instructed the novices to give him as much soup as he would eat.

Tess plucked at the nun's yellow sleeve as she walked past. "Two ruffians, Reg and Rowan, want to take him away, but don't let them. He doesn't deserve that fate."

"I agree he does not," said the nun sternly. "It's curious, though: he's indisputably one of Heaven's innocents, and yet so bursting with guilt that he confesses his sins to every passerby."

Griss looked as innocent as an openmouthed chick, awaiting the next spoonful of soup.

Mother Philomela went to an occupied bed to check the bedpan. "Tell me something, boy," she called over her shoulder to Tess, who hadn't followed her. "He's not your father or grandfather, but you risked your safety to bring him here on such a night, with dangerous men pursuing. What drove you to help? Guilt? Pity? Something else?"

Tess considered, averting her eyes from the messy business Mother Philomela was now engaged in, cleaning up her elderly patient. "He reminds me of my grandmother," offered Tess.

"Love, then?" said the old nun, tucking the quilt back around her patient, who quietly thanked her. She patted his frail hand and carried the slops to the next bed. "Love is a worthy motivation, although you see how quickly it can sour into guilt. He loved his sister, after all."

Jeanne involuntarily, painfully, leaped to Tess's mind. Will wasn't far behind. "Are they really separate things?" Tess asked, glancing up. "I can't seem to tease love and guilt apart."

"You've been thinking about it," said Philomela, sounding pleased and surprised. She busied herself with the next patient, an old woman. "You'd never guess, but hospice is an excellent place for thinking while your hands, almost incidentally, do good. I'll tell you this: love and guilt are like ham and eggs. So many people enjoy them together, but there's no rule saying you must have one with the other. They don't even come from the same animal."

She emptied another pan. "Here's an analogy I like: guilt is a runaway wagon down the mountainside. It may carry you a long way, but it usually ends in disaster. Love, on the other hand, is much slower—just your own two feet, really," she said, casting a meaningful look at Tess. "But it's more likely to take you somewhere worth going."

Tess had never met anyone who talked like this, all up on the abstract plane, and she didn't know quite how to respond. "I do like walking," she said at last, limply.

"You've got good boots for it," said the nun, bustling over to the last patient.

Tess smiled wryly. "And callused feet. Walking the road gives you time to think, too."

"I could tell you were a philosopher," Philomela said warmly. "Let's hear what you've come up with, then."

"*Walk on,*" said Tess, feeling unexpectedly shy as she said it, as if she were showing the sister the inside of her heart.

Philomela was silent as she emptied the pan, then said, "What, that's it?"

"It's harder than it sounds," said Tess, folding her arms. "Whenever I start feeling like I want to . . . like I'm not going to make it, I decide to walk on until tomorrow, at least, and—"

"And then you do it, eh?" said the old nun. "Sounds a bit like running away."

"No!" cried Tess, stung. "It's the opposite of running away."

"Running toward?" said the nun, hefting the slops bucket. She gestured toward a double door with her head; Tess opened it. Outside, in the courtyard, rain spattered noisily. Mother Philomela left the bucket under an overhang and shut the door again. "I'm not saying don't run—or walk, as you say—only that it sounds incomplete, as a life's philosophy. I meant to prompt you to think further." She dried her hands on her apron. "What do you do when you get there?"

"You don't *get there,*" Tess said, growing crabbier. "You're on the Road, and the Road goes ever on and on." Tess felt herself capitalize *Road,* as if it were a person; she hadn't realized she felt this way until she said it aloud.

"Now we're getting somewhere. We're all on this road, met-aphorically," said the old nun, returning to the hearth. "This is our lot. Is that what you're getting at? And one must choose to walk on, rather than petulantly sitting on one's rump and pouting?"

Why did it sound stupid from Mother Philomela's mouth when it had felt so profound while she was walking? "I guess," said Tess, who was beginning to pout, and almost certainly would have sat down petulantly if there'd been a chair available.

"It's a start," said the old woman, washing her hands in a basin near the fire. "Tell me something, though: is walking the only virtue in your philosophical system? What if someone decided to stay in one place and not walk on—on purpose? Would that be bad?"

Tess considered. "I have been walking, literally walking, for two months, and I feel . . . *right* when I do. My mind is clear; the world makes sense. Walking is a good in itself."

"Of course it is," said Philomela brusquely, "but it's not the only good. Since we're being literal now, have you felt clear and sensible at other times during your travels?"

The question startled Tess into thinking. "While turning hay. Swimming in the river, crawling through caves . . . once I was lying under a cattle guard, eating bread, and the sky was blue and there was a bee—" She cut off, embarrassed. It was hard to explain about the bee.

"Right," said Mother Philomela firmly. "Working, swimming, eating. Walking."

Tess blinked, unsure what she was getting at.

"You feel whole when you're doing things, Jacomo. When you're in your body," said the nun slowly, as if Tess were stupid. "The mind may hare off in all directions, but truth is centered in the body, ultimately."

The body sounded like a corpse at a funeral. "The body, as in . . . the wellspring of sin? The author of excess and misery? That body?" Tess said, trying to plumb the nun's meaning.

"Don't quote me St. Vitt," snapped Philomela, her face like

a bulldog's. "That is *not* what I mean. We don't subscribe to his contemptuous credos here."

"'The flesh is but a sack of goo'?" Tess sang badly, batting her eyes.

The nun raised her jowly chin. "*Goo* is a description, not a judgment. How could I do this work"—she encompassed the ward in a broad gesture—"if I held the body in contempt? Our sisters are midwives, too, you know." Tess did know. "We usher bodies into this world, and we usher bodies out. As your aged friend here so poignantly reminds us, the mind goes. The soul . . . who can say what it is or where it's located? In the end, often as not, our bodies are all we are."

Tess's chest felt suddenly very tight under her jerkin.

"I would guess, based on your knee-jerk quotations, that you were raised to despise the flesh and all its fleshly doings. So tell me, young gentleman," said Philomela, putting a light emphasis, not quite sarcastic, on *gentleman*, "in your philosophical estimation—or in St. Vitt's—is the body born evil, or does it do evil for the sheer anarchic joy of it?"

Tess went cold. Philomela was quoting her father. She'd seen through Tess, deduced who she must be. She shouldn't have sung that snatch of song. "Born evil," said Tess, heart pounding. "St. Vitt says explicitly that the female—"

"Wrong," snapped the old nun, her sharp green eyes taking in every nuance of Tess's reaction. "First, I gave you two choices as a test: there are never just two choices. That is a lie to keep you from thinking too deeply. Second, and more important: the body is innocent. Deeply, beautifully, fundamentally innocent."

"That isn't true," Tess half whispered. "Every one of

Philomela's words was a knife, prodding a deep, unhealed wound.

"Third," said the sister, as if Tess hadn't spoken, "consider children, who merely follow their natures. They may be born difficult or contrary, but never evil. The ones who enjoy misbehaving can be taught better. Too many, alas, have parents who hold them in contempt."

Tess trembled so hard her teeth chattered.

"So it is with the body," said the nun, eyes narrowing fiercely. "The hated innocent becomes hateful. Goodness withers when it is continuously ground underfoot. We fulfill our parents' direst prophecies, then curl around our own pain until we can't see beyond ourselves. You want to walk on? Walk out of that shadow. Walk, girl."

Tess wrestled back tears.

"I saw what they thought of you," said Mother Philomela, her voice gentling. "I rejoiced that you'd struck out on your own, but you've a long way to go still. Your kindness toward this one, when you needn't have troubled yourself"—she gestured at Griss—"shows me the true heart of you. Your credo goes further than you realized: walk on, yes, but don't walk past people who need you. Uncurl yourself so you can see them and respond."

Tess was too distraught to take everything in. The words bounced off her like a stone skipping over the surface of a lake.

A stone may skip a long way, but it always sinks eventually.

"How did you know who I was?" said Tess when she could speak.

"I wasn't sure until you confirmed it, but it seemed possible," said Philomela. "Your case stuck with me. Your parents, when they learned you'd gone, were like characters in a bad play, overacted and overwrought. They were embarrassed to have brought me out for nothing. It didn't have to be for nothing; I might've counseled them on handling the loss of you, or how to improve themselves for your eventual return. They weren't interested. Underneath the huffing and puffing, I suspect they were relieved."

This made Tess feel no better. "What about my sister? Not Seraphina, but—"

"Your twin?" Old Philomela's memory hadn't dulled a bit. "I met her, and her softhearted husband. I won't lie: you cut her. She's got walking and uncurling of her own to do, and without the boots and stubbornness. She'll find her way. If she can't, it isn't your fault."

Tess felt cut herself; a lukewarm wash of guilt made it sting. "But how did you come to be all the way out here?" she asked, feeling about for a less painful subject.

Mother Philomela laughed. "Would you believe, your departure got me thinking. I've never gone far afield myself, and I haven't many years left. I'm on a farewell tour to as many hospices as I can reach upon my own ass." Her eyes twinkled; Tess remembered her donkey. "Three down, and I feel hale as a cowherd. I may get all the way to Samsam before I'm done."

Mother Philomela turned to Griss and laid hands upon his woolly head. "As for you, old friend: Annie chose that hilltop," she said. "The dragon was an unlucky happenstance. You didn't kill her. You each wanted to do right, and it all went wrong."

"Wait, you knew his story?" said Tess. "It happened the way he said?"

"More or less," said the old nun sadly. "I was born and raised in Trowebridge. Everyone of my generation knew the tale. It became a popular ballad." She began to sing:

Then Johnny ran off, ne'er did repent,
And left his brother's poor heart rent,
Left him there to rant and rave
At Annie's nonexistent grave.

Griss perked up at the sound of her singing and joined in:

The years roll on, the worms fly by,
Our Annie's tomb is in the sky.

Mother Philomela smiled wanly. "When the rest of the mind has fled, sometimes there's music left. We'll take care of him, daughter. But what do you intend to do next?"

Tess glanced back. Rain still drummed on the roof, but the outlines of the windows were becoming visible; behind a quilt of clouds, the sun was rising. "It almost feels like a sign from Heaven, finding you here," she said. "I almost feel like I should stay."

"Almost isn't good enough," said Philomela. "Just like guilt isn't good enough."

She was right, and Tess felt a weight come off her heart. She threw her arms around Griss and held him a moment. He smelled terrible, but Tess, friend to quigutl, didn't mind such things. "You'll be safe here," she said, "away from Wreck and Ruin. I'll miss you, though."

Griss was weeping. "Oh, Annie, goodbye," he sobbed. "I never said goodbye."

"You just did. Goodbye, old love," said Tess. She kissed his forehead, wiped her eyes, and was ready to go. The novices resumed spooning soup (the old man was a bottomless hole). Mother Philomela led Tess out to the courtyard, through drizzle and gloam, toward the front gates. It was still noisy outside, even though the thunder had ceased.

"You could stay and rest until the sun's properly up," said the nun, slowing her steps.

"Thank you, but I have promises to keep," said Tess, although the noise was beginning to concern her as well. It had begun as thuds and clatters, but now there was shouting and snarling.

Mother Philomela detoured to one side of the courtyard and knocked on a door. "Sister Mishell," she said, her voice light and calm, "ring the bell. Now, please." Philomela gestured for Tess to keep still. A bright bell tolled, whereupon Mother Philomela took up a rusty fire poker that had been left near the gates, unbarred the doors, and swung them slowly inward.

At the gates of the hospice, Reg and Rowan battled two quigutl. The first quigutl leaped at Reg and got a frying pan to the face. It sprawled out cold on the ground. The second quigutl dodged left, feinted right, and then clamped its jaws upon Rowan's meaty thigh.

His scream tore the air like lightning.

Sixteen

It was Pathka who'd fallen to the ground.

Tess fell to her knees in the mud beside him, scrabbling for the hot pulse at his throat, praying to every Saint she knew (except her sister) that he wasn't dead. He shuddered and then took an enormous breath, but his eyes didn't focus. His throat pouch had a three-inch gash in it that bled copiously.

Tess shielded him with her body from the mayhem that continued on all sides. Reg was shouting obscenities, Philomela was brandishing her poker, and Rowan was screaming incoherently. Then villagers descended in a flock, summoned by the bell, waving hay forks.

Mother Philomela ordered the villagers to seize Reg and haul him to the stocks, crying, "I will see him later, and he will be sorry to see me." She approached Rowan cautiously, as if he were a roaring, thrashing bear with a quigutl clamped to his thigh. "Be still, or I'll have to knock you out," she said in a voice of unassailable authority. Rowan struggled to hold his roar to a whimper and his thrashing to a violent shudder.

"Little neighbor," Mother Philomela said to the second quigutl, "if you release your grip, will his femoral artery gush and kill him? Hang on, if so."

The quigutl carefully opened her mouth and moved away, leaving Rowan's leg in the grip of a steel contraption, a set of false jaws as strong and spiky as a wolf trap.

"Teth," said Kikiu, "tell her that he will bleed out as soon as anyone unclamps him."

"What is that thing?" cried Tess. "And what are *you* doing here?"

"Bite enhancer," said Kikiu mildly, as if it were not some heinous contraption of death. She drew nearer and pressed her hollow tongue to each of Pathka's eyes, checking some unknown quigutl vital sign. "And my story can wait. My mother-*utl* needs care most urgently."

Nuns bundled Pathka and Rowan onto portable cots and fetched them into the hospice. Tess helped as she could, keeping one eye on Kikiu. Why would the hatchling have come back with a steel trap in her mouth unless she intended to bite Pathka again?

Kikiu, as if she could read Tess's suspicions, cocked her head spines sarcastically and gave Tess a *fthep* around the knees with her tail as she turned to follow the nuns inside.

The sisters specialized in palliative care, but they knew their way around surgery. Rowan was easy; they had him stitched and locked up with his companion in the village pillory by the end of the day. "Conspiring to commit violence against nuns" was the official charge. Reg and Rowan would be tried at the local lord's convenience; the entire village of Muddle-on-the-Fussy was ready and eager to testify.

Pathka required more extensive interventions. In addition to his throat pouch perforation, he had a concussion and a dislocated dorsal arm. "It could be weeks before he can travel," said Philomela, never one to honey-coat things. "But you're welcome to stay until he's fit."

Thus Tess ended up staying among the nuns longer than anticipated. She didn't begrudge it, and unexpectedly she wasn't bored. She explored Muddle-on-the-Fussy, the nearby fields and hills, the black raspberry patches along the river. She told stories to Griss and the other hospice patients. It had been a long time since she'd stayed in one place with enough to eat and no urgency to get anywhere. Apparently she'd needed rest as well.

Tess felt some guilt over Pathka's injuries. Following Reg and Rowan, getting Griss to safety, had been entirely her project; Pathka had participated reluctantly and paid a heavy price. She needed to make it up to him. If she could locate a large cavern in the vicinity, Pathka might finally be able to do his *kemthikemthlutl*, to dream with Anathuthia and call to her.

Tess asked around. If there were large caves nearby, there would be stories. Surely cows sometimes fell down them, or young lovers got lost. Nuns and villagers alike gave the same answer: she should try Big Spooky, a cave so enormous it had swallowed an entire castle.

She told Pathka about the cave after he'd been in the infirmary a couple of weeks; he still seemed to be in a lot of pain, and she thought he could use the encouragement. "It's only a couple of miles away," Tess told him. She'd nearly said *an hour's walk,* but she wasn't sure how quickly he'd be walking, or how soon.

Pathka, curled in the nest of quilts the nuns had made him, didn't respond.

"You still haven't found your subterranean monster?" sneered Kikiu, who was just sauntering in from wherever she slept at night.

Kikiu was still here after two weeks, leaving Pathka's side only to sleep. Tess had eyed the hatchling with skepticism at first, unsure what Kikiu intended, but the youngster had made no threatening move. The nuns had locked the bite enhancer in a strongbox, which eased Tess's mind considerably.

Pathka raised his head for Kikiu, at least. "Did you get it?" he rasped. The hole in his throat made it difficult to speak.

Kikiu bent over Pathka and bared her teeth. They glistened coldly.

"Don't you dare!" cried Tess, almost before she understood what she was seeing.

Kikiu was wearing the bite enhancer.

The young quigutl swiveled her eye cones, looking shifty, but Pathka interjected, "It's all right. I asked *ko* to . . . show me. Wanted to . . . understand."

"Those teeth were under lock and key," said Tess, still not trusting this.

"Not a very sturdy lock," said Kikiu slyly. She turned back to Pathka and opened her nightmarish jaws, letting her mother examine them from different angles. "I gave them good shear strength," she said. "They're fast-snapping. Won't rust or jam."

Pathka held out a cautious finger; Kikiu held still and let him touch the jagged steel.

Tess squirmed, and yet she had no reason, surely. They seemed to be getting along.

"I did what you said," said Kikiu quietly. "You were right about Trowebridge. It was a false nest. I couldn't go back."

"What *I* said?" said Pathka with effort. "Seeking your true nature?"

Kikiu nodded eagerly. "I think you'd approve of how I've been living. No money, no—"

"If that's true," hissed Pathka viciously, arching his back, "then why the . . . enhancer? You're . . . making yourself *unnatural.*"

Kikiu recoiled from Pathka's ferocity, looking so abashed and awkward that Tess couldn't help feeling sorry for the hatchling.

"Why did you really . . . come back?" Pathka roared, his pouch perforation adding an extra whistling wheeze to his utterance.

"Where else was I to go?" said Kikiu hotly.

"But how . . . did you find me?" wheezed Pathka.

Kikiu looked away, avoiding his gaze, mumbling something Tess couldn't hear.

"That's not it," said Pathka. "You knew . . . where I was."

Pathka lunged fiercely, without warning, and bit the front of Kikiu's face, her whole muzzle, nose and mouth, so she couldn't speak or breathe. Kikiu thrashed and tried to pull away, eyes rolling in panic. They writhed together on the floor, Pathka heedless of his open wounds, Kikiu flailing with the frenzied energy of someone who believed this might be her last struggle.

"Pathka, stop!" cried Tess in absolute horror. She picked up the stool she'd been sitting on and bashed him over the head with it.

Pathka let go.

"Are you mad?" screamed Kikiu, scuttling backward toward the wall, away from Pathka.

"There," said Pathka, panting with agony. He'd torn his throat pouch afresh, and it was oozing. "I needed . . . one more. *Fatluketh* didn't work . . . we were still bound. Finally . . . free."

Kikiu's snout was bleeding. She could have lunged at Pathka with her metal jaws—Tess feared as much—but instead Kikiu said bitterly, "We still won't be free. You'll see. There's something wrong between us, and always has been."

Kikiu bolted toward the door. Tess looked frantically at Pathka, appalled by what had just happened, but Pathka made no move to go after Kikiu.

Tess knew quigutl bit each other, and that it looked crueler than it was, but this was different. Kikiu's reaction told her that much, and the fact that Pathka could have killed the hatchling.

She wasn't sure he would've let go if she hadn't brained him with the stool.

Tess dashed after Kikiu into the courtyard. The front gates were shut; Kikiu had climbed to the top and was ready to leap down. When Tess cried, "Wait!" Kikiu paused, spines flattened like a chastened dog's.

"Pathka isn't himself," said Tess, jogging up to the gate. "He's still hurt. He's not thinking clearly. I know him, and this is not like him, and I'm sure he couldn't have meant to—" Tess paused to catch her breath, and to wonder at the litany of unsolicited excuses she was making for Pathka's violence. At last she said weakly, "Are you all right?"

"I have never been all right," said Kikiu evenly. "I came here hoping *ko* would be proud of me, if you can believe it. I am making my own way through the wilderness, through my own nightmares. But what good does it do? *Ko* isn't interested in the slightest."

"Nightmares?" said Tess, a spark of hope blossoming. "You're dreaming, without your nestmates around you. Have you dreamed of the serpent? Tell Pathka that. I think he'd—"

"Give me another wrongful bite?" said Kikiu, peering down at Tess like a cat in a tree. "Hear this, human: I have always dreamed, even back in Trowebridge. I worked so hard to make my place there, to follow the rules and fit in there. And still I dreamed, even with my brethren piled around me, as if I were old and senile. I was so ashamed.

"Then Pathka had that dream—that *call*—and bragged about it, as if it were a miracle and not proof that *ko*, too, was irretrievably alone."

"But then that's something you've got in common," said Tess. Surely this was a misunderstanding. Pathka couldn't have meant to be cruel, wouldn't have been if he had known. "Come back and talk to him. You can still be nest to each other."

"We have never been nest," said Kikiu. "And never will be."

"If you're dreaming of the serpent, then you're called," said Tess, pleading now. "You belong with us, searching for the Most Alone."

"*I* am the most alone," hissed Kikiu. "Exactly as my mother made me."

With a serpentine tail ripple, Kikiu twisted around and leaped from the gates, out of the hospice, and away.

Tess stared at the spot where Kikiu had been. "Mother" had hit her like a slap, and she finally saw what had been there all along: Pathka, her best friend in the world, had been a wholly inadequate parent.

Kikiu, conceived in violence, whose birth almost killed Pathka, would have been eaten if Tess hadn't put a stop to it. Pathka hadn't wanted Kikiu, or loved her, or been nest to her. Tess didn't know what was considered good quigutl parenting, but if Kikiu had been so alone that she was dreaming, Pathka couldn't have been doing his job.

It was completely understandable, and it was a heartbreaking shame.

Tess stumbled back indoors, stricken with a kind of vertigo, wondering whether there was anything she could do.

Pathka's impatience to get going outstripped the speed of his healing, and they set off for Big Spooky four days later, on a warm, clear morning, before he was really ready to travel.

The two miles took half a day because they stopped

whenever Pathka's breathing grew too labored. Tess had brought all her gear, plus rations the nuns had kindly packed, hoping not to go back to the hospice, but Pathka crept so slowly that she began to regret not staying another week. It was midafternoon by the time they spotted the ruins on the ridge.

The denizens of Muddle-on-the-Fussy, who had a special talent for naming things, called the shattered keep Old Haunty. It looked like a collapsed soufflé, crumpled in on itself, sunken and shrunken down through the middle. The stone walls bowed and bulged dangerously. Vines snaked over the walls, and saplings grew in the crevices of the ruined battlements. The caverns beneath the castle had collapsed a century ago.

Had the castle's people had any warning, or had they suddenly fallen down a hole and died? There might still be bones in the caverns, or treasure. Tess felt a vestigial piratical twinge.

Big Spooky's most accessible entrance, the nuns had insisted, was south of the keep, a fifty-foot pit lined with vegetation. It was a hard climb down for Tess, even with rocks and vines to hold on to, which made her wonder about these nuns. They must be tough as goats.

Pathka, even injured, outclimbed Tess. He was already preparing a torch for her by the time she reached the bottom of the pit, aching, scratched up, and proud of herself.

"Finished these . . . the night of the storm," said Pathka in the harsh, sore whisper his voice had become. He gingerly drew from his throat a pair of what looked like large cockroaches. They were thniks, roughly moon-shaped; Tess had mistaken untidy wires for legs. "Only hands and tongue. No tools," Pathka rasped, amazed at himself.

Tess stowed her bug—she still found it insectoid—down the front of her jerkin. Pathka lit the torch, and together they descended into humid, chilly darkness.

These were caves on a different scale than they'd encountered before; they walked for hours. Pathka chose large passageways, looking for someplace deep and majestic enough to perform his calling. He'd know it when he saw it, he insisted. They found a vast lake, which horrified and fascinated Tess, and discovered rooms full of crystalline wonders: frozen waterfalls, gypsum snowballs, pale needles of stone. Nothing suited Pathka.

They reached a chamber like the nave of a cathedral, its ceiling and walls far beyond the torch's reach. An enormous flat rock, like a dais, lay near the center; it had fallen from the unseen ceiling an age ago.

"Here," Pathka said approvingly. "Help me, Teth." He paused, hand to his throat, until the pain passed.

"Of course," said Tess warmly, wedging the torch between two rocks so she could have her hands free. "What do you need?"

"Pierce my artery," said Pathka, pointing out a tender spot under his arm. "Collect blood. Sprinkle around while I sleep."

Caves, it turns out, are incredibly quiet when you're too stunned to speak.

"Use your knife," said Pathka gently, as to a frightened child. "Your skillet. I can do the . . . stabbing, if it's too hard." His throat pouch quivered as he spoke.

The stabbing was one place Tess had snagged, certainly, but not the only place. It was too grotesque to fill the skillet with blood, as if she meant to boil it down for quigutl black pudding. What else did she have to catch blood in? Her water skin was in use. The nuns had sent a jar of sauerkraut. She couldn't possibly eat it quickly enough.

She glanced around in frustration and noticed two odd whitish stones a ways off. They were identical, curved like shallow bowls, roughly the shape of a fingernail and the size of two cupped hands. She'd never heard of such formations in any geology lecture.

They'd hold a good dribble of blood, though.

"Teth!" cried Pathka. "Now. Quick."

He was already bleeding. Tess grabbed the bowl-stones, one in each hand, and moved them to catch the silver blood. "What are those?" Pathka cried, his arm gushing.

Tess examined the bowl-stones anew. They didn't feel like stone, in fact. They were too light in her hands, milky and translucent and . . . flexible? A little? "They feel like fingernails, honestly," she said, feeling foolish about this observation.

Pathka, with some difficulty, reached his non-bleeding arm across his body and touched the rim of one of the bowls. "Ohhh," he sighed. "Teth, you're right . . . that was . . . living matter."

"A shell?" she asked, because the only other living matter she could think of that was this shape was too strange. It couldn't be. The bowls were too small.

"Anathuthia," gasped Pathka as if the name took everything he had.

"A shed scale?" There was no way this had come from a great serpent. "It's too small."

"She's been young . . . many times. Renews herself . . . parthenogenesis. Must've passed this way . . . long ago."

Tess didn't know the word *parthenogenesis*—in Quootla or Goreddi—but she knew when her friend was suffering. "Is this enough?" she said, swirling blood in both bowls.

"Probably. It's all a guess," said Pathka. He seared the wound with his flaming tongue and then flopped back against the flat stone, exhausted. "Wait until I'm asleep."

"Do I pour it on or around you?" asked Tess, trying not to sound appalled.

"Try both," he said faintly. "Listen to your instinct. Do what seems right. Intention is more important . . . than details. Probably."

Tess sat carefully, a bowl—scale?—full of blood in each hand, and waited, listening for his snores. They came like a trickle, then a roar.

Before she'd made up her mind to start pouring Pathka's blood, it began to glow. The bowls in her hands glowed pale blue. All around the cavern other blue orbs shone, like a hundred moons reflected in a lake, breathtakingly beautiful. The chamber was full of these . . . scales?

Pathka had surely guessed right. What besides World Serpent scales would glow in sympathy with a quigutl's dreaming? Tess, remembering her task, rose awkwardly and circled Pathka's stone, dribbling blood around him. Every spatter made a constellation.

She flicked the last drops across his body, and Pathka, too, began to glow.

Tess sank to her knees just as the torch sputtered out. The pale blue light of a hundred shining scales suffused everything and was enough. It ebbed and flowed over Pathka like the

Southern Lights, flaring upon his throat pouch, his dorsal arm, his skull.

Before her eyes, the hole in his throat closed up.

Tess watched, mesmerized. Then the light began to fade, so slowly that Tess couldn't tell if the glow still lingered or if it was an afterimage on her eyelids.

Finally the darkness was total. Pathka stopped snoring, and the silence was total as well.

For a moment Tess imagined she didn't exist. It was surprisingly soothing.

"Teth Teth *Teth*!" Pathka cried, just beside her. "We did it! I dreamed with her! She's expecting us now. I can hardly believe it worked—"

The stream of enthusiasm was forestalled, momentarily, by the sound of Pathka vomiting.

His voice sounded stronger. "Are you all right? I can't see," said Tess, feeling around.

Pathka reignited the torch and vomited once more. Tess saw what his voice had made her hope: his throat was whole again. She knelt beside him and held up a tentative hand; Pathka stilled himself and let her touch his skin, his arm, the dome of his head, every place that had glowed with extra brilliance. He was whole all over.

Will had hypothesized that the serpents could heal—pagan and Pelaguese myths hinted as much—but seeing the evidence was still a shock. "How is this possible?" Tess said, stroking Pathka's scarred flesh. "This wasn't some kind of ... of supernatural—"

"No, friend," said Pathka gently. "If it exists in nature, it is natural, not *thupernatural*. The world is different than you thought, maybe. We quigutl *are* the serpents, Tess, made from their dreams and bones, and they are us. They sent us after the great dragons, to bring them back, but we never made it home. I don't know why. We forgot who we were, and I suspect the serpents forgot us. What do you call that thing you do to remind your Thaints that you exist? You say special words, like waving a flag for them to find you."

"Prayer?" said Tess. "This was a prayer to Anathuthia?"

"I am the *prayer*," said Pathka, repeating the Goreddi word. "To the Most Alone, from my people."

This was the Pathka she loved, full of myth and wisdom and enthusiasm. The serpent had restored not just his body but his spirit as well.

If ever there was a time to bring up Kikiu—that other most alone—it was surely now. Kikiu was suffering, had suffered for years; Pathka would care, if only he could be made to see it.

"Kikiu told me something before she left," said Tess. "Did you know she dreams?"

"On the road? Of course," said Pathka. "Without the nest to mute them—"

"No, no. It started back in Trowebridge," said Tess, "before yours did. She was ashamed to tell anyone. She thought it just showed how misplaced and disconnected she was."

Pathka stared at Tess hard, saying nothing.

"I thought you should know," Tess persisted. "You have this quirk in common. If you reached out to her, the dreams could be a bridge between you, a way of being nest to—"

"I was *called*," Pathka snapped. "I'm the one who's been

alone, ever since Karpeth died. I'm the one who's lived in pain. Kikiu has nothing to complain about."

It was an unsympathetic, waspish reply, like something Mama might have said. Her acute suffering—real suffering, Tess couldn't pretend otherwise—had always blinded her to everyone else's.

Tess could tell by the set of his spines that there was no discussing this now.

"We must keep walking south," said Pathka sourly. His tail was twitching side to side with barely concealed anger. "Anathuthia says the world will bring us to her, and I have faith that it will. I'm called to find her."

Tess swallowed her disappointment and shoved the bowl-scales into her pack, in case they were needed again. Pathka led her in irritated silence through the maze of caverns, toward some distant egress that only he could discern.

Seventeen

They emerged on the other side of the ridge, which put them, according to the nuns, a couple of miles from the Ninysh border. Now that Pathka was healed, they made good time.

Borders are curiously fluid over centuries. Like a river carving a wide valley, this border had rampaged all over, however docile it might look in its present channel.

A Goreddi castle guarded the boundary these days. In times of Ninysh ascendance, when the border had passed farther north, the fortress had been called Palasho du Mornay, but now it was plain old Castle Morney. Tess spied it in the distance, a crusty wart on a hillside; the road led around it to the west. She would know she was in Ninys, land of her mother's people, when she had to look over her shoulder to see the battlements.

This was a milestone worth taking note of, and not merely because she'd have to shine up her rusty Ninysh to communicate. Crossing an international border—upon the solstice, no less—felt like an accomplishment. She'd walked a long, stubborn way, without stopping, chickening out, giving up, or needing anyone's help. She was a child of the Road.

"We should celebrate," Tess said to Pathka's shadow in the tall grass. "There's a village in the valley under the castle, looks like. Let's stop for a proper meal."

The words were out before she'd thought it through: Pathka couldn't eat in a public house. "Just bring me out some cheese," he said, cutting off her apology.

He was still cross with her. It wasn't like him to stay annoyed; Tess had really stepped on his tail, bringing up Kikiu, and she didn't know how to fix it.

And she couldn't apologize. That much she felt sure of.

The village, made up of fewer than a hundred households, was a two-church, four-tavern affair and, Tess quickly learned, bilingual. That explained the doubles. This close to the ebb and flow of the border, everyone would be jumbled together yet fiercely separate. Judging the inns by their names, Tess settled on Do Flaquette, a Ninysh establishment with pancakes painted on the sign. Her Belgioso aunties made glorious pancakes; Tess had hopes.

The tapmaster hailed her, and she understood him perfectly—"What will it be, my bravo?"—but was hard-pressed to dredge up an answer from the reluctant sludge of memory.

Mama spoke Ninysh with her aunties all the time, so Tess

had considered herself decent at it. Understanding was simpler than finding the right words and stringing them together, however. "I, er . . . give at me the pancake and the cheese and the . . . not the beet. Not the bee. *St. Daan in a pan, I know this!*"

She'd uttered that last phrase in frustrated Goreddi. The room fell silent; heads turned toward her. "*That* language, *here?*" somebody called. "Do you need me to punch you, Puco?"

"Hush," said the barkeep, glaring at this rude patron. "He's clearly from the uncouth north and has no idea what he's doing. Ferdono, lead him to one of the Goreddi bars."

"Aw," said Ferdono, a freckled scullion, drying a glass. "Can't I put him with the horses? His money's still good."

"Make it quick," cried someone else. "Every word is an earturd, stinking up the room."

Tess, who'd begun in embarrassment, now faced her detractors indignantly, hands on her hips. She could not have said where the words came from—maybe Aunt Mimi—but they'd clearly been stored up a long time, fermenting. "Foul-mouthed child!" she cried. "The devil's in your eyes, but I'll beat you till he comes out your nose. Think I won't?"

There was a shocked silence as thirty patrons tried to figure out where on earth Tess could have come from. "Eh, he'll do," said a big man beside her at the counter. "A little mad, perhaps. What do you call yourself, bravo?"

Tess archly gave the Ninysh name Kenneth had bestowed upon her: "Tes'puco."

A titter went up, and then another, and then an avalanche of laughter swept the room clean of all resentments, and Tess was proclaimed a "child of Heaven." She sensed that this wasn't a compliment, but if they'd decided to let her be, she couldn't complain.

"Friend, what is it called, this drink?" asked Tess, plucking at the big man's sleeve.

"Beer," he said, lifting his mug so she could see inside. "You've spent more time in deep Goredd than is good for you. We don't make it with bees or beets here in Afale."

Tess, unexpectedly, felt like she'd been slapped. "Forgive me," she said, fighting a tremor in her voice. "What did you call it, the name of this village?"

"A-fa-le," he said, enunciating exaggeratedly. The final vowel was a light schwa after a languid el, just enough to sound slightly different from the Goreddi version of the name.

But not so different as all that.

Tess had arrived in Affle, Will's hometown.

And then—the next thing she was aware of—she was outside Affle, beyond it, laboring up a hill. The last rays of daylight cut across her path, staining it orange.

She paused, breathing hard, and looked back. Will's village nestled into the valley. All was calm; nobody had followed her. Had she stormed out of the tavern? Slunk? Run, clutching her stomach?

She sat heavily in the dirt, stunned. Broad leaves rustled beside her, and then Pathka crawled out of the underbrush. He let her finish crying—or let her face finish, anyway; it had begun without permission. Tess barely noticed until she had to blow her nose.

Her body had been making decisions on its own, again.

"What is it, Tethie?" Pathka was saying. His irritation

seemed to have been swept away by concern for her. "Are you sad? Angry? Sick?"

"Are you checking off a list?" said Tess, trying to joke but only managing to sound bitter.

"Yes," said Pathka. "You're wearing a negative face I haven't seen before, so I'm trying to narrow down what it might be."

Indeed, what was it? Something akin to panic. Realizing she was in Will's village (she peeked again; it was still there) had rent her mind from body, right in two. All she'd done to put herself together—walking, swimming, hay turning—undone in a lightning strike of fear.

She owed Pathka an explanation. "That's Will's village. I— It took me by surprise."

It had reminded her that Will still existed. He was somewhere in the world. He was real.

It was a frightening thought.

"You never talk about him," said Pathka. It wasn't a question (Quootla made questions clear with an interrogative particle), but Tess felt a dozen questions pressing behind it.

"I don't want to talk about him," said Tess. "I don't want to remember those days."

She'd crammed every memory into darkness, the oubliette of her mind's dungeon. It did no good. The past was never really past if being in Affle could bring it all rushing back.

Pathka laid his head on her lap, and they sat like a parody of a unicorn tapestry. "Did you *thluff* him?" asked Pathka, using the Goreddi word *love*. "You humans prefer to *thluff* your mates."

"As opposed to what?" asked Tess.

"Answering the call of the pheromones," said Pathka breezily, as if it were nothing. "They call, we pile on. It's fairly uncomplicated."

"No," said Tess, appalled. "It's not like that at all."

She was lying, though, a little bit. She swatted that thought away as if it stung her.

And then she told Pathka a story.

⚔

Her most vivid, shining, Will-ful memory was the evening they'd tried to steal Spira's notes.

Tess had been sneaking out of the house for about a month at that point. Kenneth had quickly gotten serious about Lord Rynald, so it was Will who met her at the shrine of St. Siucre, and Will who walked her back again at the end of the night. He sneaked her into lectures and the faculty library, introduced her to scholarly luminaries, and let her participate (over some grumbling) in the raucous debating around his table at the Mullet.

It was more like a scholarly drinking game than a proper debate. Tess loved it, and not just because she often won. It made her feel like one of the lads, bold and adventurous.

It had emboldened Will, too: he'd kissed her beside the fountain in the old cloister courtyard, the stars dancing overhead. It had been a perfect jewel of a moment, and she had felt in her heart that all her hopes were coming to fruition.

If she couldn't be Dozerius—she'd accepted this at some point—there was still adventure and some semblance of freedom to be had at his side, as his ladylove.

The night in question—the adventure of Spira's notes—she and Will had been coming out of a geology lecture. Will was doing an impression of Saar Fikar, the female dragon geologist, saying *naphtha* hungrily, like it was something to put on toast. Tess took his arm and laughingly called him naughty.

Roger Ivy was waiting for them in the corridor, pamphlet in hand.

"Roger, favored nest-comrade of my youth," cried Will, continuing his impersonation. "Won't you accompany us to the Mullet for a flaming jar of naphtha?"

Tess smiled at Roger and leaned her head against Will's shoulder.

"You need to see this," said Roger unhappily, pressing the pamphlet into Will's hands.

It was called *Part 3 of 4: On the Folly of Relying upon Quigutl Falsehoods and Children's Imaginings,* by Scholar Spira.

"Damnation," said Will. "Not another one."

Roger took off. Will drifted up the corridor, skimming Spira's treatise; Tess at his elbow read as much as she could before he turned each page, feeling increasingly alarmed and humiliated on his behalf.

Will noticed her reading. "Don't bother, Therese," he said, tugging her braid in gentle admonishment. "It's rubbish. Spira's out of arguments and now resorts to ad hominem attacks, publishing as quickly as possible in order to bury me while I'm still rebutting the first one."

Will rolled up the pamphlet and smacked it against his palm, mouth flattened in frustration. "There's a fourth part coming. I need to stop it."

Tess read his tense jaw, his distant gaze; these pamphlets hurt him deeply, though he feigned bravado. She said, "Could you anticipate Spira and have a rebuttal ready to go?"

Will's blue eyes darted toward her; he wagged a finger slowly, like the tail of a cat about to pounce. "That is not a bad idea. 'Children's imaginings,' indeed. Spira can go pound sand."

He grabbed Tess's hand and, with customary quickness, ducked upstairs to the faculty wing. Tess bumped along, trying to keep up, like a kite on a string. "Spira's notes are in a locked cabinet," Will was saying. "I can't say I've ever picked a lock, but how hard can it—"

He stopped short as they turned a corner. Ahead, a patch of light stretched across the darkened hallway; Spira was up late working.

"Saints' flippers!" muttered Will. "But no, this could be good. I might not have to pick a lock after all. I'll need your help, though, little bird."

"Anything," said Tess stoutly.

His smile in the semidarkness grew sly. "Even sit on Spira's lap and flirt with him?"

Tess's face fell. She'd said "anything" without considering that he might ask something so repugnant of her. She hated to break her word, hated to disappoint him, but how could she . . .

Will chuckled lightly, as if her inner tug-of-war was transparent to him. "I know you're not that kind of girl. But I won't think less of you—it was my idea, after all—and you couldn't be safer. A sexless organism like Spira won't take liberties. He'll be mortified and, more importantly, distracted while I rifle through his cabinet."

"Isn't there something else I could do?" Tess began weakly. "This seems mean."

Will circled his arms around her waist; his jerkin was perfumed with some Zibou scent full of spices Tess couldn't name. "You're right, it would be mean," he said, warm breath in her ear, "if Spira could feel it, and if he didn't abundantly deserve it. You are such a sweet, sensitive little bird, correcting me and being my conscience. Of course you should never have to do anything you don't feel comfortable with. It's all right. I'll break his lock tomorrow."

He still held the rolled-up pamphlet. Its title was obscured, but Tess remembered it—an insult not only to her but to Pathka and all quigutl. Dragons were always kicking their smaller cousins around, killing them, using them. Saar contempt for quigutl was far worse than Will's contempt for saar; dragons had corresponding power to hurt. It wouldn't hurt Spira in the least to be taken down a peg while Tess stood up for quigutl in a small way.

And it would mean so much to Will.

"Fine, I'll do it," she said reluctantly. "But I'm no good at flirting."

"That's patently untrue," said Will, kissing her ear. Tess pushed him playfully away.

Spira, slumped at the desk like a bagged pudding, was solving equations as they entered. "Ah, you've seen it," said the scholar, noting the rolled pamphlet. "Now, William, you mustn't take these things so personally. Professor Ondir requested me to explore the practicalities of such enormous creatures existing, how they might be hidden, even from us. And even you have to admit that most of your sources are rubbish."

He meant the quigutl, and this helped Tess feel a little less sick about what she meant to do next. She steeled herself and valiantly sat upon Spira's lap. It was soft, as were the shoulders Tess snaked an arm around. The scholar's guano-colored bowl cut smelled of goose grease close-up. Spira's eyes bulged like two eggs.

"Remove yourself from my person," said the saar.

Tess pretended not to understand by telling herself she'd sat upon a bagpipe, which had squeaked in protest.

Will had crossed swiftly to the cabinet; Tess didn't dare watch him, lest Spira turn to look. She gazed into the scholar's myopic gray eyes, feeling ridiculous. Flirting with Will had been hard enough, given her upbringing, but this felt downright unnatural.

"I admire your treatises," she said hopelessly.

Spira, clearly startled, said, "Thank you. They're a bit pedantic for some tastes, but it's important to be thorough."

Tess had inadvertently stumbled on the way to keep Spira's attention. She continued: "I'm not sure you've been thorough enough, in fact."

"What are you suggesting?" said Spira, brow furrowing.

Tess shifted her weight; it was like sitting on dough, and she was in danger of sinking in. "You claim a World Serpent couldn't get enough energy to move, even if it ate coal or tar, but what if it delved down to the mantle of the earth?"

Will paused in ransacking the cabinet to look at her; Spira's expression sharpened.

"We were just at a geology lecture," Tess explained, "which made me wonder whether such a creature might bask upon the earth's hot core like a snake in the sun, and take strength from that."

Spira stared into the middle distance, cogitating. "You raise a point I hadn't considered. It would be worth calculating, to be sure."

Tess batted her eyes and patted his pasty cheek. "Are you *sure* you should do that, Spira? I read somewhere that it's folly to take such childish imaginings seriously."

Spira paled. Will didn't dare laugh, but grinned, brandishing a flat leather case. He had what he'd been looking for. Tess had merely to hold Spira's attention until Will could duck out.

Will puckered his lips, clearly suggesting that she kiss Spira. Tess balked—that was beyond the pale. Spira must have noticed the disgusted look on her face. "What's he doing back there?" the scholar cried, trying to turn and see.

Tess, in desperation, grasped Spira's head and planted a kiss upon those thick, clammy lips. It was like kissing a trout. Spira squirmed, but Tess held on.

"What is this, Saar Spira?" boomed a terrible voice. Tess pulled away from Spira and leaped to her feet. Professor the dragon Fikar stood in the doorway, glaring icily.

Will was already twisting the story. "Spira just grabbed her. He's a maniac. He needs his brain pruned."

Tess was so shocked and ashamed that she didn't hear half of Saar Fikar's scolding. Before she knew what was happening,

Will had taken her hand and they were running down the hall-way. He pulled her around a corner and through a door, which he slammed behind them.

Will leaned against the door, laughing so hard he almost couldn't stand, and then Tess started laughing, too, the stress and anxiety of the last minutes pouring out in one long torrent.

Will grabbed her face and began kissing her warmly, fiercely. "You are extraordinary," he said breathlessly between kisses. "My little bird."

Tess forced herself to pull away, holding his hands so they wouldn't wander further. She dared not lose herself or let him go too far; whatever little rebellion she might be waging against her family, she had not simply abandoned her morals. She was not that kind of girl. Even kissing him was questionable, but she'd rationalized it to herself: it was not the Final Thing, as her mother ominously put it, and the Final Thing was what she had to avoid, according to the letter of the law. Tess was half lawyer; she knew what a loophole was.

"Is Spira going to be in trouble?" she asked, trying to bring them both back to earth.

"Terrible trouble. Old Fikar was writing up a reprimand as we left," he said gleefully.

Tess must have looked as sick as she felt. Will caressed her cheek, his brows bowed in overstated sadness. "Of course you feel bad for him, love. I'd expect no less. You'd pity a slug squished underfoot, or a fish flopping in the net, so capacious is your heart.

"Still, this went better than I could have hoped." He un-tucked the leather case from under his arm. "Spira carries this everywhere. It contains either his notes or something horrifyingly personal. Either way, we've got him."

Tess followed him toward a moonlit window. They were in the museum, her favorite place, a former monastic dormitory now lined with taxidermied animals—badgers, stoats, lions, swans—and shelves of amber jars where stranger things bobbed. The smell of dried rose petals covered a darker waft of decay; the moonlight brought feral shadows spookily to life.

Will threw open the casement to the chilly night and sat on the window seat; Tess sat across from him, watching his elegant hands unbuckle the straps. He winked at her and said, "Now, at last, we reveal the ugly heart of Spira's—"

There were no notes. Will froze in apparent confusion.

The case was full of little glass vials, wrapped in cloth so they wouldn't clink together. Tess picked up one of the vials and rattled the dried herbs inside.

"Spira's tea-smuggling operation?" asked Tess. "Spira's oregano addiction?"

Will, in an unexpected burst of anger, threw a vial out the window. It shattered upon the bricks of the old cloister walk. He threw another, then tipped the rest out.

"Will!" Tess cried, appalled.

"I'm sure he can get more," Will said, shrugging it off.

It wasn't the scattered herbs that had alarmed her, though, but Will's blaze of anger. She'd never seen him act so impulsively. It was almost violent.

But surely it was understandable—she, of all people, knew him and could see the good in him. He was frustrated not to have found the notes. Spira's intellectual attacks must also be taking a toll. His moonlit profile looked like a statue of a tragic king, betrayed and bitter. What was rage but a cover for some secret fragility, some sorrow?

Tess felt strangely privileged to have glimpsed his pain.

She leaned across the window seat to kiss him again, and then, who can say how, she was on his lap, which was much solider than Spira's. This would have alarmed her, but she'd already crossed that river, it seemed, and nothing untoward had happened. This was not the Final Thing.

Then Will's hand was inside her bodice, cupping her breast through her linen chemise.

Tess all but levitated off his lap and landed three feet away. "Will!"

"Oh, my love," said Will, clapping a hand to his chest, his blue eyes wide and ingenuous. "I've overstepped. Forgive me—I got caught up and forgot what I was about."

Tess frantically rehooked her bodice, tears in her eyes; her mother had refused to buy her a gown with "harlot hooks" down the front, so Tess had altered the dress herself, and now look what had happened. She should have worn proper, decent laces.

Will extended his hand like a peace offering. Tess pointedly didn't take it.

"Would you believe, little bird, that this is what I love about you most?" he said, his voice hushed and awed. "You're so *good*. Who else, in the midst of kissing, could keep virtue in mind? I hope you know I admire that."

Tess looked away, a ticklish feeling rising in her chest. She knew she wasn't that good, especially after what she'd just done to Spira, and yet—

"You're a rare and beautiful thing," Will was saying. His fair hair haloed his head in the moonlight. "I wish I could build you a cage, little bird, or a beautiful tower, to keep you safe from the corrupt, cynical world. You don't know how precious it is to be naive and innocent. I only want to protect you, so you can sing and be free like the golden bird you were born to be."

It didn't matter if he was wrong; she was hungry to be told exactly this, that she was not a waste of space or a born trouble-maker, not a spank magnet or a little devil girl. That she wasn't failing all the deepest wishes of her heart.

Will beckoned. She hesitated, and then returned to his lap.

"Your virtue heals me, and makes me want to be better," Will whispered in her ear. His warm breath on her neck made her shiver. "Even a kiss"—he kissed her lingeringly—"could be a sordid thing, but you refine it into something radiant and pure."

She fell into his kiss again. And when, soon after, his hand returned to her breast—outside her bodice, this time—she let it lie, reasoning that this, too, was not the Final Thing, and that someone who so valued her might be granted a little more liberty. Maybe this touch, too, was within her power to purify, like a refiner's fire.

⚔

Night had fully fallen over Affle, starless and overcast. Tess shivered, despite the heat.

"I used to look back on that evening and laugh," she said

in a hollow voice, like the wind through reeds. "I thought of it as a hilarious Dozerius tale, 'Wherein Our Heroes Trick Spira, Who Had It Coming.' We were lively and alive—how could that be wrong?—and I thought I'd done something genuinely helpful for Will, who was haunted by some hurt he wouldn't explain."

Like the romantic hero of almost any story. She felt embarrassingly transparent.

"But the harm we did outweighed everything," Tess continued. "Spira had to stand before a dragon tribunal for deviant behavior. Those herbs were medicine. He—" No, that was wrong. She still wasn't treating the scholar like a person, saying *he*. "*Ko* had Tathlann's syndrome. No maternal memories; no male or female parts; weak immune system. We made *ko* sick."

Pathka shifted his head uncomfortably in her lap.

"It's one of my biggest regrets. I wish there were some way to make it up to Spira," Tess added, hoping Pathka didn't think her a terrible person.

Pathka raised his head sharply and said, "You won't like hearing this, but sometimes you can't fix what you broke. Sometimes you just have to live with it."

He was so riled up there were sparks coming out of his nostrils.

She'd made him angry again.

Tess backed away, mostly so she wouldn't catch fire, and said hesitantly, "I didn't mean to—are we talking about the same thing now?"

"About responsibility, and making up for past mistakes?"

said Pathka, and there was a bite in his voice that Tess had never heard before. "Oh yes. You were subtle, but I'm sure we understand each other."

"Pathka!" cried Tess in frustration. "I'm confessing my sins. I can regret how I treated Spira without it being an underhanded criticism of . . . of you and Kikiu."

Pathka was done listening. He turned, tail snaking ominously, and walked off into the descending night. Tess called after him, to no avail, until he was almost out of sight.

She had no choice but to follow, into the uncertain darkness.

Eighteen

They camped, eventually, and by morning Pathka seemed to have forgiven her, or at least recovered his equanimity. They followed the road south in silence.

The roads in Ninys were better than those in Goredd; this was a fact, and an artifact of their different histories. Faced with marauding dragons, Goredd hadn't prioritized things such as paving stones, roadbed grading, or drainage. Indeed, for generations it had been safer to stay off the roads. Dragons knew to look for you there.

In this era of Queen Glisselda's Peace, Heaven let it last, Goreddi roads were finally receiving some attention. Improvements spread from the capital outward, like a seed sprouting shoots, but they had not yet reached the far corners of the realm.

It would be an exaggeration to say the roads grew immediately straighter and tidier the moment one crossed the border, but that was because the border had moved so often. The roads around Affle were hearteningly decent; a few miles beyond, the paving stones took on a geometric regularity. The roadbed acquired a curve, encouraging water to sluice off the sides instead of accumulating in the middle as a paradise for mosquitoes and stink. Tess, who'd become something of a road connoisseur, appreciated the greater ease of walking.

The flavor of the thing was hard to get used to, however. Ninysh roads smacked more of civilization than mystery. Tess had to squint to see the potential, to keep believing that anything might be around the next corner. All roads were one, surely, even if their textures differed.

Was she as varied, a part of herself as rough and rutted as the Goreddi roads, and some other part as efficient as the Ninysh? She often felt, early in the morning, when the world seemed most malleable, that she contained these different potentials, and more. It wasn't merely that she could be anything, but that she was everything, all at once.

When Tess came across the road crew, therefore, she approached with curiosity. Here was a different way of engaging with the road, and it seemed as open to her as any other.

Pathka, without a word, dived into the wheat to hide.

The workers had a big encampment, a dozen tents and nearly as many wagons. As Tess drew nearer, she saw workmen clustered around a yawning sinkhole in the middle of the roadbed. It had been there long enough that passing travelers had carved wheel ruts through the adjacent wheat field as they gave the hole wide berth.

Tess walked up beside a ruddy young man who was leaning

on his shovel and chewing a blade of grass. A wagon, opposite, dumped gravel into the chasm, raising clouds of dust and making everyone cough and complain. When the dust cleared, the hole looked as empty as ever. The redheaded fellow spit into the abyss.

"Was the rock eaten by water?" said Tess, edging up and peering into the darkness. She couldn't say *limestone* in Ninysh—but this wasn't limestone anyway. This far south was all Ninysh Shield, as she'd heard it called, an expanse of basalt. It didn't erode as readily as limestone; a sinkhole was rather surprising.

The lad—scarcely older than Tess—flicked a glance at her and rubbed his freckled nose. "We dug this ourselves," he drawled. "It's a latrine."

Tess ignored the sarcasm. "What causes this?"

He shrugged, instantly bored with her if she wouldn't laugh at his jokes. "Our geologist don't know. It's a giant cave, like nobody from the Academy ever seen before. He's got a bee up his bum, cuz Boss Gen won't let him down there after the cave-in killed Daniele." The lad pointed across at a man in a leather apron, long hair tied back, on his stomach lowering a rope into the hole. "He's sending down a wren in a cage. Not much else he can do."

Men worked around the geologist, shoveling gravel down the hole. "Felix, you son of a donkey, there's nothing to do on that side!" one shouted, glaring across at the lad who was talking to Tess. Even the geologist looked up and frowned.

"I was only telling this lout to talk to Boss Gen if he wants work!" Felix shouted back, thumbing his nose. "Excuse me for trying to find someone to replace poor Daniele."

"Daniele wasn't a lazy git, at least," said a muscular gray-haired man, rounding the side of the wagon. The others pretended to have been working hard rather than leering at Felix.

Felix grudgingly straightened, muttering, "I *was* working, Arnando, till I got interrupted." He glared sidelong at Tess—that rude interruptrix—and began picking his way around the perimeter. Big Arnando, clearly the foreman, crossed his arms and watched Felix like a hawk.

Tess stared down the hole. This cave might be even larger than Big Spooky.

"Boss is in the main tent," called Arnando; his deep voice carried effortlessly across.

He'd believed Felix that she was looking for work. To Tess's surprise, she found herself tempted. This was honest work, paid in money, not lunch. There was something to be said for that. She couldn't live hand to mouth forever.

Wheat stretched to the horizon. It was just the kind of place Pathka had said Anathuthia would be in. The little quigutl had ducked out of sight the minute they saw the crew working, but he'd be nearby. Tess scanned for the telltale wiggle in the grass, but the plants stayed eerily still.

Then she spotted him. He'd crept to the edge of the chasm, in broad daylight, in front of all these men. Pathka clung to the lip of the hole, immobile as a stone, doing nothing to draw the eye; only Tess's scouring gaze had enabled her to spot him. She rounded the hole toward him.

He lay flat, sniffing the subterranean wind, one eye on the men. The other reeled back toward Tess. His tail twitched side to side with barely contained excitement, and she knew: this was the place. No wonder the cave had baffled even the geologist. A World Serpent had made it.

She would ask for a job. They needed an excuse to stay right here.

The canvas tents were cleaner than one might have expected. She found the biggest tent easily enough, but the door flap hung closed. What was correct tent etiquette? Knock? Holler? Walk in? She glanced around for someone to ask, but another gravel wagon was backing up to the hole and all eyes were focused on that.

Tess took a deep breath and flung the flap aside. Across the dim interior, she saw a woman. Apparently this was the wrong tent, and she'd rudely intruded on someone.

"Oops, sorry," she mumbled, and let the flap drop.

The woman called, "Well? Are you coming in or not?"

Tess peeked around the flap and saw that the woman was sitting behind a folding camp desk, a ledger book in front of her.

"Whatever you're up to," said the woman crossly, "it smacks of nonsense, and I truly do not have time for nonsense today. Especially not the nonsense of beardless boys. If you're coming in, come in."

"I'm looking for Boss Gen," said Tess, in a voice very like a beardless boy's.

"Are you indeed?" said the woman, pausing to push up her spectacles. She was squarely built, with a snub nose and a blond braid wrapped around her head. "Will you be amused or alarmed to know that Boss Gen is looking at you?"

"You're . . . you're the boss?" said Tess, coming all the way into the tent.

"Oh, bravo," said Gen, underlining something emphatically, "you may almost be smart enough to work here, although I warn you, I will boss you until you bleed."

"I want a job," said Tess, before it had quite sunk in that Gen might have already implied that she was hired. "That is . . . did you just offer me one?"

Gen raised one terrible eyebrow, and Tess felt something wither inside her. "I did, but you're rather dim on the uptake. Unfortunately, that means you'll fit in very well. We need to replace Daniele—rest he merry in the arms of Heaven." Boss Gen grimaced at some memory. "If you're to work here, understand that there is to be no exploring of that tunnel during off-hours. We're trying to fill it, not get ourselves crushed like cockroaches."

Talk got technical then, as Gen explained what grueling physical labor Tess was to perform in exchange for money. Even after all the farmwork, Tess wasn't sure she had sufficient muscles for these tasks. Gen anticipated this objection, saying, "You're kind of weedy, but don't worry if you're not strong yet. You will be soon enough, my boy."

There was something sarcastic in that final word. Tess stared hard at Gen, trying to decide whether she could tell what Tess was hiding. Gen stared back with a burning glare that suggested she could see through Tess's clothing, in fact.

Tess fidgeted with a button on her jerkin. Keeping up her pretense while surrounded by men would be a challenge. It might be useful if somebody else knew the truth, somebody she could go to in an emergency. If the boss was a woman, surely Tess could trust her with this.

"There's something you should know about me," Tess began.

"You're a girl in disguise?" said Gen, obviously struggling not to roll her eyes. She pulled out a penknife and sharpened her quill.

Tess self-consciously touched her hair, which was still quite short. "You could tell."

"No, but there are only so many guesses when someone furtively tells me there's something I should know," said Gen, peering shrewdly over the top of her glasses. "I, of all people, couldn't care less what you are. I tamped roadbed for five years and fitted stone for ten, and there is nothing you can't do on this crew once you've built up some strength, except piss standing up—and even that is possible with practice, I'm told, though who wants wet shoes in the meantime?"

Her casual vulgarity shocked Tess into silence. Boss Gen dug through a trunk and found Tess a broad sun hat and a leather apron. "You've got good boots already, and the jerkin will do. You're going to sweat, make no mistake, and they'll tease you for keeping your shirt on—oh, don't look so alarmed. They'll assume you're embarrassed by your hairless, caved-in, little-boy chest. Unless you tell them the truth, but I don't recommend that."

"Of course," said Tess with a knowing, one-woman-to-another nod.

"You mistake me. You'd be perfectly safe with my men," said Gen shrewdly. "If they touched a hair on your head, I'd make them *castameri* with this left hand." Tess didn't know the term, but Gen made a clawed, cupping gesture, leaving no doubt as to what she would grasp and pluck like fruit. Tess flinched, and she didn't even own the requisite anatomy.

"Now ask me what I'll be doing with my other hand," Boss Gen stage-whispered.

"Uh, what will you be doing, uh, with your—" began Tess, not sure she wanted to know.

"I'll be writing a sonnet!" cried Gen, slapping her desk. "But do keep pretending to be a boy. They'll only give you trifling tasks otherwise, and I need hard work out of you." Gen began drawing up a contract. "What name do you go by, Sir Road-worker?"

"Tes'puco," said Tess without flinching.

"Stupid-head?" said Boss Gen, writing it down. "What are you, eight?"

"Are you asking because you need to put my age in the contract?"

Gen laughed delightedly. "Not so stupid, perhaps. But you've a ways to go before you'll impress me, *boy*. Sign this and get gone. Take Daniele's old bunk, with Mico, Aster, and Felix."

Tess read the whole contract, which caused Gen to emit annoyed and impressed grunts by turns. The term was one month, a reasonable trial period for both sides (Tess had no idea how long it might take to find Anathuthia). The weekly salary seemed enormous, until she noted deductions for food and board and apron rental. Still, she'd be glad to have money. Winter was months away yet, but it would be good to have something saved up toward some kind of shelter. Once Anathuthia was found, she was probably on her own, and Tess had no idea how far it was to Segosh, or if she'd want to walk there through the snow.

When Tess emerged from the boss's tent, Pathka still lay at the lip of the hole, on the far edge. Tess couldn't just saunter over and talk to him. She had to find her tent, and if they were labeled in any way, she couldn't tell. She looked for Felix. His rust-colored hair didn't stand out here, but his tendency to lean on his shovel and stare into the distance certainly did.

"I'll show you," he said when she asked where the tent was. "The sooner you're settled, the sooner you can be out here, taking Daniele's place. Until then you're deadweight, and we don't need any more of that. That's my job. What did you say your name was?"

Tess hesitated. Her childhood nickname seemed like less and less of a good idea, but she'd already given it to Gen. "Tes'puco," she said, affecting a devil-may-care attitude.

Felix's brows shot up. "Either you're some kind of simpleton, to let people call you that, or you have *bollos* the size of dragon eggs."

"It's the latter, I assure you," said Tess, somewhat stiffly. "More . . . more of those bits you mentioned than you can shake a stick at."

Felix laughed, his scrawny turkey neck bobbing. "C'mon then, Dunderhead. Let's get you settled so you have time for an honest evening's work."

Tess followed him toward the tents. Some intuition led her to glance back at the hole, just in time to glimpse Pathka's tail disappearing down it.

Nineteen

Before bed, Tess slipped away from the tents, followed a footpath through the nodding wheat, and sat behind the wall of the neighboring meadow, where she wouldn't be seen. Night fell late this far south. The salmon sunset persisted stubbornly; the stars had to shout to be heard.

She pulled out Pathka's thnik, the little moon-bug, and flipped its switch. "How is it down there?" she asked him. "Any sign of her?"

"She's everywhere," his voice hissed and popped back. "The smell of her, I mean. She passed this way recently. It's so overpowering that I'm having trouble determining how to search. If they keep dumping gravel down the hole, it's going to force me to choose a direction before I know where she went."

"Don't tell me Anathuthia has moved on. How far will you

have to go to find her?" said Tess in dismay. She'd just signed a contract to stay right here.

"I don't know," said Pathka. "I'm half tempted to wait here. The dream was very clear: a wheat field, it said, and here we are. But maybe I'm supposed to follow her?"

Tess scuffed the toe of her boot in the soil, wondering what the odds were that Pathka would take off after Anathuthia and not come back.

Was Pathka still cross with her? They hadn't had a chance to clear the air before Pathka dived down the hole, and now Tess didn't know how to ask. Kikiu was a raw wound, it seemed, and she didn't know how to avoid poking it again.

"Be careful," was all she managed to say. "I don't want to lose you to a cave-in."

"Stop the wagons, then," said Pathka. "I'm more likely to be buried by a heap of gravel."

Tess switched off her thnik disconsolately and tucked it down her jerkin. How was she supposed to stop the gravel wagons? She could think of no surer way to get fired.

Later, listening to her tentmates snore, Tess managed to think of several surer ways to get fired. She could throw Felix, Aster, and Mico down the hole.

Tess spent the next day dead on her feet, and it was a minor miracle that she didn't end up falling into the pit herself. Gravel, though it is made of tiny pieces, is heavy in the aggregate—far, far heavier than hay—and while shoveling may seem a simple matter at first, each scoop weighs more than the last. By the end of the day, her neck and shoulders burned; she could barely turn her head or lift her spoon to eat her soup.

If Aster, Mico, and Felix snored that night, Tess snored louder.

Tess didn't have to stop the gravel wagons, it turned out, because by the end of the second day, it was clear that their efforts were futile. The cavern floor sloped in two directions, and the gravel was sliding into oblivion on either side. At this rate, they'd have to fill the whole chamber with gravel, and there wasn't enough gravel in the world.

Boss Gen held an emergency meeting with the geologist, the surveyor, and Big Arnando, the foreman. Because the meeting was held in a tent, everyone in camp could hear what was going on—particularly the shouted parts, which were many. Felix waved Tess over to the shady side of the tent, where he and Mico and Aster had set up a crate and were playing cards.

"Deal Tes'puco in," said Felix, offering Tess his spot in the deepest shade.

"Can 'Puco even hold the cards? His arms are like noodles," said Mico, a dark-complexioned fellow. He wore the same chin beard as Felix and Aster, but his ponytail made a curly pouf like a water dog's tail.

"I'll hold them with my toes," offered Tess. "What are we playing?"

"No, we can't just build a detour!" shouted Boss Gen from behind the tent wall. "Do you know how much paperwork that would involve? How much money, for the new rights-of-way? It would take months, and meanwhile this hole is gaping at us. Cows are falling down it."

Felix chuckled. "She's so tenderly concerned for her fellow

steers. 'Puco, the game is called Madeleine's Arse. Queens are high. . . ."

Tess, initially put off by the name, soon realized the game was a variation on Crespina, which she'd played a thousand times with Lady Farquist. She bid hesitantly at first, feigning surprise at her "beginner's luck," but by the fifth hand she was openly trouncing them, and after the eighth, Aster leaped to his feet, kicked over the crate, and drew a knife. "You cheat, Penoio!" he cried, the first words Tess had heard him speak.

"Whoa! Hold on!" cried Mico, wrapping his muscular arms around Aster's heaving middle. To Tess's surprise, Felix grabbed her the same way. She hadn't risen to meet Aster's challenge—choosing instead to cower—but clearly Felix expected her to.

"You're not cheating, are you, 'Puco?" said Felix. He was sweaty and rank, and she wished he'd let her go.

Tess said quickly, "No, no. I pretended to be stupider than I am, though."

"That's not against the rules," Felix pronounced, like a judge. "That's strategy. I pretend to be lazy all the time, so that when I do any work, everyone's pleasantly surprised."

"I'm pretty sure you really are that lazy," said Mico, still clasping Aster around the middle. The red drained from Aster's face; when he stopped struggling, Mico let him go. Aster wouldn't look at Tess, but dug the toe of his boot into the dirt.

In all the brouhaha, they'd missed the conclusion of the meeting. Suddenly Big Arnando was there, telling them to get back to work. "Doing what?" Felix demanded, incensed at the injustice of being asked to do his job.

"Licking cats," said Arnando. Mico burst out laughing. Tess guessed this was some rude Ninysh idiom, but Arnando kept a straight face and unwavering calm. His very mildness suggested they didn't want to see him riled. Mico stashed the cards, and they got to it.

The crew were herded away from the hole, to the western side, where horses and wagons had beaten a makeshift detour through the wheat. The next wagon had been redirected onto that path, and men were already spreading the gravel with rakes. "I hate this plan!" the surveyor was shouting. "The road was perfectly straight. This is a pimple on the face of my road!"

"Get out your equipment and mark us a perfect semicircle," said Arnando, cool as morning dew. "Make the best of it, you geometrical tyrant."

He did it, sputtering all the while. Tess envied the surveyor's assistant (who was also his daughter); that was a job she could have done, holding the measuring string, dangling the plumb line. Felix grumbled, clearly thinking the same thing.

Tess got a lesson in road building over the next several days; she learned about grading, leveling, layering, banking, tamping, laying stone. She still ached when she lay down to sleep, but the aches were more varied and interesting than when she'd merely been shoveling.

She learned the hierarchy, too. She and her tentmates were the bottom of the heap. Above them were the senior graders. Above them were the stonefitters and then the stonecutters. Above them all was Big Arnando, the foreman, and above him,

Boss Gen. The surveyor ranked with Arnando, but he couldn't reprimand anyone except through the foreman.

The geologist stood apart from everyone. He wasn't part of the crew, Felix explained, but had been brought in specifically to deal with this hole. "Dunno why he's still here, honestly," said Felix, on the third day of detour grading. "We've stopped messing with the hole."

But that wasn't entirely true. Tess had seen the geologist, called Nicolas, visit the edge after dark when Boss Gen wouldn't notice him. He lay on his belly like Pathka and gazed into the depths, his face dimly illuminated by a lantern he'd lowered on the end of a string.

He was the first learned man Tess had encountered in her travels, and she found him unduly fascinating. Not that she found him handsome, to be clear: his face was heavily weathered, like a bit of craggy cliff. It was more that his quirks—reading at the mess table, getting impatient and snappish when the other men said stupid things—made her oddly nostalgic.

She liked scholars. They'd been the best thing about her youthful misadventures. Surely it was possible to talk to one without everything going bad?

She needed to prove this to herself. After dinner on the fourth evening, Tess eschewed the card game and went out to the hole. Nicolas was on his stomach; the hole glowed eerily.

"Spot anything?" asked Tess, nearly startling him into dropping the lantern.

"Don't sneak up like that," said the geologist, scowling. "Who are you?"

"Tes'puco," said Tess, seating herself carefully beside him, letting her feet dangle into the yawning chasm. "I like geology."

"Oh you do, do you?" he said, as welcoming as blackberry bramble.

She was going to bump right up against the limits of her Ninysh, talking about rocks. "We've got caves in Goredd, worn away by water. I've crawled through lots. They're beautiful, and sometimes they collapse. This, though . . ." She tossed a rock into the depths; it made sharp, sweet echoes. "I can tell this is different. Water didn't make this hole. What do you think?"

"Nothing could have made this," said Nicolas, raising himself on all fours. He began reeling his lantern up. "That's solid *basalto,* no sign of erosion. We're not mining this part of the shield." His tone softened slightly: "I'm fascinated and baffled in equal measure."

Tess smiled to herself: he was a quintessential natural philosopher, prickly until he realized she was interested. Nobody else had cared about the *basalto,* evidently.

"At least we're not still trying to fill it," said Tess, looking down the hole.

"Who told you that?" said Nicolas.

"Well . . . why the detour, then?"

He shook his head. "That's temporary. They don't even have the landowner's permission. They're trying to make it passable until the boulders get here." The lantern was up at last. "The gravel slides aside, into the depths of the cavern, so they're hauling in some very large rocks from the quarry at Dulouse. It should take about a week."

"That seems like a waste of stone," said Tess, although in

truth she worried about Pathka being sealed in. "Wouldn't it make more sense to build a bridge over it?"

"A . . . bridge?" said Nicolas, confused, as if he'd never heard of such a structure.

"If this were a river, that's what they'd do," said Tess. "Not fill it in."

"Filling a river would have consequences," said the geologist. "Filling this hole—"

"Would have consequences," said Tess. "You'd never learn what made it."

"You have some crackpot theory," said Nicolas shrewdly, eyeing her sidelong.

She did. He was going to think her mad, but Tess found she didn't care. She had nothing to prove to this man, and there was a certain pleasure to be had in shocking him. "Ever heard of the World Serpents?"

The geologist laughed. "Oh no, not this. Don't tell me this mania has reached all the way to Goredd. It's bad enough that some of the Academy's best and brightest have gone tearing off after the one in the Antarctic, but—"

"Since when do naturalists take World Serpents seriously?" asked Tess, put out. She and Will hadn't convinced anyone, but Nicolas was claiming the Ninysh were interested? Never.

Nicolas shrugged. "Only in the last few years. Countess Margarethe of Mardou is on a voyage as we speak, scouring the waters around the Archipelagos."

Tess emitted a bitter sound, halfway between a laugh and a snort. It figured. The countess had said *megafauna,* and Tess had fallen down a hole in her own mind. If she'd said *World*

Serpent ... would it have made a difference? Was there really any chance that Tess could've been sailing the Antarctic right now? She probably would have found a way to stab herself in the foot no matter what. She'd been so resentful that day, biting everyone indiscriminately.

"What's this Academy you mentioned?" said Tess, pushing away her regrets.

"The Academy of Segosh, older and more reputable than your St. Bert's," said Nicolas archly. "We're ahead of Goredd in most endeavors, but even our finest minds may fall prey to fads and manias. Before this, they were trying to replicate St. Blanche's mechanical marvels. They made some inroads, and Ninysh clockwork is now superior to any in the Southlands, but in the end, no one could do what St. Blanche does. She's a Saint; she puts a piece of her soul into everything she creates. Mere humans simply can't."

"The quigutl accomplish a great deal without involving, uh, souls," said Tess, pulling Pathka's insectoid thnik out of her jerkin.

Nicolas turned it over in his hands. Wires protruded at strange angles. "I've never seen such an ungainly one."

"It was made on the road," said Tess, taking it back and stashing it again, wary that he might want to dismantle it. "The quigutl didn't have his usual tools along."

"That device would interest the Academy very much," he said. "That we could learn from. If you're ever in Segosh, consider donating it."

"And you should consider taking my bridge idea to Gen,"

said Tess, standing up. "If the hole is left open, you could come back later with proper gear and explore its depths yourself."

Nicolas raised his lamp and stared into the black pit. Tess left him to his considerations.

"You're a clever bastard, I'm told," said Boss Gen the next day. She'd called Tess into her office, to the unexpected envy of Felix and Mico; the sun was particularly strong that afternoon. "Vessi the surveyor loves your bridge idea. Now the road can run tediously straight, like his imagination. Count Pesavolta will send another crew with an engineer and masons, which suits me fine. Once we finish the detour, we can get back to doing our job, which is filling potholes, not the earth itself."

"Do I get some kind of cleverness bonus?" asked Tess, cocky from the unexpected praise.

"You do not," said Gen, "and this isn't really why I called you in. I wanted to ask"—she lowered her voice—"one woman to another, whether you're adequately prepared for your monthlies. I don't know how you've been taking care of yourself out on the road—"

"Moss," said Tess.

"—and I don't *want* to know," said Gen, glowering at the interruption. "But now that you're among men, pretending to be one, laundry becomes an issue."

"Moss works surprisingly well in a lunessa, and you can burn it in the fire," said Tess.

"There is a dearth of moss here in the wheat country," said Gen, clearly regretting this conversation. "I have proper wool lunessas in that trunk. Use them as needed, and wash them in privacy, here in my tent. That's all I wanted to say. You're welcome."

"Won't there be gossip? They're going to think young 'Puco is your lover."

"How are you not dead of stupidity?" cried Gen, apparently irritated that Tess had thought of something she hadn't. "The moss has taken root and grown into your brain. Get out!"

Still, the offer had been kind, and Tess intended to take her up on it. She trotted back out into the hot sun, lamenting the fact that she couldn't take her shirt off like everyone else.

⚔

The detour was finished within two more days; they were to pack up the tents first thing in the morning and move on. Tess, clever as she was, had inadvertently hastened the crew away from the hole, and away from Pathka. Upon that final evening, she sneaked out to the meadow wall and called Pathka on her thnik again.

"I'll stay here with you," she said. "I'll break my contract and slip down the hole and—"

"It's no good staying here," Pathka's voice came back tinnily. "I don't think she's coming back. I'll follow her scent underground while you travel with the road crew."

"We're on this journey *together*," Tess cried.

"On parallel roads, for now. Stay topside. I'll check back

every few days, and when I find her, I'll come get you, Teth." He paused, then added, "I watched you working today. You looked happy. It will be better for you to stay with creatures of your own kind, in the sunshine."

That sounded too much like goodbye. "Don't do anything that could kill you," said Tess, her voice thickening. "Otherwise I will find you in quigutl Heaven, if there is one, and I will bite you like you've never been bitten before."

A clapping sound was Pathka's laughter, and then the thnik buzzed, disconnected. Tess picked herself up, threw a rock at the moon, and stumbled back to camp.

She fell into routine, the daily rhythm of tamping, rolling, grinding, filling, chipping. Tess had never worked so hard in her life, but her blisters turned into calluses, her aches into smaller aches. Twinges, really. The heat grew almost unbearable as summer careened drunkenly toward fall; she wet her hat and drank water. Honestly, keeping her shirt on beat being sunburned. Her tentmates, even dark brown Mico, were crisped around the edges like roast beef. Their muscles rippled under the sun. She tried not to stare at them too obviously.

This labor was as much like digging into herself as digging into the roadbed. Every fiber of her body seemed connected to something else, an emotion, a memory, a snatch of song. This persistent ache was Will, and that one her mother; her sisters hid in unexpected twinges. Motion broke up chunks of anger and sorrow, and sweat washed them away. She felt empty and full at once, an odd condition. Labor silenced the gadfly voice better than wine. Wine muted it, but it also dulled her defenses and made that buzzing monster feel enormous; hard work made it shockingly clear that the fly was only fly-sized, and might be crushed.

Felix liked to sing a song that ran at the pace of roadbed-pounding. The rhyme scheme made it easy to improvise verses between thumps, even if one's Ninysh was shaky:

> *Sweet Jessia's so fair* (thump, thump)
> *With golden flax for hair* (thump)
> *I'd give away a whole year's pay*
> *To see her standing there* (thump)

Most verses continued in the same tedious vein. Tess's verses, which began as quiet rhyming exercises muttered under her breath, were noted by Mico, who spread them to the rest of the lads, and soon the flavor of the entire song had gone a shade darker:

> *This clod is like my heart* (thump, thump)
> *I smash it all apart* (thump)
> *I had one goal, to keep it whole*
> *But that's beyond my art* (thump)

Felix, a little envious of Tess's versifying, sometimes changed the last line to "But no one gives a fart," which made everyone laugh and seemed to cheer him up.

Tess was liked well enough, but weeks passed and Aster

didn't warm to her. The others shortened her name to 'Puco, "stupid," but Aster called her Penoio, which meant (to put it bluntly) "penis." Tess hadn't known the word, but when she figured it out she felt rightfully insulted. She took the matter up with Felix one day as they waited in the shade of a poplar tree for their turn at the water wagon. "Why does Aster call me that?" she fumed.

"Call you what?" said Felix pigheadedly.

"*You* know," said Tess, elbowing him.

"On my mother's grave, I do not," said Felix, grinning in a way that showed he knew perfectly well but was determined to make her say it aloud.

Just as Tess had been when Jeanne asked about her wedding night. She deserved this, but she'd show that Felix. "Penis!" she cried, far louder than she meant to. Everyone fell silent and looked at Tess, who'd gone alarmingly crimson. A ripple of appreciative laughter rolled down the line, and they went back to talking as if nothing had happened.

Felix was laughing his ruddy head off. Tess glared at him. "Oh, you're serious!" he said, throwing up his hands. "I don't know. Why do you call yourself that?"

"I don't call myself that," she said tersely.

Felix sighed. "Tes'puco, who taught you Ninysh? Sometimes you speak like you suckled it at your mother's teat, but other times you know nothing. Apparently I have to spell out what every five-year-old knows: here is your smart head." He took off his hat and swatted Tess about the ears with it. "And there is your stupid head." He mimed punching her in the crotch.

She dodged, then hit him in the stomach.

"Ow! I didn't touch you!" he cried, and punched her in the bicep.

"Are you lads having trouble standing in line?" said Big Arnando, looming behind them.

"No," they squeaked. Arnando walked on; Felix burst into giggles. Tess wasn't so merry. She'd always assumed Kenneth called her Tes'puco because it started with *Tess*, but now she wasn't sure. Had he known about this double meaning? Was this how he'd repaid her for making him stick his face in the fountain, or marry Jeanne, or twenty dozen other stupid ways she'd preyed on his compliant nature? It would be just like him to take revenge so subtly that she might've gone to her grave not realizing he'd done it.

The next time Aster called her Penoio in the middle of a card game, though, she took a jaunty little bow. She'd named herself, after all. She might as well claim it. The lads burst out laughing, and even Aster had the smallest arc of an unaccustomed smile on his narrow lips.

After cards, Tess sometimes sneaked off to call Pathka on the thnik. He was usually in some lightless tunnel that he couldn't describe except through smell, but one evening he said, "Do you still have those scales from Big Thpooky?"

"I do," said Tess warily. "You're not thinking of doing that ritual again? I thought you couldn't do it alone."

She disliked the idea of him bleeding in the dark, far from help.

"I'm not alone, if you must know," Pathka said. "At least, I hope I won't be, if I can persuade *ko* to help me." There was a long pause. "I've found Kikiu."

"Oh?" said Tess cautiously, unsure whether to be alarmed or optimistic.

"I sensed *ko* up a side passage in an old iron mine," said Pathka. "*Ko* was there, making more ... unnatural enhancements. Anyway, since you were so critical, you should know that we had a very civil conversation. And I was right: Kikiu wasn't called. Not like I was.

"But maybe you had a point. Maybe we could dream of Anathuthia together if we perform the *kemthikemthlutl*," said Pathka. "I want you to understand that I'm making a good-faith effort to be nest to my hatchling. Since you were so critical."

"That sounds reasonable," said Tess, unsure whether any of this would work. Still, it was surely a good sign that he was trying. She did as he asked and left the scales in the field, under the wary eye of the moon.

In the morning they were gone.

Tess worked all day and slept like the dead. It was, perhaps, the most fulfilling existence she'd ever led. When she'd been with the crew for almost six weeks, though, something happened to spoil her idyll.

A colorful two-horse cart crossed the horizon into view, sending a raucous cheer through the pothole crew. "What is it?" Tess asked Felix, but he just grabbed Mico and danced a little jig. Tess saw nothing too remarkable about the conveyance: it had four wheels, a roof and door, a crooked tin chimney poking up. One horse wore a straw hat; the other looked down his sloping nose at this.

The wagon trundled closer, and its bright paint job proved to be a mural of whorls, butterflies, and plants not found in nature, like a scene from a dream. Letters among the mayhem spelled DARLING DULSIA. Dulsia herself had the reins firmly in hand, and she had two outriders, bruisers with swords, ahead and behind.

The cart rolled to a stop before the torn-up roadbed, to cheers and hats thrown in the air. Felix ran for Gen, who emerged from her tent, shading her eyes from the noonday glare.

"Who's Darling Dulsia again?" asked Tess of no one in particular, as if she'd been told once already.

"The itinerant priest," said one wiseacre, winking at her.

"My wife," said another, "but she's too much for me alone."

"I can help you out, brother," said one of the stonecutters, clapping him on the shoulder.

There was a great deal of laughter at this. Tess gauged the flavor of the laughter and disliked it. Nor did she quite approve of the plump little lady driving the cart. Dulsia wore gaudy jewels and a flouncy skirt, not practical for driving at all; her hair was curled elaborately and her face made up. Tess's hands tightened around her tamper and her eyes narrowed.

Dulsia waved at the men and cried, "Did you tear up the road to stop me from rolling past? Oh, darlings, I would have stopped for you in any case. Gen keeps the finest crews."

"We love you, Dudu!" someone shouted.

Dulsia tossed her auburn curls. "And I love you, lordlings," she said. "With the boss's permission, of course."

"Please," said Gen dryly. "Put them out of their misery."

There was uproarious laughter at this. Tess felt sick. Any doubts she might've entertained as to the profession of this woman evaporated. She was exactly what she seemed to be: a harlot. A lady of the night. The word Tess had punched Jacomo for.

Damaelle, the crew called her—"small, dear lady." It was politer than any Goreddi epithet, and certainly not the usual word in Ninysh.

Tess had glimpsed such creatures in Lavondaville, where they were required to wear black and yellow and skulk in crannies after dark. Their existence seemed to pollute the very air; the streetlamps flickered with shame. Tess had always scrupulously pretended not to see them.

It was hard to look away from Dulsia, though. She was short, adorable, and round, like a pumpkin on legs, and so lively she seemed to glow. Tess couldn't guess her age. Dulsia leaped from her wagon and glad-handed her way among the men, letting them kiss her dimpled cheeks. One—a new fellow—tried to take greater liberties and was immediately hauled aside by Dulsia's muscular outriders, her brothers.

Gen shook Dulsia's hand, to Tess's shock. Then again, Gen was always shocking, so maybe she shouldn't have been surprised. "How long can you tarry?" the boss was asking. "Are you headed toward some appointment?"

"No rush," said Dulsia, smiling. Her teeth were endearingly

crooked. "I'm due at a patron's on the equinox, but that's three weeks away. I could spend a few days, if anyone can afford me." She eyed the fellows behind her. Several waved, not bashfully.

"As you see, *damaelle*," said Gen, "they've been saving up, just in case."

Tess could listen to no more of such talk. She returned to her task, pounding roadbed. Nobody else was working except Arnando, who eyed her quizzically. She avoided his gaze, pinched her lips together, and hefted the heavy tamper stone.

Her crewmates spoke of nothing else at dinner: who'd saved up, who (lamentably) had to send money home like a responsible person, who'd enjoyed Dulsia's favors before and could give lascivious descriptions of the delights in store. Tess kept her eyes on her stew, hoping no one would speak to her. Her boorish friends, alas, couldn't tell to leave her alone. Felix threw an arm around her hunched shoulders. "Do you have enough saved up, Tes'puco? Not unless Gen pays you better than the rest of us."

"Gen has a thing for him. He goes to her tent some evenings. Who knows how he gets paid?" said Mico, making a suggestive gesture.

"Shut up," said Tess through her teeth. Hadn't she warned Gen that people would talk?

"Give 'Puco some credit for taste," said Felix. "He likes them younger, and not so bovine. I bet he's got three girlfriends back in Goredd—one blonde, one brunette, one redhead, all with breasts like—"

"Stop talking," cried Tess, grabbing the front of Felix's shirt and shaking him until his teeth chattered. She let go abruptly, shocked at herself.

"What are you, some kind of prude?" said Felix, straightening his shirt.

Mico laughed. "He's a virgin. Not a whisker on him. I bet he can't even—"

"Of course he can!" cried Felix, coming all unwanted to Tess's defense. "If he never has, it's only that he hasn't had the opportunity."

And that was how the "Let's Get Tes'puco Laid" fund got started, everybody chipping in to finance the loss of Tess's presumed virginity. She prayed no one would contribute to such a ridiculous project, but apparently the more ridiculous the project, the more fervently Felix felt he needed to evangelize it. Bizarre stories circulated about the size of Tess's manhood and the deprivations of her childhood that had led her to be, at the ripe old age of seventeen, still disgracefully envirginated.

The consensus was that Tes'puco had been raised by the Order of St. Vitt. Tess might have found this amusingly accurate if it weren't an argument for sending her to the traveling harlot.

Boss Gen had strict rules about who could patronize Dulsia. She made the men bathe; if they'd been violent or ill-tempered or had gotten on her last nerve, she blacklisted them. If she overheard anyone being crass or disrespectful, she'd mime writing a sonnet, slowly and ominously. They all seemed to understand what that meant, and shuddered at the sight.

Tess complained to Gen about the "Let's Get Tes'puco

Laid" fund, but the boss found her predicament distressingly hilarious. "You have two choices, my dear," said Gen, not looking up from her paperwork. "Either put your foot down and tell them you won't go—"

"Or?" said Tess, arms folded.

"Or *go*," said Gen, rolling her eyes, "and stop complaining that your lack of action had consequences. Honestly. This isn't alchemy."

It might as well have been. Tess protested, but no one would listen. "You've got cold feet," said Felix. "Dulsia will warm those up for you. You'll see."

Dulsia camped nearby for three evenings. Only on the final morning, when she was nearly packed and ready to go, did the lads finally scrape enough money together (in fact, they were slightly short because some idiot donated a button and some other idiot pretended to believe it was a half crown). Dulsia stood at the door of her caravan and cocked an eyebrow at poor Tes'puco's story of tragic inexperience—as narrated by Mico, who added a wicked stepmother, an order of self-flagellating monks, a rooster, and a bull. Tess's face grew redder and redder, which Dulsia seemed to find more interesting than the story. When the narration finally ceased, Dulsia weighed the small sack of coins in her hand and said, "Why not? But this is the last one; I have to move along, lordlings."

Everyone feigned weeping. Dulsia took Tess's icy hand and led her up the caravan steps.

"Don't be afraid," said Dulsia, closing the door and bustling past Tess into the tiny, colorful room. "Gen told me what you are. In fact, she bet me that you would 'take the coward's way out,' meaning you'd come in rather than tell her lads where to stick it." She smiled, her eyes crinkling. "But I don't think it was cowardly at all. I think you're being rather brave."

Tess, dazed, sagged into an armchair draped with green and purple scarves. The room took up only half the caravan; the rest was behind a locked door. The walls were painted with oddly suggestive flowers, the ceiling hung with fancy lanterns. There was a feather bed with a tidy quilt upon it; cupboards, from which Dulsia took a teapot and cups; and a tiny table where she set them. A little iron stove muttered to itself in the corner. The kettle had just reached a boil.

"I thought you could use some tea," said Dulsia, winking conspiratorially.

Tess took the proffered cup, hot in her cold hands. Her fear was dissipating—indeed, the *damaelle* up close could have terrified no one, so plump and cuddly was she—but still Tess jittered as the dregs of panic drained out. The cup clinked against her teeth.

Dulsia divided the money into five piles on the bedspread. She clucked her tongue at the button and stuck it down her bodice. "For me and my brothers," she said conversationally, putting three stacks of coins into a wooden box beneath the bed. "One for the future." This went into a metal strongbox in the cupboard. "And one for my comrades-in-bed, the red ladies of Segosh, who aren't as free as me." This last went into a leather bag, behind the locked door.

"Now," said Dulsia, returning to the bed with a flounce, like a young girl. "We can have tea at the lads' expense, but I'd prefer to have earned my money. I assume, gauging by your wariness, that you'd quite balk at my usual services for ladies, but I can answer practical questions if you like, or massage your poor, hunching shoulders. I see you carry your troubles there."

Tess knew she should scorn such a disreputable person—bad enough to be drinking her tea—and yet her back and neck ached terribly, now that Dulsia mentioned it. Tess was surprised to find herself tempted.

Her mother and brothers had said she'd end up a harlot, and Tess had known—everybody knew—that it was a fate worse than death. And yet here was this woman, who seemed . . . she seemed fine. She seemed kind, and Tess knew from experience that kindness was hard to manage if you were filled to the brim with bitterness.

Dulsia shouldn't exist. Tess had questions; the only way to ask was to stay a bit longer. "You may rub my back, but don't touch the rest of me," said Tess, holding up a warning finger.

"Never," said Dulsia firmly. "Unless you ask it."

Tess lay on the bed with her jerkin off (though not her shirt). Dulsia's strong fingers moved the hills of Tess's shoulder blades, exalted the valley of her spine, made the crooked straight. Sometimes it hurt, and Tess cried out; Dulsia paused until Tess bade her continue.

"All your sorrows are bound here. I can feel them," said Dulsia sagely, proceeding with a gentler touch. "Don't be surprised if you weep. I'm warning you in advance."

Tess finally worked up the courage to ask: "How did you end up a . . . a whore?"

Dulsia's hands grew heavier; she didn't like that word, or

didn't like remembering. "When our father died, he left us this cart, a horse, and nothing else," she said. "My brothers thought to join the army, or sign on as private guards. They meant to sell their bodies, and possibly their lives, and we would be separated. I couldn't bear it. So I said, what if you were *my* guards, and I was the one who sold her body, and nobody died?

"It seemed simple, but nothing ever is." Dulsia kneaded like a cat. "I'd naively stepped off a cliff, expecting to walk on air. I went to Segosh, hoping to apprentice—like any baker or ribbon maker—and was nearly entrapped. The ladies there are contract-bound to unscrupulous bosses. The law won't protect them; they fear for their lives. I was lucky to get away."

Tess remembered the money Dulsia had put away. She must be buying out contracts, freeing her sisters in town. Tess wriggled a hand into the pouch at her hip, grabbed the first large coin she found, and handed it over. The *damaelle* stared, as if she didn't know what it was for.

"For the red ladies," said Tess. "To make up for that button."

Dulsia smiled then—all dimples—and put the coin down her bodice. "Thank you," she said, resuming work on Tess's neck. "I know how fortunate I've been. We've found some modicum of independence on the road; I'm not suffering, like my sisters."

"But isn't the work . . . terrible?" said Tess into the pillow. "Doesn't it take a toll on you?"

"Of course it does, just as pounding roadbed takes a toll," said Dulsia. "Even a painter, spreading his own heart upon the canvas, gives it up for money and weeps afterward. There is no pain-free path, sweet girl. Choosing is what makes life bearable.

Every month, my brothers and I count our money and decide whether to quit. When I can't do this anymore, they'll have a turn supporting me. They talk about opening a ribbon shop."

It was such a delightfully incongruous image that Tess laughed, and then Dulsia's thumbs on either side of her spine found a pocket of tension that almost brought her to tears. This backrub had her bouncing between extremes.

"I couldn't have survived without my brothers," Dulsia was saying, "or without friends like Gen watching out for us. She gets hers for free, forever, in gratitude."

Tess turned a skeptical eye. "What could you possibly do for a woman?"

"Are you being nosy, or are you requesting something specific?" said Dulsia, pausing with her hands below Tess's rib cage.

"Neither," said Tess hurriedly. "But our part in ... marital relations"—she felt supremely ridiculous saying that to Dulsia— "is all duty and pain. St. Vitt repays our endurance of it tenfold, provided we keep faith and don't stray, and thus the bitter trials of womanhood are *worth* something, in the end."

"Dear little virgin—" Dulsia began, a smile in her voice.

"I'm not a virgin," said Tess. "Truly. I've borne a child. I know what goes where, and why, and so I know that there's nothing two women could possibly—"

"There's something crucial you seem not to know. A woman may take as much pleasure from *relations* as a man," said Dulsia. "She may even do this on her own, no man required."

And then she told a tale so outlandish that Tess's mind rebelled and rejected it. There was no such thing as a *nupa*—Tess couldn't even translate the word into Goreddi. It had to be a lie.

Tess would have hotly refuted this nonsense if the *damaelle*'s skilled hands had not, at that very moment, reached the tightest and most terrible of her muscles, the fibers of her lower back.

Where Tess had hurt, exactly, excruciatingly, when Dozerius was born.

The memory had been locked in her back, like coins in a strongbox, like a prisoner in a dungeon, and pounding road-bed had bound it tighter. Feeling the same hurt again set the memory free. Pain sprouted across the ready ground of Tess's body and bloomed: pink clover pain, bright buttercups of sorrow, flaring poppies of agony.

Violent sobs, like barking, burst from her throat. She could not hold them back, or she'd split down the middle.

"What is it?" cried Dulsia, pulling her hands away, but too late. Tess was wrecked on the rocks of memory, and there was no returning from this. She shoved the *damaelle*'s hands aside, clutched her jerkin to her chest, flung wide the door, and rushed out into the blinding sunlight.

Her workmates looked up from pounding roadbed and burst incongruously into cheers, until they saw her face.

Twenty

Tess rushed to her tent. She heard Gen snapping at everyone to stop gaping and get back to work, and then heard the soft sound of the flap as someone came in.

Tess looked up from her cot, face streaming, but it wasn't Gen who'd come after her, and it wasn't Felix (her second guess). It was Big Arnando.

He sat cross-legged on the ground near the head of her cot until her sobbing stilled. Then he ran a hand through his graying hair and said, "I told those fools, Felix and Mico, that you seemed unenthusiastic about the *damaelle,* that maybe you were a Daanite—like me—and didn't want to tell them. They didn't listen, and here you are. Felix has a good heart, even if he has no sense. He'd have rushed in here, but I thought you might not want to see him yet."

"Thanks," said Tess, who never cared to see Felix again, and hoped he fell down a hole.

Arnando lowered his voice. "Gen's prowling around, keeping everyone away. Nobody's going to overhear you. You may tell me anything, comrade, if it would help. Dulsia didn't make you do anything against your inclinations, did she?"

Tess shook her head, but started crying again. Arnando took her small, newly callused hand in one of his enormous rough ones.

He asked for no further explanation, but still she wanted to give him one. The memory was loose in her, and she was too wrecked to fight it down and lock it up again. The only way to release it was to utter it aloud.

It wasn't the sort of thing one tells a stranger, and yet there was comfort in the fact that Arnando wasn't a friend. It would be like confession to a priest or, based on the size of him, a mountain. She could hand him her pain, she felt instinctively. She wanted to.

"She made me remember my baby," said Tess, and then she was off her cot and in Arnando's arms, weeping against his mighty chest.

And he didn't say, *Wait, you're a woman?* or *Your name isn't really Tes'puco?* You didn't become the foreman of Boss Gen's crew unless you impressed her, and you didn't impress her unless you were smart.

Arnando cradled Tess to him, a rock in her stormy sea, and said, "Tell me your story."

Grandma Therese had been a comfort during Tess's pregnancy, but Chessey the midwife had been solid as granite. At their weekly checkups in the cherubic panopticon bedroom, she was all business. When she said, "Gown off," Tess obeyed. Chessey would prod and palp with devastatingly competent hands, listen to Tess's belly through a tube, and measure the latitude and longitude of her bump.

If Tess felt sorry for herself and began to weep—as sometimes happened—Chessey snapped, "None of that. You may've played the dog in getting this baby, but you'll play the princess delivering it. This is not defeat, not 'illegitimate,' whatever your family says. Heaven brought each of us forth into this world, and you can't tell me Heaven don't know what it's doing."

The night Grandma Therese died was the night the contractions began, three months early. The memory was blurred now: Tess screamed in the garden; Uncle Jean-Philippe brought her indoors; a scullion was sent running to the village for the midwife; someone must have carried her grandmother's body indoors, but Tess was privy to none of that. She was sent to the cherubic chamber, where servants buzzed around her like bees, fetching towels and boiling water. By the time Chessey arrived, they'd swaddled Tess like a mummy.

"No," barked Chessey, shooing people out and excavating Tess from the mess of linens. She laid hands upon Tess's belly, reading it with her fingers. "That feels serious," she muttered, flinging back Tess's chemise. Tess was too racked with contractions to protest.

Chessey shook her weathered head. "Saints' bunions," she

said. "You're determined to have this baby right now. I don't like it, but you're so far along the tea wouldn't stop it. Might even hasten it. Can you stand with an arm around my shoulders?"

Tess answered with the negative, or tried to, but all that came out was a steam-kettle shrill of panic. Chessey wedged a wadded rag into Tess's mouth.

"Be quiet and listen," she said in a voice that brooked no compromise. "You can give birth the agonizing, terrible way, or you can do it the less terrible way. The latter involves listening to me and doing what I say. What's it going to be?"

Tess, tears streaming down her cheeks, pointed urgently at Chessey.

"Good," said the midwife. "Now stop screaming. It wastes power you'll need later. Stand up." She pulled Tess firmly upright and plucked the rag from her mouth. "It's less frightening on your own two feet, I promise. Walk with me—I won't let you fall—and when your time comes, you shall face it upright, like a proud young lady, not flat on your back like a cowering hound."

They walked, paused for pain, walked some more, paused again. Every time they paused, every time Tess began to flag and fear, Chessey whispered: "You are the traveler, taking this journey. You are the hero, writing this story. When the trickster Pau-Henoa wandered under the earth, what did he find?"

"The sun," Tess gasped when the contraction had passed and she could speak again.

"Right," said Chessey firmly. "Even the pagans knew: you will wander the dark places under the earth, but you will come back with the sun."

The image of the sun, the idea of light, sustained her. She walked when she could and waited when she had to, Chessey guiding her through the labyrinth of pain.

By the time the baby came, Tess had walked herself toward proud young lady, every trace of terrified, subjected dog long gone. Chessey caught the baby, as she'd caught generations of sun-stars, and she cut the cord and bathed the child. Tess—who, having striven and conquered, was permitted at last to lie down—arranged her exhausted limbs on the bed, and yet she wasn't entirely exhausted. Her heart soared with unexpected euphoria, like she could do anything, like nothing would ever hurt again.

Chessey brought the bundle, and Tess gazed for the first time upon that tiny, wrinkled face, like a wizened old man's. His hands were perfect. A warmth rose in her chest, the purest, most aching love she had ever known. Her baby stretched his neck like a tortoise, eyes closed, feeling for her with his mouth, and Tess thought she might die of joy.

"I'm here," she whispered into his damp, sweet scalp. "Always, Dozerius, my heart."

His breathing wasn't right. Every intake was raspy and irregular; Tess felt the sound like cuts against her skin. "What is it, Chessey?" she cried, but the midwife shook her head grimly.

"He came too soon," she said. "Like bread too early from the oven. He's unfinished in the middle."

At Chessey's urging, Tess tried him at her breast—"Not that you've much to give yet, but let's see if he can suckle." His mouth was so weak and tiny that he choked and turned blue. Tess panicked, but Chessey, unflappable, revived him. She had goat's milk brought from the village and showed Tess how to dip the corner of a handkerchief and let milk dribble into his mouth. Some went in, some came up. Dozerius didn't open his eyes and didn't sleep, either, mewling fretfully like a kitten.

By the next day, his limbs, never strong, grew floppy; his skin, never bright, grayed alarmingly. Uncle Jean-Philippe had sent a fast rider to Lavondaville as soon as Tess's confinement began; Mama arrived without Papa, Jeanne, or Seraphina, and the little bit of sun Tess had managed to retain went out. Mama stormed in, a cloud, and glowered over the bed.

"It's a mercy," she said at last. "I prayed to St. Vitt that you'd miscarry, but this will do."

"You talk like he's already dead," said Tess, clasping Dozerius to her chest.

"Steel your heart to it. I'll fetch a priest to do his psalter so some Saint may petition for his entry into Heaven, irrespective of your sins. We'll need to name him."

"I've already named him," said Tess coldly. "He's called—"

But she couldn't say Dozerius, when it came down to it. She couldn't say that she'd named her child after the adventure stories Mama had never approved of, that had propelled her into the world to get herself in trouble. She knew what Mama would say and couldn't bear to hear it, so she sat there, gaping like a fish, trying to come up with a quick substitution.

"Julian," Tess said at last. "After your grandfather, the count."

"That old devil?" said Anne-Marie, frowning, but she didn't suggest another name, so Julian he stayed, officially. The priest came, and the baby's psalter Saint was determined—St. Polypous, the devious one, apropos for both Dozerius and Count Julian. After that, as if reassured that he had a good advocate for entry into Heaven, little Dozerius began to fade away. His skin grew nearly transparent, his breathing so light and shallow that it could barely be heard, and he died in Tess's arms upon the morning of the third day.

She couldn't . . . remember how she knew. Only that she lay clasping him to her chest, hoping against hope that this had all been a dream and that, in accordance with the logic of dreams, he might melt into her heart.

"You've been given a gift, even if you don't realize it," said her mother softly, taking the tiny body from her arms. (Where had she come from? How did she know?) "We only had to hide this pregnancy; now we won't have to hide an embarrassing bastard, too."

Tess could not reply; she had no muscles left, no will.

"When you're well enough to travel, we shall return home, and you'll follow your sister to court. She needs you to keep her to the righteous path, for you know it now. Maybe someday the Saints will hear your prayers, and your penance will be enough."

No penance could be more terrible than this. Her very heart was dead.

"I went numb," she said, raising her head from Big Arnando's shoulder. "I could see my sorrow in the distance, and I knew that it would kill me, so I didn't let myself feel. I cut it off—cut everything off—like taking a cleaver and hacking off my own—"

Foot. Like in her dream at the Queen's summer palace, except in the dream it had been an act of courage, not cowardice.

"You did what you had to do to survive," said Arnando, pressing his cheek against her forehead. He smelled like the dusty fields. "One thing I've learned about grief: it's like a creditor's bill. You can put off paying, but it eventually falls due, and exacts usurious interest."

"Do they send someone to break your fingers?" said Tess, thinking of the Belgiosos.

Arnando laughed softly. "You find a way to break them yourself." He paused to let her think about what that entailed; she had some idea. "There's a room in my heart full of unpaid bills," he said. "We all have one. It's useful to go in occasionally and open a few."

Tess pulled away and wiped her eyes. "Then they're paid? Am I done with Dozerius?" Her voice broke as she said his name, and she knew that she was not.

"That's a big one, so I doubt it," said Arnando, his blue eyes mournful. "You might have to pay it in installments, but now you know you can. It won't kill you. You have the funds, 'Puco." He paused, embarrassed to have called her Stupid.

"Tess," said Tess.

"Tess," he agreed, taking her hand and squeezing it. "You're stronger than you were when it happened."

She nodded, inhaling one last sob-breath. They sat in silence a moment, and then she said, "I would like to get to work now."

"Good," said Arnando, standing and extending a hand. "There's always more to do."

He pulled her to her feet, and they went out together, into the blazing noonday sun.

Twenty-One

Arnando, true to his word, never told anyone what had passed between him and 'Puco. In fact, he went back to being her foreman, to Tess's great relief, and not her particular friend. Having disburdened herself, she wasn't sure how to talk to him afterward.

Mico joked with her as if nothing had happened, but Felix, at least, felt guilty for sending her to the *damaelle* against her inclination. He cringed like a kicked dog with big, sad eyes, as close as he could get to apologizing. She didn't forgive him, quite, but she might have if he could have brought himself to ask.

✄

Tess was awakened one night by chirping, as if a cricket had crawled down her shirt and started singing. She sat up, half-panicked, swatting her chest, before realizing it was the thnik. Pathka never called her—it was always the other way around—and she hadn't expected it to sound like a cricket. She clapped a hand over the device to muffle it, grabbed her boots, and sneaked out of the tent without waking Felix, Mico, or Aster.

"Pathka, what's happened?" she asked when she was far enough from the tents not to be heard. It was well after midnight. Gen set watches along the road, so Tess had run perpendicular, into the wheat. She stopped and wiggled bare feet into boots.

"There's a windmill downwind from your camp," said Pathka faintly. "I'll be there."

Its triangular sails were outlined against the rising moon, half a mile off by her estimate. "I'm on my way," cried Tess, hastening her steps. Pathka didn't answer.

Tess had been watching the windmills on distant hillsides for weeks, fascinated by their majestic slowness. Up close, this one groaned and flapped; some internal trundling mechanism kept up a persistent thump. The door was locked.

Tess scoured the perimeter, and finally looked out at the wheat on the far side of the ridge. A trail of crushed plants was just visible; it ended twenty feet downhill from her. She plunged into the field and found Pathka, collapsed, the bowl-scales clasped to his back.

A glittering among the stalks gave the tableau an aura of enchantment until Tess realized it was the moon reflecting off a puddle of silver blood.

Pathka's eyes were squeezed shut, and he had three more broken head spines. The blood was coming from a series of punctures in his side, all the same depth, in a tidy curve.

Tess knew only one thing that could make such a wound: Kikiu's bite enhancer.

Tess fell to her knees and laid a hand on Pathka's head.

"You came," said Pathka, his voice faint and gritty like sand underfoot.

"What happened?" said Tess, stroking his drooping spines.

His breathing sounded strangely doubled, a gasp followed by a hiss, and Tess realized with alarm that his lung had been punctured.

"Don't speak," she cried. "Tell me after—"

"Might not be an after," he croaked.

"Did Kikiu do this?" said Tess furiously, uselessly.

"Bit me like an animal." Pathka paused, panting. "Not like a quigutl at all. That monster—"

Pathka's voice sputtered and his eye cones rolled. He was out cold.

Tess's mind raced: he needed care. She'd take him back to the tents, bind his wounds, explain him to Boss Gen somehow. The odds of the road crew accepting Pathka's presence were dismally small, though, and she couldn't even vouch for Gen with certainty.

And frankly, she wasn't sure he'd make it.

Anathuthia could heal him right now, if Tess could get the ritual to work aboveground. She didn't know if it was possible, only that she had to try.

She gently took the scales from Pathka's unresisting arms. The wounds in his side still oozed sluggishly. Tess caught the trickle as best she could, shared drops between the bowls, and hoped it was enough.

Hoped *she* was enough. Pathka had been a more active participant last time.

She squatted in the wheat, elbows on her knees, holding the two bowls like offerings.

Nothing glowed.

Could he be too deeply unconscious to dream? Tess didn't dare sprinkle the blood around him if it wasn't glowing.

She'd never been good at prayer, and Anathuthia was surely more monster than goddess, and yet. She could think of nothing else to try.

"Anathuthia," she said to the empty air, "I am nest to Pathka, insofar as a human can be. Nest and not-nest. I call upon you, since Pathka cannot."

There was no sound but the thunking and flapping of the mill.

Nothing was happening. She didn't know what to do. Last time Pathka had said to listen to herself, but that was surely useless. She wasn't a quigutl. She didn't have the kind of connection that—

A terrible idea struck Tess. She blinked, as if the thought were dust in her eye and her vision might clear, but it was still there.

Pathka wasn't conscious enough to dream, let alone vouch to Anathuthia that Tess was his nest. The only way she could think of to show the serpent she was serious involved ingesting poison.

Tess swirled the blood, took a deep breath, and put the scale-bowl to her lips.

She took a single drop into her mouth and was overwhelmed by astringent bitterness, like earwax and green persimmons. It numbed her tongue and seized her throat so she couldn't swallow. Her whole being seemed to shrivel and pucker, except for her stomach, which lurched violently. Tears streamed down her cheeks; she couldn't do this, she'd failed.

She retched into the wheat. A thin stream of drool hung from her lips.

It began to glow.

"Never," she whispered, and the wind whispered back through the wheat, as if in answer.

She took another tiny dram—less terrible because her mouth was already numb—and she spit it out messily, all over Pathka. The droplets glowed like fireflies, and then the blood he'd spilled crawling through the wheat began to glow as well, like the long blue tail of a comet.

"Anathuthia, I call you," Tess cried hoarsely, feeling it. "Most Alone, who is not alone. Singular-*utl*. Pathka needs you. Find him and soothe him and let him come home."

The wind picked up; the wheat rolled in waves like the ocean. Tess was too logical to believe it was an acknowledgment, and yet . . .

Pathka's limbs twitched as he finally began to dream; his wounds began to close.

Tess crawled a little ways and vomited in the wheat. Then she lay beside him and slept.

⚔

Her mouth still tasted terrible when she awoke, but she seemed to have suffered no other ill effects. She was going to have to take this up with Seraphina, if she ever saw her again.

On the other side of the ridge, muffled shouts told her the crew had begun to stir.

Tess looked down at Pathka, who was still sleeping like the dead. It was time for their roads to be reunited, there was no question about that, but first she had some loose ends to tie up. Her pack was back at camp, and she didn't like leaving with no explanation. She owed Gen that, at least.

If she went quickly, Pathka would never know she'd been gone. She dashed back across the fields toward camp, steeling herself to say goodbye.

Tess retrieved her pack from an empty tent; Mico, Felix, and Aster must've been at breakfast already. She had absent-mindedly carried the scale-bowls back with her, so she shoved those inside her bag, along with her savings, her dirty laundry, and the rest of her gear. She crossed camp to the mess tent and entered, scanning the crowded trestle tables for Boss Gen.

"Where'd you sneak off to, 'Puco?" called Felix.

Mico hollered after: "Sleeping with the boss again?" Laughter went up all around.

Tess thumbed her nose at them. A gust of wind shook the

tarps of the dining tent, and then an eerie, inhuman scream and a very human shout of alarm sounded from the road.

Everyone leaped to their feet and rushed out to see what had happened.

One of the cart horses was screaming, eyes reeling white, bucking against the traces. Its drovers tried to calm it as it reared, overturning its wagon and scattering gravel everywhere.

The drovers cursed, scrambling to right the cart again.

The crew wouldn't be able to move on until the road was cleared. They ran for shovels while Boss Gen barked orders.

This was not the time to approach her about quitting.

Someone pressed a shovel into Tess's hands, and then she was rushing to the roadward side of the gravel pile, ready to do her job one last time. The wind grew wilder and whipped her short hair around.

She'd reached the far side of the gravel when a flood of animals surged across the road in front of her: field mice, frogs, rats, chipmunks, badgers, snakes, crickets, a flock of starlings, and finally a small battalion of deer surged out of the wheat. The animals swarmed east, reaping a swath through the fields on both sides of the road. The crew gaped in dumbfoundment. It was like a story or a dream, these animals united in direction and purpose.

The mill was east, Tess suddenly realized. Were they running toward Pathka, or away from something else?

That was when the earth began to shake.

The tremor snatched Tess's feet from under her, and she belly-flopped hard on the paving stones. Men fell like timber behind her, crawled on elbows and knees, cried out in terror. Tess's brains seemed to slosh in her head; she clung to the stones, feeling upside down, as if someone had grabbed the world like a big ball and was trying to shake the ants off it. She hung on with everything she had.

The shouts around her took on a new meaning. She heard her name—"Tes'puco!"—over and over. She raised her cheek from the stones and saw her comrades wildly waving from the gravel pile. Tess blinked uncomprehendingly. Felix shouted through cupped hands, and she could discern his shrill words through the cacophony: "Stupid-head! Get your stupid body over—"

She didn't hear the rest. A thunderous rumble, like the earth's intestinal tract, jerked her up and down and side to side, and then the solid ground disappeared from under her, stone and earth turned into empty space. A deafening roar, darkness and dust; she couldn't orient herself in space. She flopped like a rag doll, bouncing around, like falling down stairs, sliding, scraping.

She hit her head and saw stars. When she finally realized she'd stopped moving, and the dust began to clear, she saw the hole, maybe fifteen feet above her. She was on top of a shifting pile of loose stone, not underneath it. That was lucky.

Her hearing slowly cleared. She heard Nicolas enjoining others to avoid the edge: "—it's not that you might fall in and break your necks—as if I cared!—but you might send more rocks precipitating down to crush Tes'puco."

Tess felt like one big bruise. Her eyes were crusty with dust. Her limbs seemed intact and uncrushed, but something had happened to her left side. Maybe a cracked rib. It gripped her lung like a vise and sent a shock of agony up her side when she tried to breathe.

"'Puco!" It was Felix screaming. "Answer me, damn you! If you're alive, answer!"

She couldn't get enough breath to scream. "I'm here," she wheezed. "Not dead." It struck her as funny, even though it manifestly wasn't. Still not dead, in spite of everything.

They couldn't hear her; they kept shouting. A light rain of gravel drummed on her head; she dragged herself out of range, down the side of the mound, deeper into darkness. They'd never see her unless they came to the edge and shone a light.

Gen's brassy voice sounded over everyone else's. "No closer, you idiots. Have we already forgotten Daniele's bad example? Will you follow each other over the edge, one by one, like lemmings? We will find her, but we'll do it systematically."

There was absolute silence for a heartbeat, and then someone said, "Her?"

Tess wanted to laugh at Gen's misstep under pressure, but the laugh turned into a cough, which was agony. Tears rushed down her cheeks, mixing with the dirt to form muddy streaks.

"Hush!" cried Arnando's echoing basso. "I hear something."

Could they hear her blubbering? Tess's heart leaped, but then she realized she wasn't the loudest thing down here. Something was scraping, like rocks down a rough incline.

The ground shook again. Chunks of ceiling fell around her; she skittered down the incline as fast as her ribs allowed, into a deeper part of the cave where the floor was solid and the ceiling wasn't shedding chunks of rock. The light from the distant hole barely illuminated the cavern around her, but her eyes were growing used to dimness.

Something moved. She couldn't understand what she was seeing: one wall of the chamber shifted—and was it glowing, or was that her imagination? It was more regularly shingled than any pile of detritus should be.

Her breath caught as the "wall" slid past, tapered to a dull point, and then disappeared around a curve in the tunnel, leaving nothing but darkness behind.

Anathuthia. That had been the mere tip of her tail.

Above Tess, voices became audible again, though it was harder at this distance to distinguish words. She caught snatches of a debate on whether to risk sending someone down on a rope, or whether they should wait to be sure the aftershocks were over.

Tess felt like she'd died indeed, and was hearing all this from a terrific distance, dispassionately detached. A curious pity stirred her heart. They were going to miss her.

Her thnik chirped. Tess scrabbled for it and switched it on. "Pathka?" she rasped breathlessly. Heaven's dustbin, it hurt to talk.

"I saw you fall in," said Pathka tinnily. "I'll be right there."

He was up and about. That was good news, at least. Tess inventoried her pack while she waited. She'd acquired flint and steel while on the work crew, and a small lantern. The lantern was slippery with oil, but she managed to light it without catching herself on fire. She muscled herself to standing, clutching her throbbing side, and looked ahead, after the serpent. The tunnel seemed to extend forever.

Shouts rang, and then a shape hurtled down the hole and rolled down the pile of broken rocks. It was Pathka, none the worse for his tumble. He frolicked around her, making grotesque shadows in the lamplight.

"The crew is trying to make a harness Felix can't fall out of," Pathka reported, "but I suspect he has untapped talents. They're going to waste a lot of time looking for you, you know."

Tess looked up regretfully but had no illusions about wasted time. Boss Gen would give them a day to search, and then they'd be back on track, sending word to the engineers that there was another bridge to be built, saying farewell to her imagined corpse if not her memory.

They still talked about Daniele; they'd be discussing her eccentricities for a long time.

The last thing she heard before staggering up the passage after Pathka was Felix shouting into the chasm: "Hang on, friend, whoever you are! We're going to find you. Don't be frightened." His voice broke a little. "I hope you've never been frightened of us."

"Never," Tess whispered, her heart unexpectedly full.

Then she turned and followed Pathka along another road.

Twenty-Two

They followed the cavern around the bend and down a steep grade, toward the center of the earth. Small side passages branched off at irregular intervals, and Tess noticed Pathka pausing to sniff these, even though the serpent could never have squeezed into them.

"Is Kikiu down here?" asked Tess, guessing what he was sniffing for.

"Not anymore," said Pathka, although he took one last, lingering sniff. "I hope you see that I tried to reach out, Teth. I made a good-faith effort and was nearly killed for it."

Tess's cracked rib made it hurt to talk, so she merely nodded.

"Kikiu is broken," Pathka pronounced as he reached the ceiling above Tess's head. "*Ko* is becoming more unnatural, deliberately. You saw those metal teeth. Now *ko* has made iron horns. If *ko* chooses to be monstrous, I don't see what else I can do. I tried."

Tess found it hard to catch her breath, as if she were tightly corseted, but she couldn't let that pass without comment: "Not at...the right time, Pathka—not back when...she needed you."

Pathka's tail gave a sharp, serpentine twitch of rebuke; he flounced ahead, across the ceiling, without another word.

Tess's lantern ran out of oil after another hour, and then they traveled by the wavering light of Pathka's tongue. Tess's ribs throbbed and constricted her air; she required frequent rest. Pathka waited with her, though every angle of his spines betrayed irritation and impatience. He could have navigated the caverns without any light.

Two hours later they found more scales, similar to the ones in her pack but many times larger. Big enough to use for a sledge in wintertime. Tess, who'd grown too sore and exhausted to go on, curled up and slept in one. Pathka kept watch.

When she awoke, however, Pathka wasn't there.

She hoped he'd simply decided to scout ahead. Surely he'd be back. She sat up carefully in the pitch darkness and called softly, "Pathka?" Her voice echoed, an acoustical map she couldn't interpret. She whistled, listening to the vastness, and experienced an unexpected frisson, a goose-bumpy thrill.

Not fear. Excitement.

She felt for the smooth edge of the scale she'd been sleeping in, moving calmly, trying to orient herself. She sat with her legs dangling off, breathing (painfully) and reasoning. She didn't have to worry about hitting her head on the arching ceiling. Assuming she hadn't rotated in her sleep—and in fact, she wasn't prone to flopping about—she would have arrived from her right.

Forward, toward the serpent, must be to her left.

In her satchel she found raisins and her water skin, nearly empty—the limits of her survival. She sipped and nibbled, put everything back, and got to her feet. Walk or crawl? Her rib cage made the choice for her, objecting vehemently to any weight on her arms. She stood cautiously and began to walk like a dancer in a promenade, patting the ground with her toe before committing to each step.

Fear still hadn't found her, but then this wasn't so different from how she'd been living since she ran away from home. If she couldn't see where she was going in this cave, well, she couldn't see the end of the Road, either. In fact, this was part of the Road, she decided. The Serpent's Road. The most useful virtues, for one who walked on, were flexibility and a willingness to improvise.

She'd just thought this—just decided she *liked* it—when the darkness ahead began to change. She paused and stared, her eyes ecstatically informing her that there was light ahead, the faintest glow. She could discern the shape of the passage. Maybe. Unless she was imagining it.

Another hundred yards along, it became unmistakable. Black was transitioning slowly to dark gray, like the moment before sunrise when the sky begins thinking about day, when the outlines of trees become visible, black upon somewhat-less-black. Tess could make out the silhouette of her hand. She quickened her pace. Anathuthia had glowed; she hadn't imagined it. Pathka must have reached her, which was why he wasn't back yet.

The ground quaked. Tess dropped and braced herself against a boulder. Sand rained into her hair, and there was a sound so low she didn't hear it so much as feel it in her chest. Her heart and lungs vibrated in concert. Her ribs, a delicate barometer of agony, left her gasping, her forehead beaded with sweat.

When the earth stilled, she walked clutching her side, breathing raggedly. Anathuthia must be ahead. Surely nothing else could sound like that, not even the earth itself.

The passage wound left and right, the eerie glow strengthening with each turn. Light prefers straight lines, so only half-light made it around the curves, the memory of illumination, a daydream of daytime. The tunnel finally opened into a chamber so vast she couldn't see the far side. In fact, she couldn't see much besides the light.

The floor was a great crater, and at the center a sphere glowed coolly blue, a now familiar color. Nothing gave a sense of scale; the ball might have been as big as a house.

No serpent. She hesitated at the lip of the bowl, then took a tentative step.

"Teth!" cried a stone at her feet. She'd almost trodden upon

Pathka, who'd been perfectly still but was now dancing around her, his earlier irritation apparently dispelled.

"This is Anathuthia's nest!" he cried. "That's her egg. Isn't it astonishing?"

It was. Tess tried to say so, but Pathka was bounding so comically that she had to put all her effort toward not laughing. Laughing was excruciating. She lowered herself gingerly and Pathka rubbed against her. "She laid it before my eyes. This must be her ancient birthplace."

"Where is she now?" Tess whispered, glancing around. Was it dangerous to invade a serpent's nest? Maternal instinct could make even placid creatures fierce.

"She left." Pathka's gravelly voice reverberated; apparently he didn't share her worry. "Maybe looking for sustenance. Laying eggs is work."

Tess could hardly take her eyes off the egg. Its light seemed to swirl and sing, like the surface of a river.

"It's her blood that makes it glow," said Pathka, anticipating Tess's question. "It will probably fade as it dries."

They watched in silence. "Pathka," Tess said at last, "I'm afraid . . . I need to go—"

"Wait until she comes back," said Pathka. "Look Anathuthia in the eye, and then tell me you have any desire to be anywhere else."

Tess shifted, wincing. "You don't understand. I fell down here . . . underprepared. Water's almost gone. I want to . . . not die of thirst."

"Oh, is that all?" said Pathka, perking up. "Wait here. I'll find a spur to the surface."

The egg's glow had nearly faded by the time Pathka returned. Kindly, he'd made Tess a torch. "I've found a way up that doesn't involve crawling across the ceiling," he said. "Follow."

He led her to a tunnel that seemed artificial, to Tess's surprise; chiseled steps curled upward in a spiral. "Maybe this was once a mine," Pathka speculated. "The chamber might have held useful minerals. Saltpeter? Is that used in St. Ogdo's fire?"

Tess didn't know her knightly lore and wasn't sure. She mounted the stairs alone.

She emerged, jelly-legged after a long climb, into a decorated grotto. Above the arched doorway was carved in an archaic script: PAU-HENOA'S GATE.

Tess knew that name: it was the pagans' trickster god, who'd gone under the earth to fetch the sun. Maybe this was where the world had given birth to daylight.

Or maybe those pagans had glimpsed a World Serpent's egg.

The inscription notwithstanding, the grotto had been converted into a shrine to St. Prue—Santi Prudia, in Ninysh—complete with altar, bas-reliefs of her life story, and dried flowers on the floor. A hand-painted sign forbade anyone but the abbot and priors to descend the stairs, which were dark and slippery and led to a meditation chamber containing absolutely no treasure of any kind. Tess wondered whether that last protestation made people want to check and see. There were contrarians in this world, and she should know.

Apparently there were also monks who knew about Anathuthia. This was much more surprising.

Outside loomed their massive monastery, surrounded by a

wall. Tess made out an orchard on the other side, and more outbuildings than she could be bothered to count. The bell for whatever monks did at twilight began to ring, and she heard pattering feet and snatches of song. She skirted the compound toward the setting sun until she reached the gates and saw that the monastery, like the shrine, was dedicated to Santi Prudia. These monks would be historians and archivists, but if she was hungry, they surely wouldn't turn her away.

The earth grumbled again. Tess steadied herself, gritting her teeth against the pain in her side, and then knocked at the bronze-bossed monastery doors.

A panel in the door slid to one side, and a pair of long-lashed hazel eyes peered at Tess through a grating. "You knocked?" said a nasal tenor. "Or was that the earth?"

Tess affected a pious mien. "Bless you, Brother, I was passing by . . . and I was—"

"Terrified by earthquakes? Wise man. Go back where you came from." The panel snapped sharply shut.

Tess, irritated, knocked again. The panel opened ominously slowly, no eyes visible now, only the darkness at the heart of the gatehouse. When Tess drew nearer to squint into the gloom, the monk popped up and startled her. "Go away. I won't be nice a third time."

"You haven't been nice once!" She had to catch her breath. "Is this how your order treats . . . hungry and indigent? Your fellow churchmen? I'm a . . . seminarian."

The eyes blinked, and she heard a mumble that might have been "Damn it." The door swung open and there stood a scrawny, slouching monk, maybe five or six years her senior, in a blue cassock. His sharp nose might've looked decisive if the rest of his face hadn't looked so resigned; it was the lone dissenter, and a little depressed about it. "Come in, then. And for the record: you don't look like a seminarian. You look like a wiseacre." He stepped aside to let Tess in. "I'm Frai Moldi—for when you report me to the abbot. What do you call yourself, Brother?"

"Jacomo," said Tess. She extended her hand, and Frai Moldi scowled. Only then did she notice that his right sleeve was empty, tied in a knot to keep it out of his way. "I beg your pardon," she said, quickly offering her left instead. He took her up on the offer, never quite losing his skeptical expression. She grimaced; her left arm connected directly to her aching ribs.

All she wanted was some food and water, but Frai Moldi wouldn't hear of handing her a loaf and letting her continue on her way—no, no, he couldn't treat a seminarian so shabbily (except the ones from St. Abaster's; those fellows could hang). He had to offer her a bed, at least. Tess protested—Pathka would surely worry if she was gone all night—but it became quickly clear that there would be no food forthcoming unless she let Frai Moldi show her the dormitories first. She followed him into the depths of the monastery, to a narrow cell.

"We have all the fine monastic amenities: narrow cot, paneless window, unpadded kneeler," he said, pointing them out. "We're not big self-flagellators here, but I can get you a knotted rope if you need one."

Tess chuckled, painfully; Frai Moldi shot her a sharp look. "Sorry," she said, her face reddening. "I assumed you were joking."

"I suppose I was," he said dismally. "I'm not used to anyone finding it funny."

They made a brief stop at the well so Tess could wash up—her face and hands were filthy, and there was grit in her hair—and then Frai Moldi led her to the refectory, a vast hall where the monks held communal meals. The bell, half an hour ago, had been for supper, but no one was eating yet. The abbot, seated at the top of the room with the priors and the most senior monks, was still holding forth on the Disquisitions of Santi Prudia.

"'We build history every day, anew,' saith Santi Prudia, but what does it mean?" the abbot was saying as they entered. Frai Moldi picked his way between long monk-filled benches, leading Tess toward the far end of the room. The only empty seats were behind the novices, who refused to shift and let Moldi sit ahead of them. A silent struggle ensued, which Moldi lost. He flipped a rude gesture at his uppity juniors, taking care that the head table couldn't see, and then grudgingly sat at the end with Tess.

One of the novices, eyes bulging in outrage, raised his hand for attention.

"Knowledge is nothing," said the abbot, ignoring the hand. An iron-haired, crease-faced senior monk, sighing heavily, rose and came toward the back of the hall; the sermon continued, unstoppable: "Interpretation gives knowledge value, but it must evolve as new knowledge emerges."

"What are you doing?" hissed the senior monk, who'd instantly identified Frai Moldi as the problem. "You have gate duty."

"Visitor," Moldi whispered loudly, pointing at Tess. "Should I have let him starve?"

The senior monk sat beside Moldi, and they held a

conversation with their faces until the end of the sermon. Tess watched, fascinated. The old monk's face went from stern admonition to fatherly concern; the younger's said piss off and then, when the old monk turned away, despair.

"... from myriad incomplete truths, a greater whole. So shall it be," said the ancient abbot in conclusion. "So shall it be" echoed reverently around the hall, and then the food came out, more than Tess had seen since her sister's wedding: roast venison, mutton, and boar, each with its own sauce; white bread; braised root vegetables; tender cabbage with apples.

"Introduce your guest, Frai Moldi," said the senior monk, helping himself to parsnips.

Moldi pulled his pointy nose out of his wine cup and aimed it at Tess. "Brother Jacques do Mort, seminarian."

Tess grinned again, but then she wasn't sure whether he was joking or had forgotten her name in fact. "Brother Jacomo," she corrected.

"Welcome. I'm Frai Lorenzi, head archivist," said the older monk, bowing slightly. The bare patch atop his head was liverspotted. "We should show you our library after dinner."

"It's the jewel of Santi Prudia," drawled Frai Moldi. Tess cringed at his tone, but if Frai Lorenzi heard the sarcasm, he gave no sign. Frai Moldi, frowning, switched his empty cup with a novice's full one. Tess knew that trick.

"Which seminary do you attend?" said Frai Lorenzi. He took small bites and chewed his food thoroughly, like an elderly rabbit.

"St. Gobnait's, in Lavondaville," said Tess. They'd surely identified her accent.

"Oh, indeed!" said the archivist with unexpected enthusiasm. "Is my cousin Bastien still prior there, or has he retired?"

Tess hesitated, causing Frai Moldi to freeze with his hand near Frai Lorenzi's cup. He'd been about to make the switch but was relying on her for distraction. He bugged his eyes at her.

"Ah-h-h," said Tess, drawing it out, trying to hold the archivist's gaze, "he hadn't retired when I left, but I've been on the road for months, so it's possible..." She waved her hands eloquently; Moldi made the switch. She may have smiled a little at this.

"Where are you traveling?" said Frai Lorenzi, noticing none of Moldi's shenanigans.

"I'm following Prior Bastien's advice, in fact," said Tess. "I lost my faith, you see—"

"Your faith, or your vocation?" said Frai Lorenzi, tenting his bony fingers.

Tess could tell this question was a precipice over a deep philosophical ocean. "Both?"

"It's a personal question, forgive me," said the old archivist, "but vocation is something I think about a lot—how is it found, what is it for? Must the call come before the work, or will any good work, done with openheartedness, slowly begin to call to us?"

Frai Moldi rolled his eyes hard, then blinked as if he'd strained something.

This was an old dispute between them, evidently. Tess only half listened as Frai Lorenzi droned on about love and work; she was riveted by Moldi's expression. It was a flat mask of scorn, and yet she could make out eddies beneath it—despair and desperation—as clearly as if he were transparent. His pink-rimmed eyes wouldn't meet hers.

He was a wreck, the human version of Old Haunty. Tess felt like she was seeing herself at Jeanne's wedding—but worse. A caricature. At least, she hoped she hadn't been so obvious.

Moldi eyed her cup. Tess slid it across to him while the archivist was occupied pouring gravy. Moldi sneered, but downed her dregs at a gulp.

A tremor made the chandeliers swing and sent the gravy boat sailing off the end of the table. The room went quiet momentarily, and then the brothers went back to eating and debating the minutiae of history as if nothing had happened.

Anathuthia might have returned to her nest; Pathka would be wondering why Tess hadn't. "Thank you for the meal and good company," said Tess to the monks across the table, "but I need to be going."

Frai Lorenzi looked mournful. "You can't mean to sleep in the cold? Stay until morning, at least."

Her ribs ached; a night indoors would do her good, and surely Pathka was enthralled with Anathuthia and wouldn't miss her right away. Tess assented, which plainly delighted the old monk. He sent a grumbling novice to take over Frai Moldi's gate duty, and then led Tess to the top of the room. Frai Moldi followed them, sullen and unsteady.

The head archivist introduced Tess to the abbot, Pater Livian, so old and frail that his skull seemed to shine through his skin.

"Stay as long as you will, Brother Jacomo." The priors

helped him to his feet. "But don't be surprised if our library inspires you to join our order. It's the finest in the Southlands."

The library was apparently a popular after-dinner destination; Frai Lorenzi led Tess alongside a crowd of monks heading the same direction. They reached a high-ceilinged octagonal chamber full of writing desks, a scriptorium, which was the first room of the library. The brothers took their seats, ready to resume work. Many had brought unfinished cups of wine, which they set beside their inkpots. Tess wondered whether they ever picked up the wrong vessel to drink from, and if they minded.

Frai Moldi could open his ink one-handed, even drunk. He sharpened his quill against a stone and did not look at Tess.

The head archivist gave her a tour of four vaulted rooms resplendent with rich, dark wood, gilt columns, and stained glass. "We have more than five thousand volumes," he said modestly. It was indeed magnificent, and if Tess had never seen the library at Castle Orison, which held the collections of St. Ingar, she might have agreed with the abbot's assessment.

"Our scribes copy any new book that comes in," said Frai Lorenzi. "Travelers like to dictate their adventures. We have books that exist nowhere else."

Tess had a few stories worth telling. She wondered whether to offer them.

"Listen," said Frai Lorenzi, lowering his voice and glancing toward the scriptorium. "Did you know Moldi before?"

"Before he lost his arm?" she reflexively whispered, guessing.

"No," said the archivist, taken aback. "Well, *yes*, but I meant . . . You're not an old comrade from his soldiering days?"

Tess must have looked as astonished as she felt, because Frai Lorenzi shook his head, frowning. "Forgive me. I thought maybe, because he brought you to dinner. Guests of your stature are supposed to eat in the kitchens. Also, you smiled at him and . . . that's not how people usually react to Moldi."

Frai Lorenzi tried to smile, but his shoulders sagged. As he led Tess back to the scriptorium, a tremor racked the library, strong enough to make the chandeliers dance and to knock large books off the top shelves. Frai Lorenzi scowled at this nuisance and found a lower shelf for the fallen books.

None of the monks commented on the tremor; they must endure these quakes often, and the sign above the stairs had called the nest a "meditation chamber." There were probably volumes about Anathuthia in this very library.

"This monastery is how old?" she asked Frai Lorenzi, loudly enough for all to hear.

"Five hundred and eleven years," he said proudly.

Several dozen pairs of eyes looked up at her. They knew. Men of knowledge, living above an enormous snake for five hundred years, keeping meticulous records? They couldn't not know—the only question was whether they'd talk to her about it.

They certainly hadn't shared their knowledge with the outside world. Will would have given his eyeteeth for the chance to interview one of these brothers, if he'd ever learned that they existed.

But Will wasn't here. Tess was. And she was grinning absurdly to herself.

A direct, respectful approach was surely best. "Brothers, I

arrived here through the caverns. I know what made them, and I want to know more. What can you teach me about the giant serpent below you?" she said.

"Ha ha!" Frai Moldi burst out, but the rest of the room fell into a silence—not angry or hostile so much as cautious. Frai Lorenzi scrutinized her face.

Tess tried again: "Clearly it's a secret you keep, and I respect that. I found the creature on my own, though, following sinkholes it made. I only want to learn more about it— you surely understand that, and you must know more than anyone else."

"Wait, *what*?" Moldi looked around wildly at his brethren. The novices seemed equally confused, but the older monks watched Frai Lorenzi as if waiting for instructions.

The archivist looked pained. "The novices haven't earned this knowledge yet," he said, flashing Tess a rueful smile. At his sign, the new recruits were led out—along with Moldi, who must've been too junior or too irresponsible. He did not submit graciously but had to be pulled along, bumping into lecterns and stools. He stared at Frai Lorenzi all the way out.

"We call it Santi Prudia's Sign," said Frai Lorenzi while Moldi was being ushered to the door. "It returns at irregular intervals, bringing tremors with it—"

"Whoa, hold on, no," said Moldi. He sat blocking the door and refused to budge a step farther. His escort tugged Moldi's arm but didn't quite dare to drag him. "You said Santi Prudia's Sign was the earth stretching itself. Nothing to be alarmed about."

"It is, indeed, nothing to be alarmed about," said Frai Lorenzi calmly.

"The devil it's not!" cried Moldi, jerking his arm out of the other monk's grasp. All around the scriptorium, his brethren kissed knuckles against evil. "A serpent that makes earthquakes and sinkholes? When were you going to tell me about this?"

"Once you'd proved yourself worthy," said Frai Lorenzi. "I had every confidence that you'd get there eventually."

Moldi leaped up and dodged his lunging escort, who fell into a bookcase. "What's it doing down there? What does it eat? What does it *want*?" Each question raised his voice half an octave.

"We'll talk about this later, when you're calm," said the head archivist.

Several more monks tried to herd Moldi out. Drunk and scrawny though he was, he'd been taught to fight once upon a time, and was surprisingly nimble. Moldi knocked one brother to the ground, dodged three more, and somehow ended up on top of the lecterns, leaping from desk to desk, scattering piles of manuscript pages. Parchments flew like leaves in a gale; monks scrambled to pick them up.

Was he upset by the serpent or trying to upset everyone else? Tess couldn't quite tell.

Frai Moldi had just decided to lift his robes and waggle his bare buttocks at the room (answering Tess's unasked question) when the doors opened and the abbot, Pater Livian, arrived on the arms of two priors. The scriptorium went silent; even Moldi froze mid-waggle, his face falling. Pater Livian, antique as he was, took in the room at a glance—parchments, chaos, buttocks, and all—and said quietly, "Frai Lorenzi, a word, if you please."

Frai Lorenzi had the wherewithal to first instruct one of the junior monks to see to their guest, and Tess, to her dismay, was led back to her cell and bid good night.

☙

The matins bell woke her—indeed, there was no sleeping through it—and she got up only to find her door locked. She banged and shouted to no avail, and so she went back to bed in hopes that maybe this was a dream and things would be different when she woke up.

Breakfast woke her the second time, a tray under her door. Tess was forced to admit that she was locked in and had no notion why.

The abbot visited her at noon, his priors looming behind him, and explained that Santi Prudia's Sign was a holy mystery, and therefore Tess could not be allowed to leave. She could, however, join the order, and once she'd earned enough seniority—

She closed the door in his face—maybe not her wisest move, as it was locked again immediately. Tess threw herself onto her cot and stayed there all day. The window, though paneless, was too narrow to squeeze out of.

She was startled awake by Frai Lorenzi sitting on the foot of her cot. He carried a roll of parchments under one arm and was wearing spectacles. The light through the window had turned orange; it was nearly sunset. Tess sat stiffly, side aching, and tried to shake off her grogginess.

"Forgive me for waking you, Brother Jacomo," said Frai Lorenzi. "But I need your help, and I believe you need mine."

"I can't join your order," said Tess, ready to explain why, if it would get her out of there.

The creases in his forehead deepened. "Well, you *could*, if you wished, but I disagree with our abbot that witnessing Santi Prudia's Sign means the choice is made for you." Frai Lorenzi lowered his voice, as if Pater Livian might overhear. "Our mandate is to conserve and interpret knowledge, not conceal it. Why shouldn't the world learn of the wonder beneath our feet? Are we alone worthy of glimpsing Heaven's majesty? I can't accept that.

"If you don't feel called, though, you mustn't be forced to stay. You and I both know you're no seminarian." He smiled a little at her discomfiture. "No more pretending, Jacomo. My cousin Bastien was never prior. He's the head archivist. Runs in the family."

Frai Lorenzi pulled a complicated key out of his pouch and laid it on the cot between them. "This opens every lock in this monastery. The front gate, obviously, will be guarded, but there's the orchard gate, where we load cider barrels, or a sally port at the end of the chapel, in case of fire. There are several others; you'll find your way." He transferred the roll of parchment to his hands, tightening it nervously. "Leave the key in the shrine. I'll find it."

"Thank you," said Tess dubiously. "But why help me?"

"Because there's someone else I can't seem to help," said Frai Lorenzi sadly. Glare on his spectacles obscured his eyes as he unrolled the parchments upon the thin coverlet. They were pages excised from books, all in the same hand (left-handed, Tess noted). At first she thought he wanted her to read them, but the pages were from different texts and he flipped them too quickly.

The margins were alive with innumerable eccentric drawings. "Look at this one," he said, pointing to a dog wearing a bishop's miter. Tess glanced at the old archivist's face, trying to understand if he meant her to be appalled or appreciative. His expression remained neutral, but his eyes gleamed when he showed her Frai Moldi's drawing of a battle between armies of crabs and frogs. Tess decided he admired these drawings, even if he was too proper to say so.

There was a nun laying eggs, a fish-headed baronet, a recognizable Pater Livian picking fruit from what could only be described as a bollocks tree. They were terrible and hilarious, and they made something ache in Tess's heart.

The old librarian pinched his dry lips together. "At first I made him redo everything. When that didn't deter him, I showed his scribbles to the abbot, who locked him in the cellar hole. Moldi never seemed to care, but eventually I couldn't take it anymore. I stopped tattling, stopped pulling pages. There are penis-demons, arse-bagpipes, every outrageous thing he could devise, scattered throughout the library for the edification of future scholars, Heaven help them."

"So . . . you want him to stop?" asked Tess, trying to understand.

Frai Lorenzi startled. "No, no. He stopped once he realized

he wouldn't be punished anymore. All this fierce, outrageous talent, and he doesn't care a fig. He wanted punishment, and he's found other ways to earn it." The librarian smoothed the pages against his knee. "He hardly speaks to me anymore. I hoped, when you smiled at him, that maybe you saw through him. That you might befriend him. You're leaving, though."

"Indeed," said Tess, studying his face.

"Good," said Frai Lorenzi curtly, rerolling the parchments. "Let me just reiterate: that key opens any lock here. All of them. You should have no trouble."

He wasn't very subtle. Tess took up the key and mimed unlocking the air. "*All* of them. Even the cellar hole."

Frai Lorenzi rose and paused with one hand on the door, his face full of grief and hope. "Thank you," he said softly. "He's the son I never had. I don't know what else to do."

He left. Tess put on her boots, gathered her things, and sneaked down the dormitory hallway, through the vaulted kitchens, and into the cellar. She found no "hole," only casks and crates and a dark stairway to the subcellars. She went deeper, through more storage rooms, and was ready to give up when she spied it behind a hogshead of ale, a depression in the floor covered by an iron grille. As her pool of lamplight neared, dirty fingers poked up through the bars like tentative shoots in springtime.

"Frai Lorenzi?" said a heartbroken voice.

"He sent me to release you," Tess said, kneeling by the hole and fitting her key to the padlock. Hinges shrieked as she swung back the grille. Moldi's eyes reflected lamplight like a frightened animal's. His chin was gritty with day-old beard.

"Give me your hand," said Tess, reaching toward him.

"*Give* it? I don't have a spare, like some people," said Moldi, making no move to get up. In fact, he flattened himself so Tess couldn't reach him.

"I'm not coming out," he said. "You needn't bother."

Tess lowered herself onto her stomach, arms folded at the edge of the hole, fascinated. His petulance wasn't aimed at her, and there was probably nothing she could do to fix it, and still this drew her like a moth to flame. "Are you angry that Lorenzi didn't come for you?" she said, trying to guess. "He thought you wouldn't speak to him."

"I probably wouldn't have, at that," said Moldi grudgingly. "I'm an incorrigible ingrate."

"Bitter as gall," said Tess. She recognized it, even if she couldn't see the root cause. "Is it because you lost your arm?"

"Lost it?" he cried. "Never. Does Goreddi have the expression 'I'd give my right arm'? I gave mine to get out of subduing the Archipelagos. Threw myself under a horse."

Tess grimaced, imagining the desperation it would take to do such a thing.

Or the courage.

"It was a foolish trade; I'd assumed I could go home," said Frai Moldi, growing quieter. "I hadn't appreciated that I was merely a coin in my baronet father's keeping. Betting me on warfare brought a poor return, but I had to be spent somewhere. I had no say in the matter. He reinvested me here and sent my younger brother to be a soldier in my place."

"You're worried your brother will be hurt," suggested Tess, still groping for the answer.

"I *hope* he'll be hurt," said Moldi, deep in his hole. "He likes killing things, and he's good at it. Mark my words: if the Archipelagos catch fire, it will be Robinôt who did it, and his pathetic brother Moldi who's ultimately responsible. We should have been a feeble soldier and a terrible priest; that was our destiny as the second and third sons of a baronet, and no harm done except to my soul." His voice broke. "Now the world is afflicted with an incapable monk and an arguably excellent axe-lieutenant, which is much, much worse."

"You're not merely a monk," said Tess, trying to sound encouraging. "You're a historian. If there is trouble in the Archipelagos, as you say, maybe someday your insights into your brother will let you write the definitive—"

Moldi's shoe hit Tess stingingly in the ear, and then it ricocheted back down the hole and got him in the face. "Damn it," he said, rubbing his cheek. "No, I'm not a *historian*. I'm trapped, as surely as I was before, but without any spare limbs to gnaw off.

"Frai Lorenzi says that if I study, the threads of truth will come together into a numinous, shining tapestry—or some cack. But you know what history looks like to me? My weeping mother and splenetic father; my sweet-natured elder brother, a Daanite, obliged to flog his serfs and produce an heir; my sisters married to wastrels just to join their lands with ours; and a little devil who's traded his homilies for a poleaxe, thanks to my selfishness.

"Here's the truth, Brother Jacomo: history is a hole, and at the bottom is a smelly drain, a damp floor, and a debauched monk who can't see his way out of darkness."

It took Tess a moment to find her voice; the word *selfishness* echoed inside her, bringing back memories and regrets. Old bitterness was never completely gone. "I've lived in that hole," she said quietly. "I promise you, that's not all there is. The world is different than you think."

Moldi made a rude noise through his lips.

"However," said Tess, pushing off the floor and brushing grime from her jerkin, "I can't make you come out. Frai Lorenzi hopes you'll leave; I just want you to have the choice."

His voice grew small: "Leave . . . the monastery? Where would I go?"

"You could come with me," said Tess, not sure if she meant it. Frai Moldi would make a dismal traveling companion, but maybe that was better than no companion. Pathka's quest was finished; she'd barely admitted to herself what that meant. "I have some business to attend to in the cavern," she said, "and then I'm off to Segosh."

"That cack-hole!" he cried, his scorn returned in force.

"Is it worse than the one you're in?" said Tess.

The silence seemed to deepen as Frai Moldi considered. "Good point," he said at last, sitting up. "Segosh is certainly worse. I'm surely meant to keep rolling downhill."

He staggered to his feet. Tess hesitated and then said, "Can you climb out?"

"What do you think?" said Moldi, reaching for her help.

He brushed cellar-hole detritus off his cassock and then led her by quiet passages to the gardens; they stopped at the well so Moldi could get a drink and dump a bucket over his head—most welcome, because he smelled terrible. The orchard door was closest, so they departed that way and locked it behind them. Tess waded through waving grass toward the shrine, Moldi at her heels. She left the key on the altar for Frai Lorenzi while Moldi studied the pagan inscription above the doorway down, shaking his head.

"I've got to go down again before we leave," said Tess.

Moldi wrinkled his nose. "Down . . . with the giant serpent. On purpose."

She'd discounted his terror in the library. "If you're frightened, you can wait here, but Frai Lorenzi will come fetch his key eventually, and I don't know how long I'll be below. I've walked a long way. . . ." Across lifetimes, she felt. "I have to see the serpent, after all I've gone through to get here. And I have a friend down there whom I can't leave without saying goodbye."

Moldi stared at his shoes while she spoke; when he raised his chin, there was an unaccustomed gleam in his eyes. "All right, then. Let's see this monster. Why the devil not?"

They descended. Halfway down, the biggest tremor yet made the stairs churn and rock like the ocean. They flung themselves flat and clung to the steps for dear life. Tess prayed to St. Prue (as seemed prudent) not to be buried alive in this stairwell.

The shaking ceased, and Tess clambered to her feet, but Frai Moldi couldn't seem to stand; he trembled as if the quake continued in his very bones. His fear hadn't all been an act. Tess grasped his hand, pulled him to his feet, and kept hold of him the rest of the way down.

So it was that Tess, hand in hand with a monk, entered the great chamber and saw.

⤫

The world was different than either of them had thought.

⤫

Tess always felt, later on, that words could not begin to touch that moment.

Not that she didn't try, but explaining was like trying to carry a river in a teacup. Or worse, that the experience was like a paper-thin, perfect sheet of ice upon a pond, and every word of explanation a heavy footfall, obliterating what it meant to elucidate. The serpent truly was *thmepitlkikiu*, the death of language.

The only approach was through analogy, but Tess didn't know many good ones.

Far to the north, on the continent of Iboia, was a chasm, a gash in the face of the world so deep and wide that one could not see the bottom, or even the opposite rim on a hazy day. Its edge, where the rock was crumbly and weak, posed a real hazard of falling in and tumbling more than a mile downward, bumping and cursing. Yet people stood at the edge, gaping foolishly, because they didn't believe it. The chasm was too big to understand.

Tess, alas, didn't have access to this metaphor.

At the end of St. Jannoula's War, when St. Pandowdy be-stirred himself from the swamp and circled Lavondaville, shedding dirt and rocks and trees and shining with the light of Heaven itself, people fell on their knees, prostrated themselves, and wept for joy and terror. His presence was so sublime that a human mind could not comprehend it.

Tess, in the tunnels when St. Pandowdy rose, couldn't make this comparison, either.

The closest she could get were the stars. Kenneth had once explained that while it looked like the sky arched above and the earth sat solidly below, up and down were mere conventions. "We're clinging to a sphere, after all," he'd said. "From some angles, up is toward the earth and down toward the sky, and everything—people, horses, cathedrals, dreams—is suspended over the ceaseless void, barely hanging on."

Tess had looked at the stars differently after that, lying with her back pressed desperately to the earth, and felt the thrill and terror that gravity might capriciously drop her into the sky and she would fall forever.

Anathuthia recalled in Tess that terror and exhilaration. The whole chamber ached with vibrant life as her luminescent blood pulsed beneath milky, translucent scales. Her massive loops and coils arced impossibly, like stone arches made of noonday sky, burning a hole in night. Tess had to squint because the light was too much. Everything about Anathuthia was too much.

And Tess was vanishingly small.

Everything disappeared. Will. Dozerius. Mama.

All your failures and hopes, your suffering and striving, the great coils seemed to say, *are inconsequential, compared with this. They are nothing.*

You are nothing.

It was a relief to be nothing; it felt deep and beautiful and true.

Tess wept.

Beside her, Moldi wept for reasons of his own. Maybe for the same reason. Tess didn't let go of his hand. They could not feel time passing.

All was nothing. It was exactly as it should be.

Moldi broke the reverie after what might have been hours. "Light requires the high relief of darkness," he said, and although Tess's thoughts had been going in other directions, she understood him. "Seeds sprout in darkness. Children are conceived, and the sun reborn. Death returns us to it. Darkness is not . . . it's not *wrong.*"

He was weeping again. Tess could think of nothing to do but hold him close, his head against her shoulder. He clung to her fiercely until his breathing calmed. "*You* are not wrong," Tess whispered into his hair. Impulsively she kissed the top of his head.

Experiencing nothingness had left her feeling unexpectedly full.

Moldi sat up, wiping his wet face with the end of his sleeve.

The blue light gave him a ghostly aspect. "I hope you won't be too disappointed, Brother Jacomo, but...I need to go back. I—" His voice broke again, but he steadied himself. "I can't believe I'm saying this, but I've heard the call."

"Your vocation?" whispered Tess, happy for him.

He shrugged self-deprecatingly and quirked the first smile Tess had seen on him, a small, ironic, unpracticed thing. "That's a rather grand word for finally noticing what's been right in front of you. But Santi Prudia's Sign was painted in mile-high letters. 'O ignoramus,' it said, 'your life is not a tragedy. It's history, and it's yours.'" He flashed Tess an apologetic look. "It made terrible yet reassuring sense in the moment. Words aren't—"

"I know," said Tess. "I had a moment of my own."

"Would you tell me about it?" asked Frai Moldi shyly.

Before Tess could answer, though, Anathuthia moved. She rubbed against the ceiling, and loose rock rolled down her shining body, boulders like grains of sand. A chunk the size of a farmhouse crashed and split with a sound like the world's end. Across the dark ceiling a darker crack appeared, like black lightning, growing and forking as it spread.

Tess and Moldi held on to each other and gaped, forgetting they had lives to fear for, until a shape came hurtling out of the shadows and shoved them toward the stairs.

"Go!" cried Pathka. "Get out! It's falling!"

Only Tess understood the words. She grabbed Moldi's arm and hauled him toward the spiral stair. The ground bucked so hard they could barely keep their feet. They climbed endlessly while stone crumbled around them. Their lantern was dashed on the rocks, but they kept moving through darkness until they burst out into another fine autumnal evening.

Only the stars stood still.

The plain undulated. Apples fell in the wobbling orchard. The bell tower flapped, clanging, as if seized by an invisible hand, and then the library of Santi Prudia seemed to melt as Anathuthia's chamber collapsed beneath it. A cloud of dust rolled out of the chasm.

Frai Moldi paused, swaying on his feet. "Sweet Heavenly home," he murmured. "So many times I prayed this place would disappear, Jacomo. But not like this."

Tess followed him into the dust cloud, coughing and choking, calling Pathka's name when she had enough breath. The little quigutl didn't answer.

When she caught up, Moldi was already directing his brethren hither and thither, organizing stunned monks into gangs to move roof beams and free their trapped brothers. He was the lone pole of calm in a blizzard of panic, touching his brothers' wet, grime-streaked cheeks and whispering in their ears.

Only when he looked into the chasm did she see him falter. At first she thought it was the shock of seeing Anathuthia again, not as the sign revealing his vocation but as the monster that had destroyed his home—and surely he struggled with this terrible paradox. However, Tess followed his gaze and saw that the surface of the serpent, its glow discernible in the deepening twilight, was littered with stones, broken shelving, thousands of books, and the wrecked bodies of everyone who'd been in the library.

The head archivist, recognizable by his iron hair and lanky

limbs, lay splayed within view. Frai Moldi sank to his knees. Tess was at his side in an instant.

She didn't know what to say, so she sat with him in silence. He sighed heavily and ran his hand over his face.

"Are you all right?" she finally whispered.

"Absolutely not." His mouth quivered. "But I'm used to it, Jacomo. They're not. I think I can show them the path out. I understand now that it's not a question of faith or hope; it exists, and we can find it. It's going to take some time, though."

He took a last, lingering look at Frai Lorenzi's broken body and pressed his hand to his heart, as if he could keep it whole by squeezing.

Then he stood shakily, holding Tess's arm, and walked back to where he was needed.

Frai Moldi was up all night, soothing his shocked brethren and aiming them in useful directions. He gently pointed out to a group of wailing librarians that the refectory still stood; they stopped crying and got the injured indoors. Moldi had learned to bandage a wound and wrap a sprain as a soldier but couldn't manage either one-handed; he calmly instructed a novice, who taught others. Pater Livian had hit his head and seemed confused; Moldi brought him to the dazed priors, who snapped out of it and organized a sort of nest for him at the head of the room.

Soon every surviving monk was either caring for the injured, being cared for, or salvaging what supplies and furnishings could be safely reached. Tess had joined the bandagers, and by dawn they were out of wounds to tend, to her relief. Her ribs ached terribly. She caught some sleep under one of the refectory tables, and when she woke she went looking for Moldi again, to see what else was needed.

She found him at the periphery of a meeting of senior monks, sitting alert as a collie; he'd herded them together and was ensuring they didn't wander. When he saw her, he quietly slipped away and led her out to the remains of the orchard.

"Did your friend survive?" he asked. "I presume it was he who shoved us up the stairs."

Tess looked away; she'd been avoiding thinking about Pathka's fate. "It was. And I don't know."

"Go down and look for him," said Frai Moldi, watching her steadily. "And then you should travel on to Segosh, if you ever mean to go."

"You still need help here," Tess began, but the little monk held up his hand.

"You've helped, and I thank you from the bottom of my heart," he said. "But you never meant to join our order, and if you're going to leave, it would be easier on me if you left now."

Tess swayed on her feet, buffeted by a sudden surge of love. Her mind raced through futile scenarios, trying to devise a way to stay, but it was impossible. She didn't belong here. She couldn't have joined this order even if she felt called to it.

Anyway, it wasn't that flavor of love. She could leave and carry it with her. Time would not put a dent in it, nor distance snuff it out.

She threw her arms around him, hurting all over. She could

hear the smile in his voice as he said, "Give Segosh my apologies, but I have my own cack-hole to attend to here."

Tess gave him one last look. Frai Moldi seemed more tired than despairing now; his decisive nose was finally coming into its own. She turned to go before she lost the will to do so.

With great trepidation, she returned to Santi Prudia's shrine. Frai Lorenzi's key lay on the floor among rubble. The spiral stair looked surprisingly intact, so she picked her way down.

Pathka had been right behind them when the cavern collapsed. She saw it over and over in her mind. But had he been crushed, or had he dodged and wriggled free?

She was afraid to find out.

The bottom of the stairs was clogged with debris, but she squeezed through a cranny near the ceiling, her ribs screaming agony. The other side, the cavern that was now a pit, was bright and airy, with noonday sun shining down; loose pages fluttered, caught by a breeze. She climbed mountains of books and rocks, which slid, shifted, crumbled underfoot.

"Pathkaaaaa!" Tess cried. There was no answer but her echo.

The bowl of Anathuthia's nest had filled with fallen debris; the serpent herself was half-submerged, coated in dust and stone. Her glow was barely discernible, but she still radiated warmth. Tess, numb with exhaustion and worry, felt herself drawn forward across the wreckage, over one last heap of ruined books. The serpent—the coils that weren't buried, anyway—loomed like a living wall, aquiver with breath and expectation. A glowing stream of blood trickled from a high-up wound, almost dried now.

Tess approached, mesmerized, and pressed her palm to the serpent's side, into the rivulet of sticky blood. Blue fire ran up her arm. Literal or figurative, she couldn't tell. Tess screamed, but the pain was already gone, only a flickering afterimage now, a gentler warmth suffusing her body. Her ribs stopped aching, her mind stopped aching, and she was filled with unexpected reassurance: *I am Pathka.*

She yanked her hand away. She'd heard the voice in her head. Impossible.

Anathuthia glowed in front of her, inscrutably.

I am Pathka? He wasn't dead—she felt certain—but he might have been . . . subsumed? Absorbed or eaten? The voice had been so reassuring that she couldn't fear for him.

This was what he'd wanted. The end of the singular-*utl*, whatever that meant. It occurred to her, not for the first time, that no matter how she'd tried to define his journey—quest, ritual, pilgrimage, religion—Pathka had always slipped the traces and eluded her. He had truly been on a path she couldn't follow or understand.

It was all right. It had to be.

"Take care of him," she told the serpent, as if her admonishment could carry any weight. One might as reasonably command a mountain.

Tess wiped her hand on the pages of a ruined book and then picked her way—less gingerly than before—back to the stairs.

She'd almost reached the stairs when a torn page blew

against her ankle and clung there. She picked it up and saw, beside an account of ancient warfare, a scribbled drawing of a monk playing what could only be called arse-bagpipes. Tess laughed and cried, both at once, and then she stuck the drawing in her pack and walked on.

Twenty-Three

The monastery had collapsed so suddenly that Tess had had no time to dwell upon her own experience of Anathuthia. She wanted nothing more than to recapture that feeling—the comfort and joy of nothingness. She stared at the sky while she walked; it was not quite the same shade of blue that lingered behind her eyelids. Thinking about Anathuthia was like almost remembering a perfect snatch of song that had made the world stand still.

It was right on the tip of her tongue. It flitted around her like a swift.

She wanted to talk about it, to tell the peasants in the fields and the nobles in their palashos—the cows in the pastures, the very birds in the air—that everything was nothing. It was a delightful thought because it meant (to Tess) that one was free to choose, or decline to choose, without shame or coercion.

For someone who was nothing, anything was possible. The pressure was off.

"What would you say if I told you we're all very, very small?" Tess asked an aged farmer as she helped him pack his barn with straw against the coming cold weather.

"Are we," said the old man, eyeing her suspiciously.

"Did you ever see something so beautiful, so awe-inspiring, that it made you look at the world through different eyes?" said Tess. "Well, it happened to me recently."

"Did it." The farmer scratched his rough red chin.

"There's a giant serpent underground," said Tess, launching into the story, but it was like pushing a boulder uphill; his silence made the slope steeper. The story felt dead in her mouth.

She didn't hear what he whispered to his wife when they'd finished work. The old woman gave Tess a whole loaf and a warm blanket and said gently, "St. Loola's runs a hospice down in the village. Take care of yourself, m'dear."

Thus ended Tess's short career in herpevangelism. If nobody believed her about the serpent, she wasn't going to enlighten anybody by babbling on about transcendent nothingness.

It wasn't true that nobody would believe her, though. The masters of the Ninysh Academy in Segosh had heard of the World Serpents; Nicolas had said so. She walked along, thinking of her favorite lectures on exotic animals at St. Bert's, how she'd hung on the explorers' every word and dreamed of such adventure herself (or of accompanying Will, who would find her indispensable). This was an important discovery; the masters would be interested, if she could find the right way to talk about it.

They'd think of Anathuthia as merely an animal—but maybe that would be easier. One could describe an animal; it had measurable qualities, like size and strength and feeding habits, and that was knowledge she could share. In fact, she had a mandate to do so, she felt, from Frai Lorenzi, who had said the world deserved to know.

She tried remembering as many concrete details as she could, reducing Anathuthia to facts. She missed the soaring feeling, but it was less frustrating not to have a snatch of song eluding her, or a bird darting just out of view.

Still, she saw pale blue behind her eyelids sometimes when she blinked. It was never really gone.

The nights were getting longer and the mornings nippier, making Tess grateful for her second blanket. The equinox had passed without her noting it; winter fell quickly this far south, by all reports. In Goredd the first frost usually hit right around the feast of St. Prue, but here it would be at least two weeks earlier, and if she kept walking south, that date would keep creeping toward her until the pair of them met for a nice kiss.

She didn't fancy waking up with frost on her lips. She needed to find a way to sleep indoors sometimes. One evening she stopped at the tavern in the village of Anshouie and asked the tapmaster, "How much for a room?"

He was drying a glass on his apron. "Two and a quarter for the night, ten per week."

She cringed. The dregs of her road-building wages weren't

going to last, and the farms wouldn't offer much once the harvest was in. She needed to hurry to Segosh.

The tapmaster eyed her from under shaggy brows. "You drinking?"

"Bitter Branca," said Tess, absently ordering Felix's favorite. That rascal. She missed everyone. While the tapmaster mixed ale and pine brandy, Tess looked around at the patrons of the pub. Most were old or idle, folks who'd likely been here all day. The evening crowd was just beginning to trickle in.

The village priest arrived, a phlegmatic young man in the rust-red habit of St. Munn, his fair hair already thinning and his shoulders stooped. His parishioners clapped him on the back and brought him a drink. When he spotted Tess, a stranger, he shook her hand and said, "Welcome, traveler. I'm Father Erique."

"Brother Jacomo," said Tess.

"Not a monk?" said the priest, giving her an unsubtle look of doubt. She was wearing Florian's striped jacket against the cooler weather.

"A seminarian," said Tess, affecting a humble mien. She told her usual tale, lost her vocation, looking for it, blah blah.

The priest got a funny look when she said *vocation*. She wondered what his story was, and whether he'd be appalled to hear about a giant serpent.

He forced a smile. "Let me know if you have questions about the Order of St. Munn."

Father Erique glad-handed his way to the end of the room, stood on a chair, and called, "Heaven keep all here. Ready for the news?"

The villagers stopped gossiping to listen. Tess nursed her piney beer. The priest brandished a ring on a chain around his neck and said, "The Bishop of St. Munn's in Modera had a lot to say this week. First, there's sheep pox in the Samsamese highlands, so be careful buying ewes."

He gave farm news from all over. The ring was a thnik, clearly. All the priests of St. Munn must have them and be sharing information through their bishop, who sat in the middle like a fat spider, passing messages along.

Father Erique ended with world news: Samsam's fleet, destroyed by Porphyry in the war, was finally restored to its former glory. An expedition to the Antarctic (Countess Margarethe's? Tess wondered) had claimed two new islands for Ninys but come up empty-handed on sabanewt oil. Last but far from least, news from Goredd: "Queen Glisselda's baby, Princess Zythia, was presented to the public for the first time at her psalter ceremony. Heaven ordained that her patron will be"— Father Erique checked his notes—"St. Polypous, like her royal mother. Heaven keep the Goreddi royal family. I think we're all entitled to raise a glass to that!"

So the baby had a name now; Zythia was surely Seraphina's suggestion, named for her Porphyrian friend, St. Zythia Perdixis Camba. St. Polypous had been poor dear Julian/Dozerius's patron, too. Tess sighed wistfully and downed her Branca without finding it too bitter, and she said a little prayer to her own St. Siucre that Seraphina wasn't finding it miserable to pass off her baby as the Queen's. As painful as it had been to lose a child, Tess suspected it took a core of steel to do what her sister was doing.

Then Seraphina's perfect for the job, was her knee-jerk reaction, but upon further consideration, she wondered about that assumption. She didn't actually know what it took to hurt Seraphina. Having a baby changed everything.

Tess decided not to take a room after all. It wasn't so cold that she couldn't stand it, and thinking about Seraphina and her baby had made her antsy. She felt a strong desire to get back on the road, where she belonged, and walk it off.

She hefted her pack and was about to duck out when a hand tapped her shoulder.

It was Father Erique. "Do you need a place to stay, Brother Jacomo?" he said, fingering his collar, which was lined with squirrel fur. "You're welcome to sleep in the church, of course, or I've a spare room at the vicarage."

It hadn't occurred to Tess that she might hop from church to church, impersonating Jacomo and rooming for free. This was worth considering.

"My Angelica is roasting a leg of lamb," said Father Erique enticingly.

Lamb was awfully tempting. Tess weighed it against the need to walk, and the prospect of a full belly won. She followed the priest through the village and past the church to a well-appointed house nearby.

The vicarage was warm and cheerful, with a roaring fire, a little dog on a cushion, and a serving lass no older than Tess just bringing supper in from the kitchen. "Another place, if you please, Angelica," said Father Erique, leaving his shoes near the door. "Brother Jacomo will be staying the night."

Tess followed suit and removed her boots. When she looked

up, she caught Angelica staring. The girl averted her eyes almost at once, but Tess knew what she'd seen. Utter hatred. It lingered like an odor in the air.

Tess's presence made extra work, certainly, but the depth of venom in Angelica's gaze seemed unwarranted. Had a previous guest left her with a terrible mess?

Tess felt compelled to reassure her during dinner. When Angelica filled her wineglass, Tess said, "Thank you, Angelica," and smiled warmly. The braised parsnips and bread pudding were remarkably delicious, so Tess made sure to say, "Angelica, you're a wonderful cook."

The girl recoiled each time. By the end of dinner, Angelica was so furious she was shaking; Tess's comments had unintentionally made things worse, and she couldn't fathom how.

Father Erique appeared to notice nothing amiss, which was not lost on Tess.

The priest offered Tess a seat by the fire while Angelica washed up. "So tell me," said Father Erique, extracting a bottle of cognac and two glasses from a cabinet near the hearth. "Are you Goreddi? Your vowels sound a little squirmy."

At Tess's murmur of assent, the priest smiled knowingly. "What do you make of this Princess Zythia, then? Is she the Queen's own, or have they adopted some half cousin's bastard?"

Tess, who knew plenty, didn't like his tone. "Why would you imagine that?"

"Don't be coy. One hears rumors, even this far south. We know the Queen and prince consort are all politics together. But the Queen and St. Seraphina? Hmm?" He made fingers on each hand into a V, locked them together, and waggled his blond brows suggestively.

"I have no idea what you're asking," said Tess, refusing to give him the satisfaction.

He shrugged it off and handed her a glass. Tess accepted it warily. Drink gave her a propensity for punching priests, and this one was almost begging for it already.

"You seem like an adventurous soul," said Father Erique, settling into his chair. "Have you considered traveling to the Archipelagos to convert the heathens?"

"No," said Tess. "I've lost my—"

"Your vocation. I know," he said, smiling wanly. "It's not uncommon, Brother, believe me. Isn't that the purpose of travel, to rediscover your convictions? It matters less where you go than that you keep moving."

Tess had often felt that. She swirled the amber liquid in her glass, wary but listening now.

"I mentioned that southern expedition. There are many such, and each one needs a priest. If those islands are ever to be fully Ninysh—as Heaven clearly intends, because why are they so close to us, otherwise?—then we need to sow knowledge of the Saints among the people there. They must be made to understand that they're part of a divine plan."

Tess must have looked unenthusiastic, because he added, "Ninysh expansion doesn't appeal to a Goreddi, eh?"

"I'm not sure spreading the scriptures, as such, appeals to me," said Tess. She'd read scripture every day as a child; it had been her mother's favorite stick to hit her with. She'd never seen any divine plan, unless the plan was to saddle her with guilt and self-loathing.

Those voices had been unusually quiet since she'd seen Anathuthia, she suddenly realized, as if the serpent had given her permission to let go of all that.

And now this priest thought she should take her mother's stick to the Archipelagos and beat those people with it? *No thank you.*

Father Erique poured himself a second cognac. "This is our time, Brother. Our faith is ascendant. Think how many new Saints were revealed during St. Jannoula's War. St. Pandowdy is out there somewhere, head touching the clouds; St. Jannoula is a traveler like you. We'll spread the word to all corners of the world. My bishop even speaks of converting the Porphyrians. What a coup that would be!"

The whole scheme sounded revolting to Tess. Father Erique laughed at her expression and misinterpreted it. "You're like I was at first. It sounds impossible. But you'll see."

"I thought only the Samsamese aspired to convert everyone," said Tess. "I thought you Ninysh were famously relaxed about these things."

Father Erique's expression soured abruptly. "We're nothing like the Samsamese! They revere strict, intolerant Abaster and Vitt, keep their women locked up until marriage, and don't even drink. What sort of civilization is that? Ninys is enlightened and tolerant—which is why we need to win this race, don't you see? The Samsamese fleet is restored; they'll be sending out missionaries as fast as they can. Would you rather live in a Samsamese world?"

Tess had lived in one, after a fashion, thanks to Mama's devotion to St. Vitt. She'd be the first to call it restrictive, but the idea of converting "heathens" repelled her. Her own father, for all his faults, was an unbeliever. It was one of the nicer things about him.

Father Erique apparently concluded that he'd won the argument, for he rose and stretched as if the conversation—or possibly conversion—were over. It probably was; Tess was too irked to argue further, and she doubted he'd listen. She set her untouched cognac under her chair.

"I've had Angelica make up her room for you," said Father Erique.

"Oh," said Tess, taken aback. "I thought you had a spare room."

"That is the spare room," said Father Erique. "You can make her sleep on a blanket in the corner if you *want* to, of course, but I highly recommend keeping her in the bed with you. She's nice and warm, my Angelica, and compliant as you please."

Tess's understanding, which had been floating unmoored down the river of her mind, was suddenly firmly tied up at harbor. No wonder Angelica hated her on sight. Father Erique apparently lent her to guests for their personal use. Tess's dinner came unsettled.

"Daanite?" said Father Erique pityingly, as if this were the only reason he could imagine for Tess's nauseated expression.

Tess couldn't speak; she felt too much. Her heart pounded, and she teetered between the urge to smash his face and to run. Flight won. She snatched up her pack and rushed blindly into the night, toward the sanctuary.

"The key is under the statue of St. Munn's terrier," Father

Erique called after. "See you at breakfast! My Angelica makes the best—"

Tess slammed the church door on his description and staggered toward the altar, where a wooden statue of St. Munn loomed in darkness like a solid shadow. Tess bent double, hands upon the Saint's oaken feet, and wrestled the urge to vomit.

Here she'd been walking around feeling light and free, marveling that the world was different than she'd thought it was, while it was the same as it ever was: a world where Julissima Rossa died for shame and Dozerius sailed on; where a woman walking alone had to fear every shepherd, whether he meant her harm or not; where Roger Ivy spied on her from behind a screen and gave student-priests permission to call her whore; where she might be ruined, while Will, who took without asking, ran off without consequence.

Where Angelica could suffer . . . Tess could barely complete the thought. It crushed her.

She collapsed before the altar and was insensible to the world for a long time, maybe hours. She awoke stiff and cold, with clammy cheeks, and gazed up at the statue, knowing she'd find no comfort there. St. Munn's eyeballs, painted eerie white, were visible in the darkness, as was a corsage of frail mushrooms growing from his shoulder. She didn't know this Saint well, only that Aunt Jenny had been married in his church and that the Ninysh side of the family revered him.

"My mother must've rejected you," Tess whispered, rising. She touched his robe, and paint flaked off; the frail wood crumbled like gingerbread under her fingernails. "That makes me inclined to give you the benefit of the doubt, but what do you tell Angelica, to reassure her that the world is more than she can see from under a monstrous priest?"

Is it, though? the statue seemed to answer. *You've gotten awfully arrogant. One glimpse of a big pagan worm, and you think there's a way out of all this. Get on with you, mooning about, wallowing in gooey sentiment. It doesn't change anything.*

"It does, though," said Tess, a blaze igniting in her heart, a blue flame. "Maybe the world isn't really different, but I am different, and I am in the world."

Not just *in* it. She *was* it.

Tess knew what to do. She was called to do it.

She thought about pushing St. Munn over—there would have been some satisfaction in that—but those mushrooms meant he was already rotting from the inside. They glowed faintly at his shoulder, like an afterimage.

Tess returned to the vicarage; the door opened readily. She didn't bother taking her boots off, and skipped checking the priest's bedroom. He wouldn't be there.

She threw open Angelica's door and there was Father Erique, who'd apparently just shed his nightshirt, climbing into the bed, and there was Angelica, squeezed against the wall, as if she might have slipped into the crack and disappeared.

Her expression cut Tess—that was a blankness she knew, that she'd lived. Angelica had absented herself, but Tess was here, uncurled, heart fully breaking.

Tess pulled the priest by the arm, practically lifting him out of the bed. He was scrawny, and Tess was strong enough, after months of road work, to have beaten him within an inch of his life. She was angry enough to have made it half an inch or less.

"Changed your mind?" said Father Erique hastily. "Take her with my blessing, Brother."

Tess twisted his arm behind his back.

Angelica rolled toward the wall, wrapping her arms around her head. Tess knew how shamed she must feel, but she had to deal with the priest first.

"You're a boor, rushing in here so violently," said Father Erique. "And you've got it all wrong. St. Munn's is not a celibate order, and we Ninysh have more enlightened attitudes toward these things than you Goreddis do."

Tess stomped his bare foot with her boot. He howled.

She could have killed him, broken his naked body into a thousand pieces. She writhed with the urge to do him violence, but . . . no. She was more than just a priest-puncher, and there was always one more trick to try.

Tess called to Angelica, "Get dressed and find me some rope. Please."

Tess turned her back to give the girl some privacy. Wrangling Father Erique took all her concentration; he was a slippery wriggler. She wrestled him into the main room, into his armchair, and waited for Angelica. It took several minutes for the serving girl to slouch in from the kitchen and hand Tess the rope.

"Thank you, Angelica," said Tess gently, trying to reassure the serving girl, who looked sick. She would still think Tess was a man, and who knew what *he* intended to do with her?

"You're safe now," said Tess, who didn't dare reveal her identity to this priest.

Angelica looked away, pushing tangled blond hair out of her face.

Tess bound Father Erique hand and foot, feeling that she ought to preach while she worked. The scriptures must've addressed the monstrosity he'd committed—how could they not?— but she hadn't been taught those lines. St. Vitt had scoldings aplenty for the woman who led a priest toward sin, though. Tess recited these, turning them inside out for Angelica's sake.

"'Woman, do not submit,'" Tess misquoted. "'If a man be tempted by thee, thou art not a temptress. If a man be led to sin, his sin is not added to your tally.'"

"That's backward," said Father Erique.

"Shut up," said Tess. She held the rope against his mouth, considering whether to gag him, but decided against it. "Angelica, please find me ink and quill and parchment."

Angelica sullenly searched the cabinet. Tess wrote a sign in a plain ecclesiastic hand: *I, Father Erique, forced myself upon my serving girl and offered her body to houseguests. I am a terrible priest. Take me to the local lord and subject me to the harshest justice the law allows.*

Tess laid the parchment between his feet so as not to blunt the full impact of his nudity. He'd feel humiliated to be found this way; no more justice than that was guaranteed, alas. Who knew what the lord would say, or what lies Erique would tell. Slippery wriggler.

"I never used force," he said, reading upside down.

Tess needed to get gone before she punched him. She gathered her things. "I will find you, Brother Jacomo," cried the priest, struggling against his bonds. "I will have my revenge."

"I doubt it," said Tess, shouldering her pack. She glanced around, but Angelica had evaporated. "Angelica?" Tess called. Quiet sounds at the back of the house grew quieter. Tess looked into the girl's room; Angelica froze like a hare scenting hounds. She'd thrown a homespun woolen gown over her chemise and taken up a bundle of belongings.

"Oh, good," said Tess, surprised to see her ready to go. "Let's get you out of here."

Angelica glanced at her open window, then put her head down and followed Tess out past Father Erique, who shouted, "Don't you dare, Angelica! Your name will be blackened in this village. I'll see your family suffer. Untie me, and all will be forgiven. We'll live as if nothing had happened."

Angelica turned back and kicked him so viciously that his chair fell backward. Tess, shocked despite her sympathy, scrambled to set him upright and then rushed into the frigid predawn after Angelica.

She wasn't on the road. Tess listened until she heard what sounded like a clumsy deer picking its way through the wooded glade behind the vicarage. Tess plunged into the brush after her, but the closer she got, the faster Angelica went, until they were both running flat out, as fast as the tangled thicket would let them.

They burst into a field of unharvested oilseed, desiccated seedpods rattling and bursting as they passed. Tess rapidly gained on Angelica now, but she didn't want to tackle the girl and terrify her even more. Tess tried speaking: "Wait, please, Angelica. . . . You can't just go running off by yourself. We've got to get you someplace safe."

Angelica wheeled to face Tess, murder in her eyes. "I'll go . . . nowhere . . . with you . . . ," she panted.

"I won't hurt you," said Tess, holding up her hands. "I'm not like him—"

"The devil you aren't," snarled Angelica, breaking off a thick oilseed stalk and slashing the air in front of her. It sounded like a whip.

"I'm not a man. I'm only dressed like one. My name is Tess." Her name felt strange in her mouth. "I've run away from home. Just like you."

For the merest moment Angelica froze in astonishment, her blue eyes wide, her hair a wild, bright corona in the morning sun. Then with a shriek, Angelica launched herself at Tess, nails, fists, stalk, and teeth. Tess was strong enough to fend her off, but slow to understand she was being attacked. She got a stinging scratch along her cheekbone.

"What's the matter with you?" Tess cried, growing angry. It had cost her considerable courage and effort to confront Father Erique, and while she hadn't done it merely for gratitude, she hadn't expected this.

"You ruined everything!" Angelica cried. "D'you think I couldn't take care of myself? I was stealing coppers from the offering plates, saving up." She pulled a purse out of her bodice and jingled it. "I had a plan, you meddling bitch. I was going to escape—me, myself. I'd've poisoned his nasty—"

"So I saved you from becoming a murderer, too," Tess burst in hotly. "You're welcome."

"You're not!" shouted Angelica, whipping the stalk. Tess had to duck to keep from getting it in the eye. "I don't have enough saved up to make a decent go of it, thanks to you, and I didn't even get my revenge. I owe you nothing, and you can just piss off!"

Tess had a momentary, terrible impulse to throw the ungrateful girl over her shoulder, run her back to the village, and dump her there. Her better nature prevailed, however. She felt in her pouch for a large coin and held it out between two fingers. Angelica eyed her suspiciously but darted in and snatched the money. Then she took off running again.

Tess did not follow, but she couldn't help calling after: "You're not safe traveling by yourself!"

No sooner were the words out of her mouth than Tess realized she sounded like Will, who'd escorted her across town a hundred times to keep her safe. What a fantastic job he'd done, too. She felt dizzy and disconcerted.

Angelica turned and made an obscene gesture. "Devils take you!" she cried. "I will burn the earth!" And then she was across the field, disappearing into a hedgerow.

Tess watched her go, feeling hollow and miserable, but wondering what she might have done if things had been reversed. She wasn't sure that she'd have been any more gracious to a knight in shining armor.

In fact, now that she thought about it, she'd been every bit as hostile. Countess Margarethe probably still hated her for it.

The world was littered with all the babies she'd thrown out with their bathwater. She'd burned bridges while standing on them. She, of all people, knew what that was like.

She kissed her knuckle and turned her face south, back to her own road, blinking hard against the stinging wind.

Twenty-Four

Tess reached Segosh upon a crystalline autumn morning that had left a chill in her bones upon waking. It was time to get indoors, though she felt reluctant to leave the Road behind.

The Road, however, was not so easily abandoned. It led straight through the gates of the city, whereupon it divided itself, strands interweaving between buildings. Here it was called Streets and Boulevards and Alleyways, but it was the same entity, and she was still its progeny.

She'd grown up in a city, and never appreciated this until now.

This felt like a triumphant homecoming, back to civilization, and Tess entered like a hero, even if no one noticed. If she'd been Dozerius, this would have been the part of the story where all her trials were rewarded, where she finally got the recognition she deserved. She'd take her discovery to the

Ninysh Academy and become the famous explorer she'd always dreamed of being.

It felt not just possible but inevitable. She'd done something truly astonishing, and had beaten a certain naturalist of her acquaintance to it. He could kiss her mud-spattered boot. She grinned impishly at the lone cloud in the sky, which was not particularly Will-shaped, and thought, *Eat your heart out, scholar.*

(The thought of Will gave her pause. The Ninysh Academy was an obvious, logical place he might have gone when he left. Heaven forfend that she'd run into him, but even if she did, wasn't she strong and capable? She'd accomplished things Will could only dream of. He didn't scare her. A whole Academy full of Wills couldn't scare her.)

Conquering the Academy would not be accomplished in a single afternoon; more urgent was securing a place to sleep tonight, and paying work. City streets had no comfy green verge for her to bed down upon. The alleys were full of rats and rubbish and elderly gents who made Old Griss look clean and polished.

She thought she glimpsed him once, but it was clothes on a line, a trick of the light.

The embroiderers' district, she quickly learned, consisted of a narrow byway called Crewel Ramble. *Crewel*, of course, referred to a style of embroidery. Tess understood *Ramble* the minute she laid eyes on the street: it was having trouble committing to being a street at all, crooked and narrow as it was. Most streets run in a certain direction, but this one stumbled and teetered between the looming half-timbered buildings, as if it were drunk.

She asked after work at several houses, but as soon as she asked for accommodation also, they all directed her toward a house at the end of the street called Fine Eyes. "Mother Gaida's got a room you can have for free, if you're strong enough, but she won't let you have it if you're working for another house," was the general consensus.

Tess didn't need to be told more than thrice. She knocked at the door of Fine Eyes (wondering whether the name was a pun on "fine work," *eyes* and *work* being quite similar words in Ninysh). Three young women, blond and giggling, answered the door. They'd spotted Tess through the corbelled window and taken her for the young fellow she appeared to be. Tess doffed her cap and gave one-quarter courtesy—more than they merited—causing a rapture of squealing.

"Forgive the intrusion, ladies," said Tess, dredging her manners up from the bottom of some deep river in her soul. It was a nice cold river; it had kept them fresh, if slightly damp. "I'm looking for Mother Gaida."

The ladies left Tess in the parlor on a densely embroidered sofa between riotous pillows. The fringed drapes were overgrown with brocade. Tess found herself grinning stupidly at a framed shepherd and shepherdess above the hearth. Smoothly executed satin stitch, she noted, and finely rendered features. Dove knots. Helical whorls. She stood for a closer look, hands clasped behind her back.

"Can I help you, sir?" said a crisp voice. Tess turned to face Mother Gaida, a diminutive old woman in a close-fitted caul, lean and tough as a strip of hide. "Are you here with a portrait commission?" The woman lifted her brows, indicating the figures above the hearth. "I do those myself. We embroider clothing, of course, and take in mending on the side—unless you're from the Guild of Tailors, in which case I deny everything."

"I'm looking for work, madam, and a place to stay. The houses up the street said—"

"That I might hire a young fellow like you?" said Gaida, quirking an eyebrow.

"I'm not a 'fellow,' first of all," said Tess. "And I know my stitches. I embroidered at the court of Goredd for Lady Farquist—"

"We'll see about that; I'll want a sample," said Mother Gaida, raising a bony finger. "You also said you need a place to stay. I have one, but *you* may not want it, not-fellow."

"No?" said Tess, crestfallen, because that was what she needed most in this strange city.

"Because of my son, you understand," said Gaida. "I need a boarder who can help care for him. He was thrown from a horse several years ago and can't walk. He'd be dead, but for the miracles of St. Blanche the Mechanic." She kissed her red knuckle. "He can do most things himself, Saints hold him, but he needs help getting in and out of the bath, for example. I can't lift him, and I'll wager a weedy thing like you can't, either."

"Indeed I could," said Tess, feeling the woman was being unfair to both herself and her male alter egos. "I mean, unless he's big as a barn."

Gaida drew herself to full height, which wasn't much, and sniffed disdainfully. "He takes after his mama in all his finest qualities, including his svelte phys—"

She got no further because Tess, tired of trying to move

426

the immovable, ducked her head under the old woman's out-stretched arm and flung Mother Gaida over her shoulder like a sack of grain. Turning hay and pounding roadbed had given Tess some strength in her arms and back. The old woman shouted shocking obscenities as Tess turned her around. Back on her feet, Mother Gaida swayed dizzily, swatted Tess's ear, and began to laugh.

"What are you?" she cried, unable to fit Tess into her usual categories for human people.

Tess wanted to say, *A child of the Road,* but feared she was already too eccentric for the old seamstress. Instead she said, "Just myself, Mother Gaida. Nothing more."

The old woman still hesitated. "But...you've seen a man naked before? I'm afraid it's not quite decent work for a young lady."

"Let me meet him," said Tess. "If he and I together feel it could work, I'd happily be his nursemaid until the end of winter." Perhaps longer, but she wasn't sure she'd want to keep that promise. Come spring, the Road would surely start calling again.

This satisfied the aged embroiderer. She tested Tess's stitches, came to an agreement about wages, and found Tess some fill work to do (shocking her other embroiderers, who found Tess less giggle-worthy now). At the end of the day, Gaida locked up shop and led Tess a short way up the crooked street to another house, bigger than the place Tess's family had been living in for the last couple of years. Its three stories were cantilevered above the street, each a little farther than the last, stone and then brick and then timber. The front entrance was a double door, like the doors of a stable.

The sun had set, but it was bright within; someone had lit the lamps. They seemed to have walked directly into the kitchen. "The house is laid out to accommodate my boy," Gaida was explaining. "His bedroom is here." She indicated another double door across the room. "Sitting room's upstairs. You'll be on the third floor, under the eaves."

Before Tess could answer, a clanking and creaking from the next room raised the hairs on her arms. She shot a glance at Gaida, whose fuzzy chin wrinkled anxiously.

The double doors sprang open together, and in the doorway stood a man with eight legs.

Tess did not cry out or gasp; if she was afraid, it was only for a moment. First she saw that the spider legs belonged not to the man but to an iron chair he was sitting in; his own legs, thin as sticks, were curled under him. In the next instant she realized she'd seen this man before.

The walking chair had been built for him by St. Blanche, in thanks for his service to Ninys before the war. He'd been a herald, and Seraphina's guide as she collected other half-dragons. When Tess was twelve, he'd come to Lavondaville to visit Seraphina; the family had met him at the home of the Ninysh ambassadress, Dame St. Okra Carmine. The chair had been new, a marvel of engineering, the only thing anyone could talk about, but Tess had been struck by his face and by the shadow of sorrow under his eyes as he looked at Seraphina.

He'd been in love with her, Tess was convinced. He'd come all the way to Goredd to see her again, and she'd broken his heart.

He didn't look heartbroken now. In fact, he looked very

well, his long reddish hair tied back, his chin beard tidy, his blue eyes smiling. If only she could remember his name.

Gaida saved her the awkwardness. "I've brought home a prospective boarder, Josquin. A lady, despite all appearances. She's called . . ."

Tess had given Gaida her name, but the old woman's memory hadn't retained it. "Tess," she said, stepping up and shaking Josquin's hand. "Tess Dombegh."

"Dombegh!" he cried. She'd forgotten how deep and pleasant his voice was. "That's a name I always like to hear," he added in Goreddi. "Your sister's well, I trust?"

Tess wasn't sure of the answer. "She had a baby," she began feebly.

"It *was* hers, then, not the Queen's," said Josquin. "I wondered."

"That's my guess," said Tess, unsure how much he knew and didn't know. "I haven't been home in six months, but I saw Seraphina pregnant."

"And you're certain the Queen couldn't have got her that way," said Josquin, with a smile that suggested he knew rather a lot, in fact. Maybe he knew more than she did.

"I am never certain of anything where those three are concerned," Tess said dryly, "and that's the way they prefer it."

Josquin threw back his head and laughed. Gaida, who didn't speak Goreddi, was losing patience. "If you knew him, why didn't you say?" she fussed, seeming to forget that she hadn't mentioned his name. "Don't deny it. All the women know him, and I never understand how."

"They talk among themselves, Mother," Josquin called as

Gaida led Tess upstairs. "They say, 'What a fine, mannerly man Mother Gaida raised, and have you seen his marvelous legs?' We can't stop them talking. I could be less mannerly, I suppose."

"Rapscallion," muttered Gaida under her breath, but she was smiling.

Tess settled in quickly; the attic room was tiny and she had only her pack. She came downstairs to stew and crusty bread, a collaborative effort of mother and son. Tess relished every morsel and helped with the washing up, and then Gaida said, "You'd better talk to him and learn what you're to do. See if you want this job. Clearly, you get along already"—her mouth pinched suspiciously—"but that will only take you so far. He needs care, and care is work. You may be too delicate for it, after all. We shall see."

Gaida toddled upstairs. Josquin clanked toward his bedroom, beckoning Tess to follow. He closed the doors behind them with a lever. One end of the room was set up as a study, with a broad desk and bookshelves; at the other end was a railed bed and an enormous round bath with a gleaming boiler tank behind it.

"More of St. Blanche's handiwork," Josquin said, noting where her eyes lingered. "A pump fills it from the well, which I can work myself, but the boiler is hard for me to stoke."

"You're lucky to get so much personal attention from a living Saint," said Tess, realizing only afterward that *Saint* might remind him of Seraphina. She didn't want to make him sad, or invite a comparison she could only lose from.

"Blanche feels guilty for trying to kill me the first time we met." He directed his chair across the room toward another set of doors. "She also built the privy in the yard. I can use it without help, unless there's snow."

"Light the boiler; shovel snow. What else can I do?" said Tess, folding her arms. "Your mother hinted, but didn't say much."

"There isn't much to say," said Josquin, falling serious. "The house is set up so I can take care of myself. I'm not an invalid." His chair crabbed toward the desk, where he started tidying papers. "Honestly, it's my aging mother who needs help. She insists on doing too much. I have to butt in to do my share of cooking; she won't hear of moving to a smaller house. Anything you could do for her—pick up the slack, take her arm on the stairs—I'd appreciate it."

Tess peeked over his shoulder at the papers he was shuffling. They looked like verses, but he whisked them away too quickly for her to read. She leaned her backside against the desk. "Your mother worried that I wasn't strong enough to lift you out of the bath, but I threw her over my shoulder, which convinced her."

"I wish I'd seen that," he said. "I don't suppose you'd consider doing it again?"

"She'd hate me," said Tess, "and I need a place to stay. I also want to properly earn my keep. You can do everything yourself, but you don't have to all the time. I'm not squeamish, and I'm not afraid. I've seen naked men before."

Josquin, who'd taken up a deck of cards from the corner of his desk, paused mid-shuffle. "You get straight to the point."

"Don't spare my imagined sensibilities, is all," said Tess, drumming lightly on the desk. "I spent two months with a road crew, turned hay, mucked stalls, helped care for a senile old man—" She kissed a knuckle Heavenward. "My sensibilities are back on the road somewhere."

Josquin eyed her with new interest. "I don't like to pry, but I remember your family and I can't not ask: why did you leave home? Not to work on a road crew, presumably."

Tess opened her mouth and closed it again, not sure how much to trust him with. "I'm just walking the road, looking for reasons to keep walking."

"The road becomes its own reason, doesn't it," said Josquin softly, and Tess met his eye again, surprised. "I was a herald for ten years, riding all over Ninys, and the thing I miss most keenly isn't the use of my legs but the road itself. Possibility around every turn; the horizon always out of reach." He grew misty. "You must have some good stories."

"I have all the stories," said Tess warmly. Here was a fellow traveler, his journey cut short by circumstance, and she felt for him. "If that's how I can help, by bringing the road to you, I'll tell every single one. Twice if necessary."

Josquin laughed and lowered his gaze. He was still shuffling cards, his large hands competent and precise. "I'd like that," he said. "That is help I would willingly take."

~⚔~

Tess quickly found her niche. Routine sorted itself around her, like a river around a new rock. She woke before dawn to make everyone breakfast. Tess and Gaida went to the workshop, while Josquin puttered around, reading and writing; they came home for lunch (Gaida's bailiwick) and then again for dinner (which Josquin had declared officially his). In the evenings Josquin had his bath, a long therapeutic soak in St. Blanche's tub. Tess ended up supervising this because the old woman put her foot down. Gaida's greatest horror was that her son would hit his head in the bath and be drowned.

It was hard for Tess to begrudge her. She'd fulfilled her own mother's worst fear, bearing a bastard; if she could ease Gaida's mind for so little effort, she'd do it.

Josquin was somewhat sour about this at first. Tess would ask, per Gaida's instructions, whether he wanted help getting in, then again later whether he needed a hand getting out, and he would answer tersely that he wasn't a child.

Tess didn't mind the snapping; it was all a formality. She was really there to tell him stories. If the bath went cold before Josquin remembered to climb out of it, Tess considered this a sign of good storytelling and felt satisfied that she was doing her part.

"Isn't this delightful," Gaida said one evening as they lingered around the hearth, too full to move on to the next stage. "You've fit yourself right in, my dear. Rebecca never made that kind of effort."

"Mother," said Josquin warningly.

Tess's ears had perked up with interest, however. "Who's Rebecca?"

"Oh, she was Jos's caretaker before you," said Gaida, scraping the bottom of her empty bowl with her spoon. "A midwife from the Archipelagos, always flitting about, attending her patients before my Jos. I never liked her."

"You loved her, Ma," said Josquin, weariness in his voice.

"Indeed I never! I *supposed* she would do, since we couldn't find a man to take care of you, and she was coarse and boor-ish enough to be one. But my gut said she was trouble. The Pelaguese always are. I wasn't the least surprised when she left and broke your heart."

"You realize that Tess will leave us come spring," said Jos-quin, rubbing his neck. "She's mentioned it several times."

"What? Oh, I know what she said," said Gaida, suddenly flustered. "But spring is a long ways off. No need to dwell on it now."

Tess listened with a certain amusement, and when Josquin retired for his bath, she followed, grinning. "So, this Rebecca," she said as she stoked the fire. She tried not to sound teasing, but almost certainly failed. "Were you two . . . you know . . ."

"Yes," said Josquin, pulling off his shirt, and then Tess real-ized she'd been too vague. There were several unspoken ques-tions he might've been answering. *Were they?* They were.

"Mother hoped Rebecca would marry me," he offered. Tess, behind the boiler, could hear the smile in his voice. "She came here to study, and then it was time for her to go back home. It was always going to happen—she told me, I knew—but she dashed my mother's hopes."

"Am I going to dash them, too, when I leave?" said Tess, tapping the temperature gauge and then opening the spigot.

"Of course you are," he said lightly. There was a long pause while he removed his breeches, something of a project from his spider-legged throne. "Can't be helped," he said at last, placing neatly folded pants on the bed and gesturing for Tess to fetch two enormous towels. "She's scared that she's going to die and I'll be all alone."

Tess's face must have reflected the same concern, because he added quickly, "I won't be alone, Tess. I've always been good at making and keeping friends. You don't need to worry, and you don't need to stay here beyond your own inclinations."

Tess nodded, a little flustered now that he was entirely naked. She usually kept hidden behind the boiler during this part, but they'd been conversing, and he'd left the towels across the room, and . . . she could turn away right now. She might do so at any time. She was entirely free to engage her good manners, starting this very moment. Or even right about now.

She was a little in awe, though, of how he lifted himself out of his seat, how he grasped spider legs and then tub railings with his hands and swung himself into the water. He had enough control over his legs that he could tense them and bring them over the edge; they helped slow his descent. His arms were wiry but strong; Tess could see every muscle in his shoulders working.

She watched the whole operation, fascinated, then forced her gaze to the corner of the room. "What can I tell you tonight?" she mused, but she already knew what she wanted to tell him. She'd been putting it off, practicing in her head. It was the story words wouldn't stick to, and she needed to say it out loud, get it right, before taking it to the Academy.

"When I was a child, my best friend was a quigutl," she began. "He told tales of seven great serpents beneath the surface of the world. I always assumed they were a myth."

Josquin closed his eyes and sank into the water up to his chin beard.

And so she told Josquin about her search, with a few omissions: how she had gone to St. Bert's hoping to learn more; how only Will had seemed to believe her; and how they'd planned to go searching for the World Serpents together, but that had fallen through (she didn't go into detail); how she'd determined to find one on her own after she ran away from home (she felt some delicacy about Pathka's pilgrimage, so she glossed over it); how she'd fallen down a hole and glimpsed the beast; how she'd followed it to its lair, met a mournful monk, and then the library of Santi Prudia had sunk into the earth.

Josquin listened without interrupting. Tess drifted around the room as she narrated, from the desk to the bed and back, until she was seated on the little bench beside the tub, with his towels. His body looked pale and contorted under the water, like some strange fish.

Tess leaned her elbows on her knees. "I want to present this discovery at the Academy," she said. "What did you think of it? Is it believable?"

Josquin opened his serious blue eyes. "I believe you, but the way you tell it is a bit personal for an Academy presentation. You'd be telling hundreds of strangers, you realize."

"Personal?" cried Tess. That was what she'd been trying to avoid by leaving out Pathka's quest, Will, and Julian/Dozerius— by concentrating on the facts. "Which part was personal?"

Josquin exhaled, rippling the surface of the water. "I don't even know what to call it. The ecstatic-revelation-alongside-a-monk part?"

"That's the most important part," said Tess, crossing her arms.

"Important to *you*," he said gently. "The Academy isn't always sympathetic to that sort of thing. If they get scornful, it's going to hurt."

Tess laughed. "I've got a mask to wear. I'll go as Tes'puco. He can take it."

Josquin rolled his eyes. "You know that name is childishly rude?"

"I revel in it," she said haughtily.

"If you're going under an assumed name," he said, "at least pick something with more dignity. What's the other ne'er-do-well you sometimes pretended to be? Brother Such-and-so?"

"Brother Jacomo?" Tess shook her head. "Not for this. He's too earnest, desperately trying not to be the terrible clergyman he knows he is in his heart. He would take it personally if they laughed. Tes'puco is sassy and bold. Tes'puco doesn't care."

"If you say so," said Josquin, clearly unconvinced.

"Anyway," said Tess, waving it off, "they won't think twice about the personal parts, not when there are so many significant *facts* for them to cogitate upon. How does it glow? What does it eat? How did it heal me?"

She blurted out the last question before it struck her that Josquin would have feelings on this subject. In fact, she'd expected him to ask about the healing, and was only now thinking that perhaps his silence meant something—but what?

"I don't know if it would be possible to . . . to collect its blood or something," Tess stammered. "Did the blood heal me, though, or was it touching the serpent that . . . ?"

Josquin pursed his lips and said nothing; his fingers drummed on the rim of the tub.

He didn't seem hopeful or excited or even particularly curious about the prospect. Tess tried to make sense of that and couldn't. She'd assumed . . . she'd assumed Angelica would be grateful. Assuming was, perhaps, not the best way to understand things.

"Would you want to be healed, if we could figure out how?" Tess asked quietly.

Josquin looked up at her, a look with uncountable facets; she waited for the words. "I don't know," he said at last. "I feel like I should, and maybe someday I will, but . . . I don't know how to make you understand. On a bad day—and there have been plenty of those—I might've said yes, please, wave your wand and make it go away. Now, though? I hate how ungrateful I sound, but I find the idea insulting, as if you were saying, 'All your pain was a mistake. Here, have everything back.' Except it wouldn't be everything, not the time, not the suffering, not the thousand ways I've changed."

He shifted in the water. "I wouldn't wish for this, Tess, but I'm not sure I'd wish it away, either. Does that make any sense at all?"

Tess couldn't speak. She remembered Countess Margarethe, swooping in like some fairy godmother with all of Tess's abandoned hopes on a plate, and remembered her own reaction.

His hand was still on the edge of the tub. Tess laid her hand over his and squeezed. And that was the beginning, though neither of them knew it yet.

Twenty-Five

Tess, who was occupied a great deal with embroidery, did not at first understand that Josquin didn't stay home all day. She'd assumed he must be a shut-in; he'd mentioned friends, but she figured they came to see him and not the other way around. Only when she noticed that Gaida never seemed to do any shopping but there was always food at home did she begin to realize Josquin had an entire life outside the house.

If the weather cooperated, he went out every day. He'd been off the herald circuit for more than five years, but he still knew half of Segosh. When Tess had an afternoon off, she began to accompany him, to market or the Hall of Archives or the Spotted Livery, where elderly members of the Brotherhood of Heralds drank.

If Tess didn't have an afternoon off, she soon learned that she could get one by saying to Gaida, "Josquin asked me to—"

"Of course," Gaida would reply. "Go."

Josquin knew the masters of the Ninysh Academy. "When you're a marvel of medicine and engineering," he explained to Tess as she followed him through the market with a shopping basket, "of course they all want a good look. I should have died, if not from my injury then from infection. Between Dr. Belestros and St. Blanche, I've been a prop at more than twenty lectures."

Tess looked at him sidelong. "'Prop'? That must get old quickly."

"It would," he said, "but St. Blanche is a darling and I can begrudge her nothing. Also, it's important. Others will be saved, thanks to my patient posing. It's a small price to pay."

He didn't say it aloud, but Tess understood: a miraculous serpent-cure would render their work and his sacrifices unnecessary. That didn't make it bad, just . . . less simple than it seemed.

Tess polished an apple on her jerkin. "Could you get Tes'puco an invitation to speak?"

"I can advise Tes'puco—if that is his real name—that Grand High Master Pashfloria wants to be petitioned in writing."

Tess got right to it, colonizing Josquin's desk when they got home. He barely had time to hide his poetry. "He who snoozeth gets his verses read," said Tess while Josquin snatched away notes, correspondence, and poems dense with scrawled commentary. Tess wasn't that interested in his poetry, which was surely all damp laments for lost Seraphina; she only meant to tease him.

"What hand would Tes'puco use? Something brash and

masculine." She wrote *I swashed and buckled my way across Iboia* in several trial scripts.

"Which hand is your own?" said Josquin, sorting his work onto different shelves.

"All of them," said Tess, choosing her manliest and setting to work.

She signed her long petition *Tes'puco the Explorer.* "You sound like a character in a children's story," Josquin teased, but Tess would not be dissuaded.

Master Pashfloria replied two days later, expressing mild doubts about her story. Tess sent him one of the bowl-sized scales from Big Spooky, a sketch of Santi Prudia and the caverns beneath it, and finally, for good measure, a wholly inadequate drawing of Anathuthia.

It took the Grand High Master a week to write back, and Tess despaired that her request had been denied. When his letter finally arrived, however, it told her she was booked to give a speech before the entire assembly at the Great Odeon in three weeks. She wrote a gracious note of acceptance in Tes'puco's best formal handwriting. Less formally, she danced around Josquin's room; he watched her with a spark of fond amusement in his eye.

Josquin had called upon his old comrades at the Brotherhood of Heralds to deliver these missives. "We need the work," he told her as they trundled down to the Spotted Livery. "Now that thniks have become so commonplace, our ranks are dwindling. We still escort dignitaries, but we're not the fastest way to carry news anymore."

Tess noted the first-person pronouns. He was still a herald in his heart.

Taking the letters gave him an excuse to spend an afternoon with the old-timers. Not that he needed an excuse; in addition to his poetry, he was writing a history of the Ninysh heralds, so he went several times a week to take notes and drink beer around the flimsy green tables.

Tess liked to go along and listen. The old heralds had ridden every road in Ninys, and there was something comforting and familiar in their tales. The Road took them from adventure to adventure; they met curious characters, left them behind, and found them again. Tess could almost see the warp and weft of a great tapestry, the world, being woven as they spoke.

Occasionally the stories got ribald. Tess's presence seemed not to deter anyone from telling such tales; she only hoped Josquin didn't see how she blushed. Indeed, Josquin's bawdy stories were in some ways the worst. Not that he went into lascivious detail—he wasn't one to wax rhapsodic about heaving bosoms or curvaceous backsides—but he was unfailingly frank. If he'd painted himself as a dashing romantic hero, she could have imagined he was talking about someone else. Tess found herself uncomfortably moved by his transparency.

"Tell me something," she said one day as they walked home to make supper for Gaida. The late autumn sky arced clear and blue above them. "Have you had a lot of paramours?"

"How many is a lot?" he said. "More than six? Less than eight? In that case, yes. Most of them after the accident, if that's your real question."

Tess gaped at him; she should have known he'd be forthright

and direct. "But ... do you have bastard children? Surely you must."

"Heavens, I hope not. No one's ever told me so," he said, raising his brows mildly as if this had never occurred to him. "It's easy enough to avoid." Tess frowned at the word *easy*.

"Remind me sometime and I'll show you Rebecca's 'basket of joy,'" he said. "Midwives know these things; she always had a mountain of herbs, Porphyrian pessary resin, you name it."

Tess could not have named any of it and was lightly appalled that he could mention such things so casually, as if they were nothing. Deep in her gut, a little flame of anger burned. She could've used such knowledge, once upon a time, if anyone had seen fit to inform her. She scowled to herself, but had no intention of reminding him to show her the basket.

And yet.

Like the metaphorical cat she was—stalked by curiosity—she finally conquered her mortification and asked. Josquin showed her everything in the basket and explained what it was for. Tess learned new words and went red as a beet, and Josquin kindly pretended not to notice.

It was probably inevitable that Tess began to feel things for Josquin that she would rather not have felt.

It wasn't merely that he was so open about his lovers and willing to answer her questions, although that certainly helped. Tess saw Josquin naked almost every day. He was beautiful, there was no denying it, even if his legs were thin and he had odd equipment. This was not a euphemism: he had a variety of apparatuses that helped him live—braces, tubes, catheters—designed and installed by St. Blanche. Tess had at first pretended not to see, but after a while it seemed no more grotesque than anything else a body had on offer—sinew, blood, or bone. There was a poetry to it, and a comedy, and much less tragedy than she would have assumed.

"The body is forever an indignity, for each of us," Josquin would say when his got complicated. "I'm working on a poem about it. 'We are the farting children of Heaven, blessed be our slippery viscera.'"

Then Tess would sing "The Flesh Is but a Sack of Goo," and Josquin would laugh uproariously. That laugh was worth everything. She could have kissed him then.

She worked very hard not to.

Not that she feared he wouldn't welcome it; she was terrified he would, and that she wasn't strong enough or together enough to keep the past from rearing up and biting her. She'd suddenly be thirteen again (against her will) and crossing that final line, unable to breathe—

She quashed such thoughts before they went further. A few nightmares still festered in her mind's oubliette, and she wasn't ready to look. She might never be ready.

Even so, Josquin occupied Tess's thoughts more than she wanted. She daydreamed. He'd be serving dinner and accidentally touch her hand . . . Or he needed help unfastening a troublesome buckle on his doublet, and . . . Or she offered to scrub his back, but she dropped the scrub brush, and then . . .

What a burden those ellipses bore. She dared not put words to what came next.

The cure for sin-bridled thoughts, she well knew, was St. Vitt's Invocation Against the Demons of the Flesh. She'd had to learn it by heart even though Mama had claimed that only men ever really needed it. "Your future husband may not know it," Mama had warned. "It might be up to you to teach him."

It went like this: *St. Vitt save me, for I have sinned in thought. Pleasure is deceit, longing is selfish, and bodily lust distracts us from our purpose, the greater glory of Heaven. I am meat, and meat is for worms; it does not deserve to want. I place my desires in your hands, for you to break upon the Anvil of Virtue—*

It went on and on, a dismal parade of recrimination and remorse. Tess rarely got past the Anvil of Virtue, which gave her a fit of giggles incommensurate to how funny it was. Laughter brought her some relief, but not enough. She couldn't sleep.

Then one day Josquin knocked his inkpot into the bath—which was entirely Tess's fault, for setting it by his elbow on the bath desk without warning him it was there. She'd been trying to anticipate him and deliver it before he asked. Anyway, it spilled into the water, which made it urgent to get Josquin out before he was stained blue-black all over. Tess efficiently removed his writing papers and the desk, without further disaster. He hoisted himself out, but needed help getting dry quickly. Josquin was laughing, good sport that he was, while Tess rubbed down the places that were hard to reach.

By bedtime, alone in her room, she was still drying him in her mind. The texture of him was fresh and vivid, the heft and give and pull. The smell of him, too, and remembered laughter ringing in her ears, and the warmth, and she imagined kissing that mouth—had longed for it in the moment, he'd been so close—how soft his lips would be, how sweet—

She wanted him. There it was, the unthinkable thought.

Saints in Heaven, she couldn't go on like this. She couldn't rush downstairs and pounce on him, and St. Vitt's Invocation was useless. She'd generally resolved or circumvented this inner struggle, but lusting after Josquin brought it back: her sordid nature was forever pitted against her longing to be good. Despairingly, she flopped around in bed like a trout out of water, until two memories struck her at once.

The first was Mother Philomela saying, *There are never just two choices. That is a lie to keep you from thinking too deeply.*

And the second was what Darling Dulsia had been saying before Tess's painful memories interrupted. She'd been too upset to listen, and yet apparently she'd retained the words, because here they were, sprung up in her hour of need: *Your body is yours, the enjoyment of it is yours, and you should never let anyone, even a Saint, rob you of it.*

Two women from her journey—polar opposites, or were they? Both worked with bodies and dispensed advice; there were more similarities between nun and whore than she could have guessed. What if those poles weren't mutually exclusive? What if opposites could be combined and transcended, paradox embraced, a whole life lived in contradictory case?

She blinked, and for a second she glimpsed it again, an afterimage of pale blue fire. City life had been so busy that she'd forgotten that other feeling, of being completely free to choose.

She had permission to let her body do and be and have what it wanted, this once. She hadn't banished Josquin with all this thinking; he came back to her, full and glorious and blazing like the sun. She touched what demanded to be touched and she let her mind fly where it would.

The endpoint was like nothing she could ever have expected, like all the beauty of the world channeled down her spine at once. Like being struck by lightning made of music. She felt dissolved all the way to her extremities.

Tears sprang to her eyes. No one had told her. The body was. All. Nothing.

There.

Afterward, though her body felt pleasantly adrift, she couldn't stop thinking (she'd never thought of herself as a thinker; Seraphina was the smart one). This, whatever it was called—Josquin probably knew, if she'd dared to ask—was one more way to put herself back together, like walking or turning hay. All right, pleasanter than turning hay.

Mama had been quite clear: men might enjoy their bodily lusts, but a woman's lot was duty and pain (although there was pleasure, presumably, in doing one's duty and knowing what rewards awaited in the hereafter). Tess wondered whether her mother had ever experienced this. She couldn't have. How could she omit to mention it if she knew?

It was possible to bear children and still not know. She herself was proof of that.

As she drifted toward sleep, Tess was struck—hilariously—by the thought that she should tell her mother. She should tell everyone, preach the word on street corners. That was absurd, of course. This was even more personal than Anathuthia. Even she did not have the brazen gall to mention this holy mystery in public.

Not yet, anyway.

Two weeks before the New Year, Tess gave her lecture at the Academy.

Josquin lent her his nicest doublet. It was a bit out of fashion (he lamented; Tess, as a Goreddi, had never seen the like) but well made, a deep brown velvet with red satin peeking through slashes in the sleeves. You could get married in a doublet like this. Tess turned her head upside down over a bucket and snipped her hair a little shorter; Josquin wore his long, but Josquin also had a chin beard and a strong jaw.

Josquin clucked his tongue at her, not for roughing up her hair but because she still insisted on going as Tes'puco.

"You don't understand," she snapped, tossing her head and looking in the glass. She looked dramatically windblown, which she rather liked. "It's better to keep pretending to be a man. I've been the lone girl among naturalists before. They never took me seriously—or if they pretended to, they were seeking something in return."

"They aren't all like that," Josquin began, but cut off when Tess gave him a look.

"Fine. Say they're not," said Tess. "Even so, I'm not outgoing and gregarious like you. Tes'puco is a shield for me to hide behind as I talk. He gives me courage."

"You might try a glass of wine for that," Josquin said, picking lint off her sleeve.

"Indeed not," said Tess, who had her reasons. Impulsively, she reached for his hand and squeezed it. "If I took enough wine to dampen my fears, I'd forget my speech altogether."

Josquin squeezed her hand back. "I wish I could come with you and be your wine."

The way he said it filled her heart with exultation, and that was just as good.

He couldn't come because the first snow had fallen, and his mechanical chair didn't like to climb the slippery hill. Tess didn't like it much, either. She hired a young porter with a sledge to haul her props and pictures across town, and she skipped alongside, full of giddiness, kicking clods of snow with her boots.

Unlike St. Bert's, the Ninysh Academy was not a repurposed church but had been built expressly for the containment of thinkers and their experiments. It boasted a grand odeon and ballroom, laboratories with gleaming soapstone countertops, a library, a menagerie, a cafetorium (providing sustenance for erudite brains), and a smaller odeon for debates (the Argumenterion, some called it, although this was a silly name). A massive dome, pure rationality made manifest in stone, crowned the building. Each of the entrance steps had a scientific virtue inlaid in contrasting marble: REASON, SKEPTICISM, EMPIRICISM, DILIGENCE. They felt like admonitions underfoot; indeed, one could hardly step on such portentous nouns without feeling wholly inadequate.

Tess hesitated at the steps, as had many sensitive souls

before, gauging her worthiness to ascend. She squeezed herself to one side and climbed without tripping over any of the words.

With Josquin's help, she'd prepared drawings and diagrams on large canvases, visible from the back of the amphitheater: a rendition of the map she'd sent to Master Pashfloria, a painting that tried to capture how Anathuthia had glowed in the dark, and a diagram of the chamber complete with made-up dimensions (it might have been a mile deep, mightn't it? This seemed plausible to Tess, who'd missed any lectures on the importance of accurate measurement and instrumentation). She'd brought the last of the small scales, of course, and a hanging her fellow embroiderers had made for her, depicting the pattern of Anathuthia's skin in gaudy colors.

Having never given a formal speech before, she'd written it all out and memorized it. She'd taken a few of Josquin's suggestions to heart, omitting not just Pathka but Frai Moldi and anything that didn't make it sound like she'd been single-minded in her search for the serpent. It made the story more sharply focused, even if it wasn't as varied, deep, and true.

Later, Tess couldn't recall the speech itself, only how her heart palpitated and her armpits grew clammy. Her voice began shakily, then strengthened. She remembered faces in the front row, old philosophers with pointed goatlike beards, an older woman in a diamond-patterned gown that reminded her of scales. She remembered how everyone held their breath at one point, and how the candles of the great chandelier flickered when they collectively exhaled.

She was a trickster-explorer in this story, a latter-day Dozerius hunting the beast with nothing but her native resourcefulness and guile. She'd tracked it across Goredd, deducing correctly that certain large sinkholes might be its handiwork. She'd disguised herself as a road worker to further her research, and met a brilliant geologist who'd given her a missing piece of the puzzle (she was vague about this piece, but definitely said "Nicolas" several times, in hopes of increasing his reputation at the Academy; she'd forgotten that he scorned the institution).

Only when it came time to describe the serpent did she falter, realizing that the moment was still deeply personal even without Moldi, even as Tes'puco. Certainly her chief impression—that she was nothing, and the comfort that had brought her—should have been unutterable at such a philosophical gathering. Her conclusion was the opposite of science, was speculative and subjective and unproved.

Still, she'd told the story with such vigor and enthusiasm to this point that her audience seemed not to mind that she was suddenly at a loss for words. Many had clapped hands to their hearts, moved by her passion. They were with her; they waited.

"There I found it," Tess said, her voice thick and overawed. "Under the library of Santi Prudia Monastery. And I fell upon my knees and wept."

The amphitheater erupted into earth-shaking applause.

She could tell a compelling story, anyway. Only afterward, when the masters of the Academy came to shake hands and congratulate her, when they mentioned her in the same sentence as the luminaries of Ninysh exploration, Nemadeaux and

Captain Foille, did it begin to sink in that they'd believed her. Many academics had been skeptical that the southern voyages (such as the one taken by Honorary Master Margarethe, Countess Mardou) would prove fruitful. Now they chattered excitedly. Anathuthia was only the beginning. There were reportedly seven of these creatures, and Ninys could be first to uncover them all.

"Its healing powers alone make it the greatest discovery of our lifetimes, perhaps of the century," said Master Pashfloria. "Are you excited by the implications, Doctor?"

The doctor he was addressing may have been a saar, because he merely raised an eyebrow. "It remains to be seen—and tested."

"If we could harness it in some way," an excitable scholar interjected, "we could—"

"Oh, um. No," said Tess with some concern. "It's not the sort of thing one harnesses, gentlemen. It's a force of nature. One might more easily harness the moon."

Everyone chuckled at this and let the matter drop.

Only one of the masters, a young pinch-faced fellow called Emmanuele, refused to credit Tess's story. "Surely we don't believe this Goreddi? He's playing us for fools. What kind of name is Tes'puco for a man of science? I smell a fraud, and I'm going to prove it."

"Do your worst," said Tess cockily. "The monks of Santi Prudia can corroborate my story. Ask for Frai Moldi or Pater Livian, the abbot. They'll tell you."

The abbot might be angry that she'd told, but this wasn't his secret to keep anymore. She thought Moldi would understand.

"I may do just that," sneered Emmanuele. He stalked off, pointed elbows jabbing the air.

It was dark by the time Tess went home. She left her illustrations behind, which was just as well. No porter could have kept up with her dancing and cavorting back to Gaida's.

They'd believed her, felt with her. She could hardly believe it herself.

Tess let herself in and would've headed upstairs, if not for the light under Josquin's door. He was probably reading or writing, but she knocked to see if he needed anything.

She opened the door a crack. He lay in bed, reading by lamplight. "There you are," he said, looking up from his book. She took that as an invitation to come in. "How was it?"

"Less terrifying than I'd feared," said Tess, closing the door behind her. She removed his fine doublet and hung it on a low peg near the desk. "Their polar expeditions have come up empty, so I'm the first explorer to find one, Josquin. The very first." She took a comical bow.

"That must be gratifying," he said, holding a hand out to her.

She sat beside him on the bed. He wriggled closer to the wall to make room for her. Impulsively, Tess lay beside him on top of the coverlet, her head on his pillow, the way she used to lie beside Jeanne for midnight conferences.

The way she'd cheekily lain down beside Will . . . It was a position with a mixed history.

She turned to look at Josquin directly, and he was so close. The disarming blue eyes, the tender mouth, the silly red chin beard. She rolled onto her side, touched his cheek, and kissed his forehead. He didn't recoil from her touch or the kiss, so she went for his mouth next and found it a welcoming harbor.

Reality exceeded all dreams. She felt illuminated.

"I see," said Josquin when she paused to catch her breath. "It's like that, is it?"

She answered with more kisses. He smiled against her demanding mouth. "Tess," he said mushily, then turned his face aside so he might speak: "What are you asking of me, dear?"

She stopped her onslaught and rested her forehead against his. "You know."

"Yes, but do you?" He took her face in his hands and made her look him in the eye.

"Of course," said Tess, vibrantly alight, moving in on him again and kissing his fuzzy chin. It was like being drunk, but better, everything sharper instead of dulled.

"Wait, wait. Listen to me, sweet," said Josquin gently. "You understand, I hope, that I take this rather seriously. If it's your first time, that's a responsibility I—"

"It's not my first time," said Tess, flushing. She hated confessing it, but could not, in good conscience, let him think her better than she was.

His pale lashes fluttered in confusion. "Your questions the other day, about Rebecca's herbs, sounded inexperienced to me."

It was rude to bring his ex-girlfriend into bed. Tess felt the strongbox where she kept her heart closing. She pulled away, and he seemed to glean that there were things she did not care to discuss.

"Maybe I was mistaken," he said, laying a hand on her

forearm, "but you are also ten years younger than me, Tess. If I should hurt you, however inadvertently, your sister—"

"I see," said Tess, pulling out of his grasp. "You're not over Seraphina."

Josquin emitted a short laugh. "Over her? She's one of my dearest friends. She critiques my poetry better than anyone. Heaven forfend I should get over her! I only meant she'd kill me if I hurt you. She'd hunt me down, and my incapacity would earn me no mercy at her hands."

Seraphina hadn't hunted Will down, Tess recalled sourly, after Will had . . . What he'd done wasn't the point. Will had hurt her, and nobody had helped. Between him, Seraphina, and Rebecca, there were now far too many people in this bed.

Tess squirmed and rubbed her eyes as if she were tired, so that Josquin wouldn't see the tears burgeoning there. "This was a mistake," she said. "You're right; I'm not ready. I've been through a lot. You don't know the half."

"You haven't told me," he said softly.

"Nor shall I," she said, turning her back to him. "I thought maybe it was time and I could heal those old hurts. You seemed harmless enough."

"Harmless?" he cried, and then he grabbed her.

What happened next happened so quickly that for a moment Tess didn't understand what she'd done. She was on her feet, looking down at Josquin, who was clutching his nose. She'd screamed; she could still hear the echo.

Her body had acted without her. Again. After all her work and diligence, her struggles to keep herself unified, how did this still happen? How could the past keep sneaking up on her like this? She reeled with despair. It was never going to be over.

Now there were footsteps outside, and Gaida arrived in her nightcap and chemise, crying, "Josquin, what have you done to this poor girl?"

"It's all right, Mother," said Josquin, his voice nasal. He removed his hand to reveal blood trickling over his upper lip. "I alarmed Tess, but she's going to fetch me a handkerchief now, and then she's off to bed."

Gaida's eyes flicked from one to the other, as if she couldn't tell whether the bloody nose was the cause of Tess's alarm or its effect. "I'll wait for you outside, Tess," said the old woman.

"Please don't," said Tess, meeting Josquin's eyes. Stopping his nosebleed wasn't enough; there was a friendship hemorrhaging, too. This was going to take some time.

Gaida left, muttering. Tess brought Josquin the requested handkerchief and then slipped out to the yard for an icicle. He let her minister to his nose; it didn't seem broken, which was cold comfort. Tess could hardly grasp what had happened, let alone fathom what to say. She'd rolled onto her side, he'd grabbed her, and she'd panicked, a full-body lightning strike. She'd apparently rammed his nose with the back of her head before leaping out of reach.

"Do you ever feel as if your mind is full of traps?" Josquin said, his voice distressingly nasal.

"Traps?" said Tess, not following.

He closed his eyes, pressing what remained of the icicle against the side of his nose. "Long ago, when I was searching for Ninysh Saints with your sister—the one I'm not over—we spotted the house of St. Blanche the Mechanic across a clearing. We didn't realize, until we were in the midst of things, that the clearing was anything but clear. Invisible trip wires crisscrossed it, each strung to a trap. Axes and logs swung at our heads, a pit opened beneath my feet, and your sister faced spiders as big as sheep."

Tess had heard the story from Seraphina, but it had felt like myth, not something that had happened to real people.

"So here's my theory," Josquin continued, folding his handkerchief back to find a clean corner. "We booby-trap our heads the same way. The trip wires can't be seen, even by those of us who strung them, until someone snags a toe and sets off an explosion.

"I think"—he held her gaze significantly—"you and I each set the other one off just now. I'm happy to explain first; I know what happened with me." He swallowed hard, his throat bobbing. "You called me 'harmless,' but my mind translated it to 'broken.'"

"I didn't mean it that way," said Tess hurriedly, although this was a lie. She'd meant it, even if it wasn't all she'd meant.

Josquin smiled wanly. "The ridiculous thing is, I *am* harmless. I was harmless before the accident. Ask your sister. I just hate the implication that I am defective and emasculated. That I *couldn't* hurt anyone. In that terrible instant, I wanted to remind you that I'm strong enough to harm you if I chose." His eyes glimmered; the bloody nose hadn't brought him to tears, but confessing did. "I'm ashamed that I felt the need to show you that. I'm sorry."

"I'm sorry," said Tess, sitting down again. She considered

kissing him, but feared bumping his nose. She settled for taking his hand and kissing the knuckles.

He watched her expectantly; it was her turn to help him understand. Her lips quivered. She wasn't sure what the answer was. That lightning-strike moment—it had been some other moment. Her mind had come unmoored in time, like Griss's.

"I don't like being surprised from behind," she said at last, feebly.

Josquin nodded solemnly. "Lesson learned, believe me." He extended an arm, inviting Tess to lie down and be held—facing him, or as she preferred. She hesitated, then lowered her head onto the pillow. He pushed himself onto his side and stroked her hair in silence.

She wiped her eyes and sat up. "I should get to bed," she said dismally. Her Academy talk felt like a million years ago, the exuberant energy all drained from her limbs.

"You could sleep here," said Josquin. "You don't have to, but know that you could."

Tess carefully kissed that fine, gentle mouth again, and took herself upstairs.

Twenty-Six

A letter arrived from the Academy, inviting Tes'puco the Explorer to a gala reception in his honor, whereupon he would be made an Honorary Master of the Academy.

"Yes, you can borrow my doublet again," said Josquin before she asked. "You'll want something nicer than those breeches, which have seen a great deal of road. Mother may have something in storage that fits you. I wasn't always so thin in the legs."

Gaida found trunk hose in one of her cedar chests, all the while clucking disapproval. "You might dress properly, child," she harped after Tess as they came downstairs. "If you tucked your hair under a gabled cap, no one would know you'd chopped it off so dreadfully."

"Leave her be, Mother," said Josquin, sampling the stew he was simmering for dinner. "She's doing what she thinks she must."

Tess appreciated this, although she suspected he felt the

same as his mother. She planted a grateful kiss on his mouth before stopping to think who was watching. Gaida cleared her throat, and Tess backed off, embarrassed. The old woman shook her head as she went back up, muttering, "First a bloody nose, now this. Let me know when you two decide to make sense."

"We have confused my mother," said Josquin, pulling Tess nearer until she lost her balance and ended up in his lap. "Yes, the chair can hold us both," he added, when she looked down at the iron arachnid legs, perturbed.

"This rain should melt the snow by tomorrow," said Tess, adjusting her backside. "Come with me to the gala."

"In my second-best doublet?" said Josquin teasingly.

"Ah, but you're the better-looking man, so it's only fair," said Tess.

The next evening found them both climbing the hill to the Academy.

The night was blustery and wet, but the halls of knowledge were full of warmth and light. Luminaries of Segoshi society—nobles, socialites, intellectuals, financiers—had come to toast the mysterious, dashing, and romantic Tes'puco and his important discovery.

Josquin spotted twenty people he knew almost immediately. He set to socializing, leaving Tess to her own devices, and ended up near the hearth, talking earnestly to a pale, slender woman with graypox scars on her cheeks and hands. Tess smiled a little; Will would never have spoken to someone who looked like that.

Tess squared her shoulders and accepted praise from all quarters. Basked in it. Glowed with it. If it had been warm water, she'd have bathed in it; if it had been wine, she'd have grown embarrassingly drunk.

In fact, this newfound fame was not so different from wine. As much as she enjoyed praise and grew heady with it, it was never enough. There was some chasm in her heart demanding to be filled, but filling it with praise was like dumping gravel down Anathuthia's sinkhole; the more they poured in, the clearer it became that praise was unequal to the task. Tess found herself approaching clusters of people, impatient for them to realize who she was and applaud her for it. She would hint appallingly—"You've heard about my discovery, I'm sure"—and await her reward like a beggar, hand held out.

She didn't like seeing herself do this, and yet she seemed unable to stop.

If someone called her discovery *remarkable*, she fretted that they hadn't said *stupendous*. If *stupendous*, why not *earthshaking* or *paradigm-shifting*? A dozen people might hang upon her every word as she told the story again, but if a single one turned away, her heart followed and she couldn't bear it. She found herself pursuing one fellow, crying, "Am I boring you, sir?"

The man, a magistrate, florid-cheeked and wearing a ruff, looked boggled. "Forgive me, Master Tes'puco. Only I wanted some pudding, and I've already heard your story twice."

Tess, embarrassed, went back for more sweets herself.

She found her mind wandering after that. What she really wanted, she began to feel, was to be back in that cavern, gazing upon Anathuthia once more. That moment had meant something; all this was a pale shadow. The praise of the world could not compare.

The torte turned bitter in her mouth, and she set it aside. She was done here. She would say her goodbyes to the masters of the Academy, find Josquin, and go.

She was approaching Master Pashfloria when a shout froze her in her tracks. "Charlatan!"

Tess turned to see who was speaking. A space had opened up in the crowd, and there, at the far end of the hall, stood Emmanuele, who'd doubted her story before. "Tes'puco, you fraud, I accuse you!" he cried for everyone to hear. "You are not who you claim to be. I followed him home last time, Masters. He lives with a seamstress in Crewel Ramble."

"You might benefit from a mistress yourself, 'Manuele," someone cried.

Everyone laughed, and the young man turned crimson. Tess's heart banged against her ribs. "What are you accusing me of?" she asked. "Living among embroiderers is not a crime."

"*You* are the embroiderer!" cried Emmanuele, triumphant. "In more than one sense of the word. Tes'puco is a seamstress, gentlemen, and *she* has embroidered this tale to fool us."

Tess felt stripped bare, as if everyone were staring through her clothes. "I—I confess my name is not Tes'puco," she stammered. She felt Josquin's eyes upon her. "But you must have assumed that? Stupid-head? It had to be a nickname." No one spoke; the room had gone stony and cold. Tess's voice barely filled the emptiness: "I work as an embroiderer because I need to earn my keep. And I am a woman. Thank Heaven your finest scholar solved that mystery."

Masters, dignitaries, people of quality were glaring at her. "What difference does this trivia make?" Tess pleaded.

"Ah, but we must consider seriously," said Master Pashfloria, rising upon the dais. "A master of the Academy, even an honorary one, must exemplify the philosophical virtues in every endeavor, and the greatest of these is truth."

"The rest of my story is true," cried Tess, fury finding foothold in her heart.

"We don't even know your real name," said Pashfloria, ignoring her question and making a gesture that apparently called forth the muscle. Two guards approached Tess from the back of the room. "How can we trust anything you say? Gentlemen, I should never have let things get this far without looking into this ne'er-do-well's background."

"The Monastery of Santi Prudia!" Tess cried, trying to shake off the guards. She could only free herself from one at a time. "Frai Moldi and the abbot will tell you I was there!"

"I've spoken to Frai Moldi via thnik," said Emmanuele, eyes glinting as he revealed this final triumph. "He was quite clear that a fellow monk, one Brother Jacomo, was there when the monastery collapsed, not an impostor calling herself Tes'puco. Frai Moldi also denied the existence of any such serpent. Master Pashfloria, I think more research is warranted, and I would like to offer up my substantial expertise—"

The guards had been pulling Tess's arms; she stopped resisting and let them lead her outside. She couldn't make sense of any of this. Nothing Emmanuele had said should have been enough to get her thrown out of the Academy, not unless Master Pashfloria simply wanted an excuse to publicly discredit her.

Of course he did. He wanted someone to go after the serpent and "harness" it, whatever that was supposed to mean. If

Tess objected to this plan, no one would credit her now. It was tidier this way.

For all the good it would do them. There was surely no harnessing Anathuthia.

Tess waited at the bottom of the steps—not daring to stand upon the scientific virtues—for Josquin to come clanking out after her. His chair was very slow on stairs.

"I'm not going to say I told you so," he began.

Tess raised her shoulders and let them drop despairingly. "You cannot imagine how often I've been told *so*. So, so, so. And still I pigheadedly do things my own way."

The rain was mixed with snow. Tess stomped down the hill, slowly for Josquin's sake, her arm linked through his. She grew damper and colder as the wet soaked through every part of her (except her feet, thanks to the miracle of good boots).

"I probably wouldn't have listened to me, either," said Josquin as they neared home. "There are lessons we can only learn by falling. But, *Tes'puco,* I do think Tess *Dombegh* is good enough to be the hero of her own story, for what it's worth."

Good enough. He'd inadvertently chosen exactly the right words. "Tess was a mess," she said, sleet beading on her lashes. "I haven't wanted to be Tess since I left home. Nine months."

Nine months, she suddenly realized, was as good a time as any to be born.

They were shivering when they arrived home. Tess followed Josquin to his room, expecting to help him with his bath as usual, but he beat her to the boiler and, even though it was hard for him to maneuver behind it, he stoked the fire.

"Er," said Tess, in some confusion. "I would have done that."

"You're so cold your lips are purple," said Josquin, "and you've had a terrible night. I think it's your turn for the bath. I can wait out in the kitchen. Or not."

She felt too much; her heart seemed ready to burst. "Stay," she said.

Josquin held her gaze, and some understanding bridged the gap between them. This time there would be no conscientious hesitations, no head-butting or springing of traps. This time was the time, was now, nobody careening unstuck through the past.

"I gently remind you that your patron Saint, Rebecca, left her basket under the bed," said Josquin, checking the temperature gauge. He opened the tap while she fetched it, and when she'd picked her poison (so to speak), he drew Tess to him and wrapped his arms around her middle.

"Thank you," she whispered, and kissed him.

Tess began unbuttoning his second-best doublet while Josquin undid the one she was wearing. There were so many buttons, so many fidgeting fingers. She felt herself released from confinement, felt the shiver-soft touch of Josquin's competent hands upon her long-suppressed breasts. She was reminded of the infant Dozerius, his mouth fluttering soft as moth wings against her skin, and for a moment she worried that she was still too full of pain, that her body held too much history to be present in the present. But Josquin kissed her again and she was there, alive to every singing nerve ending, to his touch like gentle rain upon the neglected, drought-racked earth.

We build history every day, anew.

The rest of her cold, damp clothing fell away. The tub filled, and Josquin let her climb in first while he finished undressing, giving her a few minutes to enjoy the hottest water alone.

She worried that she'd fall apart, as she'd done under Dulsia's hands.

But as she entered the water, she found to her surprise that her parts had taken on new meanings. These were the shoulders that had carried Griss to Mother Philomela; these, the arms that had broken clods and turned hay. The hand that had held Frai Moldi's. The callused feet that had carried her across the border into a new set of stories.

She was Tess of the Road, bathing in rivers, relishing the water's rush between her thighs.

Warmth entered her heart, which had been as alone as the Most Alone beneath the earth.

She still held sorrows, but she was not made of them. Her life was not a tragedy.

It was history, and it was hers.

When she had thawed, Josquin joined her, swinging his legs together over the side and lowering himself slowly. She caught him in her arms and kissed him again, and together they were broken/unbroken. All/nothing. And any chasms left between were swiftly bridged.

<hr/>

The Academy was behind her now, done and gone, and she felt like she'd been freed of a terrible burden. Now she could be nowhere but here, no-when but now, no one but Tess. The sun came out and glittered upon the surface of the freshly fallen snow, and Tess felt every bit as clean and new.

She embroidered with joy. She accompanied Josquin to market, and to his Brotherhood of Heralds meetings; she helped him cook and fetched wood and water. She kept Gaida company in the evenings. And at night, even though she insisted upon maintaining the charade of going to bed in her own room, she would creep downstairs and sleep in Josquin's arms.

She asked Josquin about all of his girlfriends, in part because she was curious, in part because she was building up the courage to talk about Will. She wanted to talk about him; he'd never seemed so distant, as if Josquin's presence had exorcised him at last, or given her something to take Will's place. Maybe the past could be past. It gave her hope.

She asked Josquin about his first time, and got a hilarious story about an inn in the Pinabra where a mother and daughter had competed for his affections. The mother had won. Tess found this shocking, which elicited a gentle laugh. "It was for the best. I knew nothing, and neither did her daughter. We don't always know what we want the first time out; we certainly don't know what to expect."

"Exactly!" cried Tess, spotting her opening. "I barely knew where anything went, and I was surprised to find myself in the middle of it before I understood what had happened."

"You—I'm sorry, what?" said Josquin, apparently befuddled. "Start at the beginning. You slept with . . . Will, was it? By *accident*?"

"I know it sounds absurd," said Tess confidentially, keeping her tone light. This could be a funny story, maybe, if she told it right.

"I'd slept with him—just slept, in his arms—a few times, and nothing had happened," she said merrily. So far so good. "I was staying out so late that sometimes it was easier to nap in his room and go home just at sunrise."

"But then one night something did happen," said Josquin, not smiling.

Tess tried to be reassuring: "I didn't intend it to. I was mostly asleep, having had a good deal of ale, and he was behind me, cuddling and kissing my ear, and it was pleasant, but really I wanted to sleep. And then—I've never quite known how—all of a sudden I realized something was different, my chemise had worked its way up and he'd slipped in, as it were."

It was getting harder to keep her tone jolly. "I didn't know what I was feeling at first, or where I was feeling it; he'd gone off the map, and anyway it was supposed to hurt the first time. The maidenhead, you know. It's supposed to break and bleed. Mama told us hers was so thick and strong that Papa couldn't consummate their marriage until a midwife came and perforated it with a knife. She was sure her daughters would be the same; I'm embarrassed to admit I was counting on it. The pain was supposed to warn me that we'd come too close.

"Anyway, he was in, like magic. I hardly felt it. Once I realized, I thought, *He couldn't have done it on purpose, we agreed we wouldn't, he must not realize.* I tried to tell him, politely, that he'd gone too far, but his weight was on me then, and my face was squashed into the pillow. I couldn't get his attention. I swatted at him, but he was behind me and I had no leverage."

This was not a funny story. Tess was feeling it now, as if she were there; she couldn't bend the tale back toward merry farce, and she couldn't seem to stop telling it, either. "Maybe I could have given him a bloody nose with the back of my head. Maybe I could have struggled harder and wiggled free somehow."

"But you didn't," Josquin said quietly.

Tess shrugged. An old familiar despair, like a leaden blanket, was descending upon her. "There was no point. I was already ruined, and it was my own fault. I'd lost my virginity in the stupidest way imaginable. Making him stop wouldn't bring it back. I only hoped he'd meant it when he said he wanted to marry me. He surely wouldn't marry me if I broke his nose."

"Tess," said Josquin, but she wouldn't meet his eye.

"I wasn't mad at him—isn't that ridiculous? He was just doing what my mother had warned me men do. If anything, I was mad at her, and at my maidenhead. I thought I'd have some warning, that there'd be time to stop him. I didn't know anything."

"Tess," said Josquin, more urgently. "It wasn't your fault."

"You're wrong," snapped Tess. "I was in his bed, in my chemise. I knew better." *I earned it,* she wanted to add, but her voice stopped working momentarily. "Anyway, it's not completely true that I didn't want it. Some part of me wanted it, just not right then. And not like that."

"If you'd told him not to," said Josquin darkly, "then it was—"

"Please don't say it," Tess interrupted. "Please. That's a terrible word, and even if it's true, then what? You'll weep for me, or get angry, and I'll feel like I have to comfort you, do you see? I can't even comfort myself."

Josquin shook his head, fuming, but held her in silence, and that was truly enough.

There was more she could have told him. The betrayal of her trust hadn't even been the most terrible part. Worse was the way Will had answered her sorrow with sophistry, informing her that true purity came from the mind and heart, not the body; that he was her teacher, not just academically but in life, and surely it was best to learn this lesson from someone who loved her; that it was not she who was sullied, but he who was redeemed by her goodness.

Worst of all was the way she'd stayed with Will for eight more months, endured more humiliations (of course he'd boasted to all his friends), and learned to absent herself as he took his pleasure with her. She dared not deny him or make him angry, because only the purifying fire of holy matrimony could restore her dignity and virtue.

And he hadn't even given her that.

⚔

Two and a half months passed, slowly and too fast. Tess's eighteenth birthday flew by without her telling anyone; she did not like to be reminded that a decision was approaching.

One day Tess came home from work, clambering through snowdrifts. She blew in with a flurry of flakes to see Josquin

470

turning a capon on a spit. "Your mother's staying late," said Tess, kissing his ear as she crossed the room. "That massive beadwork for the Contessa Infanta, the peacock in full feather, is taking forever."

"Does she want dinner at the shop?" Josquin called after Tess, who was making a beeline for the back of the house.

"No," Tess called back. "Give me a minute, eh? I need the privy."

"Do you hold it all day?" he asked laughingly. If he teased her more than that, she didn't hear. She was in the yard already, the door swinging shut behind her.

In fact, she did hold it all day. Josquin's privy was the nicest in Segosh—not counting whatever they used at Palasho Pesavolta—and it was worth a wriggle of discomfort at the end of the day to come home and use it. It had its own commodious house, with a charcoal fire in winter (Tess stoked it morning and evening). St. Blanche the Mechanic had outdone herself; there was hardly any smell. It was still a pit, like every garden privy in town, but everything washed into the storm sewers with the pull of a handle, ingeniously reusing last night's bathwater.

It was so marvelous, in fact, that the neighborhood children were always trying to use it. Josquin didn't mind, as long as they cleared out when he needed it. Today three children were hallooing down the hole, trying to see to the bottom with a lantern. "Hey, shoo," said Tess, but they paid her no mind. She didn't have Josquin's clout—or his intimidating eight-legged chair.

"I mean it, unless you want to watch," she cried, holding the door open.

Most of the little miscreants bobbed out, but the youngest paused in the doorway, her eyes enormous, and said, "There's a monster in the sewer!"

"I'm the monster," said Tess, lightly swatting her backside. "Now get gone."

Tess got straight to business, not giving the warning a second thought. When the flame struck her backside, therefore, it came as a complete surprise.

She screamed and leaped to her feet. It was dark; the children had taken the lantern, and the only light was glimmers of the full moon through the ventilation slats near the roof. Tess yanked up her breeches and called, "Hello?" into the jake-hole, feeling stupid. Had she imagined fire in the commode? What a thing to think.

No, there it was again. A flicker in the pit. Saints' bones, what was it? Swamp gas? Some kind of sewer malfunction?

It occurred to her that this might be a quigutl. She hadn't seen any this far south; if it was alone, it might be lost and scared.

Tess said, "Who's there? I understand Quootla. You may speak to me."

"I am speaking—with fire," said the creature.

Tess recognized the voice and jerked back. She'd all but forgotten Kikiu, but apparently her reflexes hadn't. "What are you doing here?" she said, keeping her distance now. "Have you come to kill me, the way you tried to kill Pathka?"

"I was defending myself," cried the hatchling, charging out of the hole. Kikiu now sported three shiny horns; her bite enhancer gleamed as she snarled. "Pathka tried to cut me and make me bleed into a bowl. What else was I to do?"

Tess felt her fear deflate. Of course they'd each been too wrapped up in their own pain to listen to the other. Maybe if she could have been there to interpret . . .

"I need your help," said Kikiu, who clearly didn't know an effective way to ask for it. "My mother's in the sewer; I dragged *ko* this far, miles through the snow, but I can't haul *ko* up through this narrow vent. You've got to come fetch *ko*."

"I don't understand," said Tess, her heart quailing. "Did you bite him again? Is he dead?"

"No, stupid human," barked Kikiu. "*Ko* is ill. It's Anathuthia who's dead."

A trapdoor in the courtyard permitted St. Blanche to visit the underworld if her innovative plumbing jammed. Tess flung it wide, took a deep breath to steady herself, and descended into the stenchy semidark, grateful that she hadn't quit her habit of breeches and boots despite Gaida's daily protestations. The ladder was nothing but notches in the slippery wall. Kikiu ignited her tongue, dissipating the smell a bit, and led Tess through a dank, arched brickwork tunnel. It occurred to Tess—how could it not?—that Kikiu was taking her down here to bite her, but then she saw Pathka lying inert in a pool of icy sludge, barely breathing.

Tess didn't let herself think about how dirty he was, or she'd have balked. She scooped Pathka out of the muck, threw him across her strong shoulders, and staggered toward the hatch. Pathka was heavier than Griss had been, and deader weight. Climbing through the trapdoor was a nightmare; Tess clung to the wall one-handed, steadying Pathka with the other, her grip slipping. Kikiu tugged Pathka's tail from above and dragged him onto the bricks of the yard.

Tess hauled water from the well and sluiced the muck off Pathka. Steam rose off him; his internal furnace still burned. Kikiu refused the bucket, preferring to scour herself with her tongue-flame. Tess removed her filthy jacket and washed her hands.

"What's all this?" said Josquin from the doorway.

Tess had been so busy she hadn't heard him approach. She was at a loss to explain, numb with cold, disgust, and worry. "I'm ... this is my oldest friend, Pathka, and his daughter, Kikiu. Pathka is dirty and ill, and I only know what to do about dirty. Where can we keep them without alarming Gaida?"

"You'll never keep me," snarled Kikiu, flaring her spines. "I won't live in a house again."

"All right, not Kikiu," said Tess. She swiped a shaky hand across her forehead, leaving a smudge.

"Tess, it's fine," said Josquin, assessing Tess's distress and coming to a decision quickly. "Let's put your friend in my room, on the tiles near the boiler. It's fireproof and warm."

Tess nodded, grateful for his decisiveness, and picked up Pathka. He was dry, the wash water having evaporated already. They made Pathka a little nest of blankets and got him settled.

Kikiu lingered in the doorway making disdainful remarks about the shape of the nest.

"That will do," said Kikiu at last. There was something in her voice Tess had never heard before, a kind of resignation. "Get my mother well, or I will exact it from your flesh. *Ko* is all I have, the only thing between me and . . ." Kikiu's head spines trembled fragilely, minutely, like poplar leaves. "Something happened when *ko* joined dreams with the serpent's—I felt it from miles away, impossibly. Then, when they killed it, I felt that, too—"

"Who killed Anathuthia?" cried Tess. Anathuthia dead had been unthinkable, but *killed*?

"Don't pretend you didn't send them," hissed Kikiu, swinging back to venom and menace in an instant. Her tail whipped the lintel as she turned back toward the sewers.

Tess closed the door shakily, mind racing. Emmanuele. It had to be. He must've gone to Santi Prudia's, maybe with an expeditionary force, and . . . she could hardly think it. When she could finally focus, she realized she'd been staring at Josquin without seeing him.

"Could you tell me what's going on?" he said once he perceived that she was present.

"I barely know," Tess half whispered, "but I'll do my best."

She'd left Pathka's pilgrimage out of her stories because there was so much she didn't understand and couldn't explain. Josquin listened solemnly, and by the end of the story she was weeping into his lap.

"Your friend is ill," said Josquin, stroking her short curls.

"Let's tend him tonight; if he doesn't improve by morning, I'll call for Dr. Belestros and St. Blanche. They say St. Nedouard was a great physician, but these two together exceed even him. They'll know how to help. Once Pathka is well, you'll have time to worry about how to make this right."

"How did you know—" Tess began, half weeping, half laughing.

"Because I know you and I know your conscience," said Josquin. "I've heard all your stories, remember? The world could end, and you'd blame yourself for it—and then you'd find a way to push on through the wreckage and save what can be saved."

Tess wiped her eyes. "Are you calling me pushy, villain?"

Josquin kissed her warmly, and then they turned their attention to Pathka.

⚔

There passed a terrible night. Pathka, in the grip of insensible delirium, thrashed and muttered and did not know Tess at all. His eyes wouldn't focus; his eye cones drooped alarmingly. Tess curled up beside him and slept as best she could.

Josquin called the physician and the holy machinist by thnik as soon as it was light, while Tess was still (or finally) asleep. An hour later, Gaida threw open the door, crying, "Dr. Belestros is here, and St. Blanche! Are you unwell, Jos? Why didn't you tell me?"

Josquin, dressed but not yet in his chair, put a finger to his lips and pointed urgently at Tess and the quigutl, lying behind the furnace. Gaida let the visitors through, but before she left said waspishly, "I'd assumed that when she wasn't in her room, she was sleeping with *you*."

"So much for not alarming her," muttered Tess from the corner, and then she was on her feet brushing herself off and trying to look presentable.

Tess recognized St. Blanche as the pale, scarred woman Josquin had spoken to at the Academy gala; her scars, up close, turned out to be silver scales. The Saint smiled shyly. Dr. Belestros, a saarantras, was taller and darker than his counterpart. Tess was surprised to find she recognized him, too, as the doctor Pashfloria had asked about the serpent's healing power.

The dragon doctor wasted no time on greetings, but went straight to palpating Pathka's throat. Belestros listened to the quigutl's chest, wrenched an eye cone aperture open with two thumbs, and then reached around and stuck an instrument up Pathka's cloaca. Tess flinched; Josquin took her hand.

"When did you last treat a quigutl, Bel?" said Blanche, her light voice carrying a note of warning. "Are you being gentle enough?"

"St. Blanche is his conscience," Josquin stage-whispered to Tess.

"I could drop this quigutl on his head," said the doctor evenly, "and he'd feel nothing." He wiped his hands on a towel. "There are two things wrong with him. First: pneumonia, which should be curable with a syrup. Second, and more perilous: a condition we dragons call inevitable quigutl quietude. I've seen it before. They fancy themselves ingenious, courting contradiction, but they may delve so deeply into paradox that their minds seize up. The wage of illogic is paralysis; everyone knows this. Blanche, I'll need your electroquietus unit."

St. Blanche rummaged in a large leather bag and drew out a device like a hedgehog, its quills all wires and switches. From two longer wires dangled what looked like meat-turning forks. Dr. Belestros pressed their tines to the little quigutl's temples, wedging them under scales and into flesh.

"Wait," said Tess. "What are you doing?"

"We'll send an electrostatic current through the brain to stop it," said Dr. Belestros, as if this were nothing. "A second current will start it up again."

"You've done this before?"

"Not precisely this," said the doctor, wrapping Pathka's head to keep the forks in place. "The machine is for hearts, usually, but I see no reason—"

"All will be well," said Blanche, turning solemn violet eyes to Tess's face. "I built this machine. No one can run it but me, because it runs on my power. It will be *my* current, softly closing his mind and gently waking him again."

"And he'll be himself when he wakes?" asked Tess tremulously. "He'll remember me, and all he's been through?"

"Oh, probably," said Dr. Belestros, waving an impatient hand. "He's a quigutl. Does it matter what he remembers?"

St. Blanche shot her colleague a look. "We'll do our best. You may wish to leave."

But Tess couldn't leave. She'd have held Pathka's hand, but they made her watch from the bed so the device wouldn't shock her as well. Josquin held her; Tess wouldn't take her eyes off her friend. Pathka twitched, died, twitched again, and took a convulsive breath. His eyes focused, though they wobbled; he raised his head an inch off the ground and said, "Teth?"

Then Tess was on her knees beside him, stroking his head, asking how he was and what he remembered and did he know she loved him?

"Stop," said Pathka, squirming in her arms. "Stop talking and listen, Teth. I was . . . we call it *tutlkikiu,* the splitting death. I will slip into it again. I feel myself slipping already."

"You should stop thinking contradictory thoughts," said Dr. Belestros.

"Quiet, dragon," snapped Pathka. "Thinking couldn't do this. It's feeling—which dragons don't understand, but you do, Teth. It's like the time you walked out of Affle in a daze, the same, except it's all the time, and I can't climb out; I will slide down forever unless I resolve it."

Pathka struggled for breath and coughed painfully. "The Academy sent a little army after Anathuthia. The monks tried to stop them—some died trying. I tried, too, but we were too few, and they were armed. They killed . . . they killed . . ."

"Kikiu told me," said Tess hastily, trying to spare him the anguish of reliving it.

"Let me say it!" Pathka wailed. "They killed Anathuthia with a ballista bolt through the eye and then hacked her into pieces. I was swimming in gore, and I *hated* you, Teth! No one else had seen her but the monks and me; it had to be you who sent them. I hated you, but I can't hate you, but I can't stop thinking about it, but you're human so I can't . . . I can't—"

"He's falling back under," said Dr. Belestros.

479

"Can't you use the machine again?" cried Tess.

"Not without harm," said St. Blanche, her pale brows pinched. "I don't understand all his words, but I think you're what sets him off, child."

Pathka struggled in Tess's arms, babbling and gnashing his teeth. It was the gnashing that made Tess understand: "Sweet St. Siucre, he needs to bite me."

"His bite is septic. It could kill you," said St. Blanche, moving as if to separate Tess from the quigutl.

"It's not a terrible idea," said Dr. Belestros, blocking St. Blanche with an outstretched arm, his voice tinged with curiosity. "That's how they reset their misfiring brains in the wild, by biting each other. The pressure of the jaw releases a de-stressing neuro—"

Tess had no time for this. She grasped Pathka's head, trying to get his attention. "I want you to bite me. I know you don't bite humans, on principle, and it's going to hurt, but if this is what you need to be at peace, then do it. Please."

She extended her arm and Pathka clamped down with tremendous force before she was ready. For half a second she felt only surprise, but then the pain caught up and was everywhere, like an immolation.

Then, mercifully, mind and body agreed she'd had enough.

Tess had a fever within hours. It raged for three days, during which she remembered only bits and pieces: Pathka sleeping beside her, Josquin feeding her broth, and Dr. Belestros making a poultice from moldy bread (surely she dreamed that; it was too bizarre).

Upon the fourth day, her fever broke enough that she knew where she was and could speak. "Next time, remind me to offer my nondominant arm," she croaked through parched lips as Josquin propped her head up and St. Blanche put a glass to her lips.

"If she's well enough to joke, she's on the mend," said St. Blanche, and some of Josquin's tension melted away.

"I'd rather have another baby than be bitten by a quigutl," Tess declaimed, teetering on the edge of delirium. "I'd rather have ten babies."

"Noted," said Josquin, dabbing her forehead and smiling.

"I'd rather marry Will than be bitten by—"

"All right, let's not exaggerate," Josquin said.

Tess and Pathka were co-invalids, together on a pallet in Josquin's room. Pathka didn't speak at first—he was recovering from pneumonia, on top of everything else—but they lay in comradely silence, nest to each other.

When they finally spoke, it was the middle of the night. Moonlight streamed in the window; Josquin snored lightly across the room. "Pathka," Tess whispered, "I'm so sorry about Anathuthia. That doesn't make up for it or fix anything, but I don't know what else to do."

Pathka was silent so long that she might have thought him asleep, except he wasn't snoring. Finally he said, "Anathuthia isn't gone. There's still the egg, buried under all that gore. The serpents are eternally renewing themselves; she may have meant to die soon anyway. I wish I knew. I was wrenched out of her dream so abruptly, it's been hard to orient myself."

"What was it like to dream with her?" asked Tess.

"All in ard, as the great dragons say," said Pathka. "I never understood their obsession with order, but there's no better word for it. I was in the right place, doing the right thing. It was all right." His eyes unfocused, staring toward the ceiling. "It will be all right."

"It must have been excruciating to lose her," said Tess.

Pathka stretched on the blanket, considering. "She's not gone, Teth. Not completely. Anyway, I feel worse for Kikiu than for myself. *Ko* arrived just after Anathuthia was killed, and saw only blood and offal."

"She said she felt it when you started dreaming," said Tess. "And she felt it when Anathuthia died. Pathka, you said she was broken, and a monster, but that doesn't sound monstrous to me. That sounds like . . . I don't know. Like she's nest to you?"

"Kikiu and I are bound together in ways I still don't understand. *Fatluketh* didn't set us free; it only bound us tighter." Pathka shifted in the blankets, reaching a sticky-fingered ventral hand to touch Tess's cheek. "I haven't done right by Kikiu. I refused to see *ko* clearly—or maybe I couldn't, until I dreamed with Anathuthia and saw everything.

"As much as I want to find another serpent and continue the dream, it's Kikiu who needs it. Something is broken inside of *ko*—I was right about that much—but I . . . I am responsible. I'm still Kikiu's mother, even if I haven't been very good at it, and I inexplicably *thluff ko*." Pathka burrowed his head under the blanket, avoiding Tess's eyes.

Tess took his hand and pressed it between both of hers until his pulse slowed. And then, insofar as it was possible for human and quigutl, they dreamed together.

Twenty-Seven

The spring thaw hit hard, turning the streets into muddy rivulets. The sewer under the privy was a torrent of run-off, making the sluice unnecessary for hygiene (although the bathwater still needed to be drained, Tess discovered, or the system backed up). The Ninysh were great devotees of bulb flowers—crocus, tulip, jonquil, hyacinth—and the stubborn things started pushing up everywhere, through mud, through cracks, wherever itinerant bulbs had sailed on the high spring tides. Tess rescued bulbs that had washed ashore in the middle of the street, against a midden of manure, and brought them home for Gaida. The yard was ringed with terra-cotta pots, ready to burst into unruly bloom.

One day a soggy messenger arrived with a letter. Josquin knew him, of course, and made the fellow stand before the hearth and have a cup of tea. They were still shooting the breeze when Tess came home from work, at which point the messenger handed her the missive.

Tess knew the handwriting. Of all the courtly, ecclesiastical, and academic hands she'd learned, there was none quite like it. It was the script of someone who'd taught herself to write at an extraordinarily young age, when her hand was too small to hold a pen in anything but a fist. It spoke of deeply ingrained stubbornness as tutor after tutor tried to correct her penmanship, their pedagogy breaking over her like a storm over a mountain. They'd eroded the fist grip to a two-fingered half fist, but they got no further with Seraphina. Tess could almost hear her, cold as well water, telling those tutors, "It's legible. You have nothing more to want."

Josquin knew the handwriting, too, and made as if to liberate the letter from her hands. "Fie, rascal, that's my name," Tess cried, dodging him and pointing to the *T*, which admittedly looked more like a *J* than it should have. She skittered past him into his room, opening the shutters with one hand and the letter with the other.

Dear Tess:

You'll be wondering, perhaps, how I know where to find you. For this you may thank Josquin, in whom I hope you have found an otherwise trustworthy friend. Don't be angry that he wrote me; if he hadn't, I believe Jeanne would have worried herself right off a cliff. She misses you terribly, but is reassured by the thought that you are alive and in the care of friends.

I don't know what you've heard in Ninys, but I had my

baby last midsummer—a girl, called Clotilde Rhademunde
Zythia (these royals and their family names! Zythia was my
choice, and she will be called that because it's the nicest of the
lot). Officially, she is Glisselda's. People seem willing to believe
that the Queen could have been so subtly pregnant that no one
could tell. Such is the magic of queenship, I suppose.

I'm presently in Segosh for several reasons, none of
which can be put to paper except that I would like to see you
at Palasho Pesavolta at your earliest convenience. I'm only
here a week (a week longer than the count would like to host
me), so do not procrastinate or dally or indulge in your usual
contrarian stubbornness.

Tess laughed so hard at this characterization that she had to
lean her head against the window. Josquin clattered up behind
her—he couldn't sneak up on anyone in that contraption—and
waited for her to finish. "Good news?" he said when Tess finally caught her breath. "Or is your sister merely being her
witty self?"

This only made Tess howl the more, because nothing was
as unfunny as Seraphina's writing. It was stiff as a board. He
surely knew this. She handed him the letter and he read it, tut-
ting lightly and saying, "Of course we've heard. We're not such
a backwater as that."

"In an effort not to succumb to my usual contrarian ob-
structificationism," said Tess with a mocking curtsy, "I'll need
something court-worthy to wear, as quickly as possible."

When Gaida came home and heard the news, she went to

her bedroom and flung open a trunk. "Unpaid alterations," she explained, riffling through linens and satins. "Folks sometimes don't collect their things. I hold 'em as long as I can, but after a certain point they're fair game."

They settled on a fine, deep green merino that Gaida had altered for an amber merchant's wife, unlikely to be claimed now that the merchant was in prison. It was nearly Tess's size, a bit tight in the upper arms and narrow in the waist; the merchant's wife apparently hadn't pounded roadbed or been much for eating. Gaida let out the waist, which she'd previously taken in, but couldn't do much for the shoulders.

It had been so long since Tess had worn a gown that she felt unpleasantly exposed. The breeze sneaked up underneath and chilled her.

"I wish I could let out your hair," Gaida fussed, running her fingers through Tess's wavelets. "A gabled cap would hide it. You don't want to give the court conniptions."

"You don't know what she wants," said Josquin.

Tess was surprised to find herself agreeing with Gaida in this case. The rules had rankled when she'd had no choice, but she was no longer a young, dependent lady-in-waiting, cowed by her elders. She'd walked the earth alone and helped them that needed it. She could deign to dress up or not, could face down courtly rules and say, *Very well, I comply—this once.*

She didn't want a gabled cap, though. "Where might I find a broad-brimmed hat, preferably with a plume?"

Three haberdashers and a chunk of winter savings later, she had what she wanted: a hat reminiscent of the one Countess

Margarethe had worn to Jeanne's wedding nearly a year ago. Tess could only afford a long, sharp pheasant's tail feather, not an ostrich plume, and a crown of felt, not velvet, but it pleased her. The hat and boots (which took polish gratefully, like Tess once took wine) gave off such an air of competent decisiveness that one might easily ascribe the same qualities to the person bookended between them.

She rose early, leaving Josquin tangled in the bedsheets, and dressed with keen awareness of his eye upon her. Before she left, she perched gently on the edge of the bed and rubbed his leg. "Do you want to come along and see her?" Tess asked quietly.

"What?" said Josquin with a start, trying to look as if he'd just woken up and hadn't been brooding on anything. "No, no. This is a sisterly reunion. I'd be in the way."

Tess quirked a tiny smile, her heart contracting sympathetically, because she understood in that moment that he was not, in fact, over her sister, and that she couldn't really blame him. "Can I help you get dressed, at least?"

"No," he said, grumpy with her now. "Go. Stop worrying about me."

She kissed his cheek and was off, up the hill toward the palasho. The rising sun crowned the buildings in gold. Tess hummed as she walked, enjoying the street beneath her feet. Its face had been hidden by snow and mud all winter, but now, with the blue arcing overhead and the cobbles dry and clean, seeing the Road was like seeing an old friend after many months apart.

She was expected at the palasho; a guard escorted her through the gate and handed her off to a footman at the palace proper. The footman led Tess to the count's library, where Seraphina waited in a window seat, reading.

Tess almost laughed. She'd been away long enough to find her sister owlishly adorable.

To Seraphina's credit (because it wasn't a given), she closed her book, looked at Tess, and smiled before she spoke. "You're looking well."

"I am well," said Tess, choosing a chair upholstered in prickly embroidered silk. The arms were gilded curlicues, ribbons, and bunches of grapes, high Ninysh baroque. Tess sat with her legs crossed at the knee, one boot swinging, hat tilted just rakishly enough, and grinned.

Here she was. Here they both were. It was delightful.

"How've you been?" said Tess.

"Fine," said Seraphina.

"Still keeping the small talk extra small," said Tess, chuckling.

Seraphina ignored this. She could be such a dragon sometimes. "I hear you've had some success as a naturalist," she said. "Word of the great serpent reached St. Bert's by thnik. The Ninysh Academy was quick to boast, our Collegium quick to envy—and to judge. It's unfortunate that they killed it."

More unfortunate than Seraphina could know. Tess felt a shadow cross her heart.

"I know you're the one who found it," said Seraphina, setting her book on the seat beside her. "Kenneth brought me the report, saying, 'Who else would purposely go by the name Tes'puco?' We had a chuckle, remembering you as a small child, the whole house a stage for some drama, directing us hither and thither. We imagined you bossing around masters and World Serpents alike, until we heard that it had died."

Tess's hands fidgeted in her lap, the only outward indication of the guilt roiling through her innards. "I never imagined they'd hunt it down and kill it."

Seraphina pierced her with a glance. "What did you think would happen, exactly?"

Tess squirmed. It wasn't an accusation, but it felt like one. "I thought that when they saw it, they'd be moved. They'd . . . understand," she said. That sounded feeble, even to Tess.

"Understand what?" Seraphina's sternness did not waver.

How could Tess explain what had happened in that cavern? Telling Seraphina was more intimidating than telling the Academy—there was history and precedent to overcome. One did not simply tell Seraphina personal things. She wouldn't care; she would logic you to death.

But Tess hadn't walked this far to be cowed again. She would tell the truth, and Seraphina could understand, or not.

"Have you ever experienced something so far beyond words that you couldn't explain it?" said Tess. "And the more you tried to tell people, the more frustrated you felt, because nobody understands unless they've been through it themselves?"

Tess had meant these as rhetorical questions, but Seraphina answered: "I have. Twice."

"W-wait, what? When?" asked Tess.

"During the war, when I turned my mind inside out and called St. Pandowdy from the swamp," said Seraphina. "And again, to a somewhat lesser extent, when I gave birth."

Tess's breath caught in her throat. Could they really both have had encounters with the numinous? She could never have imagined this.

"I found my vocation in that cave," said Tess at last. "Side by side with a monk."

"Tell me," said Seraphina, in almost a whisper.

"I feel called," said Tess, feeling it again, groping around for words to clothe it in. "To walk into the world, to see what's needed, and do it. To uncurl myself and respond."

Tess held her breath, afraid Seraphina would scorn the very idea—what reasonable person wouldn't?—but her sister nodded solemnly. She was taking this seriously.

"Well, then, I may just have a need for you to respond to," said Seraphina. "Word of all this has reached the Tanamoot. The dragons, who denied the very existence of World Serpents, are now quick to point talons of blame. They condemn the killing and mean to find the other serpents themselves, ostensibly to protect them."

Tess raised an eyebrow at *ostensibly*. Seraphina nodded minutely.

"It's unclear what they intend. Dragons aren't usually gentle with things they don't understand or can't control. It's possible they don't so much object to the killing as to the fact that they had no access to the corpse. Or that they'd hoped to kill the World Serpents themselves, quietly, before humankind found them.

"In any case, Queen and Ardmagar agree on one thing: this can't happen again. And here is where your Queen has an assignment for you."

Tess sat up straighter, as if the Queen herself had entered the room and not just her name.

"Goredd can't permit another serpent to be slaughtered," said Seraphina. "For the creatures' own sakes, yes, but also because the dragons are roaring. Our treaty shelters Ninys, to some extent, but it certainly doesn't apply to the Archipelagos or the Southern Ocean."

Tess's heart leaped. "You want me to find another one."

"Countess Margarethe has new funding and means to sail after the Antarctic serpent again," said Seraphina. "Selda wants you on that boat."

Tess laughed, a short, bitter bark. "The Queen does understand that I was horrible and the countess hates me? She won't want me along."

"I've been sounding her out about Tes'puco. Marga is intrigued by this mysterious adventurer—all the more since learning he's a woman. She admires such mischievous gall. Besides, you're one of the few who've seen a serpent, which makes you an expert. She'd be a fool not to take you.

"And there's more to it than I've yet revealed. Lucian thinks the Ninysh are up to no good in the south, making a power grab and expanding their influence. Could Ninys harness this serpent to their bidding, or use the threat of its demise to subdue the pelagic peoples, who purportedly revere it?

"Make no mistake, friend that she is, Marga is nevertheless in this as deeply as any of her countrymen, and she's taking along a Goreddi baronet, Lord Morney, whom Selda doesn't trust.

"We need eyes on that boat, but they mustn't see the Queen's hand in it. You—estranged from your family, an experienced traveler—might plausibly seek to go along. They embark from the port of Mardou in three weeks. Selda won't be able to get you aboard; you'll have to talk to the countess yourself."

There would be payment, and a thnimi—which sent images as well as voice—in the shape of a cloak clasp. Seraphina had the device on her; she showed Tess which curlicues did what, and Tess, with no cloak to clasp just now, pinned it to her bodice like an ungainly brooch.

"If they're acting against Goreddi interests—particularly Lord Morney—you are to record it and report," said Seraphina. "Do not interfere or intervene, or put yourself at risk in any way. If you meet trouble, disembark on an island and call home with the thnimi. The Queen will send someone for you, though I suspect you could find your own way back."

Back, to Tess, didn't mean back to Goredd, not anymore. It meant back to Josquin. The reality of leaving him behind hit her in the stomach. "Oh," she said.

Seraphina raised her brows, awaiting an explanation. Tess stared past her, out the window, at red tulips in the courtyard. "Josquin told you I was here," she said cautiously, "but he, ah, didn't tell you anything else?"

Seraphina grew preternaturally still. "Are you sleeping with him?"

"Ha," said Tess, not sure if she was alarmed or amused. "Can I answer by not answering?"

"Josquin is one of my favorite people, so I congratulate you on having chosen well this time." Seraphina's expression grew serious as she considered the implications. "But that complicates matters. It never occurred to me that you wouldn't want to go—"

"No, no," said Tess quickly. "Don't misunderstand. I do want to go." She put a hand to her heart. "And, also, I'll be gutted to leave Josquin behind. So runs my entire life."

"We'll send someone else," said Seraphina. "I don't mind breaking your heart, but Josquin's—"

"Shut your smug mouth," said Tess, but she was smiling.

The door flew open, and a petite blond woman burst in carrying a wailing baby. A chagrined nursemaid trailed in her wake, arms extended, trying to argue.

"No, thank you," Queen Glisselda said imperiously. "Only her auntie can calm her when she's like this. Dismissed!"

The nursemaid turned pink and left the room. Glisselda bounced the baby in her arms, chanting, "Doo-doo-duties! Cu-cu-customs!" as she crossed the room toward Seraphina and Tess.

The baby flailed hysterically.

"Darling, I'm so sorry," said the Queen to Seraphina. "I wouldn't have interrupted your time with your sister, but as you can see, she's having quite a day. It's the trade treaties. She's such a little protectionist."

"It's fine," said Seraphina, her voice low and calm. She reached up and took the child from Glisselda. The Queen looked unsubtly relieved; her golden curls were askew and, if you looked carefully, there were beads missing on her bodice.

The Queen smiled wanly at Tess, who stood and gave full courtesy. "I'll leave you to it, then," Glisselda said. "I've got to go arm-wrestle Pesavolta for that egg."

"Anathuthia's egg?" cried Tess, appalled. Pathka didn't know; he'd be devastated.

"The serpent had a name?" asked the Queen, narrowing her eyes shrewdly. "That may be useful. But don't trouble yourself; this is between me and Pesavolta. Seraphina will tell you how you may help."

She slipped from the room without further goodbyes.

Seraphina had set Princess Zythia upon her lap and they were gazing seriously at each other. Zythia's face was still red, but the tears and squalling had stopped. She smacked Seraphina on the chest with her tiny fat hand.

"If you need to give her the breast, don't hesitate on my account," said Tess, folding her arms over her own, remembering how they'd ached, how Chessey had stuffed cabbage leaves down her bodice to relieve the swelling.

Seraphina flicked her a mournful glance. "Alas, that part didn't work for me." She ran a hand over Zythia's downy head. "I'm sorry I didn't tell you she was here. I wasn't sure . . . I'm never sure what's going to hurt you."

Tess sat beside Seraphina on the window seat, never taking her eyes off the little face. Zythia shoved a fist into her mouth and gnawed on it, tears welling in her big dark eyes again.

Tess held out a hand, and Zythia grabbed her finger.

Something terrible and wonderful and painful swelled inside Tess, but she could bear it. Tentatively she laid her head upon her sister's shoulder. "You never meant to hurt me."

"We sisters have a particular talent for hurting each other without meaning to," said Seraphina. She hesitated a moment and then leaned her cheek against the crown of Tess's head.

They sat that way for some time, watching the baby, talking quietly. They spoke of childbirth like they were veterans of the same war, comparing wounds, and Tess felt some of the scars on her heart loosen and dissolve.

Phina kissed her cheeks when she left. Tess marveled that she could feel so hurt and comforted at once, so empty and full. Hers was a life lived in joy-*utl*, and she was capable and capacious enough to endure it.

Tess turned her steps toward home, and the additional heartbreak awaiting her there.

✕✕

She didn't know quite what to expect when she told Josquin she'd be leaving for the Archipelagos sooner rather than later. Josquin had been insisting all along that she would leave him—and that she should—but she hadn't quite believed he meant it.

"Of course I meant it," he said that night as he held her in his arms, moonlight streaming in the window. "Heaven knows *I* wasn't ready to settle down at seventeen. I know one lovely innkeeper who thought me a cad for it."

"I'm eighteen," said Tess, forgetting that she hadn't told him about her birthday.

He poked her in the ribs. "When trying to prove you're not a cad, maybe don't admit that you lied about your birthday. My point is"—his low voice deepened with emotion—"I know the Road still calls you. I lived for it at your age: I slept in the saddle and ate on the gallop. I'd lick my lips and know where I was by the taste of the dust. It still whispers to me, especially in springtime, only now I can't follow. How could I keep you from it, in good conscience?"

"How can you be so sanguine?" said Tess.

"I'm not, Tess, but I've passed this way before," he said. "I'll miss you every day, the way I miss Rebecca. The way I miss walking. But this is my road. I'm so happy you came and traveled with me."

"I'll come back," said Tess, growing emotional.

"I know you will," he said, smoothing her hair with a strong hand. "And you'll have had other paramours by then, and so will I, and we will be dear old friends, happy to see each other, full of wondrous stories."

"I love you," she said weepily, and kissed his lips. He wrapped her in his arms and pulled her on top of him, and that was the last time before she went.

Twenty-Eight

Tess and Pathka reached the great southern seaport of Mardou two weeks later. So did Kikiu, Pathka reported, though she did not travel with them. "I feel *ko* following," said Pathka reassuringly. "*Ko* pushes and pulls but will not run away. Have a little faith."

Pathka himself seemed different in a way Tess could not put her finger on. There was no more frolicking and vomiting and rubbing up against her knee—and no easily wounded irritation, which was a relief. He seemed to float along on some unseen, tranquil river. She chalked it up to Anathuthia, that the dreaming had given her friend a wider perspective, or that he was no longer quite of this world.

She couldn't bring herself to mention the capture of the egg, not yet. Pathka seemed fragile, like a cobweb, and she did not know what would send him back into the splitting death.

The town of Mardou had a harbor large enough to hold ships from around the world as well as river barges from the interior. Tess, who'd led a thoroughly landlocked existence up to now, gazed in awe at the forest of masts and sails, the cargo cranes creaking and straining, and the wide, dark sea.

It touched sky at a far horizon. She remembered how, when she'd first left Trowebridge, the sky had looked impossibly huge over the plain. The blue dome seemed even vaster out here.

Tess took a room at a dockside inn, Do Gabitta (The Gull), and set to learning whatever she could about Countess Mardou. Crucially, the expedition had not yet departed; the countess's Porphyrian baranque, the *Avodendron,* still languished in harbor, waiting on the delivery of "Lord Morney's contraption," whatever that might be.

The countess herself was easy to find: you had only to follow the excitement and cheering, and then look for the bobbing plumes of her hat. She scorned carriages and could frequently be seen striding through the center of town in her shiny boots, kissing babies and accepting gifts and adulation.

Tess tailed her at a distance, studying her and looking for the best angle of approach.

The easiest thing would have been to call on the countess at home, so of course Tess rejected that out of hand. Seraphina had told her exactly what to do—beg forgiveness and list her serpent-finding credentials—but Tess was Tess, however far she walked, and no less pigheaded than the day she'd set out. She would do this her own way.

If she could figure out how. There was always Seraphina's way to fall back on if intuition failed, galling though it was.

Upon her third day in Mardou, an enormous crate arrived in a wagon hauled by six heavy horses. It took the largest crane in the harbor to get it aboard the *Avodendron*. Lord Morney's contraption had arrived at last; Tess's time was up.

The tide would be right for departure at sunset. She had eight hours to come up with the best way to approach Countess Margarethe. Tess paced the piers, trying not to fret. Trying to empty her mind, in fact, on the principle that she knew the answer already and needed to give it a chance to come to the surface, unimpeded.

Tess's peregrinations took her past a contract house, where sea captains and shipping companies signed agreements before a lawyer. The top half of the door was open, in celebration of the warm morning (it wasn't that warm, but one of those spring days that feel balmy compared with the previous months), and conversation was spilling out. One voice, in particular, like a nail on slate—a grating, nasal whinge—pulled Tess out of her reverie. There was no mistaking it. She stopped short, backed up a few steps, and squinted into the dim interior.

A solicitor, pale and narrow as a moonbeam, sat behind a broad desk, scribbling diligently. To his left stood a frowsy sea captain; to his right, a cluster of four saarantrai, silver bells dinging tinnily. Tess's eye went straight to the dragons, to the one whose voice she knew, though she could barely believe it. Scholar Spira, like a lumpy dumpling, hair of indeterminate color curling at the ears, pedantically instructed the solicitor about some fussy contract detail.

Scholar Spira and three other dragons were hiring a ship.

The solicitor stated the obvious: "I've never contracted an

exploration vessel for dragons before. I wonder that you don't just fly south under your own power. You've no treaty with the islanders stating you can't."

"Bah, they wouldn't want to fly," grumbled the sea captain, who had an interest in their not flying, to be sure. "Nothing for them to eat in the far south but Voorka tusk-seals."

"My paramour is Pelaguese," said the solicitor tartly, "and he makes a delicious Voorka-flipper pie."

"Forgive us, sir," Spira interceded in a syrupy voice. "The seals are fatty, as you know, and they upset our tummies."

That comment was so Spira, so patronizing and obsequious at once, that Tess had to stifle a laugh. It came out as a snort.

Scholar Spira looked up sharply and met Tess's eyes.

She turned and ran, which was probably unnecessary. Surely Spira wouldn't have recognized her, four years later, with her hair short? And even if the scholar had known Tess's face, or smelled her at that distance, what was going to happen? Would Spira exact long-delayed revenge for the theft and reprimand?

Tess's feet slowed. Guilt had propelled her, and a reflexive association of Spira with Will. She owed the scholar an apology, certainly, but that was nothing to be afraid of.

In fact, Spira's presence might be a blessing.

Tess had barely formulated this idea when she thought she heard her name. She'd reached the end of the pier, where the wind whipped flags around their poles and suspended furious, flapping gulls in midair. Only snatches of her name got through at first: a *T* and then the vowel, which might have been a barking seal. The *-ss* was lost altogether.

She turned, expecting Spira, but a tall, stout man was

approaching. The wind harassed his longish dark hair into his eyes. He wore a gray cloak and sturdy boots and had traveled far on foot (she could spot another child of the Road).

Tess crossed her arms, not sure what to think.

"You seem not to recognize me," he said in Goreddi as he stepped up beside her. He had a familiar, aristocratic accent. Those haughty vowels had been present at some terrible moment, but she couldn't . . .

Oh yes she could. Her eyes snapped to his face, and there were the beetling brows, the sharp crow's eyes, the nose she'd broken. "Saints' bones," she said warily. "What are you doing at the butt end of Ninys?"

Jacomo—Lord Jacomo, the student-priest, often imitated—smiled. That had not been a custom of his, to her recollection, and she didn't trust it. "I've only come where you led me," he said, shivering against the intrusive wind.

"You've been following me?" This couldn't be good.

He held up his hands as if to fend off a blow.

Tess refolded her arms, which had indeed risen to defend her.

Jacomo said, "Not . . . not the way you make it sound. Your sister sent me."

"I just saw her," said Tess incredulously. "She couldn't call me on the thnimi?"

"Your other sister, Tess. Your twin."

Of course he meant Jeanne. How had Jeanne evaporated so completely from her worries?

"Could we go indoors?" Jacomo asked. "The wind is blowing my words the wrong way."

Tess ushered him toward Seaman's Row, a convenient line of taverns awaiting sailors home from the south. Singing wafted from the first public house they reached, bawdy verses punctuated by abundant *yo!* and *ho!*—the universal syllables of maritime mirth.

She wouldn't have been able to hear Jacomo in there, which was tempting, but she led him past it to a quieter, dumpier bar called Des Mamashuperes (The Squids).

The place was appalling. The sawdust on the floor had possibly never been changed; it might have been the original sawdust, the first ever invented, and as such historical. Objects were hidden in it—broken bottles, fish heads, vomit, cats—so you had to watch your tread.

If Tess hoped Jacomo wouldn't deign to drink in a place like this, she was disappointed. He led the way, intrepidly hopping over a large lump (a corpse, perhaps; no one would know). He bellied up to the bar, acquired them both ale, and found a spindly table beside the lone window, a square of gritty glass that glowed with daylight but seemed to begrudge any of it actually getting through.

Jacomo's chair broke—it must have been halfway there already—so he tossed it away and fetched another. Tess found it hard to balance hers, as if there were no floor under the sawdust, just sawdust all the way down.

Jacomo began: "I'm not here to avenge my nose, if that's what you're worried about."

"That never occurred to me," said Tess, who was lying. "I assumed you were here for a second helping. I've kept in condition by punching sheep."

Jacomo's smile was unexpectedly self-deprecating; Tess felt unbalanced in more than just her seat.

"Let me tell you how I come to be here, Tess, and then you can decide whether to hit me again. When you ran away, Jeanne was beside herself. We all searched, for her sake: Richard, Heinrigh, our fathers, every man and hound we had. We tracked you to Trowebridge, where you disappeared."

"You didn't question the quigutl," said Tess, secretly pleased.

"Ha! Your father suggested that, and the rest of us pooh-poohed the notion. He persuaded Seraphina to talk to them, but she learned nothing."

Nothing she'd revealed, anyway. Tess made a mental note to thank her for that someday.

"We'd reached a dead end. Jeanne took to her bed, disconsolate," said Jacomo. "But then we had an unexpected break: a young grist lout called Florian showed up with a note—supposedly written by me—claiming he'd done me a favor and was owed some clothing."

"Saints' dogs," said Tess. "You were still at home when he arrived."

"The search had delayed my return to Lavondaville," said Jacomo, turning his mug in a fidgety circle. "Father thought the lout was trying to scam us, but he gave what the note demanded, little enough, and it made us look generous. I had my suspicions, however, and questioned Florian in private. He'd encountered 'Lord Jacomo' in a barn south of Trowebridge."

"That rascal!" cried Tess, slapping the table. "He was supposed to say I was thrown from a horse. Much more romantic than cowering in a barn."

"He was honest, unlike the villain he'd met," said Jacomo, black eyes twinkling. He took a sip of ale. "I determined then and there to go after you myself."

Tess blinked, baffled. "Why would you do that?"

Jacomo lowered his eyes, smiling into his beer, and it was as if a curtain parted. Tess could not put her finger on it, but he was changed. This was not the angry, priggish priest-to-be she'd punched at the wedding. This was someone gentler, someone she had never met.

"I was desperate not to go back to seminary," he said quietly. "You have no idea. I never wanted to be a priest, but for a third son—"

"That's destiny," said Tess, remembering Frai Moldi.

There was a light in his eyes. "If my father had gotten wind of your whereabouts, he'd have sent armed men to bring you back. I could escape my studies by circumventing this. I told only Jeanne and Richard what I'd learned. Jeanne begged me to find you; I pretended I couldn't refuse. Richard agreed to keep my departure secret, and our parents assumed I'd returned to school—until my exam results came back null, but that took two months."

"You ran away," said Tess, fascinated.

Jacomo nodded gravely. "I did search for you, in the most halfhearted, desultory manner. You weren't hard to follow; people remember a thieving knave in a striped jacket."

"I was a terrible thief," said Tess, shuddering. "I had to change my strategy."

"Indeed you did." Jacomo leaned back in his chair. "You met Blodwen and Gwenda, took my name in vain again, and then things started to get interesting."

"They weren't supposed to tell, either," Tess burst out indignantly. "You might've been the junior Duke of Barrabou, come to kill me."

Jacomo threw back his head and laughed. "You know, up to that point I believe I had been looking . . . not to *kill* you, but to exact revenge. To drag you home in disgrace."

He leaned on the creaking table, suddenly serious. "I was small-minded, Tess. I was bitter and narrow and appalling. You told me I was going to be a terrible priest—which was true!—and I wanted you to suffer for saying that. I wanted to punch the world in the face, starting with you. But the farther I walked, the more my rage seemed to cool and blow away as vapor."

Tess's heart was in her throat. "Mine, too."

"I know," said Jacomo. His dark eyes gleamed. "Once I understood whom I was following—it became clear in what you left behind—I wanted to keep following, never quite catching up."

Tess had been unaware of leaving anything behind, but to hear Jacomo tell it, he'd played a long, slow game of connect-the-dots, and each dot had been a kindness, farm chores, laughter, a story told. She'd passed through the world, and the world remembered.

"More than that," said Jacomo. "You found Fritz. So many tavernmasters told me how kind you were, and in the end you got him to safety. You can't know what that means to me."

"You're right, I don't know," said Tess, mystified. "Who's Fritz?"

"Our old game-warden," said Jacomo. "I called him Griss

when I was little; I'm not sure why he adopted the name in his dotage. He taught us to hunt. The bear in Heinrigh's trophy room was his."

Tess remembered now: Fritz's bear, where she'd found the crème de menthe.

"He got lost coming back from Trowebridge months before the wedding. We'd given him up for dead."

"So he really did know a boy called Jacomo! And baby Lion—"

"My father, Duke Lionel, as a boy." Jacomo fidgeted. "I arranged to have him sent home. The sisters think he's fit for the journey, though he may not live long beyond that. At least he can die among his people."

Tess met his eyes and had the eerie feeling that she and Jacomo were family now, not so much through marriage as through Griss. It was as unsettling as it was undeniable.

"Mother Philomela sends her love," said Jacomo, brightening. "As does Nicolas the geologist, who's exploring a cave system beneath the northern Ninysh roads. Big Arnando showed me the hole that swallowed you up. I heard the legend but did not meet Darling Dulsia," he added with a wink. "If she could take on an anxious, uptight lad like you, surely she'd have known what to do with a runaway seminarian."

Tess still could not believe he was joking with her this way.

"Who else ... I met Frai Moldi," Jacomo continued. "In fact, I stayed at Santi Prudia most of the winter, snowed in. The serpent, alas, was dead before I arrived," he said, meeting Tess's questioning gaze. "Moldi is struggling with its death, as you might imagine."

Tess imagined very keenly. But there were two more people she needed to know about: "Father Erique?"

"Was he the priest accused of rape?" said Jacomo, rubbing his chin between a thick finger and thumb. "He'd left the village by the time I arrived, and I wasn't welcome there. Apparently you humiliated him in my name. I'm not complaining."

Tess laughed and finally drank some of her beer; the odds of punching Jacomo again had diminished to almost nothing. "Angelica?"

"That's a name I don't know," said Jacomo.

No news was good news, maybe. She hoped so.

Tess drummed her fingers on the table, something still perplexing her. "If you never meant to catch up with me, why are you here?"

"Ah," said Jacomo, turning serious again. "I have news. Jeanne is pregnant, and scared. She wants you to come home."

For a moment Tess couldn't speak. She felt too much at once, love and fear and duty and, beneath it all, an old, familiar despair.

Then, to her surprise as much as Jacomo's, she laughed.

"Is that funny?" said Jacomo, and Tess caught a glimpse of his old, judgmental self in his eyes.

"It's not," said Tess, wiping her eyes. "It's just . . . the absurdity, when you think how far I've traveled, of finding the very same choices at this end of the continent. Do I go exploring with Countess Margarethe or go back to Cragmarog and take care of Jeanne's children?"

"At least the Sisters of St. Loola had the good sense to give up on you," said Jacomo dryly. "I also recall that your answer last time was to run away from everything."

Last time she hadn't been able to see her choices clearly, Tess now realized, only that they were being made for her by other people. She'd been dead wrong about nuns; she hadn't understood where the countess was going, either. Maybe she still couldn't see what it would have meant to stay home with her twin.

"You must have some way to contact Jeanne," said Tess.

Jacomo pulled a chain out of his shirtfront; a plain square pendant dangled from it.

"Let me talk to her."

Jacomo warily handed over the thnik. "If you don't intend to go back, you don't have to tell her yourself. I don't mind being the bearer of bad news. In fact, I kind of assumed—"

"Don't assume anything," said Tess, a little waspishly. "I need to talk to her first. She's my sister. I owe her that, at least."

She went into the yard behind The Squids in hopes of finding privacy. At the far end was the privy house, stenchy even from a distance. Tess gravitated toward the woodpile instead and sat on the axe stump, sticky with resin and gritty with splinters. The sky had clouded over; a cold, halibut-tinged wind gusted from the harbor.

She turned the charm over in her fingers and switched it on. It hardly had a chance to chirp before Jeanne answered, "Yes?" The word brimmed over with hope.

Tess forced words through a tightening throat. "Hello, Nee. It's me."

And then they were both crying, two sisters, hundreds of miles apart, together in grief.

"I'm so sorry," Tess said, her cheeks streaming. "I know I've caused you a lot of worry."

"Oh, Sisi, don't speak of it," said Jeanne. "All is forgiven, if only you'll come home!"

"Of course I will. I always meant to," said Tess warmly, her heart burgeoning with generosity and affection. "It's just a question of when."

"How long it takes to get from there to here, you mean?" said Jeanne. "Where are you?"

"Mardou, on the Ninysh coast," said Tess. "But distance isn't the main—"

"How long does the journey take by fast coach?" said Jeanne. "Don't worry about the cost, His Grace the duke will pay for all. Only you can't imagine how miserable I am without you. Mama and the duchess are already eyeing each other jealously. I don't know how I shall manage to raise a child with its grandmothers circling like vultures."

Jeanne talked on and on, about her mother and mother-in-law, how each expected her loyalty, how she could never satisfy both at the same time. As she talked, she answered Tess's un-asked questions one by one. Tess couldn't leave her in foolish hope.

"Jeanne," she said gently, "my love, I'm so sorry. You've mis-understood. I will come back, but not yet. Not for the birth."

"But I need you here," said her sister.

Tess could hear every mile between them now.

"You want me there," said Tess, "to deflect the ire of those two vultures, as you called them. The minute I crossed the threshold, they'd peck at me and leave you alone."

"That's *not* why I want you here!" cried Jeanne. "I'm scared, and I miss you."

"I miss you, too," said Tess quietly, "and I would love to be there, holding your hand, but I can't go back to being everybody's goat. You don't have to go through it alone, though. Seraphina will be back soon. She's had a baby more recently than I, and you know she'll be an expert on the whole business."

The joke fell flat; Tess's heart wasn't in it.

"Seriously, Nee, call upon her for any sisterly duty. We were wrong about her all those years. I think she wanted what we had so effortlessly in each other, but she didn't know how to ask."

"What we had in each other." Jeanne sounded like she was being strangled. "Us against the world. What a mockery you've made of that."

"It was always a mockery," said Tess, flattening the quaver in her voice. "It was really Tess against the world, shielding you from Mama's rage, hard decisions, and everything else."

"You, shield me?" cried Jeanne. "I ran interference and cleaned up your messes for years. Who covered for you when you'd stay out all night at St. Bert's, so sleepy you'd nod off during lessons the next day? It was me soothing Mama's broken heart and trying to hold our entire family together, who had to be a perfect angel to make up for your relentless selfishness."

"*Selfishness* lived in your closet for two years, sewed your clothes, and found you your husband," Tess snapped back. "Self-ishness took spankings for you, lied for you, held her breath so she wouldn't tarnish your reputation by association."

"Oh, poor you. After fourteen years of doing whatever you wanted, like an impulsive animal, you did two years' soft labor in penance. Now, when I really need you, in this terrible house with these terrible people, you punch Jacomo and run away. Yes, you are selfish, and irresponsible, and—"

Tess had never heard such raw hurt in Jeanne's voice, and she found herself sitting back and marveling at this litany of crimes. Jeanne had always been so quiet and good—who knew what rancor had been accumulating inside her? Maybe Jeanne herself hadn't known.

Tess had taken Jeanne's goodness for granted, assumed she was naturally angelic and loved being so. That had been the story their entire lives, and it was deeply unfair.

Jeanne's rage combusted into heaving sobs. Tess said gently, "When did you mean to tell me, Nee? If I'd leaped to your bidding and come straight home, would you have stewed forever?"

Jeanne sobbed louder. Tess's eyes prickled sympathetically; she'd been there, full of futile rage, trapped.

"I'll call you on this thnik while I'm traveling," said Tess. "You can bite me—in the quigutl sense—as needed, and maybe we'll work out how to be sisters aga—"

"I hope you drown!" cried Jeanne, and the thnik went dead.

Tess stared at the device in her cold hands. She felt sliced up, cut upon cut upon cut. She breathed slowly and deliberately, the way Chessey had instructed so long ago. Saints' bones, it hurt. She curled up, resting her head on her knees, but she didn't split, didn't absent herself. She stayed and felt everything.

And when the pain had abated somewhat, she uncurled.

Jacomo loomed in the doorway of the tavern, rubbing the back of his neck and looking embarrassed. "I wasn't trying to listen in," he began.

"Yes, you were, Lord Dirt-on-Everyone," said Tess, but not angrily.

"That sounded bad," said Jacomo, leaning against the doorframe and folding his arms.

Tess stood and brushed sawdust off her behind with numb fingers. "Oh, I don't know. You've witnessed the first known instance of Jeanne yelling—a historic event. Maybe even a small miracle." She rubbed her nose, considering. "You know that feeling when someone punches you and you don't completely deserve it, but you also suspect you do, a bit?"

"Believe it or not," said Jacomo with a wry half-smile.

Tess sighed shakily and held out the thnik to Jacomo, to return it.

He waved his refusal. "Keep it. Call her whenever you want."

Tess jiggled the chain impatiently. "You heard the lady. I'm impulsive and irresponsible. I want you to carry it for safekeeping, so I don't throw it into the ocean."

"But I'm going home," said Jacomo weakly, pointing over his shoulder with his thumb. He was pointing south toward the sea, in fact, and seemed not to realize it. "The game is up. I found you, and now I've got to face the . . ."

The sentence fizzled; he didn't mean it.

"You *could* go home," said Tess mischievously, a strange feeling rising in her chest. It might have been the tiniest hint of anarchic joy. It had been such a long time, she wasn't completely sure. "Or you could walk on. By which I mean, come on a ship. With me."

In the half-light of the overcast afternoon, his eyes gleamed like a fox's. "What would I do on a ship?"

"That would be up to you," said Tess, "but I've heard these Ninysh expeditions are always looking for priests. You'd lend some credibility to my petition to the countess."

"Your petition? You haven't secured a place on the expedition yet?"

"I wanted something more compelling than 'Please, please, please forget I insulted you and let me tag along,'" said Tess. "Thanks to you, and a piece of luck I had earlier, I think I have it. But will you come? You're not ready to go back to seminary yet."

"I'm not," Jacomo admitted. He worried his lip with his teeth.

Tess ushered him toward the door. "Let's discuss this where it's not freezing, brother."

They went back into The Squids and finished their beers.

⌖

Tess fetched her belongings from The Gull and put on her rakish hat; the long pheasant feather had gotten bent, to her dismay, but she trimmed it down. It stood straight up and made her look like a walking exclamation.

She met Jacomo and his baggage in the street. Tess summoned Pathka, who'd managed to find Kikiu, who now wore a pair of buggy goggles in addition to horns and bite enhancer.

Tess glanced over her entourage—the enormous, mournful not-quite-priest; the small-for-his-age quigutl; and the quigutl who looked like she'd fallen into a bucket of sharp objects.

They were perfect.

She set the pace around the harbor's edge, chin up, not glancing back to make sure they were following. It would look better if they were scrambling a little to catch up. Tess walked like she owned the earth, indomitable, feather tickling the chin of the sky.

The sun, through a crack in the gray, lit up the underside of the clouds a transcendent salmon pink. She took it as her fanfare.

The gangplank of the *Avodendron* was still down while stevedores hauled up the last of the supplies. The countess was already aboard, Tess could tell, because her laugh carried on the wind. Tess knew full well that she ought to send up a message with one of the stevedores and wait for the countess to come to her. Yelling for the countess's attention would be rude. She'd never been specifically educated on ship's etiquette, but she felt instinctively that walking aboard the countess's ship uninvited would be rudest of all. It would be like climbing aboard someone's carriage, or walking into their house as if you owned the place. It simply wasn't done.

So that was what she did, her anarchic heart thrilling with every step up the bobbing ramp.

The ship, which had been full of merry chatter in Ninysh

and Porphyrian, went silent. Dozens of eyes stared at Tess from all directions—sailors, stevedores, an elderly bearded gentleman, and the keen-eyed countess herself. The noblewoman was dressed in black, with white slashes in her sleeves; her copper curls were cut off severely at chin length, which made her silhouette look a little like a mushroom.

She pulled a cutlass from her belt and held it at arm's length, pointed directly at Tess's face. Tess couldn't tell whether this meant she'd been recognized. She guessed not.

"Countess Margarethe," said Tess, giving eleven-sixteenths courtesy—odd enough to keep everyone on their toes. "I have come with my entourage to join your expedition."

She spread an arm to indicate the demi-priest and two quigutl. Jacomo, at least, strove to look stoutly loyal. Kikiu bristled; she'd just climbed out of the storm sewers, and she smelled like it.

The countess narrowed her eyes as if she knew Tess's face and voice but couldn't place them. She did not lower her weapon. Tess noted sailors shifting position, readying themselves to spring at her should the countess give the word.

"I'm Tess Dombegh. We've met," said Tess, posing with hands on her hips and feet apart, drawing upon her inner Dozerius.

The countess's sword arm drooped in confusion. Tess took this as an encouraging sign and plowed ahead. "Allow me to present the quigutl Pathka and Kikiu, and Father Jacomo, who—"

"Not . . . Lord Jacomo Pfanzlig?" said the countess, sheathing her cutlass. She apparently hadn't quite recognized him, either, with his dusty cloak and his dense hair nearly to his shoulders.

To Tess's surprise and delight, Jacomo stepped up, gave a foppish bow, and kissed the countess's jeweled fingers.

Margarethe's brows drew together, as though she were trying to solve a riddle. Tess hoped they'd begun to capture her curiosity at last.

"You may not have heard: it was I who found Anathuthia, the great World Serpent, coiled beneath Santi Prudia," said Tess.

"Never," said Margarethe, retrieving her hand from Jacomo and reviving her scornful expression. "It was some charlatan, they said."

"Right. *Me*," said Tess modestly. "The Academy killed it—those bastards." It was a calculated risk, insulting the masters, but the countess's smirk told her she'd figured rightly. "I know you're going after the great Antarctic serpent, milady; I can't let the same thing happen to it. I'm going to be there, by hook or by crook. I'd prefer to sail with you on this lovely ship, but if need be I'll sail with the dragons or hop over the ice like a puffin."

"Dragons?" sputtered Kikiu, behind her. "Never!"

Pathka took pains to calm his daughter; to the countess and her crew, they must have looked like two snarling monsters.

A mutter went up as the sailors shifted uncomfortably.

"What dragons?" said Margarethe, fingering the hilt of her sword, her eye on the squabbling quigutl.

Tess gazed at her coolly. "You have competition, or did you not know? Scholar Spira, my old comrade from St. Bert's, will embark tomorrow with a boatload of saar. I hear they're outraged in the Tanamoot that Ninys killed Anathuthia. If the

saar find this Southern Serpent first, you'll never get near it."
Tess examined her nails. "I'd prefer that didn't happen; I'd like
humanity to have a chance to see and study this living marvel.
But, if I can't sail with you, I'll have no choice but to lend my
talents to—"

"And what talents are these, precisely?" said the countess,
clearly irritated by the news of Spira's expedition. Tess had
hoped for as much.

"I understand Quootla, and I've brought two deep fonts
of lore with me," said Tess. "The quigutl know more about the
World Serpents than anyone. Pathka led me to Anathuthia and
taught me to approach respectfully."

She gestured toward mother and daughter, who were scrap-
ping on the deck like feral cats.

Kikiu screeched, "We'll never tell the dragons anything!
Never!"

Pathka pounced on her head, knocking off one of her steel
horns.

The countess pointedly ignored them. "Lord Morney has
read everything there is to—"

"Books aren't enough," said Tess, flicking a glance at the
bearded old gentleman standing beside the countess. "The texts
are all conjecture. Even Santi Prudia's library"—here she made
a conjecture of her own—"had nothing of use, and those monks
had seen the serpent with their own eyes. A creature of that
magnitude and majesty is hard to commit to paper. The quigutl
approach it obliquely, through myths, and get nearer to the
heart of the matter for all that."

Tess nodded to the old man beside the countess, who'd been observing her with an expression of detached amusement. "Your pardon, milord, but these quigutl know things you don't, and I'm the only human I know of who's bothered learning how to talk to them."

The old man cracked an enormous grin, and Countess Margarethe snapped, "That's not Lord Morney! That's my *napou,* captain of this ship."

"Mestor Abaxia Claado," said the countess's Porphyrian uncle, his eyes crinkling merrily. "I am amused to be mistaken for his lordship, but we are of distinctly different complexions, as you'll see when you meet him."

His niece gave him a sidelong look. "*If* she meets him. I've yet to—"

"You've decided," said Claado. "Admit it: she reminds you of an irrepressible eight-year-old who sneaked aboard my ship and wasn't discovered until we were three days out of harbor. The Regent of Samsam's fine furniture got delayed while we sailed that naughty child home. By the time we got back to Mardou, she knew her knots and lines, had got the hang of the sextant, and could dance a ripping hornpipe. The worst of it, though—"

"Is that she did it again when she was ten," snapped the countess. She seemed deeply displeased by this story.

"You know your sister trickster when you see her, Marga," said the old captain, sticking his thumbs in his belt.

"What I know," said Countess Margarethe, folding her arms across her bosom and narrowing her eyes poisonously at

Tess, "is that the last time I saw this miscreant, she insulted not only me but every man on this ship."

Her uncle rolled his eyes at this, but some muttering went up among the men.

"I am shocked, Tess Dombegh, that you have the gall to stand and face me. How are you not on your knees, begging my forgiveness?"

And Tess saw clearly then that this wasn't so much about the insults as about the story her uncle had told. There had been a sweet, mischievous girl in that tale, but here was a grown countess who expected to be obeyed. She did not want anyone mistaking her for that girl, and yet (Tess knew from experience) that girl was always there, threatening to bring past humiliations crashing down around her ears again.

That girl didn't have to be a liability.

"I am sorry for insulting you," Tess began, measuring her words carefully. "I was drunk and deeply unhappy, and if I could erase that day from history, I would. But I hope you wouldn't forgive me simply because I begged on my knees or fulfilled whatever conditions you set. I can earn your forgiveness without also earning your contempt. In fact, there's no other way to do it."

Countess Margarethe held her eyes a long time. "Keep those beasts under control," said the countess at last, gesturing at the quigutl (and possibly Jacomo) with her chin. "Can't have them popping out unexpectedly and scaring people."

"Thank you," said Tess, noticing the sway of the ship beneath her feet for the first time. It made her a little light-headed.

She was here. She was going. It was real.

"Don't make me regret this," said Margarethe. She turned on her heel and barked orders to the crew.

Tess turned her face to the wind with an irrepressible grin as the world set itself in motion around her.

Acknowledgments

The four points of my compass, this time: Karen New, Arwen Brenneman, E. K. Johnston, and Max Gladstone.

My intrepid beta-reading, boot-wearing, butt-kicking work crew: Rebecca Hartman-Baker, Laura Hartman, Susin Nielsen, Phoebe North, Arushi Raina, Pavel Curtis, and Els Kushner. Extra thanks to Becca and Els for accompanying me on one extra side quest full of peril.

Rainbow Rowell, whose novel *Fangirl* got me out the door.

Justina Ireland, whose essay "Windows, Mirrors, and the Spaces in Between" kept me going when the road was rockiest.

Mishell Baker, Amal El-Mohtar, Rebecca Sherman, and my mother, who gave my weary head a place to rest.

Cam Larios, who gave Kikiu her bite enhancer.

The birds in my trees: the QuasiModals, Spock's Beard, Dream Theater, YES, and always, always Iarla Ó Lionáird.

Mallory Loehr, Jenna Lettice, Michelle Nagler, and all my quigutl friends at Random House.

Dan Lazar, amazing agent, always ready to spring into superheroic action.

Jim Thomas, peripatetic editor, who had his hands full with this one and acquitted himself admirably.

And finally, Scott, Byron, and Úna, who are always waiting at the end of my road.

Cast of Characters

Tess Dombegh—the one most likely to get spanked

Jeanne—her twin sister, the pretty one

Seraphina—her older half sister, the smart one, sometimes called Phina

Claude—her father, a disgraced lawyer

Anne-Marie—her mother, long-suffering

Paul and Nedward—Tess's younger brothers, aspiring bullies

Kenneth—Anne-Marie's brother; an honorary cousin and aspiring astronomer

Mistress Edwina—a dowager baroness who resorts to teaching

Faffy—short for "Fast Taffy," a noble snaphound

Count Julian, Aunt Jenny, Uncle Malagrigio, Great-Aunt Elise—just a few of the many possible Belgiosos, Anne-Marie's side of the family

Grandma Therese—Claude's aged mother
Jean-Philippe, Baronet Dombegh—Claude's older brother, a
    bully and a cad
Chessey—a midwife, like one of the family

The Pfanzligs of Cragmarog Castle

Duke Lionel—the leonine patriarch
Duchess Elga—his pious wife
Lord Richard—the handsome one
Lord Heinrigh—the smarmy one
Lord Jacomo—the priggish one, at seminary

Royals, Nobles, and the Like

Queen Glisselda—the young Queen of Goredd
Prince Consort Lucian Kiggs—married to Glisselda; it's
    complicated
An infant princess—to be named as soon as all her parents
    can agree
Regent of Samsam—the regent of Samsam
Count Pesavolta—the ruler of Ninys
Lady Farquist—an old darling, auntie to all the eligible
    bachelors
Lady Eglantine, Lady Morena, Lord Thorsten—a chorus of
    courtiers
Lord Chauncerat—a closeted Daanite, willing to play along
Countess Margarethe of Mardou—a famous and fashionable
    explorer

Lord Morney—he of the mysterious contraption, coming to a sequel near you

Ardmagar Comonot—leader of dragons (the big winged ones anyway)

At St. Bert's Collegium

Professor the dragon Ondir—crankily oversees the doctoral candidates

William of Affle—a handsome cad, long gone

Harald and Roger—Will's best mates, aspiring cads

Scholar Spira—a pedantic dragon graduate student

Rynald, Baronet Averbath—a beautiful astronomer

In Legend and in Faith

Dozerius the Pirate—a swashbuckling Porphyrian storybook hero

Julissima Rossa—his ladylove, deceased

St. Vitt—always ready to let you know how badly you've sinned

Pau-Henoa—trickster rabbit of pagan provenance

Anathuthia—the first of seven World Serpents

On the Road

Pathka—a quigutl, Tess's oldest friend

Kikiu—Pathka's challenging offspring

Karpeth—Kikiu's other parent, unsettlingly

Florian—a grist lout

Blodwen and Gwenda—a pair of shepherdesses, lively and shrewd

Mumpinello—their mysterious friend, definitely not made up

Reg and Rowan—a pair of villains, plain and simple

Griss—their aged victim, probably not a nobleman

Boss Gen—imperatrix of the road crew

Felix, Aster, and Mico—the aforementioned crew, uniformly useless

Big Arnando—the foreman

Nicolas—a geologist

Darling Dulsia—a traveling minister of mercy

Those Who Pray

Mother Philomela—a traveling minister of mercy

Sister Mishell—rings the bell

Frai Moldi—a debauched monk

Frai Lorenzi—the head archivist of Santi Prudia Monastery

Pater Livian—the abbot of Santi Prudia

Father Erique—bad apple in a small barrel

Angelica—a wonderful cook

In Segosh

Mother Gaida—a diminutive embroiderer

Josquin—her lovely son, now a writer, formerly a herald

Rebecca—his former girlfriend, still a midwife, gone back to the islands

Master Pashfloria—preeminent natural philosopher of the Ninysh Academy

Master Emmanuele—somewhat less eminent, anxious to make his name

Dr. Belestros—a dragon physician, no bedside manner

St. Blanche—the mechanic, also good with plumbing

Glossary

Allsaints—all the Saints in Heaven. Not a deity, exactly; more like a collective

Archipelagos—islands south of Ninys, extending to the Antarctic

ard—order, correctness (Mootya); may also denote a battalion of dragons

Ardmagar—title held by the leader of dragonkind; translates roughly to "supreme general"

aurochs—large, wild cattlebeast, extinct in our world; existed in Europe until the Renaissance

Bitter Branca—Ninysh drink with ale and pine brandy

Blystane—capital of Samsam

bollos—balls (Ninysh)

castameri—eunuchs (Ninysh)

Castle Orison—Goreddi seat of government, in Lavondaville

coracle—light boat made of hides stretched over a wooden frame

Cragmarog Castle—home of the Pfanzligs

Daanite—homosexual, a follower of St. Daan

damaelle—small, dear lady; a courtesan (Ninysh)

doublet—short, fitted man's jacket, often padded

dracomachia—martial art for fighting dragons, invented by St. Ogdo

Ducana province—Duke Lionel's duchy

fatluketh—coming-of-age rite, wherein quigutl hatchlings fight their mothers and try to bite them, thereby ending the parental phase of the relationship (Quootla)

fthep—to deliver a stinging rebuke with your tail (Quootla)

fthootl—quigutl toy intended to build up ocular dexterity (Quootla)

furze—also called gorse; a tough, prickly shrub

Goredd—Tess's homeland, one of the Southlands (adjective form: Goreddi)

Heaven—Southlanders' afterlife, as outlined by the Saints in scripture

houppelande—robe of rich material with voluminous sleeves, usually worn belted; women's are floor-length; a man's might be cut at the knee

Infernum—Hell; not all Saints believe in it

ityasaari—half-dragon; the Saints of old were revealed to have been half-dragons, and so half-dragons are now considered living Saints (Porphyrian)

kemthikemthlutl—ritual to connect one's dreams with a World Serpent's (Quootla)

kikiu—death (Quootla)

ko—ungendered pronoun that quigutl use for each other (Quootla)

Lavondaville—Tess's hometown and the largest city in Goredd, named for Queen Lavonda, who made peace with dragonkind

lunessa—it's hard to find much concrete information on medieval feminine hygiene, so I invented my own

marchpane—marzipan, a confection of almond paste and sugar

megafauna—large animals, such as aurochs and dragons

mercer—textile dealer

Mootya—language of dragons, rendered in sounds a human mouth can make

Most Alone—epithet for the World Serpent Anathuthia

naphtha—flammable liquid hydrocarbon, sometimes eaten by dragons

Ninys—country southeast of Goredd (adjective form: Ninysh)

nupa—opal; euphemism for clitoris (Ninysh)

ogham—ancient alphabet of carved hatch marks

oubliette—claustrophobic pit used as a dungeon

oud—lutelike instrument, often played with a pick, or plectrum

palasho—palace (Ninysh)

parthenogenesis—asexual reproduction

Pelaguese—from the Archipelagos

penoio—penis (Ninysh)

Pentrach's Dun—hill fort ruin

pessary—form of early birth control; inserted vaginally; not as effective as modern kinds, but better than nothing

Pinabra—vast pine forest in southeast Ninys

Porphyry—small city-state northwest of the Southlands

psalter—book of devotional poetry, usually illustrated; in Goreddi psalters, there's a poem for each of the major Saints

Quighole—dragon and quigutl ghetto in Lavondaville

quigutl—small, flightless subspecies of dragon with a set of dexterous arms in place of wings and a tube-shaped tongue that can produce a flame

Quootla—language of the quigutl; sometimes inaccurately described as "Mootya with a bad lisp," as the two languages are mostly mutually intelligible

saar—dragon (Porphyrian)

saarantras—dragon in human form; plural: saarantrai (Porphyrian)

St. Abaster—staunch defender of the faith, loves smiting sinners

St. Agnyesta—patron of cheesemakers

St. Bert (Jobertus)—patron of natural philosophy; collegium named for him

St. Clare—patroness of the perceptive

St. Daan—patron of romantic love (along with his partner, St. Masha)

St. Fredricka—a living Saint and muralist who now lives in the Archipelagos

St. Gobnait—patroness of the persistent; Lavondaville cathedral named for her

St. Ida—patroness of musicians; music conservatory named for her

St. Jannoula—a living Saint, helped instigate the recent war named for her

St. Loola—patroness of children, the sick and indigent; hospices named for her

St. Munn—patron of merchants, popular in Ninys

St. Nedouard—the physician, recently deceased

St. Ogdo—founder of dracomachia; patron of knights and of all of Goredd

St. Pandowdy—a giant Saint who rose from the swamps near Lavondaville at the end of St. Jannoula's War

St. Prue (Prudia)—patron of history; monastery named for her

St. Seraphina—what Seraphina is sometimes called, to her chagrin

St. Siucre—patron of sweet memories; helps find what is lost

St. Willibald (Wilibaio)—patron of markets and news; cathedral named for him

Samsam—country southwest of Goredd (adjective form: Samsamese)

Santi merdi!—holy shit (Ninysh)

sarabande—slow, stately dance in three

Segosh—capital of Ninys, center of art and culture

snaphound—rather like a whippet

Southlands—Goredd, Ninys, and Samsam together

Tanamoot—dragons' vast country north of the Southlands

Tathlann's Syndrome—serious medical condition afflicting dragons who received no maternal memories, usually due to the untimely death of the mother

tes'puco—stupid-head, also a euphemism for penis (Ninysh)

thmepitlkikiu—something so transcendent there are no words for it (Quootla)

thnik—quigutl device that allows the transmission of voices over long distances

thnimi—thnik that also transmits images

thuthmeptha—when a quigutl metamorphoses from one sex to another, which happens several times across their lifespans (Quootla)

Treaty Eve—annual commemoration of the treaty between Goredd and dragons

Trowebridge—largest town in Ducana province

tutlkikiu—splitting death, an affliction of quigutl (Quootla)

-utl—Quootla suffix indicating contradictory case, wherein a word also means its opposite

World Serpents—vast creatures out of quigutl mythology, believed to have created the world and to hold it together

Yawning Nancy—pagan sculpture similar to an Irish Sheela-na-gig

RACHEL HARTMAN is the author of the acclaimed and *New York Times* bestselling YA fantasy novel *Seraphina*, which won the William C. Morris YA Debut Award, and the *New York Times* bestselling sequel *Shadow Scale*. Rachel lives with her family in Vancouver, Canada. In her free time, she sings madrigals, walks her whippet in the rain, and is learning to fence.

rachelhartmanbooks.com

@_rachelhartman